**Tara Pammi** can't remember a moment when she wasn't lost in a book—especially a romance, which was much more exciting than a mathematics textbook at school. Years later, Tara's wild imagination and love for the written word revealed what she really wanted to do. Now she pairs alpha males who think they know everything with strong women who knock that theory *and* them off their feet!

**Rosie Maxwell** has dreamed of being a writer since she was a little girl. Never happier than when she is lost in her own imagination, she is delighted that she finally has a legitimate reason to spend hours every day dreaming about handsome heroes and glamorous locations. In her spare time she loves reading—everything from fiction to history to fashion—and doing yoga. She currently lives in the North-West of England.

# TWINS TO TAME HIM

## TARA PAMMI

# BILLIONAIRE'S RUNAWAY WIFE

## ROSIE MAXWELL

MILLS & BOON

First published in Great Britain 2024
by Mills & Boon, an imprint of HarperCollins*Publishers* Ltd,
1 London Bridge Street, London, SE1 9GF

www.harpercollins.co.uk

HarperCollins*Publishers*, Macken House, 39/40 Mayor Street Upper,
Dublin 1, D01 C9W8, Ireland

Twins to Tame Him © 2024 Tara Pammi

Billionaire's Runaway Wife © 2024 Rosie Maxwell

ISBN: 978-0-263-32007-7

05/24

This book contains FSC™ certified paper
and other controlled sources to ensure responsible forest management.

For more information visit www.harpercollins.co.uk/green.

Printed and Bound in the UK using 100% Renewable Electricity
at CPI Group (UK) Ltd, Croydon, CR0 4YY

# TWINS TO TAME HIM

TARA PAMMI

MILLS & BOON

# CHAPTER ONE

"Maybe after three years the shine is wearing off your marriage, Ani," Sebastian Skalas drawled from his seat at the brunch his sister-in-law, Annika Alexandros Skalas, had dragged him to that bright May afternoon with any number of threats.

Even the mention of that day three years ago when he'd disappeared on Ani because of *that woman* still made him angry. Luckily, it had ended up in forcing his brother to the altar. "It's not too late to dump Alexandros and come back to me."

Ani shook her head while his twin glared at him.

Her uncharacteristic quietness worried Sebastian. In the beginning stages of her pregnancy she should look radiantly happy. Instead, since he'd arrived at the Ska-las villa near Corfu two days ago—upon her urgent re-quest—she'd been withdrawn, irritable, even avoiding Sebastian. Which had never happened before.

They had been friends for years, as she had visited their estate every summer since she'd been an infant, as their grandmother Thea was her godmother.

He had assumed his twin had been overly concerned when he'd relayed Ani's request to see him—Xander was protective and possessive on steroids when it came to his wife. Now Sebastian realized Xander's worry was very much valid.

Since the three of them had sat down, Ani had watched the gates to their estate, looking excited and terrified in equal measures, every other second. And the fact that she had summoned, cajoled, threatened and begged him to be present for lunch for the last three days seemed like the signal for something big.

Suddenly, a car stumbled in through the electronic gates to the estate. Ani shot to her feet at an alarming pace that had both him and Xander rushing to theirs. As if the driver couldn't decide whether to go forward or backward, the car shot forward, then stalled and repeated the strange dance a few more times.

"Is it the baby?" Xander asked, a terrified look in his eyes that Sebastian had never seen before, and never wanted to see again.

Ani shook her head, grabbed Sebastian's hands, her eyes full of big, fat tears. A beat of dread pulsed through him, like he got before one of his migraines inevitably showed up. "What's wrong?"

Behind her, Alexandros looked thunderous. "What the hell did you do, Sebastian?"

Ani shook her head, half smiling, half crying. "No, Xander. It's not him…" She turned to Sebastian again, and threw her arms around his waist. "Just remember. I… I've been trying to do the right thing, okay? By all of you. I couldn't bear it if you…hate me for it."

Sebastian wrapped his arms around her trembling form and met Xander's gaze over her head. His twin shrugged, looking as baffled and scared as Sebastian felt.

Ani pressed her forehead to his chest, soaking his shirt

with her tears. "You've always been my first and true friend, Sebastian. Please, just… Just remember that I had to keep it from you."

"Ani, you're scaring me," Sebastian said, the sensation making his words sharp.

"This cannot be good for the baby or you, *agapi*. Calm down, please. Whatever it is, I'll make it right," Xander ordered in a gruff voice, his hands coming to land on Ani's shoulders.

Annika nodded.

Outside of their little tableau, Sebastian was aware of the little car finally reaching the courtyard. Heard the sound of the engine gunning, as if the driver wanted to turn the car around and run away. It sidled back and forth for a few more minutes, the tires digging grooves in the rain-drenched soil.

Irritated by the driver's hesitation, Sebastian caught his twin's gaze. "Are you expecting guests?"

Xander shook his head as Ani said, "I invited her here."

Finally, the driver opened the door and stepped out. Sebastian's nape prickled as he watched the woman. Instinct that had once helped him escape his father's brutal fists made Sebastian brace for some unknown.

Recognition hit him at first glance, a solid punch to his gut.

Tall and impossibly curvy, the woman was shabbily dressed in wrinkled pants and an oversize T-shirt, with thick, wild corkscrew curls. A high forehead and stubborn beak of a nose and a wide mouth, currently in shadows by the sun behind her, would follow. He'd have known the prideful tilt of her chin and the straight, aggressive set of her shoulders anywhere.

It was the woman he'd been searching for, for three years. Only today she wasn't all dressed up in a slinky red number, with her curly hair straightened into a waterfall, that mouth painted a lush red, the beautifully distinct amber eyes hidden behind brown contacts.

Memories came flooding back to Sebastian, suffusing his body with an instant heat. The silky swath of her skin that he had kissed and caressed with relish. The soft, sweet taste of her lips and how she'd clung to him after their kiss. The strange combination of open guilelessness and intense passion with which she'd begged for more of his words, his fingers, his caresses.

This was the woman he hadn't been able to forget for three years.

The woman who'd disappeared on him after an explosive night together, the woman who had stolen the one piece of leverage he had over their old chauffeur, Guido, who was the only person who had known where their mother had disappeared to two decades ago. He had been finally so close to finding her whereabouts, only for this woman to snatch away the opportunity from him.

What the hell was she doing here now?

*He had no doubt that he didn't even know her real name.*

Before he could ask Ani, she walked the few steps off the patio toward her guest. *Her guest...*

She must know this was his residence. And yet, she was here, willingly. Why?

Did she imagine he'd forgotten that she had stolen from him, that she had blackmailed him to stop him from coming after her? She'd been clever enough—no, brilliant, actually—to get one over him, and in staying under the radar for the next three years.

"Ani, what's going on? Why is that woman here?" He hated that he couldn't hide his urgency.

Xander stared at the approaching woman and then back at his wife, scowling. He cursed, finally picking up on the tension radiating from Sebastian. "Ani, *agapi*, what did you do?"

While she'd been near sobbing with Sebastian, Annika glared at her husband, her crotchety temper of late flaring. "I did what I had to do, Xander. I'd like to see you handle something like this. It's not always black-and-white, you know, and I'll thank you to consider—"

In a public display that still shocked Sebastian to this day, Xander pressed his mouth to her temple and said, "Breathe, *pethi mou*. I would never question your intentions."

Nearing them enough to hear the marital spat and the miraculous making up, the woman hesitated.

This close, the woman's amber eyes—intelligent and incisive—glinted like rare gems in the sunlight. As did the golden flecks in her hair. For all that she dressed without the minimum concern toward fashion or basic hygiene—there was an orange stain near her breast—there was that same vitality about her that had drawn Sebastian to her three years ago.

She was beautiful in a way a feral creature that stalked the woods was beautiful—without artifice, and with all her ragged, sharp edges intact. Even now, with anger thrumming through him, he noticed so much about her.

A tremulous smile wreathed Ani's lips. "Laila, welcome to our home."

*Laila*... Her name resonated through Sebastian like a gong.

The woman's smile came out a mix of a grimace and a baring of teeth.

Ani extended her hands, as if afraid *Laila* might be spooked enough to flee if she didn't tether her. "I'm so glad you came."

"I wasn't sure I would. Not until the last minute," Laila said, rubbing her belly in that nervous gesture he remembered so well. "I don't like decisions made on instinct, but..." She shrugged her shoulders, and with an implacable practicality he found fascinating, she straightened her spine and kissed Ani's cheek. "You're well? I have missed our chats."

"Yes. I've been ordered bed rest and haven't left the estate in three weeks." Ani's smile grew wider, genuine affection replacing her dark mood. "I've been so...eager for you to get here."

Alexandros threw him another glance before pulling a chair out for Annika. Sebastian did the same for Laila, who wouldn't quite meet his gaze and walked around the table, just to avoid being near him.

And yet, there was no doubt that her sudden appearance had everything to do with him and their encounter.

"This is Alexandros Skalas, my husband," Ani said.

Laila shook his twin's hand. For the first time since she'd walked up, a smile touched her lips. It felt like a slap to his face. Her body language was relaxed, easy around Xander, as if she were a porcupine that had retracted its prickles for the moment. "Ani said very few people can tell you apart, especially when you don't want them to know."

"Can you?" Alexandros asked, clearly digging.

Laila blushed and it was incongruous next to her serious expression. "Oh, I'd never mistake you for...him. You're serious and thoughtful and almost coldly logical, from what Ani tells me. Like me. Now, I can see it in the set of your mouth. Your brother, on the other hand, has a..." Then, looking thoroughly mortified at what she'd been about to say, she turned away.

"You know Sebastian, of course," Ani said, as if she couldn't let a moment's awkwardness land.

Laila finally met his gaze. Panic, nervousness and then a steely resolve flickered through hers, as if someone was changing channels to her emotions. "Hello, Sebastian."

The huskiness of her voice only made him angrier. "Come, Ani, finish the introductions," Sebastian said. "I'd like to know why it was so important that I meet your guest."

"You kept your promise," Laila said, looking shocked.

Ani floundered, then recovered, her cheeks a dark red. "Yes, well, this is Dr. Laila Jaafri, a statistics scientist. Laila got a PhD when she was twenty and has won so many awards in her field that it will take me the whole day to list them out."

"And why is she here, at our home?" Sebastian asked, rudely interrupting his sister-in-law.

"That's for Laila to tell you," Ani said, standing up.

For just a second, Laila's face crumpled, as if Ani was abandoning her at the cave's mouth to the big bad lion.

"I think your very brilliant friend is afraid of me, Ani," said Sebastian, watching her. "Maybe you should stay so that I don't gobble her up."

"It is ridiculous to assume that I'm afraid of you," Laila

said, turning to face him, finally. "I'm simply unused to situations where I'm at a distinct disadvantage and there is no social precedent to follow."

"And yet you look like you're a second away from running."

"Sebastian, let her—"

He shot to his feet. It was extremely rare that he lost control of his temper, but the very sight of this woman made him feel unbalanced. "Clearly you're here to confront me, and yet you will hide behind my very pregnant and very kind and probably naive sister-in-law. Why do I feel like you befriended her knowing she's *my* brother's wife? What kind of a scam have you been pulling on Ani?" The more he gave voice to his suspicions, the more Sebastian knew he was right. "Alexandros, call security. Ani doesn't know that this woman is a thief and a cheat and—"

"Stop it!" Ani said, "Just give her a chance to—"

"You're upsetting her over me," Laila whispered, standing up so suddenly that her chair toppled over behind her. Then she poured a glass of water and brought it to Ani. Waited with a stubborn patience until Ani took the glass and drank several gulps from it.

Then Laila faced him, pulling a cloak of calm around her, even as he noted the erratic flutter of her pulse at her neck. "I came to tell you that 'our encounter' three years ago, where I seduced you, stole from you and blackmailed you, to protect an innocent man from your plans..." Her chin tilted up in a direct challenge, amber gaze pinning him to the spot "...had consequences...twin boys. I came here because I thought you had a right to know about them. To ask you if you wanted to be a part of their lives. And if you're not interested in that—" her shoulders straightened "—to ask that you contribute monetarily to their upbringing."

*Consequences in the form of twin boys...his sons?*

Sebastian's ears rang as if someone had set off a series of gongs near his head. He felt dizzy, disoriented, like he did during one of his migraines. He had two sons, with this woman who had approached him under false pretenses, slept with him and then stolen an important document from him.

Truth shone in her eyes, as real and bright as sunlight picking out the golden strands in her hair.

His emotions surrounded him in a dizzy whirl that he felt like he was in some kind of vortex. Like when his migraine medication didn't kick in fast enough and he needed to throw up. Like he was being battered from all sides and he couldn't escape fast enough.

*Sons... He had two sons. Two-year-old boys. Twins, like Alexandros and him. Twins with a father who didn't know the first thing about being one and a mother who... had told him the truth two years too late.*

He stared at her.

What kind of a mother was Dr. Laila Jaafri? What new trick was she playing on him this time?

Questions buzzed through him, but he refused to give them a voice. Refused to let her see how she'd shaken the very foundation of his life. Refused to let her see how thoroughly...inadequate he felt to meet this moment.

*What are their names? How do they look? Were they rambunctious like he'd been or quiet like Alexandros? Did they get along with each other? Did they talk? Did two-year-olds talk?*

More questions tumbled through him and his throat closed up in an instinctive, self-preservation response. All the conditioning he'd had in childhood and as a teenage boy came in handy because the last thing he wanted was to scare this woman off by showing his volatile emotions and his anger. He'd made a study of never losing his cool, of never letting anything matter to him so much that it touched his temper. It was the only way he'd known to survive his father's abusive rants and his meaty fists.

He turned away and his gaze fell on Ani. A jagged sliver appeared in his control. "How long?"

"Three months," Ani said, understanding his question, her face flushed with guilt.

*Three months...*

She had known for three months and hidden the truth from him. His one friend. His sister by everything but blood. He let her see how betrayed he felt, hardening himself against the flood of tears on her cheeks.

"Don't blame her," Laila said, taking a step in between them, as if she meant to protect his very pregnant sister-in-law from him.

*Cristos, what did this woman think of him?*

"If it wasn't for Annika persuading me that you..." She licked her lips, calling his attention to the beads of sweat dancing over her thick upper lip. "...I'd have taken longer to approach you."

"The better question is—" Sebastian rounded on her, some of his frustration leaching into his voice "—would you have told me the truth at all?"

"Yes."

"I don't believe you."

"I don't need you to believe me, nor do I have anything to prove to you, Sebastian. It has not been an easy decision to make."

"I don't believe that, either. I know how duplicitous you can be, Dr. Jaafri. How easy it is for you to spin lies, to fake interest, to get close with the intention of stealing from me."

"I did that because you were ruining an innocent man!" she burst out, her own temper finally breaking the surface. "And I never meant to sleep with you. It was..." Flaming-red streaks gilded her sharp cheeks and her mouth opened and closed like a fish out of water. "... unplanned."

"What a stroke to my masculinity that Dr. Laila Jaafri of the brilliant brain and the unending logic fell prey to my charms!" he bit out, sarcasm punctuating every word. "Since we're being honest finally, tell me, was it punishment for my sins that you would hide the truth from me?"

"Of course not. Would I like to have sailed through single parenting without a hitch and forgotten about the sperm donor who actively hates me because I stole from him to stop him from ruining an innocent man? *Yes!* Did I constantly, every minute of every day and all the sleepless nights, struggle with the fact that I was being unfair to my children *and* their father by not giving them a chance to know each other? *Yes!* Did I then gather copious amounts of data by stalking your friends and the woman I thought you cheated on the night before the wedding *with me*, looking for reassurances that you would not turn into a monster—as powerful men usually do when inconvenienced—who would take my children from me when I did tell you the truth? *Another resounding yes!* Did the fact that it is hard to raise two boys as a single woman with no parental or community support, financially and emotionally and physically, make it inevitable because I will not let my pride and misgivings about you become obstacles to the benefits my children will have with a father around? *OMG, we have another yes!*"

All of this she said softly, evenly, without inflection. And yet, the very lack of emotion in them convinced Sebastian of the truth.

"So you approached Ani with the intention of finding more about me? Where?"

"At the university where she takes music classes. After talking to her once, after she told me that your wedding to her would have been nothing but an arrangement between friends to help her out, I told her the truth." Her chest—delineated clearly even in the ugly, loose T-shirt—rose and fell, the only sign betraying the depth of her emotions.

And Sebastian realized one thing about Dr. Laila Jaafri. For all the games she'd played with him, she was logical. Maybe what she wanted from him...*was* what she'd outlined.

He looked away and his gaze clashed with Alexandros's. Like him, he looked stunned. So, Ani, as loyal to her new friend as Laila had been to the man she had been bent on rescuing, hadn't even told her husband.

As different as they were, in his twin's gaze, Sebastian found the answer he didn't want to admit.

Alexandros had spent his entire life trying to define who a Skalas man could be, *should be*, while Sebastian had tried to shrug off the oppressive expectations of the very name from the start. And yet, here was a crossroads he'd never thought he'd stand at.

This woman he didn't trust was the mother of his children. Whether he wanted them or not was irrelevant. Whether he wanted *her* in his life was irrelevant. Whether he felt equipped in any way to have a role in their life was also irrelevant. It was his reality now.

The Sebastian Skalas that had survived his father's abuse without losing his sense of self, the Sebastian that had dreamed of an affectionate, loving family as a young boy, the Sebastian that had spent years looking for a mother that had abandoned him and Alexandros to a monster she couldn't survive herself, would never turn his back on his...sons.

"Where are they?" he asked, in a surprisingly steady voice.

"With their nanny about two and a half hours from here," Laila said, probing his gaze. "Annika booked a luxury suite for us at this...posh hotel in Athens."

*Two hours away...*

At least Annika had the good sense to persuade this stubborn woman to stay at a good hotel and not some seedy hovel. He had a feeling that wouldn't have been an easy task.

"I thought you would want to see them," Laila continued, "As proof, if nothing else."

"Proof?"

"Proof that they are yours." Laila stared at his face in that clinical, academic way of hers, he realized now, and then at Alexandros. "They have your nose and that hair but my eyes. Of course, I understand that you'll do a paternity test."

He bristled at her matter-of-fact tone but managed to contain his irritation. "We will bring them here, now."

"I'd prefer to do it by myself." When he'd have protested, she hurried on. "They're two, Sebastian. While Nikos, older by three minutes, is friendly and trusting and very well-adjusted, Zayn is moody and sensitive. I can't just throw you in their faces. It will take…time. And I'd prefer to…"

"Nikos and Zayn," he repeated, feeling as if he was in a trance.

Instantly, they morphed from abstract two-year-olds to boys with real personalities.

Nikos was friendly and trusting and well-adjusted.

Zayn…was sensitive. Like Sebastian himself had been once and punished relentlessly for.

It was a miracle he could swallow, much less string words together. "My chauffeur will bring them all here."

Laila shook her head. "It will be easier if I go—"

"You're not going anywhere." He opened his phone. "Which hotel?"

She studied him and then sighed. "They will be okay for a couple of hours more. We can discuss our…plans before we introduce them to you. I like to be prepared—"

"They're my sons. Whether they understand it immediately or not, it's irrefutable."

"Yes, but I would like to know how involved you want to be. I have my own life and we'll have to figure out sharing custody and other co-parenting—"

"Ah… Dr. Jaafri. Now I know you didn't really pay attention to Annika."

For the first time since she'd arrived, a flicker of confusion showed in her amber eyes. Sebastian lapped it up as if it were life-giving ambrosia. "What do you mean?"

"I will not be relegated to weekends and holidays."

"It's better if you chew on this before you make grand declarations. Parenthood is a one-way road with very little incentive in terms of excitement. It means giving up quality time for yourself."

"So you think I should cancel my date tomorrow night with the hot lingerie model?"

She blinked owlishly. "No, you do not have to be celibate to raise your children well," she said, adding her own silken thrust knowingly or unknowingly, though he had a feeling that it was the latter, "but it demands some sacrifices. It's not my expectation that you upend your life."

Behind him, he heard Annika's sigh and Alexandros's choked outrage. "How very magnanimous of you, Dr. Jaafri. Why the change of heart after two years?" he said, biting down on the last words.

Hesitation danced across her face but she pushed it aside with the practicality he was coming to both like and abhor. "I would like financial assistance," she said, sticking out her index finger, as if she were highlighting bullet points. "Being a woman in an extremely competitive academic field with two little boys means I've already lost my edge, even before I returned from maternity leave." Out popped her middle finger to count out the next one. "I would also like some kind of reassurance that the boys will have a home in case I die suddenly." Third finger out now. "I would also like for them to have extended family. I grew up mostly fending for myself and it has dictated how I relate to people in general, although nature versus nurture is not completely out of the scope of our discussion. After meeting Annika and learning of your brother's strong family values and your grandmother's hand in raising you both, I felt reassured that

Nikos and Zayn would benefit from being part of such a tight-knit family."

This time, the sound that escaped Ani was that of a wounded animal. If Sebastian hadn't had a father who'd tried his damnedest to break him as a boy with his incessant taunts and meaty fists, he might have made the same sound.

"Are you unwell, Annika?" Laila said, completely and clearly missing the nuance in Ani's response.

"She's dismayed at how, in all of your myriad considerations in coming to such an important decision," Sebastian drawled, "*I* seem to have very little role to play."

Fiery red streaks painted Laila's high cheekbones, and a soft "oh" escaped her mouth.

He didn't know whether to be relieved or horrified that he was a genuine oversight on her part.

"I will not lie to save your pride and say that you were a big consideration. Ani reassured me that you would never harm the boys or me, in any way. But not harming is not being a good parent."

"I know the distinction very well, Dr. Jaafri. And it's a good thing, no, that I don't give a damn about how much consideration you gave me in all this?"

"What do you mean?"

"I don't have to feel bad about railroading you into what I'm about to do. Even Ani couldn't have foreseen this, so don't blame her."

"Railroad me into what, Sebastian?"

"My sons will be legal Skalas heirs. Which means we'll have to get married."

"That's…unnecessary," she said, her amber eyes widening into large pools. A strange mixture of outrage and innocence shone from them. "You don't trust me and I… have no interest in marriage."

"Your wishes and dreams and plans don't matter anymore. Isn't that one of the first lessons you learn about being a parent?" He took a step toward her, gentling his voice. "I do not give a fuck about whether you intended to marry or if you have a loving fiancé back home, wherever that is. Only my sons matter now."

# CHAPTER TWO

LAILA WALKED AROUND the enormous bedroom she'd been shown into, feeling untethered from her own life.

Sebastian had walked away after telling her he would *see* her when the boys arrived in an infinitely polite voice. If she hadn't seen and understood the scope and depth of his art, she'd have thought him the uncaring, ruthless, powerful man who had exploited an old man's weakness and driven him to losing his home.

But that night three years ago, she had not only stolen the promissory note he had taken from Guido as guarantee for his gambling debts, but had also gotten a glance at what Sebastian Skalas hid from the world.

The true core of the man he hid beneath his useless playboy persona. The profound beauty of his art had stolen her breath, pulled the very foundation of her assumptions about him, making her wish she'd met him under different circumstances.

But that kind of stupid wishing was not her. Neither had it stopped her from taking pictures of his art on her phone, to use as further guarantee that he would leave Guido alone. Even then, flushed with guilt and pleasure at sleeping with him, she had known that he wouldn't want the world to know who he truly was.

With that perspective that she had of him—that she knew no one else in the world did—Laila shouldn't be surprised by his easy acceptance. But she was.

Apparently, he believed her sons were his just like that, and it *was* a big deal that he had two sons. She'd expected, at least, garden-variety accusations thrown around about her character, her sexuality, her conduct and her tactics for gold-digging.

Instead, she'd been left standing in the middle of the patio, her stomach growling because she hadn't eaten anything since finishing Zayn's smushed toast hours ago, and the lingering feeling that he'd never forgive her. Which was strange because she didn't want his forgiveness in the first place.

Alexandros had pressed a quick kiss to Annika's temple and walked away, without meeting her eyes. Clearly, the Skalas men didn't abandon self-control even when they were angry. It was so reminiscent of her father that it soothed Laila, amid the gnawing confusion.

Her boys would have good male role models in their father and uncle at least. She added it to the positive column in her head, much like how Zayn collected his precious rocks.

Knowing she had a husband *and* brother-in-law feeling betrayed, Annika had looked as emotionally worn out as Laila had felt, and ordered the staff to show her to the guest suite.

So here she was at two in the afternoon, hungry and tired and sleep-deprived.

*When was she not, to be honest?*

Her brain glitched at the anticlimactic silence surrounding her. It wasn't just that she was away from the boys—she'd returned to work when they were three months old. Or that she had spent most of her adult life, and a good bit of her teenage life, looking after her father, then her mother and her sister and even Guido and his sister Paloma.

It was seeing Sebastian again. And knowing that all her preparation—stalking every piece of news and watching videos of him on social media in an unending loop— hadn't made an iota of difference to her reaction.

She'd had three years, and few enough moments without mom brain, to dwell on how decadently gorgeous he was. How his mobile mouth could mock even as his gray-eyed gaze stripped layers to see beneath. How he could be both entirely charming and exhilaratingly cunning with his quips. How some mysterious, magical thing she didn't understand had driven her to seek pleasure in his arms, bypassing all logic and rationale.

She'd thought she'd be…immune to his brand of physicality after all this time.

She wasn't and her brain didn't know what to do with this unforeseen glitch.

He was the most interesting man she'd ever met and three years and thousands of sleepless hours hadn't made a dent in her fascination with him.

He was still lean and yet somehow impossibly broad. There was a new sharpness to his gray gaze, a tightness around his mouth that she attributed to her arrival. He moved with a lazy grace and talked with an ease that she rarely saw in men who tried to dominate the people and situations around them.

No trying to intimidate the opponent for Sebastian Skalas. His power thrummed in the very air around him, making her prickly and aware. He'd tamped down his anger as easily as if he were closing his eyes.

Neither did she have any problem understanding his intent. He had meant it when he'd said, *"We'll get married."*

He meant for them to marry and live in this gigantic villa and play happy families for Nikos and Zayn. And she would be his plain, tall, big-boned wife burying her head in statistics, raising her boys in his gigantic home, feeling like a fish out of water while he…so beautiful that it hurt her eyes to look at him, went off to date stick-thin models, have sophisticated affairs, all the while laughing at her and the world. The very picture in her head made Laila want to run away and hide. Fortunately, the chirp of her phone pulled her out of the absurd reality of her marrying Sebastian.

The text was from the twins' nanny, Paloma, saying they were on their way and that the boys had settled into a nap. So, at least one stop to change their diapers and give the boys a minute—especially hyperactive Nikos— to stretch their chubby legs.

And she had three hours and one chance to convince Sebastian that his proposal was nothing but an invitation to disaster.

She found him swimming laps at the overhang pool out on one of the multiple terraces on the second floor, after walking the maze-like grounds around the silent villa, to the beach and back, and finally going up the open stairs that had a gorgeous view of the Ionian Sea.

The villa was built into the very side of the mountain, looking like it very much belonged there, with the Skalases reigning as undisputed kings. Of course, she had known he was wealthy, and in the last few months, she had come face-to-face with the fact that the Skalas family's wealth and power rivaled some of the richest people on the planet.

So what did a man like Sebastian Skalas—who had all this and the millions of euros that his paintings were in circulation for—need from an old chauffeur like Guido? So much that he had lured the old man into a gambling debt using his weakness against him, holding the threat of ruin on his head?

It was a question Laila had pondered for three years with no satisfying answer. And now, it came back to her again, given his easy acceptance of her claim. A missed step on the stairs brought her jarringly back to the world around her.

Her awe and admiration for the sea and the beaches and the near-floating palace that was the villa only lasted a few more seconds. Suddenly, all she could see were the dangerously open ledges and unending terraces and open stairs—a million places where her boys could get hurt.

When she reached the overhang pool on the second floor that seemed to stretch right out into the middle of the very ocean, though, she promptly forgot all her reservations.

Sunlight pierced through the bluest blue water and painted the man's muscled limbs and smooth strokes with splashes of golden light. It would be better to approach him after he showered and dressed, give him some more time to cool down, although he hadn't really let his emotions show.

Despite the noise of her warnings, Laila simply went to him, feeling as if there was that hook under her belly button, tugging her toward him. Memories of sleek limbs and soft touches and hard nips... The one night she'd spent with him came back in a thrumming buzz, making her skin feel tight over her own muscles. A loose, lazy kind of heat thrashed through her and she tugged her T-shirt away from her breasts. The orange stain near her left boob—from when Zayn had thrown mango pulp at her—broke the spell and she came back to herself.

That night, that role she'd played to get his attention, had been a fantasy. Reality was that she was right now very hungry, and her rationale needed to be fed. She smiled as she noticed the covered lunch tray. Grabbing it, she opened the cover to find a colorful salad, pasta in thick white sauce and a slice of thick chocolate cake.

With an easy practicality that came with dealing with two prima divas all her life, and now two very energetic toddlers, Laila had learned to eat her food with gratitude and urgency. Also, it was a timely reminder that this would be her lot if she agreed to his ridiculous plan.

He would be out there living his usual, bored playboy life and she'd be left wondering where he was.

Not that it stopped her from groaning as the rich white sauce melted on her tongue. She attacked the cake next, her eyes going back in her head at the richness of the chocolate. The salad and sweet, tart lemonade were last.

If she wasn't aware of the sudden narrowing of Sebastian's gaze on her like a soft hum under her skin, she'd have spread her legs, unzipped her mom jeans, patted her belly and fallen into a much-needed nap before the boys arrived.

For a moment, she wondered if that was the best way to discourage him from his ridiculous proposal. Wasn't Mama forever telling her that no man liked a woman who ate like he did? Who was at least as smart as him if not more, and stood just as tall, argued logic all the time and made no effort to hide any of those obnoxious traits?

She ticked at least two boxes with most men and with Sebastian, she could also add the "men want their women to be at least as good-looking as themselves" rule Mama kept throwing in her face.

So maybe all she had to do was be herself.

After all, she was nothing like the woman who had taken on Sebastian Skalas. She was not beautiful—that routine with false lashes and hair straighteners and rented clothes had taken her two hours that evening—she was not a helpless damsel in distress and she was definitely not the wide-eyed, naive, out-for-a-good-time party girl she'd pretended to be.

If she was ruthlessly honest, though, he had thoroughly reduced her to the last part. Once she'd started chatting with him, she'd forgotten the whole reason she was there.

By the time he stepped out of the pool, she had a battle plan. Or so she'd thought.

Clad in black swimming trunks that outlined every inch of his chiseled body—taut buttocks and muscled thighs and a lean chest with a smattering of hair and bands of abdomen muscles—he made it impossible to not remember how that body had felt on top of hers. How much care he'd taken with her. How he'd taught her that she was meant for pleasure, too, and how he'd wrung every ounce of it out of her.

"I do not know if the hungry way your gaze travels my body is indicative of the fact that your defenses are down or if you've revived your act."

It was the last thing she expected him to refer to. And

in that smooth-as-sin voice that wrapped itself like a warm tendril around her flesh.

Laila tilted her head back and licked her lips, feeling hunger of a different kind bloom in places she hadn't thought of in a while. Not since that night. "I have no energy left to put on an act. If you'd spent a little more time in the pool, you'd have found me snoring with my mouth open, drooling away."

"So you're eating me up with the same eagerness you showed the cake because you're lusting after me," he returned in such a reasonable voice that it took Laila a few seconds to process his taunt. "I feel like I have an upper hand for the first time since you appeared."

She blinked and looked away as he wiped himself. "I know you're not so starved for the female gaze to make this a scoring point between us."

"I'm not hearing a denial, Dr. Jaafri," he came back, lightning fast.

Laila would have docked him a point if he addressed her like that to mock her—she'd met enough people in life who used her brains as a weapon against her femininity—but he said it like it was his nod to her. "It's an exercise in exhaustion to deny things that are fact. Annika tried her best to do the right thing for all of us. I didn't tell you about the pregnancy or the boys all this while because I didn't know what you would do in retaliation for what I did to you first. And yes, I'm horny as any woman would be, especially since you're a super-stud on steroids and no, it's not a good thing or a bad thing between us." She sighed as his grin got wider. "Except it seems to stroke your ego as if you were a randy teenager in search of validation instead of a thirty-seven-year-old man."

"Now you sound like my grandmother Thea."

She didn't want to remind him of his grandmother. But maybe that was a good thing, too. "*Please*, will you put some clothes on? I can't think straight with all this…" She moved her arm in the air signaling at his torso.

Flashing another grin, he walked away.

Laila could breathe again and tried to take stock of the situation. Clearly, whatever shock he'd felt at her news had been handled. Because he believed her? Because it was that easy and of not much consequence to him? She groaned out loud. It was hard to remember she was dealing with a chameleon when he blinded her with that megawatt smile or that naughty twinkle in his gray eyes.

When Sebastian returned, his hair was slicked back, and he wore gray sweatpants that sat low on his lean hips. He sat down on the lounger opposite her, his legs caging her in, without touching her.

*An invitation but never an imposition.*

Sebastian Skalas toed that line so well.

"I'm not sure if I should enjoy your refreshing honesty or search for a deeper motivation."

"Then why tie yourself to me in marriage?" Laila probed.

"Because my children will grow up with me." His dictatorial tone would have bothered her if she didn't see the resolve in his eyes. "If you had come to me immediately after you discovered you were pregnant, I'd have demanded the same."

"You're the last man I can imagine to happily settle into matrimony and domesticity, and my sons…" Whatever fake warmth was there in his eyes turned to frost, and she backtracked. "Fine. *Our* sons are not hobbies you pick up because you're in the mood to play father for a season. They're a lifetime commitment and—"

"You claim to rely on cold, clear facts and not emotions, no?"

She nodded.

"From all the data you collected from Annika, you must already know that whatever my beliefs about you, and marriage and all those relationship traps, I would never let any harm or negligence come to any child, much less my own, *ne*? You're basing your character profile of me on nothing but vague impressions. So, no, I will not let you cheat me out of what is mine again."

There *had been* such warmth in Ani's words when she'd talked about Sebastian that Laila had found herself weaving fantasies about what it would be like to share her life and her sons with such a man.

Baba had been kind, fun, down-to-earth for a distinguished poet, and had showered her, and even her half sister, Nadia, when she'd allow it, with such unconditional love. After losing him, it was Guido, their housekeeper and papa's childhood friend, who had looked after her while her mother romanced man after unsuitable man, teaching Nadia to prize beauty and wealth and power over everything else.

Without Guido to hold her through the grief of losing her father, Laila might have unraveled completely.

"The picture I have of you is based on the fact that you'd have ruined an innocent man. You used his weakness for gambling to rob him of his home, the only thing he had, threatened him with ruin. All for what, Sebastian?" Laila said, glad for the reminder. "Guido wouldn't speak of what you wanted from him—"

"Where is *this innocent man* in all the hardships you faced?" he said, cutting her off. "Was he worth the elaborate farce? Was he worth sleeping with me?"

And there was the anger she'd expected, though only a small ember. Laila almost felt relieved at his silken thrust of a question. The deceit she had pulled on him had never sat well with her. Especially when he was the father of her sons. Especially when her entire life had been about taking care of others. Sometimes at the cost of her own well-being. That woman who had schemed to meet him, with the intention of getting close to him, the woman who had then lost all common sense and followed him to his apartment and slept with him... That was not her. Only desperation to somehow save Guido from his clutches and the genuine connection she had felt with him had driven her that far.

She hadn't realized until this moment how much she'd craved to explain her actions, how much she needed to hear his own reasons. "Guido died of a heart attack six months to the day after the boys were born. He was the first one to hold both of them. He spent hours on the floor playing with them. He stayed up with me so many nights when I couldn't get Zayn to settle down, when I'd have broken down and admitted defeat. The boys' nanny, Paloma, without whom I'd never made it through last year, is his sister. So, yes, the little I did for him, he paid it back a thousand times over, even before the boys, Sebastian. He was the one who watched out for me when I lost Baba, the one who held me steady through grief and pain. Nothing I did would have been enough to pay back the care he showed me and then my sons."

"It is your own fault that you had to depend on strangers." His polite mask slipped, and a hardness entered his tone. And yet, Laila had the strange, or delusional, notion that it wasn't directed at her. "Now, Nikos and Zayn will have my name and everything that comes with it."

"That's not possible if we share custody?" Laila asked, knowing that he had neatly sidestepped her question about why he had nearly ruined Guido. She wanted to push and prod until he answered. But right now, she needed him to back off this ridiculous wedding dictate even more.

"I'm not willing to share custody," he said without missing a beat. "You have admitted that it is hard to manage a career and the boys and all the financial responsibilities. I'm offering a solution that will satisfy both our individual requirements and…their well-being."

"So, I'd be free to devote myself to my career, with the added advantages this marriage would bring?" Laila said. Despite her best intentions, tendrils of curiosity swept through her. "If I were to be gone for days, or weeks, you would be present full-time for them? You would not use my career against how good of a mother I am?"

"Of course you would be free," he said, leaning forward. "There are a lifetime's benefits for you."

"Now you sound like an insurance salesman," she said, the very logic she trusted tasting like sawdust when it came out of his mouth.

This close, she could see the lines on his forehead, the thick sweep of his lashes and the lushness of his wide mouth. His very male presence and the heat it evoked in her and the logical offer he made—without a hint of anger or emotion peeking in—her own mind and body felt the cognitive dissonance. "A marriage like that becomes bitter. Nikos and Zayn will suffer."

"Not if we set clear expectations. What is that you truly want, Laila?" Her name on his lips, after all this time, made her feel dizzy.

"I've never dreamed of a partner or a husband or a family or anything remotely traditional. Nikos and Zayn are blessings I didn't know I'd want. But that's as far as I can stretch my imagination."

"Why not?"

"Because those things happen to normal women. Not women like me."

He cursed and she flushed at how she was painting herself. She'd never been a victim before in her life, and she refused to be one in front of this man. She'd command respect in this relationship, if nothing else. "I'm stating facts, not looking for your sympathy. In fact, that expression in your eyes feels like an itch on my back I can't get to."

He laughed and it fanned tiny spiderweb-like crinkles around his eyes and his gorgeous mouth—a sign that he laughed a lot. At himself *and* at the world, in that sly, self-deprecating tone. That same quality pervaded his paintings, too.

"Maybe a husband would be handy with scratching that itch."

She pursed her mouth even as a smile wanted to blossom. He was disarming her one smile, one declaration, one question at a time, and they weren't even really for her.

"Unless the problem is that you already have a man in your life and theirs?" he probed, sounding so smooth that she almost missed the feral undertone to his words.

Laila stared, stunned at how he could change moods and masks.

"I will not play second fiddle to another man in their life."

"I don't have enough time to sleep or eat, much less romance some—"

"But you will have extra support now that you have come to me, *ne*? I don't think you comprehend how your life will change when it comes out that they are my sons and Skalas heirs. You have set something in motion you cannot control."

Laila leaned away from him, heart pounding loudly in her chest. "You're scaring me on purpose."

"No. I'm showing you reality as I see it coming. From staff you hire to long-standing colleagues, friends you've known forever to strangers you meet ahead, people will see you differently, want things from you, will take advantage of your elevated station in life. They will invade your privacy and the boys' hoping to sell the tiniest tidbit of their lives, your life, my life to some tawdry magazine. The only way to protect the boys from that is to protect you. To make sure no one takes advantage of you with the intention of getting to them or me."

"You don't have to clarify that it's all for the boys. There's no chance of me misunderstanding it," she said, sounding miserable and confused to her own ears.

Whatever he saw in hers, something gentled in his expression. "I believe that you didn't hide them from me with malicious intentions. That you came here today seeking very little for your own benefit."

Laila stared, stunned. For just a second, she wondered if he was manipulating her by giving her that. But he wasn't. Whatever his reasons, even with the past tangled in knots between them, he was willing to believe her reasons for showing up today and spilling a life-changing secret. It was more than she'd hoped for. "Thank you for that."

"Now, *you* have to see that I do not go around offering to marry women who hide big, life-changing things from me."

His words made perfect common sense, but Laila was afraid to go with her gut feeling, even when it made her feel good. Especially then. And something about Sebastian had always found a weakness in her.

"Tell me what would sweeten the deal," he added, leaving no doubt in her mind that he'd do anything to ensure Nikos and Zayn's future was tied to his.

"Nothing you offer could make me interested. I don't believe in love and marriage and…'all those relationship traps' for me," she said, using his own words.

"We're at an impasse, then," he said with a shrug, olive skin gleaming across taut shoulders, inviting her fingers for a touch. "The boys won't leave my side in the foreseeable future. And knowing the part you play in their lives, I'm loath to separate you from them, even for an afternoon."

If he'd said that in a threatening way, Laila would have sprouted thorns. But all she heard was his sense of loss at not knowing about them, his need to make it right. Was that the thing that drew her to him even now when she didn't truly know what kind of a man he was? Because she had seen that keen loss and that sense of purpose in another man's eyes?

"Baba…my father…" She cleared her throat. "He was

a man who loved deep and true. I'm...sorry for depriving you of the boys until now. I only did what I thought was right for them."

His gray gaze held hers, a flash of emotions passing through, far too fast for her to catch any. For a second, Laila had the sense of standing at the edge of a cliff, looking into an abyss that promised untold delights if only you jumped. She wanted to run away with her sense of self intact just as much as she wanted to take a leaping dive.

Then his gaze flattened, leaving behind a touch of warmth. "You loved your father very much."

She nodded, feeling the loss deeply, even after all these years. "I did. Really, I've been fortunate..." She swallowed the sentimental words.

Even with all of Baba's love and care, she'd missed her mother. She'd desperately wanted to be part of her colorful life, wanted to drink in her exuberant personality, wanted to travel with her to all those fancy places that Nadia constantly teased her about. But that wouldn't be her sons' fate. "If you promise that Nikos and Zayn will have that... That's more than enough."

Sebastian's hand came up to tuck a curl behind her ear and every inch of Laila's body wanted to bow into the touch.

She shivered and swallowed, wondering how she was supposed to resist a man who could set her alight with one innocent touch, who was everything she shouldn't want and couldn't have. It was the same fight she had fought that night and lost.

The more time she'd spent with him, the more she'd realized there was more to Sebastian Skalas than the charming playboy or the ruthless predator of innocent men. So much so that she'd done the unthinkable and followed him to his bedroom and lost herself with him in a way she'd never done with a man, or even wanted to.

Now, again, he proved he was so much more even without answering her burning question. Even with the thorny knot of lies and half-truths between them, Laila felt that connection flare to life with one single touch, felt the need to give herself over into his hands. But there was so much more at stake between them now, more than just each other.

The worst part was that he was dangling himself in front of her, just within reach—a delicious, decadent prize, in some tragic parody of her deepest wish.

"Stay a few months here at the villa," he finally said. "Take as much time as you need to revive your career. Then you'll see that marrying me is giving the boys the best chance to thrive, with their parents together under one roof."

The need to ask his expectations if they married, to demand he promise her fidelity and more…hovered on her lips. Was it even possible after everything they had done to each other? Even now, he refused to tell her why he had targeted Guido in such a ruthless way. Even if he promised her the world and she accepted it, he'd soon tire of her. And she'd rather not face that inevitability.

"I agree, to stay here for a few months," Laila said, cautiously.

He leaned closer, temptation incarnate.

Laila dug her teeth into her lower lip to catch any wayward question and his gray eyes danced with a wicked light as if he knew how tempted she was.

"I hoped to provide some more data for your reassurances. But let's do this instead. How about I grant you three wishes, Laila?"

"Like my very own genie?" she said, unable to contain her excitement. She'd grown up living on those stories, hearing them in Baba's voice, always fervently wishing for the same one thing. "Except you're far too stud-like for any genie I ever imagined."

He laughed. It was a real laugh with deep grooves on the sides of his mouth and it tugged at her heart and somewhere else. "Yes, like that. Please feel free to rub me any which way you want. Though I will grant you three wishes without that, too."

She flushed and he grinned, the rogue. "You're a billionaire. A world-renowned artist, even if the entire world doesn't know it. You could probably charm the panties off a woman by smiling at her. Whatever I ask for, you can grant it to me easily."

"But there's the catch, Dr. Jaafri. I'm giving you a chance to up the stakes. You get to decide what you will ask me. But if I do grant you something...that truly makes you happy, that should count as a point in my favor, *ne*?"

"You can't...cheat your way through this, if that's what you're planning," she said, getting into the spirit of the challenge. It was a ridiculous bet, they both knew that. And yet, the spirit of playfulness beneath it had her arrested.

"I'm not the one who began our relationship on that note."

Laila sighed, knowing she deserved that. "So if you grant me three wishes that I truly want, I have to marry you," she said, laughing at the absurdity of the challenge. "If somehow you fail to grant me these three wishes, then you will agree to do this my way?"

He shrugged. "Yes. It is that simple."

Something about his confidence was heady and invigorating and so damned sexy. Something about the way he played with her, flirted with her, taunted her… was invigorating.

Laila wanted to bite that lower lip, and then kiss him. Only to find out if he truly wanted her, in this plain incarnation of hers. "Fine, I agree," she said, feeling a lightheartedness she hadn't known in years.

He walked away, leaving Laila feeling as if she was suspended upside down in a pool of honey, even as every inch of her thrummed with anticipation, with a new energy, just like last time. Except somehow it felt like, this time, he was the one casting the lure, and openly inviting her to walk into it.

And Laila was going to walk in with her eyes wide open.

# CHAPTER THREE

SEBASTIAN HAD ASSUMED he was prepared—mentally and emotionally—by the time the chauffeur-driven car pulled into the courtyard, as close as it could get to the wide steps, where he and Laila were waiting. But his heart—lodged in his throat—made it impossible to lie to himself.

He was excited and terrified in equal measures. For a man who'd fought so hard to not be molded into a template of his perfect twin, he found himself wishing Ani and Alexandros hadn't given him privacy to face his sons for the first time.

As some sort of buffer to guard *them* from him—what if he reacted wrong? What if, like all the times Konstantin had mocked and torn into him, something was wrong with him? What if he felt nothing for these two innocent children that were his responsibility?

The what-ifs were endless, but fear was not new to him, and Sebastian refused to let it cow him now when he hadn't let it when he had been a powerless, innocent child.

He wrapped his hand around Laila's wrist, right at the moment when she'd have flown off the steps to meet them, to anchor himself rather than to stop her. An instinctive weakness he couldn't hide.

Her entire body stilled, and her head tilted down to

look at his fingers. Then, as if they'd done this very ritual countless times, she laced her fingers around his. Her fingers were soft against his but there was also strength in them.

Without turning to look at him, she said, "For almost a month, after they were born, I was terrified every time I had to hold them. It's normal."

He simply nodded, unable to parse his feelings, wondering at how easily she offered reassurance when she had had none for the very same situation. Or rather, she'd had support, in the form of the very old man he'd been intent on destroying.

A woman, in her sixties, was the first one to step out of the car. She bent and time seemed to move inexorably slow as she plucked out a boy from the car and set him on his feet.

Smiling and stooped, she held his shoulders as his fat legs in shorts stumbled for a second like a newborn calf. Then, with a sudden whoop at the sight of his mother, he shrugged the nanny's hands off and ran full steam toward Laila.

From the wide smile and eager, inane chatter he kept spewing, Sebastian realized this was Nikos. His firstborn. His easy, affectionate, well-adjusted son.

Laila had been right about their physical resemblance, too—his son had the jet-black hair and the sharp nose of the Skalas family. But his eyes were like his mother's—a warm amber that practically glowed and changed the very landscape of the toddler's face, as if in defiance of the mighty Skalas genes that his father had been so proud of.

When Laila folded her legs to sit on the lowest step so that she was face-to-face with Nikos, Sebastian followed suit gladly, his legs nearly folding under him like they were made of matchsticks. He felt hollowed out with fear and something more, as if his insides were held together by strings outside his own body, as if this little boy or his brother could pull them as if he were a puppet and Sebastian would move and act as they bid him to.

Nikos reached them with eager cheer and easy smiles and wrapped his arms around his Mama's knees. For all his exuberant personality, it was his tiny size that struck Sebastian like a fist to his chest.

"Mama, Mama…on the way, I see horsey. Can I pet? Can I ride? Please, Mama. I be good boy for Granny."

Laila pressed her mouth to his temple and laughed, her hands moving over his tiny frame. The sound was full of such pure, incandescent love that it sounded alien to his ears. Sebastian had to swallow so that the strange, husky cadence of it didn't cling to his throat.

"Hmm… We'll have to make sure it's safe first, yeah, baby?" Laila said, running her fingers through his wind-ruffled hair. "Because horses are big and wild."

Dutifully, Nikos nodded. "Safe, yeah." Then he pinned those amber eyes on Sebastian, quite like how his mother had done that very morning, and Sebastian thought something he hadn't known inside him had been cracked open, never to be patched up or closed again. Like a vast abyss full of prickly things like vulnerability and joy and love and pain. An abyss that seemed to spring out of himself, one he'd avoided looking into for so long.

A gap-toothed grin appeared as Nikos said, "Hi."

Sebastian croaked out a "Hello, Nikos," as if he was the one who didn't know how to form words yet.

"You know horsey?"

Sebastian laughed. The sound seemed to come thrashing out from below his chest, through his diaphragm in an action his body was unaware it could perform until now. "Yes, Nikos. I might know horsey."

His good cheer growing, Nikos turned to his mother. "Friend, Mama? Not stranger?"

Hands squeezing Nikos's shoulders compulsively enough that the little boy bristled against his mother's hold, Laila trembled. But she met Sebastian's gaze over his head, ever the brave one. Then she gathered Nikos closer to her chest, kissed his temple again, before she said, "Nikos, this is your papa."

"Papa? My papa?"

Laila nodded, tears spilling out from her eyes.

"Hi, Papa," Nikos said, as if this was as easy and understandable as the sky was blue and the horse was big and then he made a jump from his mother's lap toward Sebastian that probably took a decade off Sebastian's life span.

Shaken to his core, he caught the little body. The scent of baby powder and dust and bananas hit Sebastian as he gathered his son to himself, his hands shaking, his breath a hurried whistle, terrified that he might do something that would spook the small boy.

But Nikos was as courageous as Sebastian himself had been once. Utterly unabashed, he threw his arms around Sebastian's neck and said, "Hi, Papa." His heart thundered like a drumbeat as he took in the stubby nose with crust under it and the wide amber eyes and the thick lashes. Now his heart felt like it was being squeezed in a vise, and that, too, was an ache he hadn't known in such a long time that it was now unfamiliar.

Nikos looked up into Sebastian's face, one grubby finger tracing his cheekbone, and said, "You take me to horsey?"

And Sebastian was laughing again, but there were tears in his eyes, too, and it was another thing he didn't know he was capable of—to laugh and cry at the same time—and he didn't care if Laila saw them. He sniffed like a baby, pressed a kiss to his son's head and said, "Yes, Nikos. Papa take you to horsey."

In response to Nikos's loud cheers, Laila groaned and laughed and told Sebastian in quite the stern voice that their sons would never learn to speak properly if she and Sebastian didn't speak in complete sentences to them, and Sebastian told her his son spoke perfectly enough for him and to hell with the entire damned world. And in the secret chamber of his heart that had frozen to ice a long time ago, he felt a crack. It felt good to belong to something bigger than himself, something purer than what the Skalas name and family had stood for, something that had this woman looking at him with a strange mixture of reluctant trust and utter openness.

His meeting with his second son was as much an emotional roller coaster as meeting Nikos but more…heart-wrenching, as if he'd been suspended at the scariest part of the ride, to hang upside down, his heart threatening to beat out of his chest.

And that's how it would be from now on, Sebastian realized. The stupid organ that he had no use for until now was to be wrenched and shaken and played around this way and that by these two little boys.

A few minutes later, Laila had spread a thick blanket

right on the acres of perfectly manicured lawn for an impromptu picnic, claiming she wanted to give the boys time to run around after their nap and before bringing them inside to new surroundings. Nikos was drinking water from his bottle, eating crackers she handed him and casting glances at and asking numerous questions of Sebastian—mostly about what the horsey ate and did and played with—when the old nanny brought Zayn, who'd been napping longer, out of the car.

He didn't run toward Laila like Nikos did. In fact, he seemed to be against the very idea of coming close to his mama, as long as she was sitting near Sebastian.

With a softly murmured, "Please give him space," and a tremor she couldn't hide, Laila got up from the blanket and started chasing Nikos across the green lawn, all the while keeping an eye on Zayn and chatting to him about the car ride and his nap.

Sebastian, feeling as if he'd been ordered to sit out his favorite game—which had been an actual punishment Konstantin had meted out to him more than once—took himself off the blanket, hoping Zayn would understand that he posed no threat.

Finally, after a few minutes of watching his mother and twin, a tiny notepad and pencil clutched in his tiny hands as if they were his precious possessions, Zayn approached his mother and hugged her legs. Immediately, Nikos grabbed his hand and dragged his younger brother forward. "Zayn, this Papa. He show horsey to us. You wanna come?"

While his twin's reassurance was enough to join in on the play and to hug his mother in this new, strange location, it didn't seem to hit the mark for Zayn when it came to trusting Sebastian. He took a step back to hide behind his twin's body, his amber eyes far too intensely focused on Sebastian's face for a two-year-old boy.

"Papa, Mama?" he said, after a long while, having heard his twin bandy about the word with a ferocious sort of pleasure.

Laila nodded, opened her mouth—no doubt to urge him to greet Sebastian—and then decided against it.

Zayn gave a grave nod in return, as if agreeing to process this new material, but promising no more, and then completely avoided Sebastian.

Like a laser pointer creating heat on his skin, he could feel Zayn's gaze on him from time to time, but the moment he tried to make eye contact, the little boy looked away. Which meant Nikos stayed away, too, because clearly, his first loyalty was to his twin.

Just as Alexandros's loyalty had been to Sebastian, all those years ago, enough to take on the impossibly powerful Konstantin, even as he threatened Xander's ruin for that loyalty. Sebastian looked away, the past and the future blurring in front of his eyes and in his head. He pressed his fingers into his temples, feeling the shadow of an ache there.

That won't be necessary with his boys, he vowed to himself. Nikos wouldn't have to shield Zayn from anything, much less their own father, because Sebastian would do it for both of them.

While every inch of him urged him to gather Zayn in his arms and cocoon his sensitive son from the very world itself, Sebastian fought the overpowering instinct. They were both here now, and he felt as if he had been swimming under water for too long, and he would not do a single thing that would upset his sons. He would not be his father, turning everything into ego, twisting what it meant to be a man, claiming they had to act a certain way to be worthy of the Skalas name.

He would not let his sons down. He would not let Laila down.

Suddenly, all the distrust he'd thrown in her face seemed like dust motes amid gratitude for how bravely she'd brought them into his life.

For years after she'd abandoned them to Konstantin's mercy, Sebastian had wondered where his mother had disappeared to, how she had fared, wondered if she'd thought of him and Xander, wondered if she was well. All he had known was that Guido, who'd worked as their chauffeur for one summer, had helped her escape, had been the only man who had known her whereabouts.

It had taken him years to track down the old chauffeur, a little more to understand his weakness for gambling, then he'd taken his house from him, knowing that shame, if nothing else, would persuade the old man to spill Sebastian's mother's whereabouts. He'd been desperate to find his mother as a young teen, but as a grown man, it had become an obsession, in the absence of any real purpose.

In pursuit of that piece of truth from his past, he'd threatened ruin for Guido, the very man who had helped Laila take care of his sons. Until now, that man had been only a step in his pursuit, an obstacle in his goal. But now, thanks to Laila, he couldn't unsee Guido as a kind old man who had once cradled his sons in his arms with tender care.

Guilt gnawed at Sebastian's insides. Having heard the

affection in her voice when she spoke of Guido now, he understood that she'd done whatever needed to protect a loved one. Just as he or Alexandros would have done.

And she also had every reason to think the worst of him and to stay away.

She loved his sons like no one else would—not even himself maybe—and she'd tangled with him to protect a man who had been kind to her. Now, she'd taken a chance on Sebastian, despite what she called calculating the odds.

It was his turn to show her that trust, to win her over, to give her everything she'd ever wanted in life for the gift she'd given him. To prove to her that she and the boys belonged with him.

Any momentary hesitation he'd felt about having two little boys to care for, to nurture and protect, dissipated, leaving behind a crystal-clear clarity he had never known in his life.

He had already fallen in love with his sons. It was a deluge, this sudden gripping, intense need to protect them, and hold them close and to have them near for every sweet and hard moment, a primal urge to walk into the now quiet bedroom where they were resting and watch over them for the rest of the dark nights and sunny days, a profound, gut-wrenching kind of relief to know he could feel so much for them, that Konstantin hadn't beaten that particular ability out of him.

Sebastian rubbed a hand over his face, shaking and shivering under the onslaught of emotions.

This was what he'd needed in his life, even if he hadn't known it until now. For the first time in his adult life, he wasn't simply meandering through it, trying his best to detach from the Skalas name and empire, burying himself in his art, wasting himself away on shallow experiences that drained his mind and body.

Now, he wanted his life to take a certain shape and he would actively pursue it.

Whatever instinct had propelled him to demand Laila marry him… It carried the weight of his deepest, most secret desire within it.

For his sons to be happy and well-adjusted and thriving, they needed their mother and he needed them in his life. Ergo, his primary goal now was to do anything to keep Laila in his life.

And while he'd have never admitted openly to his brute of a father, Sebastian had always known he could be just as ruthless as Alexandros, for all that he wore different masks for the world. He simply hadn't cared about anything enough, except finding his mother.

While his twin had devoted his ruthless will to ousting their father and rebuilding what it meant to be a Skalas man running the prestigious bank, Sebastian's own willpower had never been interested in anything. Until now.

He was keeping his sons and he was keeping their mother in his life, even if it meant he had to seduce every inch of logic and rationale out of Dr. Jaafri. And he would make sure she not only enjoyed the seduction but that she had everything she'd ever wanted in her life. He would make all her wishes and dreams come true. It was only a matter of getting her to admit them.

For himself, there was nothing he enjoyed more than a challenge with high stakes. Despite her lies and her one attempt at blackmailing him—all to protect Guido— he hadn't stopped thinking of her for a single day since she'd disappeared. So, it wasn't as if it was a hardship to seduce her.

As it was usually with him, she'd become an obsession, not just because she'd left him wanting more, but also because she'd gotten the closest to the one thing he held sacred in his life—his art. Now to know that she'd done it all to save a man he'd been bent on ruining...just for a piece of information that would unlock his own past. To reach a woman who'd abandoned him and Xander years ago.

*Cristos*, even for him, it was twisted.

But now that she was back in his life, with a gift unlike he'd ever received and not even known he needed, he would fix it all.

# CHAPTER FOUR

IT SHOULD HAVE felt strange to have Sebastian shadow her and the boys for the evening. Laila had found it nerve-racking when Mama and Nadia had visited a month after the boys had been born. And then when the boys had turned one.

Mama had criticized her about everything—that Laila was sharing the bed on alternate nights with Nikos and Zayn, that she didn't impose enough structure on them or that they had too much playtime or that she let them eat from her plate.

It had taken all her goodwill to not point out Mama's own flaws and faults in how she'd raised Nadia. For Laila, it was Baba who'd taken care of everything.

First, she hadn't even expected him to show up. She had compulsively followed enough of his wild, playboy exploits to know that he was a man who was bored easily, who thrived on unconventional risks, who chased every high like his life depended on it. And really, on their best day, her boys were exhausting and demanding. So, she'd been shocked when he'd arrived to get them ready for sleep.

When she got over that initial shock that he actually wanted to be part of their actual routines and rhythms, she'd braced herself to be watched under a microscope, to be weighed and judged and criticized. To be questioned.

He turned her assumptions upside down, yet again. The man had possessed a knack for making Laila feel good in her own skin in just a few hours. He'd made her laugh, step out of herself for a night. Now, she had none of that polish and fake sophistication, and yet, that same sense of ease lingered with the warm, easy energy he put out.

Through playtime and dinner and bath time and story time, he had been a quiet, easy presence in the background, keeping up a soft, slow dialogue with all three of them, without quite crossing the invisible boundary that Zayn had drawn.

It helped that Nikos, as ever, kept up their little unit's momentum, demanding to play, to eat, to be read to, on schedule and that he gave Sebastian one-word answers even as Zayn quietly observed them. By the time they'd settled into bed, Nikos had extracted another promise about the horsey from his papa.

Laila went to shower, leaving Sebastian standing outside the vast bedroom that had magically been arranged with two cribs, a changing table, a number of stuffed animals and toys in shiny new packages, and any number of paraphernalia that the boys could need, in just a matter of a few hours. Without Laila even broaching the topic, he had arranged for Ani and Alexandros to move to the second floor since the numerous open terraces and stairs were dangerous for the boys.

Being a caregiver apparently came easy to Sebastian Skalas, as easily as stunning art and that wicked, sinful smile. As hot water pounded through her tired muscles, Laila couldn't help but wonder if being a good husband would come easily to him, too.

Having dressed in an old T-shirt and a pair of shorts that suddenly felt too tight across her butt, Laila arrived in the attached bedroom to find Sebastian standing on steps that led directly to a private strip of beach from their suite.

With the moon full and high in the sky, silvery light danced on his hair, delineating the breadth of his shoulders and the taper to his waist. He was simply dressed in a linen gray shirt and black trousers and yet, somehow, he managed to highlight the powerful masculinity that seemed to thrum around him.

Laila felt tired to her bones. It had been an especially trying day, and she should have crawled into bed and let exhaustion take over. While Paloma would be the first one to wake usually if one of the boys was up during the night, Laila had given her tonight off. It was a new, strange place and she wanted to be the one they saw if they woke up feeling disoriented. Or maybe it was she who needed the comfort of snuggling one of them in her bed, since she felt more out of element than either of them. Even Zayn, while his usual reserved self, had been constantly taking everything in with those wide eyes.

The loneliness she'd endured for so long came back with a sudden bite, keener and sharper now. As if something inside her knew that what she'd wanted all along was within touching distance. Which was strange, because as she'd told him, Laila had never entertained ideas of romance or marriage. After giving birth to twins, it had become even more distant, for no man wanted to raise another man's twins. Not that she'd even considered the option of dating or fun or anything that didn't remotely concern her sons and her career and how to juggle it all.

But something about Sebastian had always called to Laila. She'd crossed so many of her self-laid boundaries back then and apparently that draw he had held for her hadn't dimmed one bit.

It was simple curiosity, she told herself, basic need for adult company, since she spent every waking hour—and some half-asleep ones—deep in dialogue with two toddlers or in statistics models she hadn't yet solved.

The stability and complexity she had sought in her career all her life suddenly didn't seem enough. Apparently, her body equated Sebastian Skalas with risk and how well and pleasurably it had paid off last time. Awareness didn't make her immune to Pavlovian responses.

She gave in to the urge and reached the cozy landing off the bedroom where he stood. Two bowls sat on the coffee table, one full of fruit and the other covered. Lifting the lid on the second, she found thick creamy yogurt with an assortment of nuts and seeds and honey in smaller bowls around it. He'd remembered the snack she'd asked for the first time they'd woken up tangled in each other that night. Warmth flickered in her chest, even as she reminded herself that the second time, she'd woken up alone and had gone through his apartment.

"Thank you for making today easy," she said, conveniently to his back. To avoid meeting his eyes, she busied herself with adding the nuts and seeds to the yogurt, and then a generous dollop of honey on top. She licked one thick streak from her thumb, and looked up to find his gaze on her mouth.

Heat licked through her blood, like the very honey on her tongue. Suddenly, she was aware of the heavy achiness of her breasts, and a loose, languid pulse fluttering low in her belly, right at the center of her core, desperate for friction.

"Is there anything else you need for tonight?" he said in such a matter-of-fact voice that Laila instantly felt foolish. It was all in her head, then—the lick of heat she'd seen in his eyes.

"No," she said, tugging the ends of the threadbare oversize cardigan she'd thrown on at the last minute over her worn-out T-shirt. "You thought of everything."

He nodded and then took the seat opposite hers, while she stirred the honey in.

A soft briny breeze was a welcome relief against her overheated skin while the yogurt was thick and creamy against her tongue. The quiet, breathtaking beauty of the setting, the sudden silence after hours of constant chatter from Nikos and Zayn, seemed to amplify the tension she felt around him. Spending too much one-on-one time with him was a bad idea, her gut said, and for once, she knew she needed to heed the instinctual voice.

"Am I speaking out of undeserving paternal pride," Sebastian said, stretching his legs, his fingers steepled on his abdomen, "or are they especially easygoing for two-year-old boys?"

Laila smiled at the lingering awe in his voice. It was good to know he was capable of those emotions, at least for their sons, and felt no shame in expressing it. "They *are* easygoing. Your paternal pride, I'd say, is not undeserving, either. You have a knack with children. Annika..." she said, hesitant to bring up the other woman but wanting to make sure he understood she'd only done the right thing, "told me you used to spend endless hours playing with her."

He shrugged, his gaze on the ocean. In profile, in repose, the magnetic quality of his presence should have been minimized, at least blunted. And yet, there was still that near-violent thrum around him, as if he was forcing himself into stillness and calm.

"Alexandros was too busy studying, doing magic with numbers and trying his damnedest to please Konstantin, to indulge in silly games with me. Ani…made it easy to escape the things I loathed. Which was everything, living under my father's thumb. Entertaining myself while I watched her for Thea and played with her…was purely selfish. It also had the added benefit of getting under Alexandros's skin, because even back then, he cared about her more than he would ever let on."

Laila absorbed every word and nuance like a sponge parched for water. There was such fondness when he talked of Annika and yet, he had refused to even look at her again after Laila's arrival. Something about how he framed it made her frown. "Is there a selfish motive in how you behaved with the boys today, then?"

He smiled. And it was the soft, disarming smile of a predator, who for some reason wanted her to feel safe with him. "Of course there is. I want them to feel safe with me, to trust me. To let me in. I know Nikos warmed to me pretty quickly, but I didn't miss how much Zayn's behavior dictates his own."

"You don't miss anything," she said, feeling both relief and a strange dread at the realization.

"You fooled me very thoroughly that night," he

quipped, one corner of his mouth tugged up. The lack of any rancor only made her want to explain.

"I didn't mean to. Or I mean, yes, I meant to corner you and demand some kind of…answer for why you were targeting Guido. I dressed up so out of my comfort zone, spent hours making myself up because you would've never paid me attention in my usual getup," she said, pulling at her T-shirt. "But everything that happened after I actually met you, that was unplanned. It spiraled into…something else. I didn't plan to sleep with you, Sebastian."

"I should feel rewarded that you did before stealing from me and blackmailing me that you would out me as the artist to the world?"

"Whether it was a reward or not, I don't know. But I'd never done that before and that—"

"You did not do what before?"

"Sleep with a man after knowing him for a few hours. Or sleep with any man," she added, though she immediately wished she hadn't. All this intimacy between them, it was forced by circumstance, not mutual want. In the normal world where she dwelled, she would have never gotten this close to Sebastian Skalas, nor should she want to.

"So you might think it's some cunning plan to seduce you but it wasn't. The moment you noticed me and started speaking to me, I lost control of everything. Including myself."

For a long while, he didn't say anything. Frustration coiled around Laila's heart. The man had a knack for making her own up to all kinds of things and yet clammed up just when she needed him to say something.

But she'd come this far, so she might as well say the rest. "I stand by what I did to protect Guido from you. But I wish I didn't have to do any of it. I would have come to you ages ago to tell you about the boys if not for the history between us. How can you insist on any kind of relationship between us when what I did will always color your thoughts, Sebastian?"

"Do you want me to forgive you, Laila? Or beg for forgiveness myself? Will it clear the slate between us?"

"I don't know," she said honestly.

He pushed a hand through his hair. "It is enough if I admit that I understand why you did it, *ne*?"

"But I want to—"

"How about we call a truce, Dr. Jaafri?" he said, interrupting her. "For the sake of our sons, we will start afresh, as much as possible. We will leave our misguided reasons behind and move forward."

It was the best she was going to get out of him—that almost admission of guilt. Something about the resolve glinting in his eyes made her ask, "What if Zayn takes longer to get close to you? To trust you? Will you abandon the whole venture then?"

Gray eyes held hers. "Patience *is* one of my virtues, Laila."

"What isn't?" she said, his words pinging over her skin.

"You'll find out soon enough," he said, his eyes taunting her yet again. "This is a novel experience for me, too. There are very few times in my life that I have set my mind to something."

"With Zayn…" Laila said, trying to parse through to the meaning in his words, "respecting his boundaries is very important and for a man who's had nothing to do with children, you made it seamless. My mother and sister usually…" She hesitated, loath to dump her frustration with them on his head.

He sat up slowly, like a predator uncoiling itself from its resting stance. "Usually what?"

"They…crowd Zayn. They constantly demand he talk to them or force playing on him or pick him up when he doesn't like to be touched. The whole thing riles him up and then he digs down into his bad mood. It usually takes me two to three days after they leave to reassure him that I won't encroach on him like they did, to get him back to a routine."

"Why not talk to them about respecting his boundaries?"

Laila scoffed. "Two-year-old with boundaries? My mother doesn't even acknowledge mine. You should have seen her reaction when I told her I was having the babies."

When the silence continued to build and he watched her steadily, Laila flushed. "Why does your silence feel like you're holding back?" she bit out.

He laughed then and this was different. This was real, with a jagged edge to the sound, as if it *had* caught him by surprise and he didn't have enough time to run it past a filter. The Charming Playboy filter. "You're very clever and perceptive, *ne*? Glad our boys have one parent to inherit smarts from."

"I know better than anyone who you are, Sebastian. But since reminding you of how I know that might spoil the mood, I shall not. Why did you laugh?"

"Because you pinned me spot-on. If you marry me, I can deal with your mother. I can deal with anyone who doesn't respect my son's boundaries. Zayn is just as special as Nikos," he said with such sudden aggression in his words that Laila felt like he'd sliced open her biggest fear for her sensitive son. "I'd hate for *anyone* to make him think otherwise."

His fierce support of Zayn made emotion surge through her. The yogurt felt sticky in her throat. "I agree. If I thought Mama or Nadia were causing him harm, I'd cut them out of our lives without another thought."

He nodded. But even their mutual agreement seemed to stir up tension between them.

Laila felt it in the pit of her belly, a taut thread tugging her this way and that. It was so new to her...this restlessness simmering under her skin. Along with the long, emotional day she'd had, it was a bit much to take in. Her breath shuddered as she tried to contain all the different emotions vying for attention.

Two seconds later, she almost jerked out of her chair when gentle fingers danced over her ankle. She looked up to find Sebastian had moved to a closer chair in front of her. "What are you doing?"

"You've had a long day," he said, bringing her foot to rest on his thigh. When she remained stiff in his hold, he looked up. "It's okay. You can let go for two minutes."

She hadn't cried on long, hard nights when it felt like the boys would never settle or when her career seemed to stall because she couldn't give it her hundred percent and when the bills seemed to pile on. And yet now... A sudden sob burst through her. Swallowing against it felt like fighting an incoming tide and a small part of her wanted to drown.

She could feel his shock in how his fingers stilled. "Are you okay, Dr. Jaafri?"

Laila tried a mockery of a smile. "I'm sorry. I don't know what's wrong with me...the whole thing is hitting me now, I think, and..."

"You don't have to apologize. I understand," he said in such a tender voice that Laila forced herself to look away. She was afraid that that tenderness, real or fabricated, might just be her undoing.

Sebastian didn't let her think, though. He nudged her foot farther into his grasp and his nimble fingers pressed into her heel and the painful arch and the sore digits, and he was kneading and pressing with such gentle, firm strokes that she felt like she was floating away on some fluffy cloud, as far as possible from hard, cold reality.

Leaning against the back of her soft chair, she threw her head back and closed her eyes. The man could weave magic with those fingers, and not just on her feet. Tension lingered but more crept in—this languorous sense of well-being she had never tasted. With her heel tucked snugly against his abdomen, which was a slab of rock, something else stirred beneath the overwhelming relief. She groaned when he switched to the other foot, hitting an especially sore spot.

"Will you throw in these foot massages daily if I agree to your condition?" She meant to sound jovial. But her body betrayed her, making her words sound like a husky invitation.

His fingers stilled on her ankle. With a lock of jet-black hair falling onto his forehead, his mouth wreathed in that wicked smile again, he looked exactly how she'd dreamed of him for three years. "Try me and see, Dr. Jaafri."

Wordless, breathless, she pulled her feet back. When she stood up, tiredness hit her like a full-body slam at her martial arts class. "Thank you for...everything."

"I did no more than the minimum expected of me today."

"You really believe that, no?" she said, picking up her spoon and the empty bowls.

Reaching her, he took them from her hands. The simple contact of his fingers lingering on hers felt so good that she had to pluck hers away. "The staff will pick those up."

"Good night, Sebastian," she said and turned away.

Behind her, he said, "Why did you decide to have the babies?"

"Why do you think?" she said, feeling instantly defensive.

"Don't worry. In all this, there's one thing that's very clear. You seek nothing from me that's not solely for the boys."

Somehow, that didn't sound as reassuring as it should have. It felt more like...scorn or mockery.

"You said your mother disapproved of your decision and I can see why, at least partly." Suddenly, he was standing too close. "How old are you?"

Laila jerked her gaze up from the inviting hollow of his throat. "Twenty-seven."

He cursed. "So, you were twenty-four when you—"

"I already had tenure at university, a clear path for my career," she said, cutting his taunt off.

"At that young age?"

"I graduated high school very early, finished my PhD when I was twenty. Academics are easy for me," she said, expecting his surprise. "Socializing, and saying one thing but meaning another, playing the polite but backstabbing games with colleagues in academia, all the strange dating rituals…not so much.

"Romance wasn't in the cards for me. Then you and I happened. When I found out I was pregnant, with twins at that… It was terrifying at first. But… I also had Guido and Paloma and the safe space to really think it through."

"It was that easy to make that decision?"

"When I was a little girl, I used to pray and wish and hope for a fun, boisterous, happy family, with parents who adored one another and siblings who loved each other. I wanted to be…loved and wanted as I was." She tried to scoff at her naïveté, afraid that he would do it, but couldn't.

"With the pregnancy, I realized this was my chance to make my wish come true. Even if the boys only had me, I thought…this is it. The logistics and reality were much, much harder than even my rigorous calculations," she said with a self-deprecating laugh, "but the love I see in Nikos's and Zayn's eyes when they look at me or reach for me or when they kiss my cheek with grubby mouths… I know I'm living my dream. No fear, or worry or overdue bill can take that away from me."

Sebastian walked impossibly closer, and her pulse began to race. She could see the deep, disorienting gray of his eyes, could smell his cologne and sweat, could feel the warmth of his lean body graze her muscles in a lazy invitation.

She held his gaze, some wild instinct she'd known only once before egging her on even as her belly took a dizzying dive.

"I've always wanted a family like that. Now we can both get what we want, *ne*?" His words were low, soft, as if he was tempering some great emotion. "You have only convinced me that I'm right, Dr. Jaafri. And soon, you'll agree."

Then, in a move that made her heart beat out a wild rhythm, his hands landed on her shoulders, and he pulled her to him.

Laila sank into the hard warmth of his body, trembling like a leaf in a storm. His arms felt like salvation, like a cocoon, like her very own safe place to land. And somehow, that deep sense of security seemed to open the floodgates to all the worries she'd been shouldering alone even before the boys had been born.

Soundless sobs shook her, washing away any embarrassment she should feel for breaking down in front of him. Sebastian didn't seem even a bit surprised or thrown off at her crying. His arms tightened, his lips whispering soft, sweet words in Greek, wrapping them around her like a safety blanket. His words, his touch, his warmth… It was a glorious gift she hadn't known she needed.

Relief filled her in soft, overwhelming waves, followed by sudden, thick fingers of sleep and she barely had a memory of sinking into his arms and the vague impression of him carrying her to bed and tucking her in, as if she too were precious to him.

Laila slept like the dead that night, thinking it curious that it was thanks to the same man who had kept her awake for countless nights.

# CHAPTER FIVE

SOMEHOW THEY SETTLED into an easy routine over the next few weeks, though it should have been impossible on paper.

Not somehow, Laila acknowledged. It was thanks to Sebastian.

There wasn't a single thing that the boys or she needed that wasn't already arranged or sorted for them, before Laila herself could think of it. He'd arranged for Annika and Alexandros to leave the villa for a whole two weeks, so that the four of them could bond as a unit, even as he admitted that Alexandros had been quite put out about moving his very pregnant wife into his penthouse in Athens, even temporarily. Laila had thought it was also because Sebastian wanted to avoid Ani, but she kept that to herself.

She would have liked to have Ani around, to avoid too much one-on-one time with Sebastian. After her near breakdown and his tenderness that first night, Laila felt as if there was no equation or model for her feelings to follow. Unless it was chaos theory, since they went up and down and around, tying her in helpless knots. Apparently, a little kindness from Sebastian could make her as fragile as Nikos's sandcastle.

He had also forbidden their grandmother Thea from visiting just yet, Alexandros had quipped, expressly for Laila's sake. Being the traditional matriarch, Thea would apparently bear down on Laila to make her great-grand-sons legitimate heirs of the Skalas family ASAP.

Laila had enough to handle with her world turning upside down, thanks to Sebastian's determination to mold himself into the father of the century and the most reliable, easygoing, close-to-wonderful co-parent.

He'd gone overboard with an army of extra staff he had interviewed himself and hired to keep an eye on the boys around the villa, and an insane number of toys and swings and slides and scooters and bicycles and inflatable castles that had begun to arrive in quick succession at the villa over the first week.

On the sixth afternoon of their arrival, Laila ran out, her heart in her throat, as Nikos shouted loudly for her from the front lawn. She skidded to a stop on top of the steps to find Sebastian on his knees, surrounded by two puppies and their sons, though Zayn was a few steps behind his twin.

Mouth hanging open, Laila reached them. "Sebastian, what did you do?" she asked, inanely.

Zayn answered for his father, more excited than she'd seen him in a long while, amber eyes dancing with pleasure. "Puppies, Mama." He held up two of his little chubby fingers aloft as if to make sure she understood the significance of the number. "Two puppies, one for Nikos. One for me," he said, thumping his chest, then turning away to run toward the tiny little bundles.

There was no way for Sebastian to answer her, though he grinned at her from the ground. Hair flopping onto his forehead, gray eyes shining with attention, he was overwhelmingly gorgeous, far too real in a way Laila had never imagined he could be. For one bitter second, she wanted to say he was manipulating the boys but she instantly knew that was unfair.

She followed the caravan—Paloma and the two helpers gleefully joining in—as Sebastian showed both the boys how to pet the tiny puppies and told them in soft, easy words how important it was to treat them kindly and to give them lots of love.

Nikos and Zayn—eyes bright and wide—followed his hands and his words and his actions, as if he was a larger-than-life hero. And maybe to her sons, he was a hero.

Maybe, sooner or later, they would have needed this, too, in their life. Laila had enough experience to know that one parent's undivided, unconditional affection could never make up for negligence from the other.

It was a long while—after he directed them to pour water in the puppies' bowls, and put a leash on them and set them all free—before Sebastian walked toward her.

Hair wind-ruffled, dark denim showing off his lean physique, he looked like he had walked out of a photo shoot. Wishing she'd put on a different top and combed her wayward hair, Laila rubbed at the banana stain on her shirt.

If he noticed her frantically grooming herself like a pet being presented to its master, thankfully he ignored it. She felt an instant thrum under her skin when he finally reached her, a thin sheen of sweat coating his face and neck.

"You didn't come to pet the puppies. The boys called you enough times."

Of all the things for him to notice and comment on... Laila was continually shocked by how perceptive he was for a shallow playboy who cared nothing about others. Or at least that was the impression he wanted to make. "I'm... I'm not used to dogs. In fact, I'm scared of them," she admitted, her cheeks going pink.

If she thought he'd laugh at her, he proved her wrong again. "You didn't have one growing up? Never played with a neighbor's dog?"

"No. I had enough people to look after without adding a dog to the mix," she said, before she could arrest the thin thread of resentment. "Baba was an academic who buried his head in research and history and my mother and sister... They would have hated the idea of a dog. Unless it was one of those posh crossbreeds that fits in a designer purse."

When he stared at her in surprise, she colored. "What about you? Did you have one?"

"No. I begged and begged but was not allowed. It was a sort of punishment."

"For what?"

"Let's just say I was a lot to handle as a kid. Giving me a dog would have been too much. And in hindsight, I'm glad I was deprived of it."

Laila stilled at the strange tenor to his words, the tight set of his jaw. But she didn't want to probe. "You're a lot to handle even now," she said, hoping to pull him out of that dark mood.

Meeting her eyes, he grinned. For the space of a second, his gaze dipped to her mouth and then back up. "I'm easy to handle if one was inclined to learn," he said, his tone returning to teasing.

"Two tiny puppies, though, Sebastian?" she said, as much to cover the heat racing her cheeks as much to speak up. He flirted so easily with her and it wasn't like it was an act, either. She knew that much. "That's a bit much for two-year-olds, don't you think?"

"A boy should always have a dog."

She heard both his resolve and something more—like a loss—in those words. It shook her a bit, the intensity he hid beneath his easy charm. "Who's going to look after them? They're babies."

"All of us."

"You're spoiling them," she said, unable to help sounding critical.

"I have more than two years to make up for." He turned to her, turning that thousand-watt attention squarely on her. Her skin prickled. "What's really bothering you, Dr. Jaafri?"

Their gazes held in a silent battle before she relented with a sigh. "Puppies feel permanent. It will be hard enough to make the boys understand when…if things don't work out."

His anger was betrayed by the tight fit of his mouth but nothing more. "I don't think you've still grasped my commitment to this and maybe that's on me. To answer your question, if you move out of here, which will be because you didn't give this a fair chance, the puppies and the extra helpers and probably even I will just follow. That's how this works, *ne*?"

With a sigh, she nodded.

But whatever he thought of her doubts, he didn't let it linger. Shooting to his feet, he gave her his hand. Surprised, Laila took it anyway. His big hand enfolded hers in an easy grip as he tugged her. "It's time you learn to play with puppies, Dr. Jaafri. Come."

"What? No. I mean... That's not necessary, Sebastian. The boys have you and everyone else to help them."

"Not to help. But for fun. For yourself."

Shocked, Laila offered no more protest and soon, her sons were shouting that she had joined and two adorable puppies were licking her chin and Sebastian laughed and held her when she burrowed into him when the more aggressive one tried to climb her legs.

Hard and hot and smelling of clean sweat and a subtle cologne, he was more than a safe haven. Under the guise of hiding from the teeny puppy, Laila clung to him for a few more seconds, and when she looked up into his gray gaze, she knew that he knew.

But he didn't mock her. With a warm flame in his gray eyes, he tightened his arms and Laila wondered at how easily he made her feel wanted.

With each passing day, Laila felt more and more out of control of her own life, even though she was doing so much more than the bare minimum. Which was strange because she was less worried about the boys' long-term security now, and had three whole hours every afternoon to focus on the paper she was writing for an extremely competitive academic journal. Paloma had two new helpers, other than Sebastian being on hand, if the boys didn't settle down for their two naps, *and*, she knew 100 percent that she'd made the right decision.

The boys were thriving under Sebastian's patient presence. Though Zayn wouldn't come out and show it just yet.

Her sensitive son watched his papa and his twin play

and run and chase dogs with his big, thick-lashed amber eyes wide and curious and longing, quite how Laila watched Sebastian, she imagined. Desperate to be part of them, but not yet ready to join in, or not knowing how.

While she was beginning to believe that Sebastian had the boys' best interests at heart, Laila thought that exact reason boded something else for her.

*"I've always wanted a family, too,"* he'd said and meant it.

Which, quite logically, led her to believe that he would do anything to persuade her to make them into a traditional family unit through marriage.

In his mind, she might as well be no more than a tool he would use to get close to his sons, to ensure their well-being and happiness, as easily as he might employ a dog or a toy. She could be any woman in the world—her defining role to him was that she was his sons' mother.

Which should be reason enough for her to resist the lure he cast. If not for her actively pursuing him, he would never have come into her orbit, never danced with her or taken her to bed. Never made an offer of marriage, if not for their sons.

Sebastian Skalas was like the sun, just as Mama once had been. He sparkled and glittered and drew others into his orbit automatically, for fun, for entertainment, wherever his fancy stuck. And then he moved on, leaving people like her sons discarded like broken toys. Just like Mama had done to Baba.

Just like he would do to Laila, given she was the exact opposite of the woman a man like him noticed.

And yet, for some inexplicable, possibly foolish and definitely naive reason that went against every bit of rationale she tried to dredge up, Laila wanted him to want her. She wanted to be seduced. She wanted more of his soft confessions and wicked smiles, and she wanted those strong arms that had wrapped around her with such gentleness to move all over her with desire and urgency and none of that smooth control.

She wanted more than his pretend hugs and polite bridge-building and fake friendship. She wanted to peel beneath the various masks he put on. Until she knew what he'd wanted from Guido so badly that he'd have ruined the older man. Until she knew why he hid his art from the world. Until she knew him like no one else did.

It was impossible to put this into a rational construct except that she'd clearly been a lot lonelier than usual since her pregnancy, and she wanted sex and companionship, and she wanted both of these specifically from Sebastian.

Whether it was because he was the father of her sons or because he'd been her only lover, or because something about him inexplicably drew her to him, she had no idea.

With a frustrated groan, she pushed away from the massive desk in the airy sunroom that had been created as her workspace. Three solid hours of free time and she was spending it daydreaming ridiculous scenarios about a man who only wanted her in his life for their sons. Leaving her to wonder what it was about Sebastian Skalas that always made her act out of character.

# CHAPTER SIX

IN HINDSIGHT, Laila thought she should have expected that Sebastian would default to form in that spectacularly dramatic fashion of his—getting caught smooching some tall, anemically thin, cheekbones-for-life model/designer/party girl.

Three weeks *was* a long time for him to act the domesticated homebody, given he'd spent most of his life in the most profligate of ways.

That some tabloid toe rag had caught him smooching said Slavic model wouldn't have been on Laila's radar, if Annika in her desperation to stop Laila from seeing it had inadvertently made Laila curious enough to seek it out.

In a smart black jacket with the white shirt underneath open to his abdomen, he had been caught in profile, with the model's mouth attached to his, her body wrapped around him like a squid's tentacles from the boys' favorite cartoon show. This was on the first night he'd been away from the villa since their arrival.

He hadn't yet returned from his jaunt and Laila wondered if he had to like…build a buffer of partying and sleeping around and causing general mayhem to sustain being the responsible, caring parent the rest of the time. Like her own mother, who'd needed parties and theater and flirting endlessly with "exciting men" because she claimed her life with Baba was boring and dull and predictable. As if it was his primary responsibility in life to provide entertainment for her. Failing that, she'd expected him to support her extravagant lifestyle.

This wasn't the same, Laila tried to tell herself. He hadn't made any promises of fidelity to her. He'd offered a cookie-cutter marriage deal that she hadn't accepted. He was free of obligation to her. They had nothing in common except the boys. He wasn't a man she could trust a hundred percent. Her excuses for him went on and on but didn't stick, didn't make the slice of hurt lessen.

Seeing him with his...flavor of the month felt like someone had picked her up and thrown her across a hard floor. Like her very breath had been beaten out of her. Like the numerous times when her half sister, Nadia, had teased her that she didn't belong with her and their mother because she was so...weird with her "not-so-slender build and over-smart brains" and a freak with her head buried in numbers and models.

Laila's first instinct was to pack up the boys and run away, which was laughable in itself because where would she run to and from what. And she wasn't the sort to run away from reality in the first place. This was her life now, even if disappointment clung like bitter bile to the back of her throat. What she needed was to get out of the villa, at least for a short while. Meet someone from her plane of reality to get her head screwed on right.

After all, this villa and the lifestyle and the man himself... They could all be from an alien planet she'd been thrust into.

She made arrangements with Paloma and her helpers

early next morning so that she could have the afternoon for herself. She refused Annika's offer to accompany her on her "shopping trip," having already divided Annika's loyalties enough to cause the rift of a lifetime. Sebastian was still avoiding her and the last thing she needed was to disclose her thorny feelings about him to her.

When Alexandros commanded in that steely voice of his that he'd arranged for a chopper to bring her to Athens, she'd almost lost her temper at him. But he wasn't her culprit. And she was working hard on convincing herself that no one was.

Finally, after what felt like an eternity but really was maybe thirty minutes, the chopper dropped her off on top of a skyscraper in the business district of Athens, close enough to the café that was her destination.

Laila took the elevator down to the boutique Annika had recommended. Not that she could afford anything more than a pair of shoelaces there, but to kill time before her friend was due.

When she stepped onto the sprawling thirty-second floor, with its shining mosaic floors and all-glass facades—clearly home to a host of exclusive, designer stores—the entire level was suspiciously empty. As was the boutique with its gleaming black marble floors, pristine white counters and a lingering expensive scent that made Laila feel like a wild creature in the plastic jungle.

Looking around the quiet space, she wondered if she'd somehow missed a local holiday. On further inspection, she found the boutique to be open, with a tall, stylish woman hovering around the entrance, looking at Laila as if she was a royal dignitary gracing the boutique with her magnanimous presence.

"Dr. Jaafri? Welcome," the woman said. "I'm Natasha. The store and I are at your disposal for the next several hours."

Laila opened her mouth, closed it, then followed the woman into the store. Now, she felt churlish for refusing Ani's company when she'd clearly arranged everything for her. She spent the next hour pleasantly surprised when she tried out the collection of frothy silk dresses, soft-as-butter blouses and trousers she preferred for work that the woman picked out to suit her unusual frame of wide shoulders, small breasts and hippy...hips.

Even though she couldn't really keep any of the pieces, Laila gave in to the pleasurable folly of trying dresses that were utterly unsuitable for her lifestyle and way out of her price range. Neither did she miss the fact that at these astronomical designer price tags, even her body could look damn good.

Two glasses of the most delicious champagne and two macarons later, she felt giddy enough to try a daring sleeveless little number in a burnt orange shade that did wonders for her golden brown complexion. The bodice was pretty much a strap around her breasts and then flared, falling a couple of inches above her knees, showing off her long legs.

Having thanked Natasha for helping her into it, Laila was about to look at herself when her nape prickled. She turned and heard the woman leave the room immediately, the door closing behind her.

Sebastian stood inside the room, immediately shrinking it in size.

In a leather jacket and dark denim that hugged his long legs, he looked like he could be one of the perfectly proportioned mannequins. Except no man made of synthetic materials could hold that warm, wicked light his gray eyes did. He looked how she imagined he'd look after a couple of nights of debauchery. Dark shadows clung to his eyes and there was at least two days' worth of stubble on his jaw. Despite his disheveled state, there was a faint buzz of sensuality that emanated from him, as if he couldn't help putting that particular vibe out.

Had he rolled out of that model's bed an hour ago? Had he come here with that woman's scent on him?

The tacky, jealousy-filled questions gave her whiplash as she fought to tamp them. *None of my business* didn't really seem to work.

Even the fact that he might have been with another woman not an hour ago could diminish his appeal, though. She had to consciously work on tugging her gaze away from the V of his T-shirt, from the corded column of his throat, that hollow she desperately wanted to…lick and smush her face against.

"Did you miss me, Laila?"

"Excuse me?"

"You have that look in your eyes, the one that says you want to inhale me whole."

Heat crested her cheeks. "That's probably the champagne on an empty stomach. What are you doing here?" Suddenly, the empty building made sense.

"Alexandros informed me about your sudden expedition. The building was evacuated. I had this store open since Ani said you wanted to shop here."

She swallowed and looked around. So, Natasha and the little surprise had been his doing? Because he wanted to assuage a guilty conscience? "Isn't that a bit much?"

"Given there were hordes of reporters here half an hour ago, I would say not."

"Reporters?" she repeated blankly. "Here? Why?"

"I'm not fond of saying I told you so. Smacks of self-righteous pride. I believe it might be because news got out that I have sons." He pushed off the wall with a smooth grace, immediately giving her the impression that he was on the chase and she was his prey. "Alexandros said he barely got you to take the chopper. You should have—"

"I didn't realize I was under house arrest. Or that I need your permission every time I need a break."

Hands tucked into the back pockets of his trousers, chin tucked down, he stared at her. "Something is wrong. Is it Zayn? Has Nikos—?"

"They're fine. Though Nikos won't stop asking after you."

Just like that, the exhaustion clinging to him vanished, changing the panorama of his face. "And Zayn?"

Two simple words and the entire universe seemed to expand with the hope pulsing within them.

For a second, Laila considered lying, then abandoned the idea. Sebastian's devotion to his sons was a rare quality and his actions toward her shouldn't be her barometer to judge him. It was easier said than done, though. "You know how his little body stills and he won't even blink when he's really invested in something?"

Sebastian nodded.

"He gets like that every time Nikos asks after you."

His chest rose and fell, his lips pursing inward and then out. And then in the blink of an eye, he switched personas. "I hear you have a hot date. Is that why you're shopping?"

"I'm meeting a friend for a drink." When he watched her, unblinking, as if she was hiding state secrets, she said, "I thought the advantage of this whole arrangement was that I could take a couple of hours out of my life for myself."

"Of course it is. Unless you told this friend who the boys' father is, and he leaked it to the press."

"Fahad would never do anything that would hurt me."

"Maybe not," Sebastian said, getting a belligerent look in his eyes that she was beginning to recognize as possessiveness. "Then how would we explain why the press was coming after you today? Alexandros doubled the security around the villa."

"Maybe they were here because they wanted to get a look at you and your arm candy?" Laila burst out.

"My arm candy?" With a curse, he rubbed his hand over his face. "You saw the tabloid?"

"It's none of my business."

When she tried to move forward, he blocked her, his hand on her elbow. Even disheveled, the man packed a punch with his magnetic presence. "You aren't upset, then?"

She shook her head, avoiding his gaze.

"If I tell you that she came onto me and kissed me, and the photographer caught us right as I untangled myself? That I have no interest in her or anyone else? That she and some friends orchestrated that whole scene in some stupid welcome joke since I've been MIA?"

Laila folded her arms, feeling that strange tension gather in her belly again. It was that irrational, inconvenient want she felt near him. "It doesn't matter, Sebastian."

He leaned in closer, trapping her against the glass wall behind her. "It doesn't matter that I propose marriage to you and then turn around and sleep with the first woman I come across that's not you?"

Laila stilled, sensing a sudden change in the very air around them. He was…angry. Blisteringly so. He hadn't been this angry when she'd revealed the news about the boys. And she knew instantly that she had made a mistake, that she had rubbed salt on a wound that clearly festered. "Since I didn't accept your proposal, it's not…"

He laughed then and it was so bitter that she felt nauseated. His lean body tightened with tension. "Maybe Alexandros is right that I'm a fool to offer you all that I have."

Laila didn't give a damn what Alexandros thought. She did care, however, that she had misjudged Sebastian through her own insecurities and created strife between them. "I hate to say this but your history made me believe the clip, Sebastian. You're notorious for this kind of behavior, for changing partners on a whim, for chasing every high, for excessively wild risks. What was I supposed to do when you disappear after three weeks with us and then show up with a woman clinging to you plastered all over the internet?"

"You could have asked me. Or is my word not trustworthy, too?"

"If you say you didn't kiss that woman, you didn't kiss that woman," she said, rushing through the words. "But we're…opposites. You thrive on excitement, and risks and bending society's rules and I'm a boring, dull statistician whose deepest, darkest wish is to stay in and listen to old maestros on precious records. That's why your proposal won't work. You'll eventually tire of me."

"All of this based on a gossip rag that caught me at a bad moment?" His tone could cut through glass and she knew this was the real Sebastian.

"All of this based on a relationship that I've once seen go up in flames, where the…parties were just like us," she said, biting her parents' mention at the last second. "We have nothing in common except the boys."

"Oh, wow, so this is the statistician extrapolating data?"

Laila sighed. "You ended up at a raucous party the first night out in three weeks. You…were itching to get away the last few days. You…"

"Because I was beginning to get one of my bloody migraines. It's not a pretty sight for anyone and they claw me under for a few days. I didn't want to frighten the boys or you. And I ended up at the bloody party because I wanted to come back to the villa and needed something to numb the pain. Like an edible. It's the only thing that helps."

Suddenly, his disheveled state, the dark shadows under his eyes, the faint tension thrumming around him made… so much sense. Why hadn't he told her? "I'm sorry. I didn't know that you suffered from—"

He stepped back from her, shaking his head. And Laila had the suddenly dawning fear that she had lost something that she didn't know she needed—his willingness to build something between them. That fear made her articulate something she'd have never allowed herself—a right to him and his secrets, to his real self. "You could have told me you were unwell. Or that you needed to get away, that you get…restless when it begins. Just one line, Sebastian and all of this could have been avoided. How do you think a marriage would work between us if you won't even give me that at this stage?"

"I will not spend another half of my life trying to prove who I am or what I'm capable of."

The bitterness in his words, the flyaway tidbits she gathered about his childhood from Annika, his disinterest in anything related to the Skalas name, his refusal to share himself with the world as a renowned painter... She was operating blind on an emotional minefield. But the thing she knew with a sudden clarity was that she wanted a map to him. She wanted to reach him.

"You said we would start over and that can't be done if you hide parts of your real self from me, and show me the charming mask you put on for the rest of the world. The boys need a father who will not hide away imperfect parts of himself. What do you think that says to them?"

A soft hiss escaped his lips and Laila knew she'd reached him. But there was more and she let it pour out. "I can't be in a relationship with a man who won't even give me easy communication in such small things. We might as well call it quits now."

His gray gaze pinned her to the spot, something dancing there. "Fine. This is my fault a hundred percent and I apologize. But instead of demanding an explanation, you decided to invite your boyfriend here in some twisted revenge?"

"Fahad is not my boyfriend," she said, suddenly understanding his anger.

"But he would like to be, no?" he retorted, with an unnerving perception.

Laila's shocked silence said things she didn't want to say.

He thrust a hand through his hair, a hardness she hated

entering his eyes. "I will make other arrangements for you to stay close to the villa while I start custody proceedings. I know you won't believe it, but I'll be fair."

"I don't want that," she whispered, grabbing his arm, the resonant truth of her words dawning on her. "I invited him because he's from my world, Sebastian, and one of the few people who doesn't treat me like a freak. I needed to find the ground under my feet."

He stilled, as if her very touch was repellant. "You can't have it both ways, by holding some unnamed condition over my head then coming to the worst conclusions in your head. You agreed to give this a fair chance."

"You can't go off to parties with models without telling me why, either, Sebastian. Or better yet, just don't go to parties with models," she burst out, and then cringed at how demanding and possessive that sounded. The words lingered between them, dancing over a line she wished she had the strength to not cross. Laila pressed her forehead to his arm and exhaled. His hand in hers was big, rough, broad, and something about the touch anchored her. Gave her strength to be honest with him and herself, as strange as that sounded to her rational mind. "I...if I'm to give our bet a real consideration, if I am to believe that a marriage between us has a chance of working, you should know I...want fidelity, Sebastian. I want it to be as real as we can make it. I can't even consider doing it any other way."

"Noted, Dr. Jaafri," he said and the serious tone of his voice told her he understood the step she was taking.

"I convinced myself it did not matter if you kissed another woman," Laila went on. "I promised myself that I wouldn't let this become personal between us, wouldn't let my weakness for you…muddy this."

"Your weakness for me would blind you to who I am?"

She scoffed, her lips trembling at the dense muscle packed in his arm. "No. It blinds me with my own insecurities. It confirms patterns that I seek to protect myself with, even when they aren't there," she admitted with little grace.

"Look at me, Laila."

She raised her eyes, feeling as if she'd cracked herself open past a door that had always been inaccessible to her.

His eyes searched hers, a steely resolve to them. "Nikos and Zayn adore you. They will believe everything you do. You owe it to me to be careful how you judge me."

"That's the thing that sticks in my craw. When it shouldn't," she said, with a snort. "You see me as nothing but their mother. I could be any woman from the long list of your lovers and you would offer me the same little package deal." She pressed a hand to her chest, her heart thundering in there. "Apparently, I'm selfish enough in all this to not want to be a placeholder."

"You think I invited you into my home, my brother's home, into our private lives, without knowing what kind of a woman you are? Without considering the fact that you nearly ruined me and yourself out of loyalty for a man who's not even related to you? Without considering that you're not only devoted to my sons, but would stand up to me if I wasn't good enough for them? Without remembering that, amid all the lies you wove and the plans you made, you responded to me with a hunger and need I have relived a thousand times over in three years?"

Laila stared, feeling more than foolish. Fingers of heat trickled through her, banishing every doubt for now.

Sebastian scoffed. "Unlike you and Alexandros, I trust my instinct. As for not seeing you..." He rubbed a hand over his lower lip and she was beginning to see it for the tell it was when he wanted her. "You live under my roof and you follow my every move with those big eyes, just as hungrily as Zayn does. You seduced me and disappeared for three years, leaving me a damn note while I obsessively looked for you. I would plan what I'd do when I caught you so elaborately, dream of the moment I had in you in my hands... I'd see your face in every woman who was tall or had that way of walking or..." His warm breath coated Laila's lips. "It is already personal between us. It was, even before the boys."

Laila felt a liquid longing well up within her at his soft words. She felt greedy, grasping, voraciously so, for more from him. *Of him.* As much as it had been an act, the one night she'd spent in his company had been the most alive she'd ever felt. The most she had lived in her entire life.

It was a dangerous game to want to matter and she had lost before and yet... She felt like Paloma's yarn when the boys got their hands on it, unspooling away into sensations and feelings, tangling into knots, changed forever.

"What would you have done with me if you had caught me?"

# CHAPTER SEVEN

HE SMILED AND it contained a multitude of promises and invitations. As if she'd asked him to reveal the secrets of the universe only to her and he'd been hoping she would ask. In that smile, Laila thought she could see her entire future, and the absurd thought nearly paralyzed her.

Grabbing her wrist, Sebastian said, "Come."

She let herself be dragged as if she was made of not bone and flesh, but want and longing. She giggled like she'd have as a normal teenager stealing away with a boy she liked, if that boy hadn't paid attention to her only because she was gateway to meeting her beautiful older sister, Nadia.

Taking her hand, Sebastian drew her inside a very upscale, very luxurious room painted in shades of soft pink and white. An intricate, vast chandelier hung from the high, round ceiling. Expensive and frothy-looking confections in bright silk—she supposed they were dresses—hung from a couple of rolling stands.

A rich purple velvet lounger stood in the middle of it, with trays of sweets and a bucket of champagne strewn about the room as if they had been expecting a...special guest.

"You planned this."

Sebastian didn't answer.

She busily mapped his broad back and his tapered waist and the outline of his buttocks in his black trousers with shameless greed, while he went around the large room turning on every light until Laila's reflection glowed in the three-fold full-length gold-edged mirror.

Since she'd left her hair to air-dry, her curls framed her face in what Mama called untamed, unsophisticated wildness. The deep rust-colored dress brought out the gold in her skin, clinging to her body just enough to hint at her small curves. Tiny golden hoops and a thin gold chain added just enough style. Her transformation from her usual food-stained loose T-shirts and shorts to this was by no means a Cinderella makeover.

But now, standing still under such soft, forgiving lights, forced to consider her reflection, Laila saw the changes in herself. Her pregnancy had left no big mark on her frame except her breasts were a little bigger. Her body had bounced back pretty easily, given she'd birthed twins, and she'd always been grateful for that.

Thanks to good genetics—which her mother bemoaned she hadn't inherited more of—she had glowing, golden-brown skin and the little lip gloss she'd borrowed from Annika made her wide mouth shimmer.

Whatever stress she'd carried along for months, weighing the biggest decision of her life, swinging back and forth, giving her a pinched look, was gone. Add the last month in with no worries about her finances or her career or the boys' well-being, the carefree nature of her present days showed in her face, as if she'd shed layers of skin. Though nowhere in the realms of Annika or her mother and sister, Laila thought she looked pretty just then, with her amber eyes glinting with excitement, her face made of strong, distinct angles, and confidence that came with living life the way she knew best, with making decisions that were right for her and her two sons.

Sebastian came to stand behind her, his head cocked to the side, his hands hovering over her shoulders but not landing.

*Completing the picture,* she thought, in a sudden bout of uncharacteristic whimsy.

"I told them to pamper you. There's a spa next door I was going to drag you to next."

"So that I can be brought up to scratch for you? For the Skalas family?" she asked, needing to know how much he cared about such things.

He met her eyes in the mirror, his gleaming with simple truth as he believed it. "Because beneath this brave, stubborn, calculating exterior lies a very beautiful woman who deserves the best."

"No need for false flattery," she whispered, even as she loved the thrum of anticipation through her body. "You've already caught me."

"Have I?"

"I… I've tried to relive that night, too. I've never been hornier, and I don't have enough sexual experience to know how to keep that separate from what we're trying to build with the boys. I know it's possible but I'm just not… sophisticated enough." She rushed on, her pulse dancing all over her body like an unearthed spark of electricity. "I left the villa today because seeing you lip-locked with that woman took me out at the knees. I needed to get you out of my head."

"What if we can keep them separate? What if I promise you that whatever happens between us, the boys are outside of this? What if you let us explore this between us? Admit it, Dr. Jaafri. A part of you loves risks just as much as I do. Or you wouldn't have played such an elaborate ruse on me."

She met his eyes, and the fight went out of her, leaving her boneless and free like never before. "You don't want any other woman?"

He shook his head.

"You want me?" she asked next, needing confirmation.

"Yes."

"Show me," she demanded, feeling a boldness she'd never felt before.

He pressed closer.

Laila closed her eyes, better to absorb all the delicious sensations assaulting her. Sweat and spice, he smelled like the decadent brew she used to relish when she'd been at college. Chest to thighs, he was hard and hot against her, his breath making the hair rise on the nape of her neck. Slowly, his arms came around her waist, as if he meant to gather her whole.

Laila stiffened.

"Shh… I can hear the gears in your head churning," he said, crooning at her ear, pulling her closer, his broad hand dancing across her not-so-flat belly. "You're gorgeous, Laila." One blunt-nailed finger traced the distinctive shape of her cheekbones, her too-large nose and her wide mouth as if he were memorizing the lines and details. "But more than that, you're fascinating and complex and brave." He rubbed his cheek against hers and the bristle scraped her skin deliciously. "You don't know what a draw that is for me. So, stop trying to put this into some equation and just…feel."

Exhaling on a shuddering breath, Laila relaxed. How an embrace could feel so arousing, she might never find out, but it was like an electrical charge running through her. Slowly, her back melted into his chest and a soft hiss escaped her mouth. His erection was a hot brand, notching up against her behind. One corded arm sidled up to lie under her breasts and then she was fully engulfed by him. His breath, his hands, his lips wound her up.

Feeling dizzy and drunk, Laila looked at his reflection in the mirror.

Those sharp cheeks dusted with dark pink, his nostrils flaring, his shapely lips slightly open, Sebastian looked as drunk on desire as she felt. The gray of his gaze deepened, into a maelstrom of hunger and need. He thrust his hips just a little and the little thrust sent damp warmth straight to her core.

"I walk around with my cock at half-mast when you strut around in those shorts, when your T-shirt gets wet during bath time, when you compulsively lick the honey from your lips every single night. When you sound sleepy and husky in the middle of the night when you check on the boys, and your hair is a halo around your face. When you're so exhausted that you can't help but lean against me and I can feel your warm, soft, silky skin." His fingers drew tantalizing trails all over her flesh—up and down, from left to right—as if waking up every nerve ending. As if it was all he'd wanted to do for a long while. "You disappeared on me and I couldn't get you out of my head. I haven't felt the faintest interest in another woman in three years. You have become an obsession." He nudged his hips against hers the same time as his hands pulled down the side zipper of her dress.

Laila groaned as his rough, broad hand completely engulfed her breasts. Her nipples poked at his palm, boldly demanding attention. "Is that enough proof for you, Dr. Jaafri?"

"Yes." Laila wanted to burrow into him. "I want more, too, Sebastian."

His long fingers kneaded and cupped her breast without touching her as she needed. "I will not be your stud because you're horny after three years of celibacy."

"I don't know how to prove to you that I'm horny *for you*," she said, half sobbing, half delirious with pinpricks of pleasure.

He laughed and it was suddenly imperative that she taste that smile.

Turning her head, sinking her fingers into his hair, she caught his lips with hers. She didn't have words like him, but she had this...deep, insistent longing to steal something of him for herself, to captivate him as he had done to her three years ago, to leave a small, indelible mark on him as he'd done to her. She traced the seam of his lips with soft, susurrating kisses and when he groaned roughly, she snuck her tongue into his mouth.

He tasted of whiskey and mint and of decadence and pleasure she had rarely allowed herself. Pleasure she had only tasted because of him, wanted because of him.

She sucked the tip of his tongue, bit his lower lip, then licked the hurt. She devoured his mouth as if he was a feast she'd been waiting for, for so long. She pulled and tugged at his hair, raked her nails over the nape of his neck until his mouth was hers to do with as she wished.

He cursed when she let go for breath and then he was devouring her, hard and fast and deep, his erection pressing insistently against her behind.

She'd relived that moment from three years ago in her head for so long and now, she wanted him deep inside her and this time, she would own her pleasure instead of feeling guilt and shame around it. She would demand everything he was and wield everything she was at him without lies and half-truths.

"Is that enough proof for you?" she said, in a breathy voice that told its own tales and gave its own proof.

Clasping her cheek in one broad hand, Sebastian grinned against her mouth. Their rough exhales joined and created a symphony of their own. "Yes."

"Now, can we please proceed to this pampering thing you planned for me?"

"Yes," he said, loosening his hold on her.

Laila grabbed his corded arms. "I want it at your hands."

"At my hands? I might ruin you for anyone else, Dr. Jaafri."

"I dare you to try," she said, grinning, and saw his gaze flare with challenge.

Sebastian hadn't meant to seduce her today, here. Not that his mind was ever *not* planning how to get Laila under him, or over him, or against the wall.

Over the last three weeks, it had become as natural as wanting to see Nikos's wide grin, feeling Zayn's soft gaze land on him like an ever-present buzz. Like breathing and eating and walking and waking and sleeping and thinking of his art.

Wanting Laila had already been an obsession, now it was torment, too.

The more he wanted her, though, the more Sebastian restrained himself, as if warned by some strange instinct whispering in the back of his head. Usually, such control was…not in his nature.

He'd lived most of his life becoming a profligate wastrel, giving in to all kinds of excesses, doing his best to shame the Skalas name, and when the noise in his head got so loud that he couldn't bury it anymore in his wasted living, he painted.

He'd never set out to be a painter, as much as Konstantin had liked to taunt him that he'd done it for express purpose of pissing on him and the prestigious family name.

In truth, Sebastian had spent a lot of his adolescence fighting the art that seemed to want to get out of him, like some poison that needed to be purged, or skin that needed to be shed. In the last few years, he'd even let his brother and Thea and friends lead him into things he had no vested interest in, for lack of anything more important that engaged his interest.

But all that had changed with his sons' arrival. With Laila's spectacular reentry into his life. He had a desire now—as bright and hot like a flame—and he had a plan to fulfill that desire.

Detours and deep dives and self-destructive plays were not allowed. He wished he didn't have to run away and hide when his migraines hit. That he didn't need to calm the buildup of that relentless clamor in his head by painting. But those detours were necessary since he didn't want to expose the pain he had to bear to Laila's or his sons' eyes.

Whatever she might say now, he couldn't let her see him like that, at his worst. Couldn't let her see the gaping void his mother's abandonment had left in him, couldn't let her see that Konstantin had managed to beat out his capacity to care, to be vulnerable, to bare himself to another in all his true tormented glory. Couldn't let her see that between them, his parents had destroyed his ability to connect like a normal man.

He'd spent so long letting it decay and rot with shallow pursuits and mockery of relationships that he knew he would not make the kind of husband Laila wanted. He doubted he could give her even the conditional happiness she was expecting from their convenient arrangement.

But he'd not let the dark void of his past destroy his future, he would not lose his sons. And that meant making sure Laila could trust him, giving her everything she needed to show her that she mattered in the logical way she understood.

His desire for her was not a lie and he would use that as his negotiating tool. He'd lusted after her for three years, been celibate the entire time—deep in his obsession with finding her—when sex had been an easy escapade all his life. For all that he had called her one, Sebastian had whored himself away from the age of seventeen, in return for escape from his own head. And yet, he had abstained for three years. He hadn't even wanted to look at another woman, much less seek out entertainment or escape.

It was as if his brain had had enough meat and material to occupy itself in search of Laila. As if on some instinctual level he had known that they were not finished.

The whole idea of scheming in the vague way he was doing and plotting each step carefully and then trying to stick to that plan… It was all very boring and self-depriving when he wanted to act on his gut. When he wanted to take advantage of the long glances and trembling gasps Laila didn't even know she was putting out.

The woman was as naive about her sexual appeal as she was no-nonsense about their arrangement. A part of him just wanted to take what she would so readily offer.

Ironic that Laila was trying to play by her instincts more while he was trying his damnedest to stick to a plan. And with the same gut instinct, he also knew that he would never need an escape from her. They would settle into the kind of matrimonial bliss that was a shallow mirror of what his twin had but that was one thing they both agreed on, didn't they?

He just had to have patience and deny himself a little more and appeal to her newly awakened instincts. To prove to her she needed him, wanted him, as much as he needed her and his sons in his life.

His momentary escape into his own thoughts cost him for Laila stiffened in his arms. When he met her gaze in the mirror, he was relieved to find it was not affront. But…concern that felt like a thorny prickle against his skin. He did not need or deserve her concern. He had spent his entire life without it.

She tightened her clasp on his wrist. "You went away somewhere. Is that a lingering echo of the migraine?"

He shook his head. "I was trying to figure out where to begin your ruin."

She laughed, having clearly decided to believe his lie. There was such a gentle generosity to her spirit that it shone out of every pore, like her skin was giving off an iridescent glow. Her large amber eyes glowed with naked desire and were so artlessly honest that it hurt to meet them in the mirror.

He stared at her, feeling a strange, overwhelming desire to steal that laugh for himself. It wasn't simple lust, for he knew how he'd twisted that beyond shape.

Sex for him had always been a momentary escape, a game to see how far he could go in his debauchery, a perversion to run away from the noise in his head, a constant chase to see if it would be enough to fight the need to emote on a canvas—which was what his painting had always been about. More an experiment than any kind of need to connect with another.

This was more. Different. A near-compulsive need to dig beneath that silky skin and learn all her secrets, to expose every nook and cranny of how she was made to his greedy eyes. The exact opposite of escape, for it filled him with renewed fervor and something that would sustain him for a long time. And when this need faded, they would have companionship, they would have their family.

"The end is a given, no? However it begins?" she said, with an eagerness that he wanted to devour. Her nipples peaked against his palms, making his mouth water.

He tucked her closer against him and had the pleasure of seeing her eyes glaze. "Yes, though I have decided to try on self-control for size."

"What does that mean?"

"That means we will pursue your pleasure, not mine." He rubbed one plump nipple between his fingers, and she arched into his touch. "And this counts as one wish I'm granting you, *ne*?"

"You're diabolical to ask me that now," she said, her words so husky that they pinged over his skin.

He tugged at the bodice until her breast in his hand was exposed to their sight and tweaked the dark pink nipple. Twisting himself around her torso, he rubbed his bristly cheek against the plump knot. "Say yes, Laila."

"Fine, but—"

Sebastian didn't let her finish.

This time, he kissed her. As he'd been wanting to do for three long years. He tasted her surprise and her soft gasp and then she softened under his mouth. In his arms. As if here, she was giving up all her rationale and all her fight, and simply caving to pleasure. Tart and sweet, her mouth invited him in with a passion he'd never known with anyone else.

With all the women he'd taken to bed, perversely, it was the Skalas name and the status, or the genetics that made him look the way he did that attracted them. He'd never allowed any woman closer than that. But Laila had jumped his defenses with her lies and her truths and had gotten far too close before he'd realized it.

With her, being wanted was a trip unlike anything he'd ever known, because she knew him and still wanted him. *Cristos*, it was a dangerous high he could chase for the rest of his life.

Sinking one hand into her thick curls, he tugged until she turned to face her reflection in the mirror. He ran his mouth over her jaw to the pulse at her neck that had been boldly taunting him for so long now. He licked at that pulse before pinching the sensitive skin between his teeth and she moaned loud enough for the woman waiting outside the door to hear.

She was unaware of how loud and wanton she sounded, lost against him, and Sebastian lapped this up, too. Feeling a potent mix of possessiveness and protectiveness, he clamped his palm against her mouth and said, "You want to see what I'd have done with you, right?"

She met his gaze, bold and brave. Always, so brave.

"This is between you and me, *matia mou*. And nothing to do with our arrangement or the future. Just the present, *ne*?"

She nodded, her curls bouncing this way and that, her front two crooked teeth digging into her lower lip.

"Tell me, Laila. Tell me what you would have me do with you. Choose your ruin, *yineka mou*," he whispered, feeling an abyss-like need for her surrender.

A fiery streak of red coated her cheekbones, like the tail of a comet painting the sky.

*Would she leave devastation in her wake somehow?*

The intrusive thought shook him up, before she caught his attention again. No, she wasn't going anywhere.

Her amber eyes glinted with flecks of gold, the irises blown up. "You're supposed to show me what you'd have done if you had caught me."

He grinned and licked the shell of her ear.

She writhed against him, her nails digging into his thighs, a perfect canvas for him to play on. "I'd have demanded your surrender," he whispered, caught up in the game. If the means itself could be so delicious and tormenting and full of pleasure, he would not even care about the end soon. "I'd have made you beg, *pethi mou*."

"Oh," she said, licking her lower lip with the tip of her tongue. "You seem to think I have ego invested in this, Sebastian. Wanting you and giving in—despite all the warnings and reasons I brought up to myself—was the easiest thing I'd ever done. The most pleasurable. When

I learned that that night hadn't hurt anyone, that it wasn't cheating, I went home and cried."

"Why?"

"Because, for so many months, I shamed myself for thinking of you, over and over. I tried so hard to forget your touch. To stop thinking about you. But I couldn't. Nothing in my life has felt so good or so real as that night with you." She rubbed at her chest as if it burned now again and *Cristos*, he knew all about shame and she hadn't even done anything to feel it.

Sebastian covered her hand with his, loving how easily she gave up her feelings and her needs. He could get addicted to it.

She laced their fingers immediately, showing him trust he didn't deserve. "That first time after I saw how happy Annika was when she talked about Alexandros and then she said you were like a brother to her, it was as if all that shame and guilt had fallen off, leaving me free to…breathe and feel and want again. I went to bed and dreamed of you. I woke up during the night feeling achy and desperate for your touch. I…tried with my own fingers but it wasn't the same. So, I switched my phone on and googled you and there you were, splashed over the internet with woman after woman…and I…"

"It was all a show. You made escape impossible."

She shivered again, and he clasped her closer. "Make me feel like that again, Sebastian."

With a groan of his own, Sebastian thrust his hips into hers, rubbing himself against her curvy bottom. Holding her gaze, he filled one palm with her breast and sent the other down to explore.

She watched, as avidly as he did, when he rolled the

hem of her dress up, revealing smooth, silky, thick thighs. *Cristos*, suddenly all he could think of was how she'd straddled his hips with those thighs. How he'd buried his teeth into the inner thigh. How she'd bucked and bowed when he'd laid his mouth on her core.

Panties made of some wispy silk covered her mound. Sebastian shoved the flimsy fabric aside and found her folds and her dampness. She was so ready for him, and it made him eager like he hadn't been even as a randy teenager.

"All this for me?" he said, gently probing at her entrance and dripping her wetness all over her folds.

Her thickly lashed eyes widened, and she must have smiled because they danced with a wicked pleasure and Sebastian suddenly loathed the fact that they were in public, when all he wanted to do was to strip her completely and drink in every nuance in her expression, every flicker in her eyes, every sweet word that fell from her lips.

"Keep your eyes on me," he said, and she instantly complied, like a kitten that knew it would get its reward.

Those big eyes held his, a promise and a demand and something more in them. He ran his mouth along her neck and her jaw, leaving a trail of wet kisses. And then he played with her damp folds. With his fingers inside her. With cajoling demands and whispered promises. With his mouth at her neck.

One arm wrapped around his neck, Laila undulated like a beautiful wave against him, rubbing that glorious ass against his shaft in a torment he wanted more of. Sebastian pinched her clit between his fingers, and she broke apart around him, digging those distinctly crooked front teeth into his forearm, her little gasps of pleasure so erotic that it left him shaking for relief and release.

Uncovering her mouth, he took it in a wild kiss. He lapped up the beads of sweat that had gathered on her upper lip, and he made her watch as he licked her taste from his fingers, and he made that blush appear again when he told her next time he was going to taste her directly. When her knees shook under her, he caught her, and when she hid her face in his chest and threw her arms around his waist with an artless, almost naive modesty, he felt a strange contraction in his chest that he buried along with a thread of unease that maybe, just maybe, for all her rules and caveats and logic, Laila did not know what she truly wanted, that something so convenient and conditional should not feel so good.

But he shrugged it away because what she truly wanted was in his power to give. For now, at least.

# CHAPTER EIGHT

"WHAT IS IT that you want from my grandson, Dr. Jaafri?" Thea Skalas demanded, startling Laila out of a pleasant daydream where she broke Sebastian's new self-control like a sorceress and brought him to his knees.

She sat up and wiped her mouth with her napkin in case she'd been drooling, swallowing the foolish answer that rose to her lips for that first question. Given she'd barely had any sleep over the past few days—both boys had molars coming in—she hadn't seen much of Sebastian except in late-night silent meetups. Definitely not for any "only them" kind of encounters. Zayn clung to her during nights and while he was usually okay to play by himself during the day, it was Nikos's turn to want his Mama.

She was tired, cranky, horny and…confused. Sebastian had said he wanted to explore this thing between them, and yet, in a week, he hadn't made a move. He certainly seemed preoccupied with something. Laila wanted to ask him about him, but she was wary of making him think she was doubting him again.

The constant drama of her parents' marriage and her mother's erratic behavior every few weeks—her restlessness that either resulted in a reckless shopping spree or a night out on the city ending up at some wild party or calling up some old friend for a glamorous date— all those memories and the fears they'd left behind in her kept intruding on the decision she had made to trust him. The niggling feeling that she was right in her Baba's place, setting herself up for heartbreak, wouldn't leave her alone.

Which shouldn't be a problem at all because she wasn't involving her heart, right? At least, that's what she had told Sebastian. So why was she constantly looking at the past instead of moving forward with her own life?

There wasn't an hour that passed since that day at the boutique without her reliving the pleasure he'd strummed through her so easily. He'd even admitted that he hadn't wanted another woman in three years. Uncharacteristic enough for his lifestyle and the public playboy.

He gave of himself freely. Or at least he was smart enough to spin that illusion. Only now did Laila realize that he hadn't told her anything more about his migraines or what caused them or how long he'd had them. Neither had he let her bring Guido up again. God, she was going to drive herself half-mad with these circular thoughts.

And at the end of it all came anger with herself. Did she have so little trust in herself? As the old woman had pinpointed, what was it that Laila truly wanted?

"Dr. Jaafri?"

Laila sighed.

The reprieve Sebastian had been able to give her— from his grandmother, from the media, from the outside world—was apparently over and she only realized now how much effort he'd spent holding his twin and his grandmother, his family lawyers and the entire world at bay, so that she wasn't overwhelmed.

At breakfast this morning, Alexandros had mentioned the need to release a formal statement to the public regarding their presence in Sebastian's life, before the paparazzi got hold of the news and spun it into a narrative that none of them could control.

He talked of appointing a secretary for Laila who could organize her life to include things like photo shoots—because he insisted it was important to release a PR-approved photo of the boys and her and Sebastian to the media to reflect a "happy situation"—and schedule her travel. Because Laila *shouldn't* go back to the university or her Baba's old house or anywhere for that matter on her own willy-nilly. And to organize a party soon with all of the Skalas extended family and friends to announce Nikos and Zayn's joining the family.

All she'd been able to do was to turn to Sebastian like a helpless little fish flip-flopping on the land. The very idea of having a PA or performing little stunts for the media or having someone organize her very boring, very mundane life…was her worst nightmare come true. All of it bringing to head the constant doubts she chewed through about Sebastian and her belonging to different worlds, the constant taunts from Nadia that she didn't belong in her world and their mother's.

God, she hadn't even told her mother and half sister for fear of having to face their reactions. For fear of cold reality crashing through whatever foundation she was trying to build with Sebastian.

Sebastian had responded by scolding his twin for ruining their appetites and informed him that Laila and he would come up with a plan together that was convenient and comfortable for them.

Before Laila could wrap her mind around all the things Alexandros demanded and how out of control her life suddenly felt, Thea Skalas had arrived, a month to the day since Laila had shown up.

The older woman's frail outward appearance had made Laila concerned for her until two minutes later, Thea had launched her campaign about the boys needing to be legitimized first thing at breakfast. The one thing Laila couldn't find fault with her was that whatever her beliefs about Laila, she'd openly and with tears flowing down her face welcomed Nikos and Zayn into the family.

"What would seal the deal in legitimizing my great-grandsons as Skalas heirs, once and for all?" Thea demanded, her impatience growing at Laila's silence.

Fortunately, Nikos and Zayn were seated far enough at the table now—near their papa and uncle that afternoon—so they didn't hear their great-grandmother's imperious demands.

"Grandmama!" Sebastian said, in a deceptively soft voice so that it didn't catch the boy's attention but delivered the warning anyway.

Thea turned her steely gray gaze toward him, even as she, too, kept an easy smile on her lips. "You might have spent your entire life mocking the Skalas name, Sebastian, but I know you damn well want it for the boys. Family matters to you too much to let it go. For whatever reason, you are letting her set the pace."

*Family mattered to Sebastian.*

It was an admission he'd made himself to her and yet, it landed in a different way falling from Thea Skalas's lips. Almost like an entity that held value in some abject form instead of gritty reality. Which she had handed him, part and parcel, by not only seducing him, then getting pregnant—yes, he'd played his part—*and* giving him two sons. Like he had himself ordered a nice, ready-made family off Amazon.

Sebastian turned to Laila, that small tilt to the right corner of his mouth.

Despite the unending string of questions in her head, that look he cast her was an instant injection of adrenaline. She adored it when Sebastian left the field to her—whether it was about the boys or other matters that concerned their life together—or when he didn't minimize her fears. For the first time in her life, she felt like she was part of something bigger than herself, like she belonged to a team or a unit, rather than operating alone as she'd done for so long.

"Maybe because he agrees with me," she said, addressing Thea, "that jumping into an outdated arrangement for the simple purpose of legality is less important than making sure the boys aren't caught up in something we're not ready for."

Thea pursed her lips while Alexandros said, "I thought you were simply taking time to get to know each other."

Laila heard his poorly concealed outrage in his tone—he disliked the fact that his nephews were not legal Skalas family members yet. Thank God, Annika had been too tired to join them for this elaborate meal. She had no doubt her friend would take Laila's side in this particular argument, and it would only alienate Alexandros toward her even more.

The last thing Annika needed was more strife in her

life because of Laila's…reluctance for matrimony. Neither was she unaware that her active resistance to the idea had already morphed into vague reluctance.

Sebastian peeled an orange and handed the juicy kernel to Nikos, who fed it to Zayn, immediately making a game of it, then stretching his pudgy palm toward his papa, for more.

"This matter is no one's business but mine and Laila's." Then he turned that intractable gaze toward his family members. "When did I ever give the impression that I will do as you two or the media or the entire damned world pleases?"

"I see you have him wrapped around your finger already. I must commend you for that," Thea said, shocking Laila yet again.

Something about her gaze said she meant it. She knew it was pointless to engage the older woman, but Laila couldn't help it. Plus, she wanted these people on her sons' side, which meant she needed them to respect her, if not like her.

"I have no intention of controlling Sebastian in any way. It's a partnership that I want."

"Ah… So you're a modern woman who doesn't respect the institution of marriage?"

"No, Grandmama," Laila said, testing the words on her lips. The older woman's gray eyes—so much like her grandsons'—gleamed with pleasure before she buried it.

"I have seen instances where it works—like Ani and Alexandros. And I have seen where it has burned down families. Sebastian and I have enough hang-ups without adding unnecessary, arbitrary structure to the mix. If I were you, I would back off. Because believe me when I say we're doing our best to make sure the boys have you all in their life."

Thea cackled and banged her palm on the table. "Fine, Dr. Jaafri," she said, respect glinting in her gaze. "You have my vote. If anyone can straighten out my useless grandson, it is you. Fate works in strange ways, *ne*?" she added as an afterthought.

Sebastian laughed, which set off Nikos chortling, which made him spew most of the orange he'd half chewed onto his uncle's shirt in a capture-worthy projectile.

Alexandros froze. Then slowly, he rubbed the toddler's face, then wiped some of Nikos's chewed-up orange from his shirt with a napkin. But the set of his face was so serious, his mouth so flat, that Nikos sobered up, watched around with those big eyes and, in two seconds flat, started wailing using all the lung power he had.

Laila sighed, knowing he was overstimulated. Her happy, easygoing baby never cried like that.

As Zayn watched his twin go off into a tantrum, his lower lip trembled dangerously but somehow, he held the incoming storm at bay, her brave, sensitive boy. Turning away from his uncle, Zayn handed another piece of orange to Nikos, who took it amid his cries and promptly started chewing on it, his chin now dripping with drool, snot and orange juice.

"*Cristos*, Alexandros!" Sebastian said, shooting to his feet with a violence she rarely saw in him. "It's just a piece of orange. You need not look like he did that to you on purpose, as if to insult you. He's just a little boy."

Alexandros Skalas, the mighty banker that all of Europe feared, looked like his brother had stricken him out of nowhere. "Of course I know that," he said, his tone whispery soft, even as he radiated tension. "I don't care if he…vomits on me, Sebastian. I'm not used to kids and I didn't even look at him straight because I was unsure of what to say or do and—"

"Yes, well. You better start learning how to handle them soon without that horrified, frozen expression or I'm going to have to raise your daughter, too," Sebastian threw back at him, only half-jokingly.

While Laila didn't much like Alexandros—so much for thinking they were similar—she felt a rush of sympathy for him. His expression made it clear that Sebastian's taunt hit where it hurt the most, and worse, it had basis in truth. Those gray eyes, so much like his twin's, watched Sebastian with such open envy that Laila had to look away. Thank God Annika hadn't been there to see it.

Laila turned to Sebastian, surprised at his cruelty toward his brother. But her chastisement never formed on her lips.

With such tender care and patience that it caught even his grandmother's attention, Sebastian was busy wiping Nikos's mouth and hands with a wet napkin, all the while talking gibberish to him, trying to make him smile, and then picked him up out of his chair. He bent down to pick up Zayn, too, as if he'd done it for years, but pulled back at the last minute, face set into a fake smile he usually put on to show that Zayn's resistance didn't get to him.

The moment struck her again with the question that came to her in those rare, quiet moments where her thoughts wandered here and there. How endless was his capacity to feel that Zayn's reluctance to warm up to him still bothered him? Would he love a woman like that, too, or was it only limited to two innocent children, who were his blood and flesh?

Tucking Nikos against his side, he looked at Laila. "Nap and pool later? I'll get this one settled down," he said, switching Nikos from side to side as if he were a basketball.

Her firstborn giggled uncontrollably, causing a string of drool to drip over onto his papa's designer shirt.

Laila nodded, still in awe of Sebastian's near-miraculous capacity to love and care for his two sons.

He gave a nod to Zayn, always making sure to include him, then raised Nikos high above his head and swooshed him this way and that as he left the terrace. Her heart jumped into her throat and a protest rose to her lips, but Laila cut it off as she slowly picked up Zayn.

Her sons needed the safety of their papa's strong arms as much as they needed to learn to fly high and take risks, knowing in their hearts that he would never let either of them fall.

It came to her then—how this whole instinct thing worked. Because her trust in Sebastian's ability to be what Nikos and Zayn needed was absolute. If only she could feel the same sense of trust that he wanted her in his life…and as more than a part that would complete the vague picture he had for a perfect family. That day at that boutique, his admission that he hadn't wanted another woman in three years, that she'd become an obsession rang true, too. But obsessions were not…whatever it was that she wanted to be to him. It sounded too much like one of Mama's fancies, unreliable and bound to be replaced soon by a new one.

Neither could she forget that his "obsession" with her

might have risen from the fact that she had pulled one on him. Once he had her assent to this marriage, once she unraveled for him in all the ways she couldn't resist, would he toss her aside? Would he push her to the margins of his life like he seemed to do with most everything and everyone? And if he did, was she okay with that?

For the first time in her life, Laila felt like her logic and rationale were of no use, and her heart definitely wouldn't follow her head.

The long summer day was finally coming to a spectacular end with the setting sun streaking the horizon with splashes of fiery orange when Laila decided to seek out Sebastian a few evenings later.

He had disappeared again, for a few days after Thea's arrival, although this time, he'd informed her that he'd be working and unavailable unless it was an emergency.

Laila had missed him—with even Zayn asking after his papa—and worried about him. Which, in itself was alarming because she was used to being alone, used to not needing to check in with anyone for days at a time. Even when Baba had been alive, he'd either be working or immersing himself in his books, putting together painstaking research on his favorite subject of Arab art of the nineteenth century.

Her intense dislike for playing the big boys' games at work meant she made few friends there. Outside of work, her life had been consumed by her sons. And yet already, she was too used to ending the day chatting with Sebastian. Already, she felt very little resistance about saying whatever came to her lips.

She had missed not only his steady presence with

them, but also the wicked invitation in his eyes when he looked at her. When he rubbed the pad of his thumb against her lower lip. When she knew he wanted her but, for some reason, was playing a waiting game.

If he was struggling with another migraine coming on, she wished he would confide in her. But for all his seemingly open nature, there was a wall she sensed in him and a host of subjects that were forbidden to her.

When Paloma had informed her that he'd returned to the villa after the boys had been settled into bed this evening, she threw on a white cotton dress with halter neck straps, another perfectly fitting dress that had been delivered as part of her new wardrobe, and pulled her unruly hair back with a clip, chiding herself all the while for dressing for him.

But she refused to be brought down by the negative voice in her head—that she was only beginning to realize now sounded too much like Mama, as if she'd internalized all the things she was always saying to Laila in the form of "self-improvement advice."

Laila had enough of letting that voice drowning out all the good things she knew about herself, all the wonderful things that Baba and Guido had pointed out about her, again and again.

She'd spent most of her teens playing second fiddle to her half sister, Nadia, always falling into her shadow, always being measured against Mama and Nadia's beauty, and coming up short. After losing Baba, she'd buried herself in her studies, in looking after Guido and Paloma. She'd never indulged in the simple pleasure of putting on a pretty dress, doing her hair, using a flick of lip gloss so that her wide mouth shimmered invitingly. She'd never primped herself, wanting to catch a man's gaze, never seen herself as an object of desire.

She did all these things now, and she did them with Sebastian's gray gaze and wicked smile in mind. It was the simplest of thrills and yet, she'd never experienced it before him. Never felt the need at all.

It was a new freedom from her fears that had tethered her for so long, a new identity even, as more than the brainy freak, the crow in the cuckoo nest, more than a caregiver for her sons and others.

As she pushed her feet into designer flip-flops, there was a zing in her belly, a pep to her step. She walked down to the beach, feeling not only carefree and relaxed for the first time in ages, but with anticipation throbbing through every inch of her. For the evening ahead and for the future.

# CHAPTER NINE

WHEN SHE FINALLY found Sebastian—much farther along the private strip of beach than she usually traversed with the boys—it was to find him staring at the sky with a grim set to his mouth. She'd rarely seen him in such a somber mood that Laila felt her curiosity increase a thousand times over.

Without disturbing him, she kicked off her sandals and scrunched her feet into the glorious-feeling sand. The sand was still warm from the hot day but the waves lapping at her felt icily cold. A childish giggle escaped her as she let the water barely touch her toes before running back. With the tide coming in faster and rougher, she felt that little lurch in her belly when the water pulled away the sand from right under her feet. Kind of how her life felt at the moment. And yet, she wanted to be here, with this man. So much for calculating her risks.

For a while, she played her game with the waves, more than content to wait out his dark mood. *A partnership,* she'd told Thea, and now she realized she'd meant it. But it had to be for more than just the boys. It had to be for them. And she was already invested deep enough to know that Sebastian fascinated her, in more than one way. It had been so from the first time she'd set her eyes and her plans on him.

Finally, she felt his attention move to her, as real as if he'd run those rough artist's hands over her skin. Like she had tiny little antennae wired specifically for his attention.

"If you have come here hoping to mellow my mood, you'll fail," he said in that soft voice he wielded as a weapon. Or was it a shield? she wondered with a fresh perspective relatively free of her own insecurities. "Unless you will let me take you on the sand…" His white teeth gleamed against his olive skin like a predator's warning. "That might mellow me down."

"Why would I want to mellow you at all, Sebastian? It is rare enough that you show your true colors. And as for taking me roughly in the sand—" her breath hitched in her throat at the image that came "—you're just being a tease. Sand or bed or wall or the pristine marble floor of my bedroom, I'm yours for the taking."

His rough curse added to the symphony of the waves.

"Is another migraine coming on?" she ventured, eager to know.

He shook his head, dislodging a lock of hair onto his forehead. "Is that why you came running?"

"Wow, you're like a prickly bull right now, huh?"

"So, you should run away screaming, Dr. Jaafri."

"I think I'll stay right here."

He shrugged, without quite meeting her eyes.

"You were hard on Alexandros the other day."

Another curse. "Of all the things to bring up… Why are we talking about my infernal brother?"

"Because I have a point to make."

"You know he does not like you."

"Of course I know he doesn't like me and that's a cheap shot," Laila said, scrunching her nose. "Alexandros likes control in all things, yes? And the fact that I will not fall into line or that you are not taking enough actions to make me fall in line, and all of this is causing too many unknowns when all he wants is quiet and comfort for Annika...does not sit with him well."

Sebastian turned to face her and admiration glinted in his eyes. "Anything more?"

"In his mind, I'm also the reason for the strife between him and Annika. Right now, I make a convenient target for him to blame, among all the unknowns."

Sebastian grinned, those thin lines fanning out from the edges of his eyes again. She loved when he smiled like that, with real mirth, without mockery. There was already a catalog of the wide variety of his smiles in her head.

"And yet you *scold* me that I'm hard on him?"

"I'm not scolding you."

"You have that stern voice you use with the boys. For all the indulging you do, that voice means business. Although, I would be up for experimenting with that voice in bed, just so you know," he said, nudging her shoulder with his.

Heat streaked through her lower belly and Laila had to retrace her thoughts. "Promises and threats, *Kyrios Skalas*," she said, taunting him.

The moment stretched between them, full of sparks and longing and...heated desire.

"What else have you surmised of my brother?"

"His dislike of me is mostly based on something other than logic. When he discovers that, it will go away. As long as he does not extend it to Nikos and Zayn—which he hasn't—I do not care if he approves of me or not."

"You sound very used to being disliked, Dr. Jaafri," he said, shocking her with his perception.

"Nobody gets used to being disliked, do they?" She laughed to bury the pain in her words, but it came out sounding hollow. But then, she had almost no pretensions when it came to Sebastian. So why start now? "Nobody should have to get used to being mocked for being odd or unconventional or differently wired or being sensitive. It's especially cruel when it comes…from people who should protect you," she said softly, acknowledging something she hadn't until now. "I'm used to it. But I'll do everything in my power to protect Zayn from something like that."

"He has to face the world on his own merit, too, Laila. Or he would never know what he was capable of."

Laila heard the almost mournful note in that and tried not to wonder what would make this seemingly powerful man sound so. The thought was terrifying even in her head. "Yes, well, that's why we both are needed, no? You can push them toward being their own selves and I can coddle them just a little."

Apparently, all it took to mellow Sebastian's dark mood was talking about them as a team. She could almost feel him put on the easy, casual mask as he replied, "Fine. Let's talk about the mighty Alexandros Skalas and why you think I hurt him."

"It comes to you naturally…being a nurturer. Which is rare enough in powerful men who're used to getting what they want. Maybe it's because you were used to Annika as a kid or maybe it's your artistic nature that pushes you to see the purity of spirit in children, I don't know," she said, clearly probing. "But it does not come easily to Alexandros, and it is also clear that the idea of being a parent terrifies him. And yet, instead of offering him some kind of comfort, you rubbed it in his face. I would say it was quite cruel of you, but luckily for me and the boys, I know that you don't have a cruel bone in your body."

"It would be dangerous to put so much trust in me, Laila."

"That's a one-eighty if I've ever heard one," she said, not heeding the very real warning in his words.

He tucked his hands into the pockets of his trousers and examined her, as if gauging her worthiness. Laila stood her ground. After a while, he exhaled and spoke. "This is the first time in our lives that I'm better at something than him. And it is a big thing, given it's a child, and his child tomorrow, that we're talking about. Alexandros is used to being perfect at everything. Except this is not a skill set you acquire overnight, is it?"

Laila slapped his arm. "That's what I'm talking about. You're…enjoying his misery. That's…awful, Sebastian."

"Well, he was good at everything growing up. The perfect heir, the well-behaved son and a genius whiz kid with numbers and stocks… For a banking dynasty's heir, that's like knowing how to alchemize everything into gold."

Her breath suspended in her throat as she got a tiny glimpse into what made Sebastian so different and so… unpredictable. "And you?" she asked, terrified of being shunted behind that invisible circle he drew around himself.

"I failed at everything he excelled at, and anything I was supposed to be good at. I got expelled out of every private school in Europe, so Alexandros had to return home, too. I made my tutors' life hell until they ran away screaming. I complained of constant headaches and visions and was high maintenance until I found something to calm me down in my teens. I drew endless amounts of art that no one could make head or tail of. Konstantin loathed my very existence, so I gave him more reasons to do so by failing at everything he set me to do."

"Your father?" Laila whispered, anxious to know more of what had made him and terrified of what it might be.

"Yes, the great Konstantin Skalas who was full of rot on the inside. He...did his best to mold me into another version of Alexandros. Because one paragon of a son wasn't enough for the egotistical control freak. The more he tried, the more I loathed it, and the more I acted out. He didn't miss a single chance to use his words and his fists against me."

Laila couldn't breathe. And when she spoke, her words were fragile, insubstantial, full of rage against this...monster of a man who would terrorize a defenseless child. Suddenly, so many things about Sebastian became clear. "What about your grandmother? And your mother? Why didn't they protect you?"

"Thea didn't know for a long time. And my mother... He'd already terrified her until she was afraid of her own shadow and lost herself in drink."

Laila felt a surge of anger toward the woman but tempered it from turning it into judgment. But the thought of no one aiding a young Sebastian, of perverting his sense of self...made her want to rage out. Somehow, she managed to sound steady. "I'm... I have no words, Sebastian. I see where your fierceness for the boys comes from. You're…" Another realization struck her. "So, you have spent your entire life shaming the Skalas name as some sort of revenge?"

He shrugged, his smile grim. "The need to dirty the name became far too entrenched in me by the time Alexandros discovered Konstantin's treatment of me. And when he did… He did his best to shield me, begged me not to fuel Konstantin's rages. For the next few years, Alexandros planned and schemed and strategized with Thea to bring Konstantin under his heel and then he ousted him from the bank and our lives."

"You resent him for saving you?" Laila bit out, before she could phrase it better.

"Alexandros did not save me," he said, a jagged edge to his answer that forbade her to probe more.

But something lingered just out of her reach and Laila couldn't quite catch what it was. "So, because he was better than you as a child, you will rub this fear of his in his face?" she said instead.

He turned toward her, finally paying full attention to her windblown hair and her new dress and her pink lips. Something hot came awake in his eyes.

He rubbed a hand over his tired face. "I reacted out of instinct. Although I do not want him to terrify my sons with his ugly face."

When she gasped, he raised his brows and grinned. Moving close suddenly, he caught one stray corkscrew curl and pulled it until it stood straight in his fingers.

Laila let him tug her closer, thick clumps of her curls between his fingers as leverage. Her scalp prickled, the remembered sensation of those fingers delving deep and driving her wild acute. "He needs you, Sebastian."

He scoffed. "Annika didn't tell him about the boys before she could tell me… He doesn't have to throw a tantrum about it."

Laila pressed her forehead into his chest, smiling at the thread of stubborn pride in his voice. "That's not what he cares about."

"No? Because Alexandros doesn't have a whole range of emotional breadth."

*And you do?* she wanted to ask but she knew the answer. Every day, every little action of his showed her what a complicated, complex man Sebastian was. And with each moment, her draw to him became stronger, nearly irresistible, as if he was a whole gravitational field unto himself and she had no choice but to be pulled into his orbit. But she wanted more than just to circle him endlessly.

She wanted a collision, an explosion, she wanted to reach his raw, burning center. Because she was almost sure that beneath all the masks, Sebastian hid his true self—a man who had to fight every day since he was a child to be himself. Just like her, but in much more horrible circumstances. Was that why nothing and no one was sacred to him? Why he moved through life the way he did?

Suddenly, whatever it was that he wanted from Guido took a new shape, an all-new dimension. She'd never wondered what a powerful, charismatic man like him could want from a poor, old man like Guido.

"Don't leave me hanging now, Dr. Jaafri," he said, watching her closely.

Laila somehow found her words, even as her mind mined for reasons. "Alexandros is angry with Annika that she upset herself over keeping it secret from you. And he's angry with you that you won't let it go. Which means he finds it impossible to confide in you that he's irrationally terrified that he might not be a great father, especially in comparison to you."

Sebastian released her hair and it popped back into its usual curls. He cupped her cheek in his rough hand, tilting her chin up to meet his eyes. "He's not terrified. My brother has never been scared of anything and he…"

"He is *now*. That's why he freezes around Nikos and Zayn."

A corded arm went around her waist and pulled her, until her breasts flattened against his chest in delicious torment. "Why do you care so much about him?"

There was almost a note of childish peevishness to it and Laila smothered a smile. "Why does it bother you so much that Annika didn't tell you about the boys when you know deep in your heart that she did the right thing?"

"Because she owed her loyalty to me at that point. Not to you."

"Is that all?" Laila pushed, pressing her cheek to his chest, seeking the kind of real intimacy that he might not allow but wanting it anyway. Slowly, she was beginning to see through his mask. Sex and seduction and sinful bets were easy for him, even shields to keep the world at bay. True communication about his needs, showing his real self to the world or caring about anything, not so much.

His heart thundered against her ear as he held her loosely, humoring her, she was sure. He was so…solid and real around her that she couldn't believe she wasn't dreaming. Only her dreams had grown bigger and more improbable since she'd arrived here.

His silence told her she'd been right about his anger toward Annika. Lifting her head, she rubbed her forehead against his stubbled chin. "I care about both of them. Annika and your brother." She had even more respect for Alexandros for taking Sebastian's side when he'd been no more an adult himself, but she was wise enough to not probe a festering wound. "She's been a good friend to me, even though I approached her with my own agenda. She spent hours reassuring me that this was right. She took a huge risk by not telling you. I've not had someone like that in my corner in a long time." She blinked away the sudden tears the thought brought to her throat. "And you…won't even look at her. Please…forgive her. Forgive her so that she's not upset anymore, so that they're not at odds with each other."

Now both his arms were around her waist, and he dipped low enough for her to feel his warm breath on her lips.

"You're a dangerous woman, Dr. Jaafri," he said, his gaze moving over every inch of her as if he meant to unlock her, piece by piece.

"I'm not, really," she said, laughing at the very prospect. "In fact, I'm terribly easy to see through once you figure out the key to me."

"Maybe the danger, then, is in my perception of you," he said, his mouth curving but the smile not quite reaching his eyes.

She frowned. "Then that would make you like every other man who called me too brainy and too competitive and too logical, leaving very little femininity behind."

His rough hand circled her nape in a hold that had dampness blooming at her core. "No one is all of one thing, *pethi mou*. Maybe you're all of those things and there is no shame in them. But I see more to you, too, and that's what makes you so…irresistible."

It was impossible to not believe him, especially when his body was radiating the same tension she felt.

He bent down and licked the shell of her ear before he said, "I'll talk to Ani tomorrow and I'll teach Alexandros how to not freeze like a deer in the headlights around his nephews. For you."

Laila slapped his chest. "For me? *Please.* You adore her. Stop making this—"

His arm tightened like a vise around her, and she loved the little cage he built. Loved the rub and slide of her curves against his hardness. "Accept that this is one of your wishes I'm granting."

"No way am I using up one of those on something you were already going to do."

"Now who's cheating?" he demanded, his mouth running a heated trail down her neck.

"Not me," she said, shivering. "Wait, I do have a question. If you answer it, then I'll admit that you've granted me another wish."

He licked at her pulse and breathed the question into her skin. "Ask me."

"Tell me about your migraines."

*And why you hide your art,* she wanted to say. But there was only so much risk or rejection she could expose herself to at a given time.

"Not much to tell. I have had them for as long as I can remember. Mama used to keep me close to her because I would roar and yell and scream when I was in throes of it. Konstantin thought they made me weak, called me a runt. Would make me run laps around the estate after I recovered as if to make up for them."

"They continue to this day?"

"I have seen specialists all around the world. They don't know what to make of it and I have learned to live with them."

"But—"

He didn't allow her to say more, capturing her mouth with his. His lips were soft and seeking, as if he was searching for something only she could give. Laila sank into the kiss, stunned at how much he seemed to need the gentle tasting as much as she did. It was a soft landing, a subtle invitation to surrender without asking, a sweet promise that he would never hurt her.

When he released her, she mewled like a cat, and buried her face in his throat. She didn't feel shy so much as protective about all these new feelings the kiss evoked. Some magical wildness in Sebastian offered both safety and excitement and she thought she might spend her whole life happily swinging between those opposing points.

"I thought you would ask me something for yourself." Desire made his words low, rough-sounding. "To get Alexandros off your delicious ass with all that stuff."

She shrugged and raised her head. "He's only doing what's right for all of us, no?"

"It is a lot to get used to," he said, nibbling at her lips. "But you don't complain. You never complain. You're a puzzle, Dr. Jaafri, one I intend to crack."

"How many more wishes do I have left, Mr. Skalas?"

"One more, *yineka mou*," he said, that roguish grin back in his eyes.

"You're so sure of getting your way, aren't you?"

"Always," he said, his fingers playing at the nape of her neck.

"Is that why you won't give us both what we want?"

A fake gasp escaped those near-perfect lips. "I'm saving myself for marriage, Dr. Jaafri. How dare you try to corrupt me with your swaying hips and sexy smiles?"

She laughed, even as she was aware that he wasn't really answering her question. It was hard to concentrate on thoughts when his hands were stroking all over her, and his mouth was nibbling at her neck. "Then I would like to grant you a wish, too."

His head jerked up, almost hitting her. Surprise made his lush lower lip slacken for a moment. "Why such generosity?"

"For being you, Sebastian." When his big body stilled around her, she added, "And okay, maybe to mellow you down a bit."

He tucked a curl away from her face with a tenderness she didn't miss. Or the sudden gravelly tenor to his words when he spoke. "And what would you grant me?"

"I want to make you lose your mind. Here, now," she said, looking around as if she could spot any rogue cameras. "Give you new memories around this place."

He cursed and grinned, though she had a feeling it was a filter hiding his true emotion. Then his teeth dug into that sensuous lower lip. "You're on. Only if you join me."

Heat streaked her cheeks and Laila instantly felt her nipples peak to attention. She rubbed her thighs, tempted beyond good sense. "I don't want to be caught by any cameras."

"And if I want us to be caught on camera? If I want more adventure and more boldness and less inhibition from my lover?" he asked, still smiling. But there was a hard, lethal edge to it as if he meant to test her limits or her trust or to assuage his own need for something.

With any other man, Laila would have backed down from the explicit gauntlet thrown down, because it would have been to expose her fears, to mock her "frigidity." But with Sebastian, she thrilled in his asking, that he would give her a chance to be what he wanted. To meet him as his equal, in this, she needed it as she needed air.

"Then I suggest you give me some time and a bit of a private location for my first time on camera and then I'll try to get into it," she said, bluffing her way to a boldness she loved within herself. "The last thing we want is to shock your very traditional grandmother with my naked ass rolling around in the sand."

He laughed and kissed her hard enough to steal her breath away. His fingers gripped the back of her head as he devoured her mouth with firm, hungry strokes, as if he was afraid she might vanish. Rough and soft, his mouth and his stubbled jaw were a contrast in pleasure and delicious pain. When he pulled back, they were both breathing hard, and his eyes carried a wild light that was different from his usual bored charm. "You're an unending delight. Though I would only want what you want, Dr. Jaafri."

"Right now, I want a little cover from the villa."

"Your genie awaits, then."

Anticipation throbbed within her as he pulled her in

the opposite direction of the villa. Running on the slipping sand, with waves lapping at her feet, with her hand tucked into his, Laila felt this…figment of joy like she'd never tasted before. It was in the back of her throat, in her chest, in her belly, in all of her, like a warm pulse. And she wanted to hang on to it, nurture it until it became a living flame that would suffuse her entire being.

Shockingly enough, Sebastian brought her to a large outhouse-type structure almost half a mile along the beach, with lots of glass walls and a high roof, answering another question that had been eating away at her. It was a recluse artist's painting cabin, Laila thought, staring eagerly at what lay beyond the small entry area where there were a bunch of unused easels and various shelves with pots of paint.

"This is your space," she said inanely.

A grunt was his answer.

Her curiosity lasted a bare second as Sebastian cupped her face with both hands and kissed her senseless. There was something new in how he kissed her, his hands roving over her body, his large, lean frame caging her against the glass wall. "You wore this dress for me?" he said, licking into her mouth.

"I wanted to corrupt you just a little," she whispered, clinging to his mouth.

When he reached for the threads of her dress strings at her nape, Laila patted his hand away. "This is my show," she said, feeling his gaze on her skin like a laser beam of want and heat. "Hands in the air, please."

He grabbed onto the beam above him, his lean hips thrusting forward in a "do your worst" pose, and she thought she might just die from the decadent sight he made. Reaching him, she unbuttoned his linen shirt—full of paint splotches—and then pushed it off his broad shoulders. If she hadn't been completely bamboozled by the man's sex appeal three years ago, she'd have noticed that he didn't have a wastrel playboy's body, or face or hands. He was all raw, rough masculinity, a man who used his body both as a weapon and a shield.

Leaning down, she pressed a trail of kisses down his chest and licked the slab of thick abdominal muscles as if he was her very own ice cream cone.

His hands went into her hair, sinking deep to hold her still. "Is this allowed, Dr. Jaafri?"

"Yes," she said, breathing it into his taut skin. Then she dragged her teeth over the same trail, marking him.

Then she undid his pants and snuck her hand in to cradle his shaft. God above, he was so hard, and he was all hers. She bit her lower lip as she fisted his erection, remembering the feel of him moving inside her. "Tell me what you like. Show me how to make this so good that you're as desperate for me as I'm for you."

Head thrown back, muscles bunched in his neck, he was all harsh masculine beauty that even her logical mind glitched. A rough grunt fell from his mouth as she rubbed a thumb over the soft head. "Squeeze harder. Move your fist up and down."

Laila complied and soon, he was thrusting his hips into her hand, in a sinuous dance *she* was leading, and she'd never felt more feminine, more in touch with her own wild cravings, just more…alive. And she wanted more. With her other hand, she pushed his pants farther down, before sinking to her knees.

She felt his shock in his stillness, rather than heard it.

Pupils blown, breathing ragged, he looked...like one of those sculptures by some great Renaissance artist. And yet, Sebastian was gloriously alive, able to feel the full spectrum of emotions unlike any other man she had ever met.

"You don't have to do this, Laila," he said, a ragged edge to his tone that said how much he did want it.

"Have you known me to do anything that I'm not into, Sebastian?" she said, teasing him with firm strokes. And then she licked the thick head experimentally. "Tell me, Sebastian. You promised you'd grant me this."

"Why?"

"Because I want the knowledge that I broke your control."

"You do it every day as you smile at me over the breakfast table with our sons in between us, *agapi mou*."

Her breath hung in her throat as she wondered if she read more meaning into those guttural words. "I want your pleasure at my hands, and your ruin, too. For making me think I was party to cheating. For making me guilty for reliving that night. For..."

*For giving her what she hadn't known she needed,* she finished to herself.

He smiled and Laila knew he understood this compulsive need to push past any previous limits with each other. To earn surrender in new ways. That he was here with her, and not just the convenient mother of his sons.

His fingers sank back into her curls and gripped the back of her head with a possessiveness she reveled in. Who knew sex could be so fun and primal and...raw?

"Open your mouth wide and take me in. Tap my thigh if it's too much. And remember, *agapi*, breathe through it."

Laila followed his instructions and soon, he had her

how he needed her. She heard his pithy grunts and his filthy curses and his ragged breaths and instinctive thrusts. When she stole a look at him, she saw this painfully beautiful, increasingly complex man rendered in strokes of stark need. And seeing him like this…was as arousing as it was revealing, for it destroyed all the lies she'd told herself about relationships and romance and sex and…love. Lies she'd spun about why she'd surrendered so easily to him three years ago.

It made her realize that at heart she was very much a simple woman with simple desires, that she'd hid behind formulae and calculations and models, that she'd buried to feel right within how she was built and thought.And somehow, Sebastian was the key to unlocking it all and there was no end to all the things she wanted to experience with him, that she wanted to make him feel.

Tears smarted when he went deep with one long stroke and breath was a mirage. Her knees felt the hardness of the rough floor, her cheeks the burn. Laila dug her hands into his thighs and doubled down. The sound of his shaft hitting the roof of her mouth was so erotically filthy that it made her core drip with need. Then he was pulling out of her mouth, and her to her feet, which were barely steady. Before she could protest the abrupt non-finish, he was kissing her, one hand sneaking under her neckline and tweaking her aching nipple.

"Come over with me," he said, rough fingers pulling the hem of her dress up over her thighs, delving deep into her folds with a gentleness that might break her. Then he hooked one finger inside her, hitting that perfect spot, and Laila thought she might be seeing stars. "*Cristos*, you're so…responsive."

They came together like that, watching each other, stroking each other, chasing each other's pleasure. Laila dug her teeth into his bicep as her climax ripped through her, turning her limbs into liquid sensation, and felt the hot lash of his climax on her belly. His satisfied grunt was a sound she wanted to hear again and again. Breath seesawing out of her mouth, she fell onto him—damp and sweaty—while he wiped her belly with the edges of his shirt.

"Are you well, Dr. Jaafri?"

The tenderness of his question made Laila swallow.

She heard a distinct ringing in her ears, which was probably her heart trying to pound out of her body because she was…so in love with this man who held her as if she was fragile and precious. The realization moved through her in far-flung ripples, turning her inside out, making her feel both new and entrenched in her own skin.

Feeling vulnerable, she tried to pull away from him, but her legs gave out from under her like a newborn fawn's. With a tenderness she suddenly, desperately wished was real, he gathered her and pulled her higher against his solid warmth. A tear ran out of the corner of her eye, and she wiped at it roughly, wishing her body didn't betray her so easily.

"I'm sorry. I don't know what's happening," she said, still battling the sudden realization.

"Shh… There's no need for words when it comes to this between us," he said, rubbing his cheek against hers. "Except praise for me for sending you to outer space."

She chuckled, but it was slight and watery, and she kept her eyes closed, wondering what he would see if she let him. He kissed her temple and then her cheek and then the corner of her mouth. "It's okay, Laila."

He'd said that before, too, infinitely patient, and so ready to grant her whatever she asked for.

God, how had she allowed this? How could she love him with this wild abandon she'd never known before? What if he tired of her while this new...emotion flickered in her chest like a live flame? What if she agreed to marry him and they were locked in a convenient, sterile marriage for the rest of their lives? Could she bear to be near him and know he might never want her for the right reasons? What was the shape of her life if she always just stayed a means for him to fulfill what he'd been denied as a child?

The more she learned of his childhood, the more Laila was sure that Sebastian had never cared about anything much, had never been given the chance to. His art and his sons were now the only things that mattered to him. What if he just didn't have the ability to care about her like she did him?

"You're still trembling," he said, tightening his arms around her.

"You rocked my world," she said, striving for a flirty tone that had never come easy even before this. So she gave in to the only avenue open to her, to feel and show this new emotion. Opening her mouth, she tasted his skin, bit into the hard muscle of his shoulder. "You never told me what had you in such a foul mood."

He was quiet for so long that she resigned herself to his silence, to the fact that there was only so much she could demand, that soon she was going to come up on his hard limits.

With a rough exhale, she tried to pull back when he said, "This…painting I'm working on…" He cleared his throat, his words sounding like they came from some far-off place in him that he never went to in front of others. Laila instinctively knew that he wasn't used to talking about this, that he was letting her enter a forbidden place in his head. "It won't come together. It's the one thing in my goddamned life I've always been good at and the one thing that…calms that noise in my head. But for some reason, this one won't come together the way I see it in my head. I hate it. And I…hate feeling like my canvas won't speak to me when it is the only thing that has always known me."

The real, unfiltered, unmasked Sebastian Skalas…

Laila nodded wordlessly, tears prickling behind her eyelids, and tightened her arms around his waist, hoping he wouldn't push her away. She didn't understand why he didn't let the world see who he was or what peace he gained by hiding himself away—even from himself, she was beginning to realize. But she felt his pain and his powerlessness as if it were her own and she loved him a little more for giving her a tiny bit more than he wanted to, clearly.

She clung to him for long moments, knowing all she had were trite words to take on what she was realizing was a lifetime's pain, so she just held him and he let her and it was enough as darkness fell around them.

# CHAPTER TEN

DAYS AFTER LAILA had driven him wild and ravenous with her words and her mouth in the very place where he had never brought another soul to, Sebastian was still feeling unsettled. That encounter had been replaying in his head like a loop, for more than one reason.

Laila with her wild hair and generous promises, granting him a wish.

Laila, who made it easy to talk about things he'd never talked to another soul about—not even his twin.

Laila with her roving mouth all over his chest.

Laila on her knees looking up at him with those big eyes and those dark cherry-colored lips.

Laila holding his gaze with a tender, possessive hunger as her soft hand stroked him to dizzying heights of pleasure.

Laila who clung to him, trembling, and shaking, hiding none of her vulnerability.

He'd never looked a lover in the eye like that, at the throes of release. Never had been pushed off the edge because of the look in a woman's eye. Never needed to hold the woman after, a little flicker of dread and a host of other emotions rooting him in place.

It was as if Laila was the genie with all the magic and

she had sprinkled it all over him, alchemizing sex into something else. For the first time in his life, he'd been left with a niggling sense of loss he'd never known before, even as his body felt fully satiated. Usually, it was all he could do to get away from his partner when he'd satisfied them both. With Laila, he had been glad that she'd clung to him because he hadn't been ready to let go of her, either.

Now he wondered if it was all so different with her because when he saw her, he saw his sons' faces first. Saw Nikos's grin and Zayn's considering stare in her features. Saw the means to the deepest wish he'd indulged in as a child who would never have his father's approval.

With a desperation that kept clawing at him every moment now, he wanted all those reasons to be true. He needed them to be true. He needed Laila to mean nothing but a means to the end.

All of it rang untrue and hollow to his own ears.

Was it the childhood shame he had shared with her? Was that why he suddenly felt raw and vulnerable around her?

He had always told himself that the shame was Konstantin's—to terrify an innocent child, not his. But he had never gone into such detail with anyone else, not even his twin. And Alexandros knew everything. For all he'd never given it voice, raking over it with her had felt cleansing rather than poking a festering wound. Like giving her the blurry, torn map to his soul.

He had spent years developing awareness and control of his roiling emotions, right from adolescence—no one was going to help him with it, and yet, now his chest felt like it was a tangle of knotted wires, pricking and poking at his conscience. Like he'd meant to paint one thing on the canvas and something else was taking shape.

Like his heart wanted, no, needed, things beyond the boundaries he'd drawn around it a long time ago. Like it craved things it didn't know how to feel and give, things it was wholly unworthy of.

There was another strange thing happening to him. But this one he didn't fight. Didn't resist. He'd been spooked enough by what had happened between him and Laila that he had gone back to his art that very night. While it had fought him for almost a month, driving him near feral, suddenly it poured through his fingers with such frenzy that he'd spent every free minute working on his painting. Despite the thing that was emerging on the canvas, it was the one thing still under his control.

But he might as well have not tried to avoid her while he untangled himself, because Laila was doing it all the same. Something about that evening had spooked her. He felt her eyes on him as always, devouring him and seeking something in turn, the easy camaraderie and partnership they had developed over almost three months was gone. There was a wary look in her eyes as if she knew now what he was up to, as if she didn't dare come close again. But desire and heat thrummed between them, arcing over with just one look, one errant touch.

"Sebastian?" Ani said, stretching her hand out to him from the grass. They were all playing in the huge meadow behind the villa that sunny afternoon. The perfect picnic spot Laila had chosen for the boys with a blanket and snacks and toys. Giant, gnarled trees that he'd once hidden behind offered spots of shade to his sons now.

Giving her his hand, Sebastian pulled his sister-in-law

up and then steadied her with a laugh as she wobbled on her feet. "Thank you," he whispered and then kissed her cheek, knowing that even in this, Laila had been spot-on.

He hadn't really been angry with Annika—he'd just given the fear inside him that label.

Without meeting his eyes, Ani wrapped her arms around his waist, like she used to when she'd been a little girl, following him across this very meadow, forever dogging his steps, making his days a little lighter.

He wrapped his arms around her, unable to meet her eyes. Now, all these years later, she'd given Laila enough confidence to tell him the truth. He thought he must have done one thing right.

Ani raised those large eyes of hers, shimmering with tears, to his face finally. "Xander won't come out and ask, as he's still upset with you. Or maybe he worries that you won't accept."

"Ask me what?" Sebastian said, frowning.

"Will you be her godfather?" Annika said, putting her palm on her belly.

Awed and ashamed at once, he could only nod.

Ani wiped the tears from her cheeks, gave him a watery smile, grabbed one of the toy water guns and jumped into the fray with the boys. Though Zayn was no less reserved with her than he was with everyone else, he had taken to calling her *Ani Auntie*, sitting close when she played the cello—clearly it soothed him—and following her around with those big eyes full of curiosity. Used to roughhousing with her own three brothers, Ani knew exactly how to engage the boys' attention.

And now to be godfather to her and Alexandros's daughter... Sebastian felt as if his cup was overflowing with all the good things he'd once desperately wanted. Needed. His wildest dreams as a child come true. Except, nothing of the innocence of that child was left in him. He might not be a monster like Konstantin, but he was beginning to wonder what his real self was under the smoke and mirrors.

His gaze shifted to Laila, who was on her knees, fixing a stuck toy gun for Nikos. The sun caught the golden highlights in her hair, made the smooth skin of her neck and bare arms glimmer like burnished gold. Her sleeveless silk top was wet after the boys had caught her with their sprays and stuck to her skin, outlining her small breasts.

Just the sight of her filled Sebastian with hunger and… something he hadn't known the taste of in years. Or never, even. And it was the newness of this thing inside him, when he'd thought he'd glutted himself on all the riches and excess in the world, that had him so out of balance.

As if aware of his perusal, Laila looked up. Emotion he couldn't name flashed through her eyes before she offered him the polite smile of the last week. He felt the overwhelming urge to pick her up, throw her over his shoulder and carry her away and kiss that wariness and doubt out of her. He'd seduce her until she agreed to marry him and this…new furor and uncertainty in his head would die down. Wouldn't it? Once he had her bound to him, what was left to worry about?

Instead, he walked back to where his grandmother was sitting, his muscles burning with the need for action.

Alexandros stood against one of the large trees, his stance rigid, watching his wife. Annika was chasing Nikos, her cheeks reddish brown in the sun, her long braid already half wet.

"Thank you for letting it go," said Alexandros, his jaw tight. Sebastian heard the emotion that his twin rarely let anyone other than his wife see. "I haven't seen her laugh like that in a while. But instead of begging you to forgive her, I've been demanding that she let this grief over you go, demanding that she be well for my sake. Even after three years, I want to control everything around her so that she isn't hurt, so that she is happy." He thrust a rough hand through his hair, a scoff escaping his mouth. "I still haven't learned it enough that to love her means to let her be who she is, and to live with this...discomfort. And I have to do it all over again with a tiny little girl who will...be my responsibility."

So that was at the root of his twin's fear—not that he wouldn't care about his daughter but that he would do it wrong because he loved her so much already.

The angst in his words made shame burn through Sebastian's chest. It had been childish and selfish of him to continue his stubborn silence against Annika.

Only the past few days, with Laila's thoughts in his head, had he been able to understand that Ani had become a convenient target for him to blame for his own actions.

His anger toward her was a shield to avoid facing the fact that he might not have ever known about his sons because of how he had almost ruined an old man. Only now, did he see shades of Konstantin in his own actions—the ruthlessness with which he had gone after Guido. He'd justified luring the old man into gambling debt, betting his little home until he lost it to Sebastian, because he'd spent most of his adult life looking for his mother, another victim of Konstantin.

But the price would have been high if Laila hadn't

taken a chance on him, despite his actions. If whatever sense of ethics she possessed hadn't driven her to seek him out. He would have lost this present, this future, by his own actions.

"Laila made me see I was causing too much strife between you both. That I was hard on you the other day."

Alexandros turned, his face slack with surprise. "Your instincts were right about her. You knew about my...feelings for Ani long before I did, too."

"Trust that feeling, Alexandros. When your daughter is here, that feeling will guide you, too."

His brother gave another nod and then a bark of a laugh. "You have always been a better man than I am."

"I fought Konstantin so hard to be myself," Sebastian said, betraying his turmoil.

"And you have succeeded. You're a world-renowned artist. Your earliest paintings are coveted even now, go for millions in auctions. You spat in our father's face for how he mocked your art, you showed him false by becoming a man in your own right without the aid of the Skalas name, without touching your legacy. And I... I've never asked why you don't tell the world who you truly are. I've never asked you to share your art with me. But Sebastian..." Alexandros turned toward him, and until this moment, Sebastian hadn't realized how perceptive his twin could be when it came to him.

After all, they'd been each other's mirror in so many ways and witness to each other's best and worst.

"What?" he demanded, sick of the dread in his stomach.

"You have been a good man, Sebastian. Until now, at least."

"And what does that mean?" he said belligerently, hating that Alexandros was speaking the same doubts he already had himself.

"Being in love with a woman like Ani... It has changed what I can see, Sebastian." His twin gave a nod toward Laila, who was squealing and laughing and running up the meadow with their sons chasing her. "Does she know that you're stalking her like a predator does its prey? That you're not interested in—?"

"She came to me. She told me what her needs are," Sebastian said, cutting off what his twin would recklessly give voice to. "I'm simply showing her what the future could be between us."

"You're just playing along, to seduce her to your way. Making a show of giving her everything."

"*I am* giving her everything she asks for and it so happens that we agree on most important things. Why is taking advantage of that wrong?"

"It's...duplicitous, because you're doing it with a goal in sight."

"And here I thought you would champion me for making this right."

"Right for whom, though?" Alexandros said, sounding more frustrated on his behalf than Sebastian had ever heard him. "Maybe, finally, I see that some risks or gambles are not just worth it, that some things are sacred. I thought you knew that, Sebastian. I thought you understood better than me that the cost is too high."

"What aren't you saying, Alexandros?"

"Either you're lying to her or to yourself. And all these lies...will crash down on you when it's too late."

Sebastian stood there, long after Alexandros deserted him to join the noisy melee. He laughed when Nikos aimed at his uncle and then took off on his chubby legs and Alexandros made a show of not being able to catch him. He smiled when Zayn followed his twin and his uncle and auntie at an appropriate distance.

He felt his heart thud when Laila slipped and fell, and Alexandros gave her his hand and pulled her up, dusted her shoulder off and kissed her cheek and he could see the twinkle of joy in her eyes from all the way over here.

He froze when Laila's amber gaze sought him across the meadow and she gave him a small nod, and mouthed thank you, for fixing *his problem* with his brother and sister-in-law.

He fought the instinct to chase her across the meadow and demand that she give him surrender. He fought the pull she had on him but refused to give up his goal.

His twin's warning resonated like a painful gong, especially since it was exactly what he'd been dwelling on. He had never meant to hurt Laila and yet, suddenly it felt like all he was doing was pulling the worst kind of deception over her. But neither could he explore the other option. He could not let himself…feel. Not when, to this day, he hadn't recovered from his mother's leaving, when it felt like a necessary part of him was missing.

Not when he couldn't risk putting himself out there again. Which left him with only one choice.

He would bury this doubt, this new…weakness and continue with his plan to persuade Laila to marry him. Maybe then, all this vague dread would disappear. Maybe when he had her legally bound to him, when he knew that she was his, it would all fall into place.

# CHAPTER ELEVEN

LAILA HAD ENJOYED a couple of more weeks of what she considered a happy, relatively functioning, well-adjusted time with her sons' new family when it all came to an end. Not to mention that her academic paper had been accepted and she had a chance to present it a conference in a few weeks. Everything was going right or everything was going wrong and she didn't know what was what.

She and Sebastian hadn't kissed or touched or…exchanged anything more than a look since her realization. They seemed to have settled into some kind of holding pattern, bracing against the next upcoming turn in their non-relationship relationship. She knew why she'd pulled back.

While the realization that she loved him only grew stronger, as if planting roots deep within her very soul, it also spurred hope and fear equally. She was afraid she would blurt it all out to him if he so much as he looked at her for too long and she didn't how to build defenses against his reaction.

If he laughed at her, or mocked her…she would fall apart. And she was cowardly enough to know she didn't want to lose his respect, or be seen as pathetic, cowardly enough to continue in this holding pattern, to lie to herself that he was preoccupied with his art.

He'd even fixed his fight with Ani and Alexandros. He'd been communicating more with her about his moods and work habits, though it felt more like ticking off a checklist.

Any hope of continuing in that way in blissful ignorance ended when her mother called demanding to know where Laila had disappeared to for months on end with "her precious grandsons" in tow. Which was laughable because Mama only visited once in six months, given her "busy career," and had only missed Laila when she'd needed petty cash or when she needed to be looked after by the daughter she knew worked damned hard.

She'd had no choice but to tell her that she was with the Skalas family—yes, *that* Skalas family—because Sebastian Skalas was Nikos and Zayn's father. Too late she had added it was not a good time to visit but it was lost in the furor Mama created at the identity of the boys' father.

She'd resigned herself to paying the price of keeping that explosive information to herself for more than two years in the form of unlimited amount of criticism in the future. She definitely didn't want them to come here and…somehow undercut Laila in an already overwhelming situation. But, of course, the model of chaos had always ruled her life. Why shouldn't it now?

They arrived one gray, drizzly evening, leaving her feeling as rootless and ignored as she always felt around them.

As it had been through her entire childhood and adolescence, Mama and Nadia's arrival caused quite the stir. Not just because they were two extremely beautiful women dressed to the height of sophistication, but because Mama had been a world-renowned actress in the '90s and Nadia was a supermodel, albeit one whose career had barely touched superstardom before spiraling down because she had the worst kind of work ethic. Also, there was not even a hint of resemblance between Laila and them.

She could see the surprise in everyone, probably wondering how Laila could be part of a family of women who looked like *that*. It was like she'd reverted back to being fifteen and gawky and awkward, her brain far too ahead of her body, wondering what she could do to look like them, how she could transform herself so that she belonged to that nest.

Before her adolescent nightmares could become truly fresh, her sensitive child came to her rescue in his own way. Reacting to Mama's frenetic, frantic energy, Zayn made his way to her, and wrapped his chubby arms around Laila's legs, begging wordlessly for respite.

Laila picked him up, hugging his small body to hers, feeling that sense of peace fall into place, like it always did when she held one of her sons. As long as she had her boys, she needed nothing. It had been her mantra since she'd held them both moments after they were born but now, as she observed Sebastian's smiling reception of her family, that conviction that she didn't need a man in her life stumbled and stuttered.

And even now, it wasn't that she needed Sebastian so much as she wanted him to need her. To want to spend the rest of his life with her. To choose it because he couldn't bear it otherwise. Apparently, her heart was just as romantic and delusional as her half sister, who kept throwing herself at men who didn't value her for anything but her beauty. But she didn't want to walk away from him, either.

Could she live in this weird limbo, then? Could she bear to marry him and live with the little he would give her while her love and her doubts niggled away at her?

Would she ever feel confident enough to even admit to him without some guarantee of return?

*No,* a voice retorted.

She'd never been able to tell Mama that she craved her attention and her affection, or to Nadia that her taunts hurt, that she wanted to be part of them even if she was different. Or even Baba that she was only a teenager who still needed his care, even after Mama broke his heart.

God, she was a coward.

She gritted her teeth, as if to brace herself against the unbidden thoughts. Zayn cried out at the sudden stiffness of her hold, and she forced herself to relax her arms, cooing wordlessly into his temple, muttering *sorry.*

Sebastian was at her side instantly, his brow furrowed, as he tried to not crowd Zayn. "Laila, are you—"

"I'm fine," she said, without meeting Sebastian's eyes.

He moved closer, his broad frame shielding her from the prying eyes. "You're not happy to see them," he said, a thread of dismay in his statement.

She pursed her lips, unable to force even a parody of smile. "They are just a…lot."

"I will send them away, then," he said, rubbing his finger over her chin, in an almost tentative gesture that raised her shocked gaze to him. As if he thought she might…push him away.

"No," she said, looking into his deep gray gaze and swallowing. God, the drama that would cause… She needed to stop being a coward. "They are family. And family is everything, isn't it?" she whispered.

He searched her gaze for a few moments, and then turned. His welcome words to Mama and Nadia told her he was *that* Sebastian again, the one she didn't want. She gingerly brought Zayn down to the floor, who instantly ran off to play with Annika, right as she was engulfed in her mother's perfume and her sister's air kisses.

Mama thanked Sebastian with the effusiveness that seemed to grow out of proportion for a man who'd simply slept with Laila—or in proportion with the Skalas name, for his gracious invitation to the villa Skalas, when her own daughter had conveniently omitted them from her good news.

Sebastian *had* invited them here, then. That explained his dismay.

*Why, though?*

"Laila has been looking lost these last few weeks. I thought seeing her family might help. And I was eager to meet her family," Sebastian replied, ever the charmer, though his gaze sought hers.

Pasting a smile to her lips, Laila looked away. For the first time since she had arrived at the villa, she wished the Skalas family wasn't all present in force. But, of course, they were curious to meet her family and clearly shocked at what she'd hidden.

She introduced Sebastian to Nadia, who demanded it with that usual diva flourish of hers, and wondered if her retinas could be damaged in the face of the radiant smile Nadia threw at Sebastian. She could sense her sister's growing interest as clearly as she could hear her own thudding pulse. Nadia shook his hand, asked after a common acquaintance and had him pealing in laughter within seconds. Nadia, who knew all about art, and high culture and fashion and business and celebrity... everything about the world Sebastian dwelled in and Laila knew nothing about, nor was interested in.

God, what was wrong with her? She'd never been jealous of her sister even as a pimply, gawky teenager. All she'd ever wanted was not to be so different from them, to belong. She wasn't going to do this to herself now, just because she was in love with him. Although, saying that to herself didn't take away sticky, ugly jealousy that consumed her.

"This is quite the pairing, no? Like a comical, reverse retelling of a particular fairy tale," Nadia said, guffawing at her own cheap joke that couldn't quite hide her upset at her sister's sudden bout of good fortune, both in looks and riches of the man she'd "*landed*." Her half sister had never quite learned to hide her pettiness. "The charming, gorgeous playboy Sebastian Skalas…"

A full-body cringe took hold of Laila as her meaning sunk. Embarrassment choked her throat as she whispered, "Nadia…"

"And our clever little numbers freak Laila Jaafri. If I didn't know your chances of succeeding were quite low and that you know next to nothing about seduction, I would've said you targeted him on purpose, Laila." She added a tinkling laugh as if to take the sting out of the words, which had never really worked and didn't now. "I mean, how else would you have met a man like him?"

Laila froze, no response rising to her lips. The hurried exit of Nikos and Zayn from the room with the ever-watchful Paloma at that exact moment meant everyone heard Nadia's comment, and her incapability to offer a token protest made it land like truth usually did—with unassailable certainty.

Alexandros and Thea stiffened. Even Annika's gaze widened as it found hers. She'd never told even her friend how she and Sebastian had met. For a weak, vulnerable moment, Laila found herself hoping Sebastian would come to her rescue.

"Oh, my God, you did target him," Nadia said with genuine shock, then considered Laila with a calculating glint.

"Fine, I did. But not for the horrible reason I see in your eyes. Not for his wealth, or his power or his…good looks," Laila bit out through gritted teeth, having had enough. Not for her sister's or Mama's sake or for her new family's sake. For her own sake. "I did it to protect Guido. Because Sebastian was…"

"Guido?" Mama and Alexandros said at the same time. His gaze swung to Sebastian and something dawned in his eyes.

"What does this have to do with that useless old goat?" Mama demanded.

Laila's gaze inexorably went to Sebastian's, even as she automatically, like a thousand times before, said to her mother, "Guido is family to me. Mama."

"You don't have to cover up my sins, *pethi mou*," Sebastian said, holding her gaze from across the room, his words smooth and yet, somehow to her ears, full of tension. "Or protect me from the world."

He chuckled and it sounded so…so broken that Laila wanted to banish the entire world and go to him.

"*I* promised to protect you, not the other way around. Though, it is clear, I failed at that, too," he said, casting a glance at her family.

But Laila was loath to speak of what he had done, loath to betray what belonged to them to the whole damned world. Suddenly, she was glad of his mask in front of her family, even with his own, and most of the world. Because the real Sebastian, he was hers. His sins and his wounds and his real laughter, they were all hers and she would not share him with anyone. "How we met is no one's business," she finally said,

"Did you get pregnant on purpose, too?" Nadia asked, as if she'd rehearsed her lines. "That's quite the diabolical—"

"That's enough, Nadia," Laila said, disgust more than anger coming to her aid. How had she always let Nadia get away with this? Why had she tried to maintain a relationship that was all work on her part and insults on her sister's?

"Behave yourself, Nadia," Mama broke in, always a little late with her warning and little too indulgent of her eldest's disgraceful behavior. "It is of no consequence how it happened. The boys belong to this family and that's that."

No one could miss the satisfaction in her voice at that statement. Before Laila could interrupt, her mother continued, "Imagine our shock when Laila told us where she and the boys were, and with whom," Mama said to fill the awkward silence, waving her manicured hands about in that way of hers, looking elegant in a blush pink cream pantsuit that draped perfectly over her tall, statuesque figure. "Three years, she hid the identity of the father. Only that… Guido knew."

Out of the periphery of her vision, Laila saw Sebastian's head jerk up at that.

"You never asked me," Laila said.

"Of course I did. Many, many times," Mama said, making a liar out of Laila. "And honestly, I don't understand why you were so adamant about doing it all by yourself when you could have had this from the beginning. It's that middle-class mentality you inherited from your father."

"If wanting to stand on my own two feet, and wanting to have control over my life is middle class, then so be it. And please, don't bring Baba into this."

Mama turned to face Sebastian, a shrewd glint in her eyes, as if Laila hadn't even spoken. "I hope you're making financial settlements for my grandsons, Mr. Skalas. They deserve a cut of all this."

Laila's gaze found the floor, wishing it would open up and swallow her whole.

"Of course, Mrs. Syed," Sebastian replied as if it weren't the crassest question he had ever had to face.

"And make arrangements to clear Laila's debts, too, I hope? My daughter has quite the clever brain for numbers and patterns and models but none when it comes to finances. She has a mountain of debts because she insists on keeping her father's old house with its massive archives instead of—"

"That's enough, Mama," Laila said, a lifetime's worth of ache and anger bursting through. As much as Mama and Nadia had had very little actual time for Nikos and Zayn, she had tried. God, she had tried so hard to make them a part of her life because her sons deserved to know their grandmother and their aunt. But not at the cost of hearing them belittle their mother.

It had been stupid of her to think anything would change, after all these years. She was the one who had to change, the one who had to find the courage to let go of foolish hopes. Even if it hurt.

Her mother looked as if Laila had struck her.

"Don't take that tone with me, Laila."

"If it's the only one you'll hear, I have no choice." She tilted her chin up and addressed them both. "You didn't come to see the boys until they were three months old. You criticize everything I do as a parent. All my life, you've never spoken one loving word to me, and you drove Baba to his death with your constant demands and criticism. And now you stand there, revealing our family's secrets, without even checking how I'm doing. You talk about Baba's research of a lifetime as some dirty secret you can't wait to throw into the garbage. I'm so done with you." She pulled in a big breath even as her throat felt like it was full of thorns. "Sebastian has no duty toward clearing our family's debts—most of which you and Nadia accrued by living far above your means. I'll not take a single euro from him or his family and neither of you will you get your hands on anything unless you plan to…rob your own grandsons blind."

"You have changed," Nadia said softly, angry splotches on her impossibly high cheeks, as if she was discovering only now that Laila wasn't kidding. Laila felt her gaze on her body like some kind of laser pointer searching for a weak spot. And right now, she felt like she was covered in holes and wounds she'd rather bare in front of a predator than her sister. "Maybe because you think you have all this?"

"Enough, Nadia," Laila said, tears prickling behind her eyes as they always did when she fought with her sister, when she realized all her childhood dreams of belonging to a loving family would remain just that. God, but not anymore. She had people who respected her, liked her, she had someone like Sebastian in her corner, and that filled her with the courage she'd always lacked. "Having all this, for me, means knowing that I don't have to worry about food and shelter and education for Nikos and Zayn. Your debts and Mama's debts would've ruined their lives. And yes, I get to wear a few new clothes and a fancy hairstyle and new makeup bought with his money. So what if I get to enjoy a few nice expensive things that have never been within my reach because you and Mama leached every last little bit out of Baba? I find no shame in accepting what Sebastian spends on me when it brings him pleasure. I find no shame in depending on him when he wants the best for our family."

"You're nothing but his sons' mother, Laila. Don't go pinning all your hopes on him," Nadia mock whispered, making sure everyone heard her.

Laila turned away. Why was it so much worse to hear your own worst fears in someone else's words? "You need to leave."

"Sebastian would marry her today if she agreed," Annika said, from across the room, forever riding to Laila's rescue, her dear, lovely friend.

Sebastian straightened from across the room and Laila shook her head to warn him off. She could see a vein ticking away in his jaw, the violent emotions swirling beneath the calm gray. This...ugly showdown with her family was long due and she had to be the one to do it.

Laila could see Nadia's shock, her mother's excitement before her sister reverted to her default setting of petty cruelty. "But you haven't accepted, have you?" Each step Nadia took toward her resonated with her heart's thud-thud. "Our dear Laila always has high standards. But that's not it this time, huh? Even you, with your head buried in numbers, must know what a prize you have landed."

"He's a man, not cattle," Laila said through gritted teeth.

"You will ruin this good fortune, just like your papa and…no, this is something else…" Nadia's stunning brown eyes widened. "You're in love with him." A tinkling laugh followed her declaration. "Oh…poor Laila. Of course you have fallen in love. But you should know that a man like that is never going to love you."

That soft gray gaze found hers in the sea of embarrassment and pain threatening to drown her and Laila didn't flinch or look away this time. She held Sebastian's gaze, marveling at the emotion beating in her chest as if it were a life unto itself, and tilted her chin up.

She would not shy away from him, now. But for once, she could not read him, either, as if he had pulled a curtain down to shut her out, too.

For all the shame she had felt all her life that she was different, all the shame she'd been made to feel by two women who should have loved her and protected her, for all the shame she'd felt that Sebastian would see how little she mattered to her own family, Nadia's petty declaration in front of everyone didn't cause that prickly emotion.

There was no shame in the fact that she had fallen in love with Sebastian. No wrong, no naïveté, no foolishness and definitely no logic to it.

But she only felt strong in her love, changed by meeting this man who had worked so hard to hold on to his true self, despite everything he'd faced as a child, no less. She'd been fortunate enough to know and love her father, to know and adore Guido, and now she was glad she had met Sebastian, even if it was through nefarious means, that she had borne his sons. That she would always love him for all the freedom he had pushed her to enjoy, whatever the future held for him.

The ache of not knowing how he felt would come soon enough, but for now, loving him was a strength holding her up.

She'd always been naive when it came to her mother and sister, forever hoping that they would change, but she wasn't stupid. And wherever she and Sebastian fell in the scheme of things, she had enough faith in him that he would always stand with her and their sons, against the entire damned world if needed.

Laila straightened her shoulders, wondering if that little spark of fire within her that was her love had changed how she looked, too. She poked her finger into Nadia's bony chest hard enough that her sister startled. "You aren't even clever enough to get on my good side knowing I could help you this time, no? Get out of my life, Nadia, and please, stay gone. Next time you decide to pay a visit, I'll have Annika call the police on you. Believe me, she's bloodthirsty enough to take you on even if I weaken."

Then she looked at her mother, who appeared pale and wan under her tan skin. Maybe finally realizing the magnitude of her errors. *Or not.*

"If you want to be a part of your grandsons' life, come back without her. And ask for my forgiveness. Then, maybe, I'll consider it, only because Baba taught me that love is more important than anything else."

Laila didn't wait to see how her words landed. Her throat burned like it had when she'd had the flu and she could barely swallow past the hurt sitting there. But at least, it was done.

# CHAPTER TWELVE

IT WAS DAWN the next morning when Laila wrapped a flimsy cashmere sweater around her shoulders and knocked hard on the door to Sebastian's painting cabin or whatever the hell he chose to call it. Cold burned her skin but she didn't care. When he'd have followed her, she'd begged him to get rid of her mother and sister.

Then she had spent most of the night awake, crying on and off, which had predictably set off Zayn and then it was hours to calm him down and then waiting for Sebastian to come find her and then walking through the damned villa looking for him like some nighttime wraith.

She had been feeling raw after that confrontation with her mother and sister. Then, to realize that Sebastian wasn't coming... All her hope and pain turned to blazing anger, fueled by his...indifference to her plight, which he had brought on. And then there was the elephant in between them he was clearly, simply going to ignore.

As if her love would just fizzle out like Nikos's cold or Zayn's bad temper.

She had to thump hard a few more times before the double doors opened with a clunk, and there he was, on the other side of the threshold, looking as if he was the one who had been through a toxic breakup with his family. She didn't wait for him to welcome her inside. Neither did she politely wait for him inside the front lobby or whatever it was.

Pushing past him, she forced herself through the open door and into what was clearly an architectural marvel of a space, because it was all glass walls and high glass ceilings and dawn was like fingers painting the horizon pink and orange.

Once her attention returned to the room itself, she could see a huge number of paintings covered with plastic sheets and a fair number, also half-covered, sitting on easels, spread around the vast room. For a second, she indulged in the idea of unveiling each one with a dramatic flourish and taking a peek. But she had once violated his privacy out of necessity. Now that she knew it was something more than just his privacy, she was loath to do it again, however angry she was with him.

Her anger was already losing steam, and when she turned around to face him, it was to see a bleakness in his eyes that she never wanted to see again. The absence of that easy smile, or the charming mask or even the more real grumpy mood he'd shown her these past few weeks, made her skin prickly with a sense of caution. But it was too late, for she was realizing the freedom to be found in truth.

She wondered if she was getting her wish, finally, if she was seeing the raw, burning center of him, and she wondered belatedly, if that meant that she was going to burn with him. But there was not a speck of fear within her.

"I knew you were manipulating me to a certain extent. I knew you only wanted me because you want Nikos and Zayn in your life but I never thought you would be a coward, Sebastian."

He said nothing. Because, of course, Sebastian Skalas the charming playboy, never lied. He only just twisted the truth enough to make it palatable, for whoever he was serving it to. She had fallen in love with him with all this information at her fingertips, and yet now she felt a strange desolation. "You invited my family here and then, it felt like...why?"

"Alexandros had an extensive background check done on your friends and family recently. He was surprised when he found out who they were, who you were."

"Wow, infringing on privacy much?" she said, wondering even now at how he didn't ask why she hadn't told him. Why she'd kept her infamous family a secret.

"I didn't look, Laila, because it didn't make a difference to me. He mentioned your father was a minor prince."

"The title was mostly honorary at this stage. He had lands, but he sold off parcel by parcel to keep Mama happy. He was a good man but an idealist. He never had a job, and he buried himself in his research of his family's art history, which was his true passion, invested the little we had unwisely because her demands were endless, and lost it all. Then when it became clear that she had left him behind, he shut himself in the flat I rented for months at a time and wasted away to nothing. I couldn't...save him. And I couldn't bear to go into that flat after. All his research, it's all sitting there."

"And you looked after him. And Guido and Paloma and your mother and Nadia."

She shrugged, not even a little surprised at his conclusion. It was a little unnerving but also liberating how clearly he saw her.

She had done that most of her life, she realized now—looked after people. She looked after Baba, at the end, when he'd been heartbroken that he couldn't keep up with her mother's constant demands, and buried himself in his archives and in his research. She'd made him meals, made him coffee, reminded him of his medication for his heart trouble. Then she had looked after Guido and Paloma, who had been dependent on her for their livelihood. She looked after Mama every time she got sick and came home because she was an awful patient and, of course, Nadia couldn't be trusted to even bring her a glass of water. She had looked after even Nadia when she would come home after another one of her spectacular breakups with men who were as shallow as she was, hoping that she and her sister would maybe form a new bond.

When Guido had told her what he'd gambled away, she'd taken care of that, too.

The only person who had ever looked after her was Sebastian, albeit with a goal in mind, but hadn't his care for her come from some other place later?

If she agreed to marry him now—knowing he would devote himself to her and the boys, knowing that belonging to him meant she would never be alone again—would she be happy? Or would she forever wonder about what he truly felt for her? Would she forever trap herself in that toxic place again like she'd done with Mama and Nadia?

What did she reach for? The known, stable contentedness or risk it all for his love?

She rubbed a hand over her gritty-feeling eyes. "Why did you invite them?"

"We were at an impasse. Something happened the last time you were here," he said, spreading his arms to span the cabin. "My goal to convince you to marry me seemed further away than where I'd started. I thought bringing your family here would be a good thing. I thought I could score another point off with you. I didn't realize how awful they are to you." He laughed but it carried no real humor. "Alexandros thought it was important to control the situation since they are in the public eye, too."

She laughed then. But it was not bitter, and she was glad because she did not want to become like her mother, who lived in ideals that had nothing to do with reality, or her father, who had given his heart to an undeserving woman and died of it being broken. "I should've known it's all a game to you."

He shook his head, frustration coloring his words. "You seemed…sad the last couple of weeks, as if you were retreating inward, going somewhere I could not… follow."

"You know why now, Sebastian," she said, throwing the gauntlet back down again. But when he let it writhe in the space between them, she tried to gather her armor back. "I guess it did turn out to be the right thing for me. That confrontation has been coming a long time and I wouldn't have done it, if not for the last three months, if not for knowing that I have you in my corner."

"You were glorious, Laila. You did what you had to do."

"I always wanted to be like them," she said, only now realizing how much it hurt to give up on those you loved.

"You're a million times more beautiful than either of them," Sebastian said, as if he could see through her to that little girl she'd been.

"You know what?" she said, seeing herself clearly for the first time in a long time. Seeing herself through his gaze helped, too, because he'd always wanted her. That much had always been real between them. "I think I'll believe you."

"I also understand how much what I did to Guido hurt you."

"After Baba passed away, he was the one who watched out for me. He...never abandoned me."

"And you didn't abandon yourself, *ne*?"

"No, I didn't. Even when it was hard. You see all this, Sebastian, and yet you withdraw here and wonder why I would fall in love with you?"

"Laila—"

"What? That wasn't part of the plan? Is it an inconvenient plot twist to the narrative you had mapped out in your head about how this would go?"

She looked like a fury he had once painted, rising out of the mountains, all stark, raw beauty and righteous anger with the gentlest spirit beneath if only one was brave enough and vulnerable enough to seek it. He had drawn it after Mama had left. He hadn't known it then, but he had drawn what he wished she could have been for him and Alexandros.

And finally, here was the woman he'd imagined once, in blood and flesh, taunting him to come closer, boldly declaring her love.

Hair flying in all directions, eyelids swollen and amber eyes red-rimmed, that wide bow-shaped mouth pinched, her frame swathed in his T-shirt, crackling with temper, threatening ruin and yet, promising salvation if only he went to his knees and surrendered.

Sebastian, as he usually did when he finished a huge piece like that, felt inadequate, small, torn apart, feeling none of the succor he thought he would have once he finished. He felt like that child again, wondering what he'd done to deserve this fate and wishing he could change it, even though it was the dream he'd once held closest to his heart.

He had set out to win Laila over to his way. He'd even found her naive and easy in one sense because she was so…fair and logical to begin with. She wanted nothing but their sons' happiness and honest desire between them. She just wanted a place for herself and he'd been happy to give it. But he'd never dreamed of her…falling in love with him, much less declaring it like this, or coming up with a fresh set of demands.

Even saying that made him want to roar and howl in a way he hadn't done since he had been a teenager who had constantly wished he was like his brother.

It had taken all his willpower to let her sister take strips off Laila right in front of him. And then that taunt and Laila's silence in the wake of it.

The bold, brave way she'd held his gaze.

He still didn't know what to make of it. Only that it terrified him to his soul, that he felt…that same sense of powerlessness he'd felt as a kid with his father in the face of her love. Like he didn't deserve it and didn't know what to do with it.

He thrust a hand through his hair. "I don't know what you want from me."

She smiled, and it was fragile and heartbreakingly

beautiful. "Why were you so determined to ruin Guido?" she said, surprising him yet again. "Please, I deserve to know. I demand to know."

And he knew that she was hacking away at all the shields he hid behind, tearing away all the blinders and smokescreens he used to keep the world at bay. She was going to bring him to his knees if he wasn't there already and there was nothing he could do to stop her.

"He used to be Mama's chauffeur. One summer, he helped her run away without raising Konstantin's doubts one bit. I wanted to know where she went."

"After all these years?" she said, tears in her eyes.

"I have never stopped wanting to make sure she was okay," he said with a shrug. Not that he had understood that compulsion, either. Like with everything else about his head, he had simply given in. At some point, it had become less about any attachment he'd still felt for Mama and more a reason to continue in the aimless way he'd adapted his life to be.

"But Guido wouldn't tell you?"

"No. Not even when I had the deed to his small house in my control."

"And now? Do you still want to find her?"

He blew out a breath. "I will not say no. But the choke hold has lessened. Alexandros told me recently that she had planned to take me with her when she fled. That she'd packed my passport and my medication in her little bag, that somehow Konstantin might have upset her plan at the last minute, and she had to flee instantly."

"And leave Alexandros behind to your father? Rip you, too, from him? That's extraordinarily cruel," she said, and he could see the rage she was working hard to temper.

"I agree," he said, remembering the bleakness in his twin's face when he had revealed that piece of the past that had tormented him for so long. "I think he thought it would bring me solace after all these years to know that she wanted me with her. I was more attached to her from the beginning and… I wouldn't stop looking for her."

"But it didn't work out like Alexandros thought it would," she said, so damned perceptive.

"Other than ripping him apart for God knows how long with guilt that he'd hidden it from me, no."

"Did you tell him that you would have never abandoned him?"

It felt like the punches kept coming, like he was already on his knees, but she wouldn't leave him until he was bloody and broken. "So sure of me, Laila?"

"I know you, Sebastian. Better than anyone else in the world. Maybe even better than Alexandros."

That piece of truth moved through him like a bullet, ricocheting through the chambers of his chest. And he was beginning to understand why he felt hunted. "I did tell him that I'd have never left him. And in the end, Mama chose her freedom over me, too. I never blamed her for being weak in the face of Konstantin's will."

One lone tear followed the strong cheek down to her chin. Strangely, her tears on his behalf didn't bother Sebastian one bit. Because she understood exactly how he felt? Because she could see who he was beyond all that he had endured?

He felt a cold chill and a hot flare at the very pit of his being. It was the freedom he'd chased all his life—to be seen as he was—and yet denied himself because he'd been determined to be far from the shadow of the past.

He'd bound himself in the shackles of the Skalas name as much as Alexandros had done, just in a different way. He hadn't outrun the name at all.

He had almost lost the chance to know about his sons. And now, when he had them within reach, within his home, within his heart, it was not enough. The means had become the end...and suddenly, Sebastian Skalas, one of the most renowned, brilliant artists of their time, a near mythical man who could alchemize emotion into colors, who could pin down the world into one blank canvas in all its glory and its disgrace, didn't know if he was enough. If he could withstand the love of this woman, if he could stand under its shadow and not freeze to ice, if he could ever...return it without conditions and contracts and...the crippling fear that he would lose it all. That something within him—some rot that his father had planted—wouldn't push her away.

"After seeing you with the boys..." he continued, determined to get it all out, because she was hollowing him out anyway, "I knew Alexandros was not wrong in being angry with Mama all these years, in blaming her as much as he did Konstantin for our ruined childhoods. A few hours after that first night, I knew how it could be. How it should be."

She took a grasping, watery breath as if she were the one living through the past.

"And yet, you're here," she said, walking toward him, "making glorious art and loving your sons right from the first minute and being a man in your own right, and being this extraordinarily kind man. I..." She smiled weakly through the tears and straightened her shoulders. "I know what I want for my third wish."

He barked a laugh out then and he thought it might be the little bit of sanity he'd hung on to all these years leaving his system, rendering him into the stark skeleton of the child he'd been born, with dreams and demons all occupying the same space within his head, able to see the world for what it was and for once, loving it the same anyway.

For all he'd blamed Konstantin as the reason, he'd been running away from life, directionless. Running away from the very spirit of the child he'd been, who'd loved endlessly and lived fearlessly.

"What would you have of me, *agapi mou*?" he said, finally beaten down and admitting defeat. All the battles he'd fought in his life, and he hadn't even seen this one coming.

She reached him and clasped his unshaven cheeks and pulled him down to meet her mouth and it was heaven and hell and the purgatory he'd existed in for so long. It was unbearable pleasure with a twist of pain in its promise. Her mouth was soft, and so incredibly sweet and he was a dying man parched of breath itself. Small hands gripped his shoulders as if she meant to anchor him to her in any way possible. He felt drenched to his soul in the affection of her kiss, in the passion of her response, drowned in her unnamed expectations. But weak man that he was, he couldn't push her away.

She touched her forehead to his, rubbed her nose against his like she did with their sons and smiled against his mouth. Her tears only reminded him of his unending thirst. "I want to marry you, Sebastian. I want to build a life with you. I want to share your art and celebrate your ups and downs. I want to have more children with you.

I want to love you for the rest of our lives, and I want it more than anything I've ever wanted in this world. And I want it with you loving me, as only you can."

"Then you might have to wait a long time, Dr. Jaafri," he said, his heart breaking, even as it felt out of his reach. A paradox if he'd seen one and he had seen enough in his life.

"I have time. You should know, patience is one of my virtues, too. I have made all the calculations here—" she tapped her head "—and here—" then her chest "—and it all adds up. My life is here with you and our sons."

"I could grant you a thousand wishes, a million and make them all true. Whatever you ask for. Except this. Don't—"

"I know what I want, and I won't settle for anything less," she said, walking away from him.

At the door, she stilled and turned around. "Remember the academic paper I submitted?"

He nodded, feeling as if he were in a trance.

"It got accepted. I get to present it at a conference in a couple of weeks in London. I'm planning to go away and leave the boys here with you."

"Zayn—"

"Zayn trusts you and loves you, Sebastian. He just needs the push to come to you and without me here acting as a security blanket, it will happen seamlessly. You trust me, don't you?"

If he didn't know her well, he'd have thought she was flexing her newfound confidence and the strength of her hold on him. But he did know her, and he was also aware that her love would haunt him for the rest of his life, reminding him of his fear. He nodded, refusing to give her the words, resentful of the understanding shining in her eyes.

"Paloma will be here just in case."

"Why two weeks?" he asked, though a part of him felt relief that she was going away. That he didn't have to face those amber eyes and the unfathomable trust in them, in the mornings, in the afternoons and during midnights when they checked on their sons. The coward in him wished she'd go away for longer, even, wished he could return to whom he had been before she'd walked into his life, blasting open every defense he'd put up against the world.

But there was also that part that hated the thought of her being out in the world without him. With colleagues and friends and some man who might see what an extraordinary woman she was. He felt torn in two and it was more painful than anything he'd ever experienced.

"I hung on to my father's flat for too long, as a way of keeping him with me. I never stepped foot inside those walls again. But now, I want to sort through his research before Mama decides she will burn it all. I want to do something with it. I want to save it so that our sons can learn about their legacy on my side, too."

"I can arrange for someone to—"

"No. I must do this. Say goodbye properly. Tell him I'm starting a new chapter in my life. And that he's given me everything I needed to thrive, that he was right when he told me that I'm worth everything the world has to offer, just as I am."

"I would have loved to meet him."

She nodded, smiling. "He would have loved to meet you, too. And he would have liked you."

Already he could feel her absence, the one person he'd ever allowed into this space.

"If I'm never ready to grant you your wish?" he whispered, feeling as if he was being attacked from all sides, swept away by a tide he couldn't fight. "If we're forever caught in this…limbo?"

"Never is a long time, Sebastian. As for the limbo, I guess we can both survive in a way, for our sons, remain stagnant and static, instead of choosing something more. But I can't…" She swallowed, her eyes searching his. "…marry you unless you—"

"It doesn't happen because you threaten or beg or demand it. Believe me, I have tried."

"No but it won't happen if you close yourself to it, either. And I want you to give us a chance, to crack open the door, to let me in. You've been hiding in shadows and secrets long enough."

And then she was gone, and Sebastian wished the coming dawn would stop and leave him in darkness for a long time because after everything, it seemed Konstantin's shadow had won and he had lost.

Because the thought of loving Laila, the thought of opening himself to her love, felt terrifying to his very soul.

# CHAPTER THIRTEEN

SEBASTIAN LOOKED UP at the tiny third-floor flat in the small coastal village, where he'd been sitting in the car for the last two hours. With the windows rolled down and a storm front coming in, he was freezing.

And he had frozen ever since he'd arrived here, with a note clutched in his hand, disappearing like a coward the moment he knew she was back.

For almost two months now, Laila and he had been engaged in a silent battle of wills when they were in each other's company. Which had been less than usual since she'd traveled out of country three separate times. With him deep in finishing a few pieces for his next exhibit and Laila traveling back and forth for work and to clear out her father's house while doing her best to preserve his research, they had crossed each other at the villa no more than for a handful of days.

And he was beginning to hate everything about their life, enmeshed together but not intersecting in any but the shallowest of ways. She didn't smile at him or argue with him or probe him or touch him. She just looked at him with that steady, relentless emotion in her eyes, whether they were playing with their sons or discussing her career or sleep-mussed from his bed, which she had taken over and he didn't mind.

Sebastian found himself shrinking, to escape seeing himself through her eyes.

His brother and Ani were baffled by the silent but pregnant stalemate between them. Even his sons, he knew, were beginning to feel the rift between him and Laila and he found himself bereft, on the verge of losing everything he'd gotten a taste of in the past weeks.

His fear of letting her in was nothing compared with the torment of seeing her in his bed and not reaching for her. Of wanting to hear those sweet words from her lips again and depriving himself because he wasn't sure he could pay the price.

Then he'd seen it, a handwritten note with two lines of address on it, left on his desk. And he'd known instantly that it was from Laila, known that she'd scoured through her father's research and Guido's belongings for this. She'd been gone to find this.

For him.

Because she wanted Sebastian to have what he'd looked for most of his life.

But now that he was here, now that Sebastian knew that his mother was in that third-floor flat, all he felt was a strange relief. A freedom. Like he was ready to set down the weight of whatever had been clinging to him.

Laila had gotten him what he'd wanted and that, too, like her love, felt like an unbinding. A releasing. A new beginning for him. For them. For their sons and their lives together.

When he heard a noise from the tiny balcony, Sebastian froze. He could hear the litany of Greek, was almost sure that it was *her*. But he didn't need to go up and confront her. He didn't need to check if she was okay. He didn't need to ask her how she could have abandoned him and Alexandros.

He didn't need any answers from her, not anymore. Not when he had an entire life waiting for him. Not when everything he had ever sought was within him. Not when a woman like Laila could see what he was truly and still love him. The reason, the struggle, the culmination of all the battles he'd taken on in his life was in his house, waiting for him. Giving him what he had needed without him asking for it. Seeing him as he was.

So, he started the engine and he bid the woman on that balcony goodbye in his head and he drove off, even as he was still shaking from head to toe.

Laila felt strong arms gently pull Nikos from where he'd been clinging to her like an octopus but felt reluctant to open her eyes. She threw an arm behind her gently, only to find Zayn was gone, too.

Instantly, she turned and blinked, remembering she had carried both boys to her bed and fallen asleep, with their arms and legs wrapped all around her. On the rare occasions that she let them both come to bed, she was usually so stiff so as not to disturb their sleep. But tonight, she hadn't cared. She'd needed them, after two months of avoiding Sebastian's gaze, only to find that he wouldn't look at her at all. Then she'd been gone again with another goal in mind. And this time, she had known he would disappear. But still, it was hard because she wanted to be with him. Because she wanted to hold his hand when his world broke apart, all over again. Because she wanted to love him.

Not even Alexandros knew where his twin had gone off to and Laila kept it to herself. She had no intention of ruining the happiness that Alexandros had found with Annika by bringing up pieces of the past he'd finally made peace with. If Sebastian wanted to tell him, that was his choice.

In Sebastian's absence, his twin had taken to reassuring Laila that Sebastian was a good man, just…maybe a little broken. Even Thea seemed to think that Laila was just being both stubborn and foolish, playing this waiting game. Sebastian, she kept telling her, would never love her.

If his continued absence hadn't sowed doubts about the future—how long did it take to drive up to the coast and find that address?—Laila would have found the mighty Alexandros Skalas's nervous declarations a little funny. Neither did she agree with him or Thea at all.

She didn't think Sebastian was broken at all. Only a little bent like her, but somehow, they had both managed to retain the best of themselves and found people to love and they had their sons to nurture and…

The door to her vast bedroom that adjoined the boys' room was closed and footsteps returned to the bed.

She gasped when those very arms lifted her not-so-slender frame and shifted her to the middle of the bed. Instant tears pooled in her eyes when she realized it was *him*. He was cold and shaking behind her and she shivered at both. She felt his lips against the nape of her neck, cold and chapped. Alarm swept through her at what he'd been up to, what he had discovered at the address she'd found. "Sebastian? You're shivering. What happened? Is everything—"

"I want to hold you, Laila. I need to..."

She grabbed his corded forearm that gripped her tight under her breasts, smushing her front against his back so hard that her breath came in rough pants, compulsively running her fingers over the soft hair there, wanting to soothe him. His other hand, she brought to her face and kissed the center of his palm. "I missed you," she said, giving up all pretense of the fight she meant to put up when he returned. "I—"

"Shh...not right now, *agapi*. Right now, I need you. I need to feel your warmth and your passion and your need for me. Only you would provoke me to this, Laila. Only you could reduce me to this—"

"I'm yours, Sebastian. Take me. Have me. Do what you will with me. I have been yours from the first moment I saw you and you showed me a simple kindness I didn't know I needed. I had been yours three years ago. I have been yours all these months and I'll be yours fifty years from now, when you're not the stud you are now."

She felt his mouth stretch against her skin in a smile, felt it reach her deep within her being, that empty place waiting for him. She felt a shuddering relief that she hadn't lost him to the past, that she could make him smile, that she...

"I want to make you promises, give you what you deserve. But I—"

"It's okay, Sebastian. Right now, all I need is to be what you need. My entire life, I have given so much of myself to people who didn't care. You... I would give you anything."

"I want you so much," he said, the tips of his fingers still cold as they dug into her willing flesh. "I'm afraid I might be rough…"

"I want you rough. And gentle. And all the speeds in between," she said, throwing her arm behind her in the dark and wrapping it around his neck.

When she turned her head, his mouth was there, ferociously demanding and desperately hungry. Just the way she needed him. His kiss was hot and hard and rough, his tongue stroking against her, his fingers on her chin holding her for his assault.

Laila moaned when his fingers snuck under her tank top and pinched her nipple. She pushed herself into him shamelessly, begging against his mouth for more. Protests fell from her tingling lips when he deserted her mouth, but his hands were all over her and she arched into his touch. For days, weeks, she'd been trying to nurture her hope, to fan it with tiny sparks that she felt living around his family, around his things, and yet it had only left her desolate. Cold.

Now, she was burning, and she wanted to go up in flames if it meant she could have him.

Soon, he'd pulled her top out of the way, baring her to him.

"I need to see you," came his ragged whisper, and then soft light from the lamp hit her closed eyes.

She kept them closed, too eager and loath to see his expression, afraid that her own hopes might dash her to the ground all over again.

His breath was a feather-light whisper against her breasts, her nipples instantly tightening. Then she felt his tongue lash her nipple in slow, tentative strokes and then, when she buried her fingers in his hair and moaned, firm, fast circles that had her panting, and then his mouth sucked her in and he suckled deep and her eyes flew open.

Pupils blown so wide that she barely saw the gray, his mouth wet around her breast, he looked like her every fantasy come true. Dark circles clung to his eyes and his mouth had that pinched look, but all she saw was his hunger. For her. His need for her.

"More, Sebastian, please," she said, arching her spine into his warmth. "Don't make me wait anymore."

He rubbed his nose down her belly, whispering words into her skin, and then he stilled.

She looked down and saw him swallow at the sight of her wispy lace panties. "They're impractical and they ride up my ass half the time and I'm not used to them," she said, breathing hard. "But I wore them for you. In case you showed up. Every night, I take a shower, rub myself all over in some freaking expensive oil that comes with being *your woman* and dress in the flimsiest of clothes with the hope you'll come to me here and that you'll see me and that you'll admit that you love me a little."

His teeth pulled at the fragile lace before he kissed the line of her pelvis, rubbed his nose at the fold of her thigh and hip, digging his teeth into the sensitive skin of her inner thigh until she was marked in his ink. A sliver of pain to punctuate the pleasure. Laila curled her fingers in his hair and tugged roughly, just as he tore them off her, and then his mouth was there.

"You taste divine," he said, his words a rumble that caused vibrations against her folds. "I remember your taste. I remember how you sounded that night. I remembered how you looked at me."

"Please, Sebastian," she said, finding no shame in begging. "You made me wait too long already."

His fingers and his lips and his filthy whispers, he drove her hard and fast and rough and so high that Laila flew up and up and away and then she fell from that height, hard. Her climax was a vortex of sensation, thrashing her around and around. And he didn't stop tormenting her.

His tongue licked at her clit, his fingers kept pumping inside her until Laila went from one orgasm to the next with no break or breath in between and her entire body was nothing but a mass of sensation.

"I forgot how you can do that," he said, coming up and smiling, his sensuous lips damp with her arousal.

"Inside me, now," she said, the words barely formed. "I started the pill."

He swallowed and then that hard, lean, beautiful body was rising over her. His mouth found hers in a soft, tender kiss as if he knew she would break apart at the tiniest of pressures and his damp, hair-roughened chest dragged over her sensitive, throbbing nipples in a graze that sent need flickering into a spark again and then he was stretching her thighs indecently wide, pushing her right knee into her chest, and Laila watched him—his intense expression, his tied brows and his swollen lips and his unwavering focus—and then his gaze met hers.

He thrust into her in one smooth, deep move, lodging himself so deeply as he'd done that first time that she'd never been able to get him out. And now, she didn't want to.

She thrust her hips up and circled them, desperate for friction, and he cursed and swallowed.

And then he was moving in and out in a slow, deep rhythm, their fingers laced, and their gazes tethered together, and Laila's selfish mind and deprived body began the dance all over again.

"I'm going to take you fast and hard," he said, against her lips, and Laila whispered another *please*.

And then he upped their rhythm.

Each stroke hit that magical point, each thrust drove her further along the line of bliss, but Laila kept her eyes on him, this beautiful, rugged artist of hers, who felt so much and who tried so hard to not love her and she wanted to say the words now.

Clasping his cheek, she said, "I love you, Sebastian."

And as if he meant to reward her declaration, he took her deeper, dragging the ridge of his abdomen over her clit, and Laila fell over.

He pumped his hips, rough and fast, into her and then he was grunting and shaking and burying his face in her neck, and his weight on top of her, for the bare second he allowed it, was the most delicious pressure and Laila pressed her forehead to his shoulder and scrunched her eyes but her body betrayed her yet again and soon, there were tears running down her cheeks and dampening his taut skin in the process.

Sebastian stared helplessly at the softly snoring woman and didn't know what to make of the fact that Laila had not only sobbed as if her heart was breaking all over again, but then fallen into such deep sleep that he was terrified of waking her.

Gently untangling her limbs from his, he pressed a

kiss to her temple, pulled on his sweatpants and quietly padded into their sons' bedroom.

Nikos was fast asleep, his toy horse clutched in his tiny fist.

"Papa?" he heard behind him.

Heart in his throat, he went to his second son, who'd pulled himself to his feet in the crib and had a hand outstretched toward him. While he hadn't run away from him or hid behind Paloma exactly when Laila had been gone, Zayn hadn't exactly sought Sebastian, either.

He was about to crouch down in front of him, wary of spooking him, when Zayn said, "Pick up, Papa. Want cuddle."

Tears knocking hard against his eyes, Sebastian sniffed and then picked up the little boy.

Tucking his little head into Sebastian's shoulder, arms thrown around his neck, Zayn didn't say much, and, in the silence, Sebastian's heart hammered out a thunderous beat.

He had no idea how long he walked around the vast bedroom, holding one piece of his jagged heart outside his body.

Two yawns and a softening of his body later, his son demanded "sleep now." Kissing his forehead, Sebastian was about to put him down on the bed when Zayn kissed his cheek. "Papa not go? Papa stay now?"

Tears crowding his throat, Sebastian said, "Yes, Zayn. Papa stay now. Papa's not going anywhere."

Zayn stared at him through sleep-heavy eyes and then two seconds later, fell into a deep sleep.

Sebastian walked between the two cribs a few times, and went off to shower, considering and discarding all the words he needed to say to the woman who'd given him more than he'd ever dreamed of.

When he returned to their bedroom in fresh pajamas hours later, with dawn cracking through the deepest dark of the night, his hair still wet, Laila was sitting up in the bed, the tank top back on, her legs folded under her, her head thrown back against the headboard of the bed. Her wide mouth was trembling, and she kept running a hand over her neck where he'd left a mark on her with his teeth, submerged in his climax.

He could sense her tension across the room as if it were his own and loathed that he had caused it. That he had made her doubt him. That he had made her wait.

She looked up just as he reached the bed. He stood there, watching her, arms hanging by his side uselessly, his heart beating so fast that it threatened to rip out of him.

"Zayn spoke to me, just now." His throat felt like it was full of needles and thorns. "He demanded a cuddle and demanded that I don't leave again."

"He missed you. He kept asking Nikos why you left and when you were returning. For the first time, I saw them fighting because he wouldn't stop asking and Nikos got frustrated. It was both...exciting because they're growing such distinct personalities and terrifying because I never want them to lose each other."

"They won't," he said, feeling, for once, more confidence in their sons than she did. "Zayn... Did he get really upset?"

"A bit, yes. Like his papa, when he loves, he loves true and deep."

"Such faith, *agapi*?"

"It's both easy and hard, this whole loving-you thing. I... I feel like I'm perpetually on a roller coaster and you know I'm not fond of risks."

He sat at the edge of the bed and took her hand in his. "I...thank you for locating that address for me. I don't know what to think."

"Guido was exactly like Baba. He never threw away a single scrap of paper. Once I remembered that, it was easy. It took only four days and sleepless nights to find it neatly written in one of his address books. I think he meant to give it to me. He knew the boys were yours."

Sebastian nodded, brought her hand to his mouth and kissed her. All his life, words had come easily to him. Of comfort and teasing and charm and seduction and... yet now... He felt like his sons, his emotions too big and too fast for his throat to work.

"Did you see her? Is she well?" Laila asked softly, taking pity on him.

"I parked outside the flat and sat there for a few hours. I didn't feel the need to go in. Even after I heard her."

And then Laila was crawling into his lap, and he heaved them both onto the bed because there was no way he could let her fall. "I'm free, *agapi mou*. Finally. Thanks to you. Free of shadows and secrets. Free to love you. And I already do. I love you so much that I find words inadequate. I love you so much and I thank the entire universe every day, every moment that you decided to lie to me, and cheat me and seduce me and have our sons. I love your honesty and your calculations and your brainy brain and how you love our sons and how you fill my life with such happiness."

Laila clung to him, her tears wetting her chest all over

again, and Sebastian pushed her into the bed and stared into her amber eyes. "Tell me again."

"I love you, Sebastian. Probably since I saw your art and how perceptive and stunning it was."

"And will you marry me?"

"Yes. Tomorrow if you want."

And then there was nothing to do but kiss her again and lose himself in her taste, and her groans and her sweet demands and her reverent promises.

# EPILOGUE

LAILA AND SEBASTIAN'S SMALL, intimate wedding—which somehow still had a hundred guests because Thea Skalas was determined to have one grandson's wedding the way she wanted it—got postponed, since Nyra Skalas, their cutest, prettiest little niece, with a full head of thick dark hair and her mom's big brown eyes, decided to make an appearance way ahead of schedule, sending them all into a tailspin of shock and surprise and laughter and a small nervous breakdown on the part of her father, who had bellowed at his twin at the top of his lungs because Sebastian had mocked him.

Even though Ani and the newborn were doing well, Laila insisted on waiting because how could she get married without her new friend/sister acting as her maid of honor. But since Ani had to have a caesarean and Alexandros was like an enraged/terrified bull on steroids every time his wife or his twin or his grandmother dared to suggest that maybe, just maybe, Ani was ready to be up and about for such a big event, they pushed it back a little more.

Which, of course, made Sebastian angry because he thought his twin was overprotective and was the main obstacle in the way of what he'd waited for his whole life.

Laila, for her part, loved it all: Alexandros's utter love for his daughter, how Sebastian—a natural at this, too—showed him how to support his brand-spanking-new niece's tiny head, how Nikos and Zayn couldn't stop blubbering about their itty-bitty cousin, about the pictures Thea insisted they shoot on day three with her two great-grandsons and great-granddaughter, and how Alexandros had nearly broken into tears when Nyra had smiled at him even as Sebastian teased that it was aimed at him—the superior uncle—and how she and Ani had hugged and laughed and cried together knowing that they'd found the kind of love that very few did.

Finally, a month after Nyra was born, the day dawned bright and sunny and Laila followed Annika, who was holding Nyra in her arms, down the aisle on Alexandros's arm—she'd been stunned and awed when he'd asked to give her away—and there was Sebastian waiting for her, with Nikos and Zayn by his side, looking like his very heart was lodged into the look he gave her.

She cried and smudged her makeup and cried a little more when he kissed her and whispered, "Six months just for us and then we're making a baby and this time, I want a girl as precious as Nyra."

"It's not a competition, you know," she said, a while later, as he kissed the back of her hand and they were whizzing away in a chauffeured car for a quick two-day getaway because neither of them really wanted to leave Nikos and Zayn just yet to Paloma and Ani and Alexandros and Thea, even though everyone kept assuring them they would be fine.

"Of course it is. That way, we could keep the bigger chunk of the Skalas fortune for our children."

Leaning into him, she kissed his naughty mouth. "As if you would take anything away from the little girl you call your princess already."

He laughed and pulled her hand up, until the two rings there shone brightly. They were unique and tiny—despite his protestations—and just right for her. He kissed the back of her hand, his throat moving on a hard swallow.

"I love you, Mr. Skalas," she said, looking into his eyes.

"I love you more, Dr. Jaafri," he whispered, and then she was squealing because he was pulling her into his lap and kissing her senseless and Laila thought her dream had finally come true' with more color and love than she could have ever imagined.

\* \* \* \* \*

# BILLIONAIRE'S
# RUNAWAY WIFE

ROSIE MAXWELL

MILLS & BOON

For my brother and sister-in-law and
my two adorable nieces, with all my love. xx

# CHAPTER ONE

DOMENICO RICCI WAS in pain. His body was heavy with it, as if his bones had been lined with lead. Even the simple act of drawing in a breath was an effort, causing his chest to burn and his stomach muscles to sharply contract.

Grief, he thought disdainfully. It had always been his considered point of view that those who cited the crippling effects of grief were simply too weak to contend with the realities of life. Death was, after all, inevitable. A basic fact of life. It was far better to celebrate a person than wallow in mournful and distressed emotion upon their passing.

But now it was his adored aunt Elena who had departed the world and all Domenico could feel was the burden of sorrow. Even the sight of his beloved Venice—home since his scandalous and uncelebrated birth—in the mauve and indigo shadows of the approaching evening offered little comfort.

In spite of Elena's advanced age, he hadn't been prepared for it. For the loss of the only woman who had never rejected him and who had spent her life guiding and encouraging him. The woman who had given him a home and the embrace of a family when those who should have loved and cared for him had been set on deserting him to a crueller fate. And now she was gone.

Just like all those other people in his life, Elena had left him too.

In the faint reflection in the window Domenico watched his lips firm and lines of strain stream from the corners of his mouth as his meandering thoughts forced him to relive the rejections and desertions he had suffered over the years, beginning with his birth family and ending with his wife, Rae.

*Rae.*

His big body clenched as he thought of her, with her heart-shaped face, her tumble of chestnut hair and eyes so startlingly, beautifully blue they could penetrate even the coldest soul, compelling Domenico to raise the glass cradled between his fingers to his lips and numb the sudden sharp pinch of bitter feeling with a long swallow of the bright amber liquid. Out of all the women who had inflicted a scar, Rae had cut him the deepest. Because he had *chosen* her. He had invited her into his life, placed a ring on her finger and made a binding vow, and she had walked out on him. That desertion burned him far more than anything he had endured from his blood relatives.

Which made it all the more inexplicable that in his moment of sadness it was her comforting touch he craved. That out of all the mourners currently in his palazzo, hers was the only face he wanted to see, only she hadn't bothered to come and pay her respects...

Domenico raised the glass to his lips again, castigating his melancholic mood for turning him into a sentimental fool. Of course she hadn't come! Rae had left him. Rejected him. She hadn't even had the decency to tell him that she was unhappy in their marriage. Hadn't offered him the chance to fix whatever it was that was making her unhappy. She'd simply walked out of the door one day and left him to find the pathetic one-sentence note she had deigned to write to explain her sudden absence.

She was the last person deserving of room in his thoughts. The very last woman he should desire. If he needed comfort, there were countless others he could turn to, women who would appreciate him and be happy to share his bed. Because that was all that would be on offer. A night. An encounter. Never again would he open up his life to another soulless, treacherous female.

The floorboard behind him creaked in a way that told him someone was outside the door to his third-floor private study and then he heard the soft squeak of his partially closed door being nudged open. He remained still. Those who knew him knew better than to disturb him, which meant it was a stranger, someone seeking something he was probably in no mood to give. A reporter possibly, looking for a quote about Elena's passing, or some grossly nosy individual...

But then the skin on the back of his neck prickled, and his nose caught a light, barely-there scent and in defiance of the command issued straight from his brain, his heart missed a beat.

And he knew it was her.

'Domenico?'

Saying his name felt strange. After such a long period of not saying it, of determinedly keeping him out of her mind, it sent a quiver through Rae Dunbar's blood.

And as for laying eyes on him for the first time in months...

Her view was only of his rear as he faced away from

her, his attention fixed on the timeless elegance and twilight romance of the city that rose from the water beyond the window, but with his strong back and shoulders so broad that they threatened to bust the seams of every item of clothing he wore, he was still magnificent to behold. So magnificent that her throat was suddenly sandpaper dry and it felt as if a swarm of butterflies had been unleashed in her chest.

Not that she had expected him to have changed, to suddenly have become lesser than the Adonis it was widely agreed he was, but Rae had hoped, quite ardently, that his effect on her would have lessened. Preferably to nothing at all. But with that single initial glance, it was painfully clear that wasn't the case.

'So you have bothered to show up. Late though you are,' he said, a visible surge of tension making the lines of his solid body even more distinct. Beneath the tailored black shirt he wore, Rae could make out the sharp definition of his powerful back muscles—muscles she had never tired of stroking her hands over—and without warning the need to feel his hot, smooth skin beneath her hands gushed through her veins, a torrent of helpless, burning longing.

'I know. I'm sorry,' Rae stammered, having to push past that overpowering compulsion to touch him in order to locate her voice. 'I've been trying to get here for days, ever since I read about Elena's passing, but an arctic storm was sat right over us. All trains and flights were cancelled. They only resumed today and I made sure that I was on the first plane out.'

The words raced out of her mouth and into one another in her haste to explain and exonerate herself of the aggravation he'd made no attempt to mask.

'I'm surprised you tried so hard.'

'I wanted to be here,' Rae responded immediately. 'To say goodbye to Elena and pay my respects to her—the wonderful woman she was.' Her words caught as she was pierced again by guilt over how long it had been since she'd seen or spoken to the older woman. And now it was too late. 'If I'd known she was ill…'

Domenico spun around, his face set in a thousand furious shadows. 'And how would you have known that, Rae? Given that you walked out on this family.'

'Please, Domenico,' Rae said, feeling his anger slam into her and almost knock her sideways, but after leaving him the way she had, she knew she deserved it. 'I didn't come here to argue.'

'Why come at all?' he demanded, some untethered emotion leaping dangerously in his darkened gaze as his stare closed around her. His fury only sharpened the chiselled planes of his face, making him more striking, and the dryness of Rae's throat intensified to an almost painful degree. 'You were under no obligation to, you made sure of that.'

'I told you.' Rae strove to keep her voice steady as she was treated to the full brutally masculine force of him. Six foot five, powerful shoulders, wide chest, jaw as sharp as a blade, aristocratic nose and eyes the shade of polished mahogany sat beneath thick, expressive brows. Looking at Domenico, no one could deny he'd been born to be a leader of men. In another time he would have been a warrior. The first time Rae had seen him, she had thought how at odds the expertly tailored suit and neatly knotted silk tie was with the man wearing it, so imposing and commanding was his physical presence. 'To say goodbye to Elena and tell *you* how sorry I am for your loss.'

The truth was she was more than sorry. That was too generic. She *ached* for him, physically and emotionally. That was why she had returned to Venice.

When she had read the news of Elena's passing, her first thought had been of Domenico. Her second had been of how to get to him in his time of suffering. Even now that she was here, closer than she had been to him in almost four months, it didn't feel close enough. The ten feet between them felt like ten thousand miles and something in her—the same instinct that had compelled her to return to Venice and Palazzo Ricci without a single beat of hesitation—longed to cross the space dividing them and wrap him in her arms.

And that was enough to trigger alarm bells in every corner of her body, because in dropping everything and racing to Domenico's side, hadn't she repeated her past mistakes? Fallen back into the dynamic that had made her so unhappy? And yes, it was an exceptional moment that she was probably right to make an exception for, but it was making her question whether she'd changed as much as she'd thought she had in the past months. And that was a very disquieting thought.

'Well, you've offered your condolences now,' he said, his eyes scraping over her in a merciless perusal which, despite their stoniness, roused tingles all over her skin. 'You're free to leave this home that pushed you into such misery. I would offer to walk you to the door, but I'm sure you remember where it is from the last time you walked out of it.'

With another scathing glower, he returned to his contemplation of the world outside the window.

A stinging heat crept into Rae's eyes and cheeks. She'd

always known Domenico could be ruthless and cutting. Managing a global conglomerate with thousands of employees required it of him at times. But he did not like to have to be so, she knew that too, and she had certainly never been on the receiving end of his cold dismissal.

It was an indication of just how unhappy he was with her, how deep his anger ran. She had left him, scorned and humiliated him. He'd probably never wanted to set eyes on her again—wasn't that why he'd made no effort to chase after her?

Yet here she was.

Rae's heart rattled with uncertainty. Maybe she should do as he bade and leave. Domenico clearly didn't want her here. And she didn't *need* to be here. Estranged wives didn't have any particular role to play in family events, after all. He had the palazzo staff to take care of any practical needs and no doubt he had…*other companions* to cater to his emotional needs.

Thinking about it now, there had really been no reason at all for her to make the journey to Venice. It had been utterly stupid of her to come!

Rae had taken a few steps in retreat when she stopped, her mind suddenly abuzz with the unpleasant awareness that she was once again being cowed by Domenico's mood, and was reacting in the same way as she always had before—letting it shut her down. *Well, not this time*, she thought, remembering the promise she'd made to never let herself be silenced again.

She had returned to Venice because she was worried about him. Worried that Elena's passing would be a tragedy so big to contend with he wouldn't know where to start. Worried that no matter how many willing companions he had, he would not express the depth of his feelings. From personal experience, Rae knew that getting Domenico to open up was like trying to pry tectonic plates apart and nothing she had seen so far had convinced her that her fears were unfounded. So she would not do as he commanded and leave, not until she had done what she'd come to do, and so with a quiet sigh, steeling herself to face more of Domenico's wrath, she turned back, her steps drawing her closer to him.

'You want me leave and I will, okay. But first I want to make sure that you're doing as well as you can be right now. That's why I came,' Rae admitted, 'not just to offer my condolences. But to check on you.'

He released a bark of derision that seemed to convey a lot more than a single sound should. It seemed to question why, if she cared so much about his well-being, had she left him? And it was a fair question, she supposed. But her feelings for him had never been the issue, had they?

'I'm fine.'

Rae swallowed the urge to scream as he delivered his standard dismissive rebuff. Why did he always have to be so stubborn, so unwilling to lower his guard, even just an inch?

'Are you, Domenico? Really? How many of those have you had this afternoon?' she demanded, striding into his side vision and gesturing to the antique crystal tumbler cradled between his long-fingered hands. 'Have you eaten at all? Have you slept?'

'My sleeping arrangements are no longer any of your business, Rae.' He threw the words at her in a way that implied it was not his sleeping pattern to which he was referring but his sleeping partners and it left the mark it intended, lodging beneath her skin like a burning bullet.

'No, they're not,' she muttered, unable to fend off the image of him with another woman and instead fighting the surge of nausea that accompanied it. 'But I know the weight that grief places on a body, on a heart and a head. I know how the day feels endless, how all you crave is the oblivion of night and sleep, but when you get there, sleep won't come. I know how hard it is to do the ordinary things, like eat and move.' Having inclined his head, Domenico stared at her as though she were a witch, knowing things she shouldn't, that he would never willingly share. 'I've lived it too. Twice. Or had you forgotten that?'

Losing both of her parents in such a short space of time had been the hardest thing Rae had ever gone through. Most days she didn't know how she had survived that turmoil and emerged on the other side of it. She didn't credit herself as a particularly strong person—a person of any particular specialness, really—and she certainly didn't feel very strong in that moment, when being back in Domenico's orbit and subject to that astonishing force of his was only threatening to draw her back in. Making all the reasons why she'd had to leave feel so very minuscule, so very far away.

Making the warning bells jangle all over again.

'No.' Draining what was left in his glass, Domenico set it down and in the dim light of the nearby lamp she could see how ravaged he was by the events of the past days. In the lines bracketing his mouth and the shadows hugging his eyes, she could see his fatigue, his strain. His heartbreak. Never before had she seen such raw, naked emotion etched into his too handsome face and once more all she wanted to do was go to him and make it better, if only for a moment. 'I haven't forgotten. The death of a loved one is a wretched thing.' Something shifted behind his hard gaze as he turned the rest of his body to face her, leaning his hip against the large desk. 'I assumed that since you knew that sting of loss, you would value your relationships all the more. But how wrong I was.' His features shifted again, rearranging themselves into an expression that wasn't difficult to translate. 'You are a million miles away from the person I believed you to be.'

'Then I guess we both suffered the sting of that particular disappointment.' He'd not turned out to be the man she'd believed him to be either!

Outrage filled his face and fuelled a heavy breath. 'What disappointment did you ever have cause to feel? I gave you everything. I offered you everything.'

Rae could not and would never dispute that. Domenico had been unfailingly generous, at least materially, but it was the price of what he had given and offered that had been fatal to their relationship.

Be at his side always. Surrender all aspects of her own life. Place him and his needs ahead of her own, every single minute of every single day.

Doing so hadn't been hard. Considering him, wanting to do whatever she could to make his life a little easier when he shouldered such huge responsibilities without complaint had been easy. Making him happy had made her happy and what had made Domenico happy was having her beside him all the time. But then one day Rae had realised she had nothing of her own. No work. No friends. No hobbies. *No life.* Nothing to sustain her should she ever find herself alone again.

It was her worst nightmare come true.

Because she knew how that scenario ended. In desolation and depression.

She had watched it happen up close. She had lived it, powerless to do anything to stop the insidious spread of pain, though she had tried everything.

The thought of returning to that emotionally empty and destructive place terrified her, and with a husband who'd been entirely unwilling to help her make the space to build that fuller life she'd craved, Rae had feared it was a very real possibility.

Her stomach knotted with the strength of the remembered feeling, but Rae chased the discomfort away. The intention behind her return had not been to sift through the ashes of their marriage and she certainly wasn't going to do so on the day of Elena's burial and with a house full of mourners to overhear.

'I think we'll have to agree to disagree on that point,' Rae muttered tautly.

Domenico said nothing, and skewered her with a look that was part exasperation and part loathing. But there was something else lurking in the shadows too, something that added a flicker of excitement to her pulse, that same undefined thing she could feel humming just beneath her own skin—something too dangerous to be acknowledged for any longer than a nanosecond.

Taking a step back from it, and from him, Rae released the breath that she hadn't realised had been building in her chest. 'Downstairs is still full of guests, you know. You should be down there with them instead of up here alone.'

Her words were met with a stubborn silence, but then

he exhaled a long breath. 'I'd rather be up here,' he said flatly. 'All anyone wants to tell me is how wonderful Elena was and I'm too furious with her right now to want to ruminate on her excellence.'

'Domenico...' Rae breathed, the admission making her heart ache for him.

His relationship with Elena had been a treasured part of his life and the moment Rae had met the older woman she had instantly seen why. Elena had had a formidable mind, a generous heart and beautiful spirit. She had also been the constant in Domenico's life and his only family, raising him from when he was a few days old and his biological mother, a young relation of Elena's, couldn't. Or wouldn't. Rae wasn't too sure. Whenever she had tried to dig deeper into Domenico's family history, she had been firmly and unmistakably rebuffed.

In fact, whenever Rae had tried to engage him in any conversation about his emotions or his life, Domenico had shut her down. From the moment they'd met she'd sensed he was burdened by whatever had occurred in the past, but whilst he'd been happy to let her close physically, to even use their sexual chemistry as a way of silencing her questions, emotionally he had never let her in, always holding her at arm's length.

At one point in time Rae had thought their respective trauma would be something to bind them even closer together. Something they could share with each other that they couldn't with others. She had never imagined it would break them apart instead. But of all the matters that Domenico had refused to open himself up about, his unwillingness to trust her with any of the details about his family situation had cut deep. Because how could she live with someone who didn't want her to know him? How could she keep giving up so much of her own life and self for a man who wouldn't show her his heart?

However, in that moment his hurt was all too easy to see and, feeling that pain, Rae could no longer keep herself from moving towards him. It was the most natural thing to want to go to him, to slide her hands up his arms, across his shoulders and wind them around his neck and hold him tight. Let him know that he wasn't alone. Domenico was a physical being and physical touch had always been the best way to reach him, to breach the weight and distraction of a long day or stressful negotiation. To encourage him to open up. And Rae couldn't bear the thought of him isolating himself in his grief, in his understandable anger.

She remembered being furious in the aftermath of her father's death. How was it fair that it was him who had been taken too soon, her father and not anybody else's? Why did she and her sisters have to go on with their lives without their integral cog? She was certain Domenico would be feeling something similar. His spectacularly strong build made him look untouchable, but he had such capacity for feeling, experiencing every emotion sharply, deeply.

But she had only just reached out to him when the lift of his cold eyes halted her as if she'd been turned to stone.

'What are you doing?'

'I'm...'

'Is this why you came?' he demanded, his eyes still pools of darkness as they probed her face, as if the answers were writing themselves across her skin, when all she could feel was a tormented, scorching heat filling her cheeks. 'Were you hoping the opportunity would arise for you to comfort me and I'd fall back into your arms?' She was too stunned to speak. 'Even grief-stricken I am not that stupid. You made it clear how little you care for me and that's not something I'll forget in a hurry, so I suggest you turn around and keep walking out of the door this time.'

He gestured towards the door with his hand, his eyes remaining fixed on her with a stoniness that turned her stomach inside out.

Rae had always known he'd be furious with her. Domenico, after all, was not used to others calling the shots. But with time she'd expected he would come to see that she had been right, that they wanted irreconcilable futures, and her leaving had been for the best. It had never crossed her mind that he'd *stay* so angry.

She hadn't wanted to hurt him. She'd just been trying to keep herself from becoming any more overwhelmed. Since talking to him had never yielded any positive results before, there'd been no reason to believe that he would *hear* her had she tried to do so again, so it had been easier to not try. To just leave. And nothing about his unwilling stance before her was making her think she'd been wrong to believe that.

But still, her throat was thick as she slowly turned towards the door and instructed her numbed legs to move.

'Actually, I think it might be a good idea for Rae to stay.'

The intrusion had both of their heads lifting sharply. Elena's lawyer and the Riccis' long-time family friend, Alessandra Donati, paused in the doorway, surveying them mildly.

'*Che cosa? Perché?*' Domenico demanded of her hotly, surveying her with his hands planted on his hips and a look that threatened to carve her in two.

Alessandra appeared unconcerned. 'I think Rae should stay for the reading of the will tomorrow. She is, after all, family and I'm sure Elena would have wanted her here.'

Rae tried to hide her surprise that Alessandra, of all people, was speaking in her defence. Having known her since arriving in Venice, she had never been given any indication that she could consider her any type of ally.

Unleashing a curse in fervent Italian, Domenico seemed to struggle with controlling his body. 'Are you seriously telling me that my aunt included her in her will?' A look of incredulity had cut itself into the beautiful planes of his face.

'I'm not telling you anything,' Alessandra parried calmly. 'Elena's final wishes will be revealed tomorrow, for everyone to hear at the same time. But my advice to both of you is that now that Rae is here, she should stay.'

Alessandra matched Domenico's hard gaze, some kind of exchange passing between them, and Rae felt a pinch of jealousy that there seemed to be no problem with *their* communication.

Overcoming his perplexed bewilderment, Domenico looked from Alessandra to Rae and then back again, his emotion building by the second if the shade of his face was anything to judge by. '*Bene.*' He threw up his hands. 'Fine. She will stay.'

'I don't…' Rae began, before falling silent beneath the quelling look Domenico dealt her. She looked instead to Alessandra. 'What time is the reading tomorrow?'

'Ten a.m. Here at the palazzo.'

She nodded her understanding, her throat tight with the thought of being such a patently unwanted guest at such a personal event. But she could hardly challenge it now, even if that was what she desperately wanted to do. 'I will see you both tomorrow then.'

Alessandra smiled at her and slipped away and Rae decided it was past time she did the same. The encounter with Domenico had left her feeling off-balance and drained and in need of a long shower and then a soft bed.

'Where do you think you are going?' Domenico queried as she took her first steps towards the door.

'Back to my hotel.'

'I don't think so. You'll stay here.'

Rae's heart slammed into her ribs at the thought of remaining in the palazzo, where memoires lurked around every corner, memories that were so incredibly potent. Walking through the front doors earlier and remembering how Domenico had once carried her through them had blocked her throat and brought her close to tears. As she'd climbed the staircase, with each step she had recalled all the times Domenico had led her up them, her hand in his, promise in his eyes whenever he'd looked back at her.

'That's not necessary. I have a...'

Domenico's face darkened. 'Don't test me, Rae. Not today. I don't trust you one bit. So you will stay here, where I can keep an eye on you.'

'Keep an eye on me?' She couldn't keep the disbelief from her voice, not when he made her sound like a wayward charge. 'What is it that you imagine I am going to do?'

'I won't pretend to know your mind,' he hit back, and

it was another heavyweight blow straight to her middle because he was the first person that Rae had allowed to know her in her adult life. She realised now that he hadn't known all of her, not the parts of herself that she'd lost or concealed in her effort to be the wife she'd thought he'd wanted, but he remained the first, and only, person she had let close to her after the horror of losing her parents. 'But until I know exactly what involvement you have in Elena's will, I want you where I can see you. I will have Portia show you where you can sleep tonight.'

It was unsurprising to her that Domenico wrested complete control as usual, blatantly ignoring her wishes and her needs. No, not ignoring—not even asking!

Rae bristled with a fury that had her opening her mouth to vent the protest already on her tongue, but she was suddenly too exhausted to argue. Instead, she nodded and let herself be led away by Portia when she arrived, content to let Domenico have his way in that moment because once she'd benefitted from a restoring full night's sleep, and felt more like herself, she had no intention of letting it happen again.

She had changed, and the days of her silently acquiescing to his decisions and wishes were well and truly over.

# CHAPTER TWO

DOMENICO PROWLED AROUND the gilded darkness of the palazzo like a restless animal. There was too much emotion coursing through his body for him to rest easily, either asleep or awake. The hours he had just spent in his private gym, pushing himself on the treadmill and punching until his knuckles felt raw, had succeeded in exhausting his muscles but had failed to rid him of his aggravating emotions.

*Damn Rae.*

Damn her for leaving and damn her for coming back.

He had far too many other matters in need of careful handling to be giving any thought to the wife who had walked out on him, and yet from the moment he had turned away from the window and settled his hard eyes on her, his only thoughts had been of her body. Wrapped around him. Welcoming him inside her.

He had very much wanted to sweep her onto his desk, part her legs, slip into the warm space between her thighs and bury himself inside her. He craved the velvet welcome her body had always offered, her muscles contracting and then clenching around him, her sweet heat enveloping him, urging him to sink deeper. He had been shaking with the force of the wanting, and the effort required to resist it.

Because he refused to want her. After the way she had abandoned him, desiring her was not an option.

But there had never been anything tame or cooperative about his feelings for Rae. The first time he'd seen her, standing outside Venice's airport, looking unbelievably attractive in an all-black ensemble, the natural highlights in her chestnut hair glinting in the low sun, he had wanted her immediately. Wanted to know who she was and to have her in his bed. Beneath him. On top of him. And in the hundred other ways flying through his mind. The potency of the desire had stopped him in his tracks on the busy pavement, bludgeoning all other thoughts from his mind, and the charge that had rocked his big body had been so electrifying it was as though he'd been struck by a bolt of lightning.

That fevered desire for her hadn't abated as he had expected it to, as had been usual in his previous relationships—if they could really be called that. Far from satisfying the craving, claiming her body as his own had only intensified his hunger for her and very quickly that scorching want had morphed into a *need* that he hadn't seen coming.

A need to keep her close. A need for her smile and her piercing blue eyes to be the first thing he saw when he opened his eyes each morning. A need to have the warmth of her body beside his all day, every day.

None of his past relationships had triggered anything so domestic in him, but none of those women had given him what Rae had seemed to be giving—her wholehearted acceptance and warmth and love. Oh, she hadn't said the words, but Domenico had known she was falling in love with him. Knew it by the way her eyes tracked his movements, by the way she took every opportunity to touch him—light brushes of her hand, tender grazes of her lips—and by the way she snuggled in close at night.

It had been addictive, so much so that Domenico had actually been unhappy about their affair ending when it was time for Rae to return home, but he hadn't expected that melancholy mood to last for more than a day, two at the most. To his surprise, however, he'd found himself missing her at all kinds of odd moments, missing her so much that eventually he'd given in and hopped on a jet to London. He'd surprised her when she finished work, waiting outside the bridal boutique where she was a consultant, and the smile that had lit her face when she'd spotted him had been dazzling. He couldn't remember a time when someone other than Elena had been that happy to see him, and as she'd thrown herself into his arms Domenico had felt something tight and knotted within him loosen, certain in that moment that life would be better if Rae was always by his side. Lowering her to the ground, he'd gazed down at her and said, *'Marry me...'* the words bubbling up inside him.

Her response had been instantaneous. *'Yes.'*

Four weeks later they had been married in Venice. Domenico had refused to wait any longer than that, wanting the marriage to be official as quickly as possible, wanting their claim on each other to be inviolable, wanting that new chapter of his life with a wife who loved him and would always be at his side to begin.

As the recollections crashed through his mind, Domenico cursed under his breath, hating the memories

enormously and that in many ways his aunt had filled the void left by the loss of her parents. One of Rae's favourite things had been exploring Elena's cavernous closet, studying her one-of-a-kind gowns, and Elena had delighted in regaling her with the story of each one. Her sudden death had to be stirring up difficult memories for Rae.

'It's fine. You're entitled to say goodbye to her. I know how much you cared for her and Elena was incredibly fond of you too. Don't rush away on my account,' he said with a sigh that was wrenched from him, because the sudden tenderness of feeling was so unwanted.

'Thank you.' Her mouth opened, only for her to hesitate before deciding to press on. 'Did Elena… I'm not aware of how she passed away…and I was just wondering if she suffered.'

'The pathologist said it was most likely an aneurism. That it would have been fast, almost instantaneous. Painless. She probably wouldn't have known.'

'Good. I'm glad. I'd hate to think that she'd been in any pain.'

Her gaze shimmered again and something erupted in Domenico's chest, a feeling of such power it felt as if his lungs were being squeezed by giant hands. He'd always hated to see Rae upset, the sight slicing right to the heart of him, and acting on the instinct firing up from a place deep within him, he reached out, curling his hand to her cheek and tenderly wiping away the tears with his thumb.

A shudder ran across his chest as the feel of the warm silk of her skin had an even bolder surge of desire pumping through his veins, forcing him to remember just how long it had been since he had satisfied his carnal cravings, since he had lost himself in the tight heat of a woman's body. If there was ever a time he could do with drowning himself in someone else, this was it. And he had never generated a more compelling heat than the one he did with Rae...

Instinct flared again, more primal than before, and Domenico lowered his thumb, tracing it across her pillow-soft lower lip, and the pure blue of her eyes exploded with a hunger that set them aflame.

With such potent desire hammering within him and forcing everything else from his mind, including all his reasons for loathing her, all Domenico could feel was his impatient pounding *want*. Raising his other hand, he captured her face between his palms and with one, two, three easy steps he had her backed against the nearest wall. Her dazed eyes held his as he stared hungrily down at her, his heart and pulse pounding in perfect synchronisation as his gaze traced the shape of her face—her flushed cheeks, her delicate jaw, her parted lips.

'Domenico...'

Was that a warning or a plea? He didn't know, or care, because his name on her tongue, in her whispered breath, nearly undid him. All he needed to do was press in a centimetre closer, lower his mouth, and he could ease the agitated ache beating in his blood and taste her on his lips again—a taste he had been craving ever since she'd left.

He froze, that final thought echoing around his brain. She had left him.

*So what the hell was he doing?*

With a quiet growl of frustration, he pulled himself back, putting distance between their bodies and trying to smother his heavy breaths. 'It's late. You should go back to your room, get some sleep. You've had a long day,' he instructed, sounding far more in control than he felt.

Rae blinked slowly, the daze slowly draining from her gaze. 'Yes, you're right. I should do that.' Slowly, almost unsteadily, she peeled herself off the wall, colour still flaming in her cheeks. She moved gingerly towards the staircase. 'Goodnight.'

*'Buona notte,'* he rasped, raking a hand through his hair and willing the beating of his blood to subside.

When it didn't, he marched back to his suite and straight into the shower, setting the temperature as cold as it would go, cold enough to kill entirely the traitorous desire that continued to burn in his blood.

The reading of Elena's will would take place in one of the large salons on the ground floor of the palazzo. It was not customary to have such a formal reading where Rae hailed from—they'd read her father's will around the kitchen table—but there was nothing regular about the Ricci family. Wealth and status like theirs, she'd long ago learned, demanded grander formalities. So, at five minutes to ten, Rae unsteadily descended the staircase, armed with her plan to slip in unnoticed, take a seat near the door and leave as soon as the proceedings were over. Her small case was already packed and waiting by the main door, so she didn't have to spend any longer in the palazzo than was necessary.

Her hopes were dashed almost immediately. The moment Rae entered the grand room, Alessandra excused herself from the conversation she was in and made straight for her, greeting her with a friendly smile and a kiss to each cheek.

'I have a seat for you,' she announced.

'Oh, I was just going to find somewhere here at the back…' Rae began, motioning to the very last row of seats, but Alessandra was shaking her head.

'Absolutely not. You're family, Rae. And family sits at the front.'

'I'm not sure Domenico will like that,' she replied tightly.

'This isn't about him. It's about Elena,' Alessandra parried, gesturing for Rae to follow her to the front of the salon and indicating a chair on the front row, right next to the seat occupied by the broad shoulders and proud back of Domenico. He was dressed in another black suit, neat and exquisitely fitted to his broad form, and he looked exceptional, far more so than anyone in a state of grief should.

'Are you going to sit on the chair or just continue to stare at it?' Domenico posed with a dark arch of his brow and, with a resigned sigh, Rae sat. But, as she did, her arm brushed against his and heat crackled through her, making her instantly feverish as remembrance of the previous night crashed through her.

She had spent the better part of the night wide awake and trying not to think about what had exploded between them. How he had framed her face in his strong hands, how she'd been trapped between the wall and his very solid, very hot body, how his lips had been right *there*, a mere breath from hers. The fact that nothing had actually happened didn't ease the alarm she felt, because something very easily *could* have happened. It had been on the cusp of happening. She had been seconds away from begging for his mouth to be on her—her lips, her breasts, her... *No!*

Rae knew her only hope now was to leave as soon as possible. If she got away quickly, she could consign the previous night's events to some dusty shelf in the far recesses of her mind and, within a matter of weeks, hopefully it would be as if it had never happened. As if none of the emotional upheaval of her ill-thought-out trip had happened.

'You slept well, I hope,' Domenico said suddenly, without tuning his head to look at her.

'The room was very comfortable,' Rae answered noncommittally, because there was no way she wanted him to have a single idea of how unsettled he'd left her.

'You didn't sleep?' he pressed, and this time he did turn his head and she was swallowed up by his bottomless dark gaze. His regard was as hot and heavy as his physical touch had been and Rae's mouth ran dry, her lips tingled and a pulse ignited between her legs.

She squeezed her thighs together, but it failed to quash the reaction pounding through her. The liquid heat of need raced through her veins, making her hunger for his touch all over again, and suddenly all she could feel was the sensation of falling. That she was tumbling head over heels into him and wanting nothing more than to be back in that hallway last night, caged by his delectable male body.

From what sounded like far away Rae heard a female voice—Alessandra—calling everyone to attention and asking them to take their seats—and she clung to it, using it as a lifeline to grip onto as she tried to drag herself from her sensual freefall.

'I slept fine, thank you,' she said, cleaving her gaze from Domenico's and fixing her attention straight ahead. She forced herself to ignore the sirens wailing in her body and listen to every single one of Alessandra's welcoming and introductory words before she handed over the duties to the other executor of Elena's estate, Elena's long-time friend and confidant, Vincenzo D'Aragona. Very quickly, his smooth baritone voice filled the salon.

One more hour, Rae estimated as Vincenzo began on the bequests, and then she would be on her way home. The thought brought a little bit of calm to her galloping heart because she wasn't sure how many more moments like that with Domenico she could withstand.

Exhaling shakily, Rae tuned back in to the reading of the will. Vincenzo was in the middle of stating Elena's wish that her donations to certain charities continued from her estate. Then he moved on to the individual bequests, monetary gifts and heirlooms for specific friends and family—none of which surprised Rae, as Elena had always been extraordinarily generous.

'Finally, to the matters of business and real estate. It was Elena's wish that all of her shares in The Ricci Group pass in totality to her named heir, Domenico Paolo Ricci. Her real estate portfolio, including but not limited to her homes in Rome and Lake Como and the apartment in Paris, will also pass to Domenico Paolo Ricci. However,' Vincenzo continued with a pregnant pause, during which Alessandra cast something of an uneasy glance Domenico's way and, noticing it, a slither of unease stirred in Rae's stomach, 'with regard to Palazzo Ricci here in Venice, Elena insisted upon the addition of a marital clause and in the event that Domenico fails to meet the stated requirements of said clause, Palazzo Ricci will pass to Elena's next closest living relative, her sister.'

The gasps of surprise from others were quickly quelled with a stern look from Vincenzo. Face tight but expressionless, Domenico leaned slightly forward, biceps straining against the confines of the suit.

'In this case, the marital clause stipulates that Domenico will only inherit on the celebration of the second anniversary of his wedding to his wife Raegan Dunbar-Ricci on October the second this year.'

Domenico went rigid, but it was an extra second before it hit Rae. And, once it did, her eyes flew wide.

*What?*

# CHAPTER THREE

DOMENICO PACED back and forth over the same length of floor. If he thought about it hard enough, he knew he would find a way out of the situation, some clever escape hatch…but each turn of his thoughts only brought him back to the same place, the same damnable words of Elena's will clanging over and over again in his mind.

'Are you okay?'

Having thought he was alone, Domenico quickly drew to a stop and raised his head. Alessandra stood in front of the closed door and Domenico pinioned her under his furious glare.

'What do you think?' Solely by virtue of the self-control honed meticulously over the years, he had managed to regulate his reaction for the remainder of the reading and the interminable process of bidding everyone goodbye, but the tether around his frustration was now frayed perilously thin. 'I can't believe you knew this was going to happen and didn't warn me,' he hissed, the sting of her treachery arrowing deeper into his skin.

At least now, however, he understood why Alessandra had been so insistent that Rae stay and attend the will reading—but he was far too angry to feel any gratitude to her.

'You know very well the contents of a will have to

remain private until after a person's death,' Alessandra reproached him. 'I was doing my job, Domenico. It's nothing personal.'

'It's personal to me,' he snarled.

'And is that all that is angering you?' Alessandra queried levelly.

'Isn't that enough?'

'So it's not about Rae's involvement in Elena's stipulation?' She allowed her words to hang in mid-air for a second before continuing. 'I won't pretend to know what's going on in your marriage, Domenico, but there's obviously something. Rae has been gone for weeks and you've been in a less than pleasant mood for most of that time.'

He spun away to stare moodily out of the window, fixing his arms across his chest. 'The state of my marriage is nobody's business but mine and Rae's.'

But as he bit out the words, Domenico knew that wasn't the case any more. A spotlight had been placed on their union—the union on which something incredibly precious to him now rested.

With superhuman effort, he swallowed the curse surging up his throat. Elena had orchestrated it perfectly, forcing his hand from beyond the grave with her stipulation. She knew Domenico would never willingly relinquish ownership of the palazzo, the only home he'd ever known, especially not to the blood relatives who had denied and rejected him, and the last thing she'd want either was her beloved palazzo ending up in the hands of her estranged sister. For both of those reasons she'd known full well he would do *anything* to prevent that from happening, including reuniting with Rae.

Which was exactly what his aunt had wanted. How

many times had she prodded him to go to London, talk to Rae and fix whatever had broken down between them? So often that he'd lost count, but, since he'd flatly refused to do so, she'd decided to take matters into her own hands.

Devious and manipulative as it was, he found he couldn't be angry with her. Even in death, Elena was still trying to protect and take care of him in the same way she always had and, eternal romantic that she was, she'd believed Rae was *the one* for him. No doubt she'd thought that she could prompt a permanent reunion by forcing them back together for an extended period of time.

But, however much Domenico hated to disappoint Elena, that wasn't going to happen.

Rae had walked out on him without a backward glance. She had shown herself to be as careless and unfeeling as the mother who'd abandoned him on someone else's doorstep. There would be no second chance.

He would never open himself up to more anguish. If there was any other option other than reconciling with Rae, he would take it. But he knew that nothing other than him and Rae being visibly happy together in his palazzo in Venice would satisfy the esteemed Vincenzo D'Aragona, the man Elena had named as executor of her will and therefore the man who would make the final decision on whether Domenico's circumstances complied with the will. He was a thoroughly unimpeachable character who had counselled Elena ever since her husband's death, with unfailing loyalty and affection. Domenico had no doubt that he would follow her wishes absolutely.

Even if D'Aragona had been a less noble character, Domenico was astute enough to know that anything less than the appearance of wedded bliss would leave him vulnerable to a future legal challenge and he wouldn't risk the palazzo in that way. It meant too much to him.

His conviction on that was stronger than anything he felt about Rae or the wretched will.

Closing his eyes and rubbing his temples, he faced the irrefutable facts of the situation and plotted his next step. There was only one.

'Where are you going?' Alessandra asked as he made a sudden and decisive move towards the door without a word to her.

'To talk to my wife.'

He really should have spoken with Rae immediately after the reading had ended, because he'd known all along there was only one way out of this mess. But he had needed a moment—several moments—to himself to process it, something he bitterly began to regret as he arrived on the ground floor salon and scanned all four corners, only to find that the room was empty.

With dread starting to roil in his stomach and that loud voice in his head berating him for leaving her alone, Domenico set his powerful legs in motion and raced into the next room and then the next, but in his gut he already knew the search was pointless.

Rae was already gone.

Rae pushed her sunglasses atop her head to keep her long hair from flying in her face as the water taxi raced across the open water to Marco Polo Airport. Yet as she imagined the violent reaction Domenico would have when he realised she had slipped away without a word—*again*—the speed felt nowhere near enough and she willed the boat to go faster.

Casting a quick look over her shoulder, the reassurance she felt that there was no sign of a vessel powering after her was hollow as she knew that by now Domenico had probably realised she had taken off and would be minutes away from—if not already—hunting her down.

Rae felt awful for sneaking away, but really, what other choice had there been? Elena's bombshell stipulation in her will had changed everything, and now that Domenico's inheritance of the palazzo was contingent on their union—on *her*—she had known at once there was no way he was going to let her leave.

And she couldn't stay. She couldn't!

She had been back in Venice less than twenty-four hours and there had been too many moments in which she'd caught herself falling back into her old ways. And not just physically, as the previous night attested, when Domenico's touch had penetrated her with embarrassing speed and ease. But emotionally too. For a brief moment back at the palazzo, after the will reading, Rae had been preoccupied with all that it meant for Domenico, reflecting on what *he* must be feeling and what *he* needed, prioritising that over what was best for herself. In the blink of an eye, she'd reverted to the Rae of six months ago, to the wife who never spoke up for herself, who hadn't been brave enough to demand that her needs be met, who hadn't known herself well enough to even know what those needs were.

But she wasn't that person any more. The issues that had arisen in their marriage had been enlightening, forcing her to take a good look inwards and consider the life she wanted to have and the kind of woman she wanted to be and, unwilling to let all the agony and heartache of the breakdown of her marriage be for nothing, Rae had wasted no time in fighting to become that person on her return to London.

Reconnecting with her ambition to become a bridal designer, Rae had dusted off her pencils and thrown herself back into the creative process of designing. No longer willing to wait for life to happen to her, she had even screwed up enough courage to contact the woman who'd once offered to invest in her should she ever decide to embark on a career in bridal design and, after her positive response, had been busy making plans for a full-blown collection. Immersing herself in her passion and with her eyes fixed on the bright future that she wanted for herself, Rae had regained her confidence and her voice.

It had never been her intention to surrender those aspects of herself, to lose herself so thoroughly in being with Domenico and the responsibilities she bore as a Ricci bride. But she'd loved him so deeply and wanted so badly to make him happy that, little by little, all else had slipped away.

When she'd become aware of how adrift she'd been feeling, she'd wanted to tell Domenico, to find a way to change. But he'd always been so closed off, always ready to retreat from any intimacy that wasn't physical, and Rae had been scared of being shut down yet again, scared of having to face how tenuous their relationship was. Running had been easier than challenging him, easier than confronting the hard truths about their marriage, but in her heart Rae knew she should have tried harder to have that conversation. A lot harder.

It was a regret that surfaced often, and whenever that thought did poke at her she comforted herself with the reassurance that she had changed and would not lack that courage or conviction again.

But she had, she realised with a nauseating thud of her heart.

Rather than stay at the palazzo and talk with Domenico about their situation, she had panicked and run away. *Again.*

The water taxi drew up to the airport. Rae thrust a handful of euros into the driver's hand and stepped up onto dry land, that sick feeling continuing to churn in her stomach as she pulled up the handle of her case and strode across the concrete concourse. Only to suddenly find she could take no further steps.

Because if she left like this she knew it would be another regret that haunted her. Not just because she would be condemning Domenico to the loss of his treasured home, but because running away wasn't the answer. It hadn't been last time and it wasn't now either. If she truly believed she had changed, and wanted others to appreciate those changes in her too, then she needed to prove herself. Prove that she was different, that she was stronger. That she wasn't a coward.

Sinking down onto a bench to allow time for her thoughts to settle, it was there that Domenico found her not fifteen minutes later. Standing before her, he towered over her, casting her in the shade of his big body that even in that moment had her breath catching in her chest.

'I expected you to be on the first flight out of here by now,' he said, his eyes flickering over her as though unsure if she was real.

'That was the original plan.'

'So what happened?'

'I realised that running away wouldn't solve anything. We have to face this.'

She saw something—surprise, perhaps—ripple through his dark eyes before he sat down beside her, her body jolting a little at the sudden nearness and the way the air seemed to change, thicken, with his presence.

'I'm glad you understand what needs to happen next.'

Rae angled her face towards him, injecting a look of warning into her eyes. 'I haven't agreed to anything, Domenico.'

'Of course you have,' he drawled all-knowingly. 'Otherwise, you wouldn't be sitting out here. You would be sitting on a plane, waiting to take off.' He looked at her almost sympathetically. 'It's only for a handful of months, Rae. Six at the most. Not an enormous amount of time in the grand scheme of things.'

He was right. Six months was not such a long stretch, but her heart gave a kick anyway because it was a struggle to spend six minutes in his proximity without a fever stirring in her blood.

'Aren't you at all concerned that we haven't been together for the last four months?' she queried, because that was a pertinent fact that he seemed to be conveniently ignoring. 'That I have not been in this city, or your home, or on your arm for all that time? Do you not think that's going to present a few problems? One day I'm not here and then *boom*, Elena's will stipulates it and suddenly I'm back.'

'Elena's will is not common knowledge. It's a private family document.'

Rae made a noise of dissent. 'You and I both know these things have a way of getting out. Making the rounds as a rumour.'

'I've never much cared for rumours,' he drawled, his eyes gleaming down at her in a way that made her head spin and all coherent thoughts scatter like marbles. 'And your argument will not be a problem as nobody is aware that you walked out on our marriage.'

'Nobody is aware…' Rae stammered in stunned disbelief, her mind doing backflips at the preposterousness of his statement. 'How is that possible? I left. I haven't been here for months. I haven't been seen. Nobody questioned that?'

'I'm not in the habit of making public declarations about my personal life,' he stated in that cool, unconcerned tone of his that stymied so effectively the questions he didn't want to answer. 'And something about my general demeanour seems to prevent the majority of people from probing too deeply. Those who did ask, I made a vague reply about you having a family situation that required your personal attention and attendance. We can continue with that line, say the issue is no longer pressing and, given the situation here, it was time for you to return home.'

'And which of my sisters do you intend to saddle with some mysterious prolonged drama that required my attention for four months?' she demanded. 'Maggie or Imogen?'

Domenico replied with a pragmatic lift of his shoulders. 'The particulars are hardly necessary. The less said, the better. All that matters is that you are back with your husband and living a happy life.'

The panic that had settled once she took control of herself started a slow climb up her windpipe again.

'Domenico, we are not just going to pick up where we

left off, like nothing has happened. We can't… I won't,' Rae stammered.

'Nor would I want to. I'm not talking about us resuming our married life, Rae,' he clarified with a sharp edge of impatience to his words. 'The idea of that is as offensive to me as it apparently is to you. I'm talking about *pretending*. Putting on a blissfully happy show—a show good enough to convince Vincenzo D'Aragona. I'm confident the pretence won't be too arduous for you. After all, you did spend considerably longer than six months pretending to be a devoted, happy wife.'

'And just how many remarks like that would I be expected to put up with in our joyous reunion?' Rae queried with a lightning flash of her blue eyes.

'The truth is painful, Rae, isn't it? But worry not, our contact over the next six months will be limited. Of course, in public we'll need to present a deliriously in love front, and we'll need to attend a fair number of public events, but in private we won't need to spend any time together at all.'

'Why six months? Our anniversary is in four and a half.'

He slanted her a brief look. 'We can't suddenly split up the day after our anniversary, Rae. Think how that would look. No, we need a buffer period too, so that when we do separate it looks real. Plus the Ricci Ball is a month after our anniversary. It would look better if we attended that together. Some time after that we can start to dissolve the marriage. Leak some rumours of fighting and unhappiness. The strain of Elena's passing, the stress of stepping into her shoes. How busy I am. There are plenty of things we could say. Then we'll divorce. I'll have the palazzo and you can…go your own way.'

'You have it all worked out, don't you?' she breathed, conceding to herself that it did sound plausible.

He tensed, impatience and determination emanating from him in one jagged pulse after another. 'I'm not prepared to lose the palazzo, Rae. It's means too much to me. So I will do whatever it takes. But I can't do it on my own. I need your help. I need you to stay here. *Please.*'

His use of that word was startling in itself, because Domenico never pleaded for anything. He would consider it an abhorrence to do so, a lowering of himself that he simply wouldn't entertain, even in thought. It revealed how desperately in need he was of her cooperation, a desperation that became even clearer when he turned the power of his gaze on her and the restless emotion brimming in the dark depths of his eyes tugged at every heartstring.

'As soon as the inheritance is settled, we will go our separate ways and I will ensure you are rewarded with a generous sum.'

'I don't want your money, Domenico.' Rae scowled, loathing that his opinion of her had sunk so low that his instinctive assumption was that she could be swayed by the promise of a payout. His money had never mattered to her.

She was, however, intrigued by the other opportunities that a return to Venice presented. The way she had departed had left matters unfinished between her and Domenico. She had shut him out of her mind as best she could, but she was not over him, no matter how much she insisted to her sisters that she was. Wasn't that why she had not yet taken the step of approaching a lawyer to initiate a divorce? But perhaps these six months could help her find that longed for closure. Perhaps being around him and not sacrificing or compromising anything of herself would reassure her that she had become a different person and that she had made the right choice in leaving. And when the six months was over she would be able to leave the right way, with her conscience and confidence intact and her emotional freedom reclaimed. Helping Domenico was the right thing to do, she didn't doubt that, but it was those ways in which she could help herself that convinced her.

'And you don't need to dangle any more incentives. I'll help you. I'll be your wife again.'

'Thank you.' The words were ground from between his firm lips, but Rae could hear the relief in them and that strength of feeling had her mind humming with curiosity about his past once more. Why did Palazzo Ricci mean so very much to him? How had it ended up becoming his home and Elena his guardian? What had happened to his parents? Why hadn't they kept him?

They were just a few of the questions niggling away at her brain, but Rae had so many more that she would have loved the answers to and maybe, she thought with a flicker of interest, the following months would give her the opportunity to find those answers. That would certainly be an added and worthwhile bonus, especially if it helped her put to rest her relationship with him.

Rae got to her feet, adopting a straight-backed pose as she quickly worked out the necessary practicalities. 'I'll go back to London, tie up some ends there and be back in a few days.'

Confusion pulled Domenico's dark brows together as

he rose too. 'What do you mean, you will go back to London?' He shook his head. 'You can't leave, Rae.'

'I need to. For starters, these are the only clothes I have with me...' she began, gesturing to the garments adorning her body.

'There are plenty of shops here in Venice,' he cut in with impatience and frustration. 'And your wardrobe at the palazzo has not been touched.'

The thought of slipping back into the clothes of that past life left Rae cold. She had no desire or intention to go backwards and as such his implacable, inconsiderate interruption had her gritting her teeth and replying with forced patience. 'I have responsibilities in London. I'm not prepared to just abandon them.'

His brows pleated even tighter, his eyes darkening as her refusal to fall in line registered. He'd never known her to be anything other than amenable and accommodating to his wishes and the change was so disconcerting to him, he couldn't hide it.

But then his eyes narrowed. 'What responsibilities?' he questioned.

'A job. Bills. My sisters.'

Domenico continued to assess her, thoughts whizzing across his eyes like shooting stars and his jaw tightening in uneasy consideration. 'Is a man the source of this need to return to London so quickly?'

'What?' Rae very nearly laughed, so outrageous was the thought.

He moved in a step closer. 'You heard me.'

She shook her head, still fighting the urge to laugh, which was so at odds with the severity of his expression. 'No. There's no one.'

'Because I will not be made a fool of by you for the second time, and that is exactly the type of detail that would undermine my claim and make this whole charade for nothing. So, if that is the case, you need to tell me now,' he commanded with godlike presumption.

Provoked by both his words and his tone, Rae stepped up to him, tilting her head back so their eyes collided, hers fizzing with anger whilst his remained darkly unyielding.

'Firstly, I don't have to tell you anything I don't want to,' she began audaciously, 'in much the same way you never told me anything you didn't want to. But, on this occasion, I am prepared to tell you that there is no one. Secondly, this isn't a negotiation,' she said, her spine and her stance strengthening with her newly acquired confidence and conviction. 'I *am* going back to London. I'll be gone forty-eight hours, three days at the most. Then I'll be back and the masquerade can begin.'

Domenico stared back at her, looking stunned and momentarily lost for words, and Rae enjoyed the ripples of her victory, because not many people could render Domenico Ricci speechless.

He composed himself within a few seconds, however, and an echo of a smile played at the edges of his too sensual mouth as he responded. '*Bene.* You will go to London.' Rae opened her mouth to tell him that she had neither asked for nor required his permission, but he held up a hand and continued in his low, silken drawl. 'However, you won't be going alone. I'll accompany you,' he asserted, reaching out to tug her closer, into the shadow cast by his body, until there was very little space separating them, 'because, *cara*, the masquerade starts now.'

# CHAPTER FOUR

THE RICCI PRIVATE JET touched down in London the following morning. On Domenico's instruction a car was waiting on the tarmac to drive them to the luxurious central hotel in which he had reserved a suite and they passed the drive through the capital in the same way they had spent the flight from Venice—in silence.

Domenico had plenty of things he could say, but he refused to give Rae the satisfaction of knowing how deeply her departure four months ago had bothered him. So he'd bitten his tongue and busied himself with work, fighting the rising urge to sit back, rest his eyes on her in the seat opposite and enjoy all the loveliness of her the way he often used to.

In her simple outfit of jeans, plain tee and well-worn leather jacket she looked beautiful, and he loathed her for it. Loathed the way the clothes hugged her slender figure, highlighting her hourglass curves and making him desperate to run his hands over them. Loathed how her freshly washed hair shone and curled over her shoulders, calling to him to once again bury his fingers in its lustrous length, to curl it around his hand and gently tilt her head back until her mouth was ripe to receive his kiss.

Once in the car, Domenico stared out of the window

rather than look at her, but every so often her reflection would appear in the dark glass and he would tense at the onslaught of longing stirred by her full lips and piercing eyes. It would be so easy to reach across and haul her onto his lap, he ruminated, to grind his groin against her and settle the ache hammering there, and it bothered him how large the idea loomed in his mind and how excited by it his body became.

Why did he continue to suffer this infernal attraction to her? Imagining all the ways he could drive her to make those delicious mewls of delight he so loved, and all the ways she could enchant him with her hands and lips and tongue. Rae had made it clear she had no love or respect for him. And that inequality of feeling infuriated him, stirring memories of another time he had yearned for something with every bone in his body…and the crushing rejection that had followed.

He'd always been fascinated by the idea of his mother. Elena had shielded him from the truth of how she came to raise him, simply telling him that his mother had had to leave him in her care, and so as a young, vividly imaginative boy he'd built a thousand scenarios around that mysterious mother figure, imagining all the possible reasons why she'd had to leave him and how it would be when she returned. When he'd finally learned her identity and seen a photograph of her she'd been even more beautiful than he'd imagined and, with a real face to revolve around, his daydreams had grown even grander. When he'd heard she was in Venice, those dreams had seemed on the verge of coming true. He'd been sure that she was there for him. To see him. Claim him. But when they had finally come face to face, she'd shown none of the joy that he'd dreamt of. Her eyes, when they had finally come to rest on him, had turned cold and cruel, before she turned her face away, as though she didn't know him at all.

The incident had left him crushed and reeling, but he'd been too foolish, too full of hope, to learn his lesson and he'd gone to find her at her home. He had begged, he remembered with nauseating clarity, for a moment of her time, a conversation, that was all, but the rejection had been swift and brutal. The look that chased him away had told him he was nothing. Less than nothing. It was a look that, until Rae, had prevented him from ever getting too close to anyone.

However, he was older now. Wiser. And this situation with Rae would not be the same, he reassured himself. He was capable of ignoring the inclinations of his body and the messages being telegraphed by his recklessly beating heart, and even more reckless libido. All he wanted from her was her cooperation to ensure he inherited Palazzo Ricci. He harboured no hopes and he would not be *begging* for anything.

That was Domenico's last thought before they pulled up outside the hotel. They were checked in quickly, his name prompting a flurry of activity, but as soon as they entered the confined space of the elevator, Rae's gentle scent hit him like a punch, making him question that resolve as it took him right back to their most intimate moments, when he was deep inside her and the world began and ended with her. To the way she moved atop him, covering his body with her own, silencing his groans with kisses, fogging his mind with that light-as-air scent— *her* scent.

The moment they entered the suite he strode over to the

terrace doors and pushed them open, partly to assess the view but mostly to flood the room with clean spring air and dilute the potency of her presence. Feeling fatigued, though it was only just past noon, Domenico availed himself of the top-of-the-line coffee machine and then carried his very strong espresso out onto the terrace. He was sipping at his coffee when he noticed Rae emerging from the far side of the suite and heading for the door, her jacket on and bag hanging from her shoulder.

'Are you going somewhere?' he demanded, quickly stalking back indoors.

She flashed him a look that said it was obvious. 'To do what I came here to do. Press pause on my life for the next six months.' Turning her back on him, she reached for the door handle. 'I'll be back in a while.'

'That's a little vague for my liking, Rae.'

Her shoulders stiffened and Domenico had the distinct impression she was counting to three and taking a deep breath before responding. Not for the first time, he caught himself reflecting that she was much spikier than she'd been before. Quicker to argue and sharper with her retorts. Thinking back to the way she had challenged him about the particulars of her return, forcing him to hastily rearrange his schedule to accompany her to London, he couldn't say he appreciated the argumentativeness but, for reasons unknown to him, he was somewhat intrigued by her new gutsy spirit. He wondered where she'd been hiding it throughout their marriage.

'I'm going to hand in my notice at work and then I'm going home to see my sisters and to pack up my things.'

Domenico searched her expression for any sign of deceit, though he wasn't sure he trusted himself to recognise it. She had, after all, fooled him for a long number of months into thinking that she was as invested in their marriage as he was.

'Very well.' He set down his cup and reached for his phone. 'I'll call for the car.'

'I don't need the car.'

'You may feel like traipsing across London with luggage. I, however, do not.'

'Since you're not coming with me, I don't see why what *you* feel like is relevant,' she riposted with a flash of temper, crossing her arms defensively over her chest, which was rising and falling with each flustered breath. Much to his frustration, the movement only drew his attention to the generous shape of her breasts beneath her shirt and abruptly all he could think about was how responsive they'd been to his touch. How Rae had loved him to flick and lick and suck. How she would writhe beneath him and beg breathlessly for him to keep going.

'It's relevant because I *am* coming with you,' he snapped, breaking free from those thoughts, but only with great effort.

Outrage glowed in her eyes like sudden flames, enhancing their naturally bright hue. 'No.'

'Yes.' Lifting his jacket from the back of the chair, he pulled it on.

'I don't need an escort, Domenico.' When he didn't bother to respond to her jibe, she huffed out an irritated sigh. 'I gave you my word that I would go through with this charade. So what is it that you think I'm going to do? Disappear into the crowds of the city and never be seen again?'

'No, I don't think that's going to happen,' he responded,

rapidly losing patience, 'because I'm not going to allow it. You may have given your word, Rae, but surely you can understand why it doesn't count for much.'

He might be foolish enough to still desire her, but he was not such a fool that he would trust her ever again. Not after what she had done.

So he would not be letting her out of his sight, at least not until she had proven herself. And on one level he was curious about the life she had chosen over him. Masochistically eager to see what had been so much more worthwhile than him. Than *them*.

'So,' he said, forcing himself to ignore the hurt clawing its way into her gaze and gesturing for her to precede him out of the door. 'After you.'

*So this was what she had left him for.*

It was the sole thought in Domenico's head as the car pulled away from the kerb outside the bistro in her home suburb of Wandsworth, where Rae had seemingly been working, and set off towards her house.

*To be a hostess in a high street restaurant and live back in the house she had grown up in with her sisters.*

It was unfathomable! He could give her the world and she had picked this?

Turning his face away from the window with a barely suppressed breath of anger, he dug his phone from his inner jacket pocket and with a frustrated jab accessed his emails, questioning afresh how he had made such an error in judgement in granting Rae access to his life. That he had ever considered her different from the women from his past was perplexing to him now, and there was little comfort in recognising that she had fooled Elena just as convincingly.

His aunt had often remarked that she thought Rae possessed a similar spirit to her own, but Rae's actions had thoroughly debunked that. Elena had been one of the wisest, kindest, most loyal people he'd ever known. She had never turned her back on him, or anyone in need, and although Domenico sometimes questioned if she had only taken him in to fill her barren life after her husband Raphael's premature death, and to give herself a once longed-for heir, he'd never doubted her affection for him.

However, it was that ugly question that drove him to work so hard, to build The Ricci Group—Raphael's business—into something even bigger than Raphael Ricci or Elena had dreamed of. To prove to Elena that she had been right to take him in when no one else had wanted him. To show her that, out of all the lost boys in the world, he was deserving of the good fortune she'd bestowed on him. Even if *he* never quite felt deserving of it, of the love and attention she had offered.

It was as though his abandonment as a newborn baby had stained him, marking him out as unwanted, and nothing he did, however hard he worked or how much he gave, could erase that mark, or the feeling that sometimes crawled beneath his skin because of it.

It was a feeling not helped by the world he inhabited, where it was never clear if the people who flocked to his side and fussed and flirted in the hope of earning his favour did so because they actually wanted to know him, or because they could not resist the lure of his wealth and status.

He'd never had that concern with Rae. Whilst instantly

recognisable in Italy and other countries across the Continent, his profile in England had been relatively low when they'd met. Rae had known nothing of his wealth or the Ricci name. Her interest had been solely in Domenico, the man. For a short while, at least, and when that had waned, even the wealth and luxury he could offer hadn't been enough of an incentive to cajole her into staying.

She just hadn't wanted him. Like so many others before her.

He hated that it hurt him, like a scalpel splitting his skin open and tearing it back so he felt exposed. Vulnerable. Domenico thought he had excised all those feelings long ago. Whatever small splinters had remained had been dealt with in the aftermath of Rae's departure, plucked out like thorns. But he could feel a fresh spill of that poison, spreading outwards and infecting his thoughts and his mood, propelling him back to that day when he had stood in the freezing, pouring rain, pleading for the chance to know his family, only to have the door slammed in his face.

It was a memory, and an insecurity, that he couldn't abide and he loathed Rae for stirring it up, for making him feel weak, especially when he had been a damn good husband to her.

As his wife she had wanted for nothing. She hadn't needed to work. She'd had the freedom to travel with him in opulence and comfort to the most exciting cities the world had to offer and to enjoy them in a luxurious manner that most people could only dream of.

Her only responsibilities—if they could even be called that—had been to represent their family and business with poise and elegance. To attend the necessary social functions and work with certain charitable organisations and, every so often, coordinate with a team of event planners to set up a party on behalf of The Ricci Group.

What cause had she had to leave?

The life flying past on the other side of the window was the life Rae had left behind to be with him in the first place. And she had left it easily, happily. So why had she returned to it? It could only be that she'd stopped loving him.

That he hadn't been enough.

The story of his life.

*But* she had been as close to capitulating to the swirling fire between them as he had, and didn't that indicate that she felt something for him? That he continued to hold some mastery over her emotions?

In which case...

*Basta!*

*Enough!*

Vexed by that dangerous train of thought because it was contaminated with too much hope, Domenico ruthlessly shut down those thoughts. It didn't matter why Rae had left, only that she had. Even if he was able to burrow inside her mind and understand her ultimate reasoning, what would it change? There was no going back for them. She had betrayed him. Broken his trust. Broken everything they had built together. So he resolved to give it no more thought, and focus only on the issues that could be resolved—like his inheritance.

Rae was beyond relieved when the car pulled up outside her family home on the tree-lined residential street in Wandsworth and she was able to escape the confines of the car and with it the intoxicating, darkly sweet scent of Domenico's supremely male body and the feel of that body so close to her.

'Do you want to come in?' she offered out of politeness.

'No. I'll wait here for you. I have more emails that I need to respond to and you probably need some private time with your sisters.'

She tried not to show her relief. After the flight, which had seemed to take double the normal time, and crisscrossing the capital in midday traffic, Rae badly needed a reprieve, and not just from her bodily reactions to him, but the disapproval that had been radiating off him in violent waves ever since realising she'd taken a part-time job as a hostess and waitress at a local restaurant. Domenico had taken one look at the frontage of the bistro and his lips had instantly compressed together in that flat line that expressed his discontent. Senior executives at Ricci lived in fear of that compression of his mouth, but Rae had only ever been subjected to it on occasion, most memorably the once or twice that she had tried to express a preference that she did not accompany him to a particular event.

Using her key to let herself into the house, Rae hadn't even shut the door before she was set upon by her sisters, demanding the answers she hadn't been willing to give them during the brief call she had made from Venice. Sitting with them in the living room, she slowly explained all that had unfolded and what would happen next.

'So you're actually going back to Venice to live with him and pretend you are still together for the next six months?' Maggie demanded in open-mouthed disbelief. 'Have you completely lost your mind?' she exploded.

'Maggie!' Imogen chided.

'Don't Maggie me!' she fired at their youngest sister. 'It's absurd and if you're being honest, you think it is too.'

'I know it's crazy,' Rae admitted, looking between her sisters. 'But helping him is the right thing to do. For him, and for me too.' By their looks of scepticism, she knew she needed to explain further. 'I want to draw a line underneath this whole chapter. I've got so many good things to look forward to, but Domenico is always lurking at the back of my mind. There's no closure there and I know the only way I'm going to be able to get that is by going back and proving that I've learned something about myself. That I've changed and I'm not going to make the same mistakes again.'

'Rae, how can you even think that? You're so different from the person you were when you were married to Domenico. Both Imogen and I see it,' Maggie reassured her urgently.

'Totally,' Imogen agreed quickly. 'You're more assertive, you have such a determined focus on your bridal collection, you're chasing it with everything you've got. We're so impressed by what you're doing and we're so proud of you.'

'You saying that means a lot,' she said, taking both her sisters' hands in hers. 'But this is just something I need to do. For myself.'

'Then do it,' Imogen said, squeezing her hand. 'We're here for you whatever.'

Content with the support of her sisters, Rae went upstairs to begin the task of packing her clothes. From the window of her bedroom that overlooked the street she could see Domenico's car outside. She could make out his figure in the back seat, gesturing with his free hand as he spoke on the phone, and the movements were so familiar to her that her heart gave a kick and nervousness fluttered deep inside her chest.

*Six months*, she reminded herself. *That's all. You can do this. There's nothing to be nervous about. You'll prove exactly how much you've changed, that you're capable of being around him and not sacrificing anything of yourself. That you don't have to suffer the way Mum did. And then you can walk away with a clear conscience and an even bigger belief in yourself.*

Buoyed by that pep talk, Rae spun away from the window and reached for her case, because the sooner she got the ordeal started, the sooner she'd be on the other side of it and that wonderful, exhilarating, heartbreaking, petrifying chapter of her life with Domenico would be over for good.

# CHAPTER FIVE

RAE HADN'T BEEN back in Venice a full three days when Domenico informed her that they would be attending a black-tie ball at the end of the week. He had given her fair warning it was what he expected and Rae knew she had agreed to it, but still the prospect of attending a function on his arm had her heart racing and chest constricting. It wasn't just that there would be dozens of sets of eyes on them, all watching to be convinced of the continued validity of their union; it was that there would be no escape from Domenico.

In the days that she had been back in Venice, Rae had seen him only a handful of times. He was staying true to his word about living separate lives in private, and that suited her just fine. She was able to devote her alone time to her bridal design business, working on new ideas as well as her ongoing orders, and when she needed a break she would take a leisurely wander of the city that had long ago captured her heart, strolling along the narrow waterways or enjoying the bustling piazzas from outside a coffee shop. However, that lack of contact or communication in private created a greater nervousness about being with him in public, because they were going from one extreme to another. From zero interaction to pretending to be in love.

Obviously, she had realised when she'd agreed to return that the pretence would be necessary, but she'd been so preoccupied with her emotions about returning that she hadn't given much—*any*—thought to the practicalities of it.

But now all Rae could think about was all the ways Domenico would be touching and holding her.

How he would casually drape an arm around her shoulders or her waist, stroke his fingertip across her cheek, brush escaped tendrils of hair from her face, all with a gentleness of touch that was at odds with his brute size and that provoked a seismic reaction beneath her skin. And he would probably kiss her, holding her captive beneath that dark chocolate gaze before slowly, so her anticipation built, lowering his lips until they met hers in an eruption of quiet, screaming passion.

As she imagined it all in excruciating slow motion, something rippled across her skin—something Rae wanted to pretend she hadn't felt or recognised. Because to give a name to it would make it real and she didn't want it to be real. Couldn't let it be real. Not if she was going to emerge intact at the end of their six-month arrangement.

Despite her unease, on the allotted night she was dressed in her finery and descending the palazzo's long curved staircase to meet Domenico. Although he had given her a new credit card to cover all of her costs, Rae had selected a dress from her old wardrobe, a previously unworn classic creation of black silk from a renowned Italian designer that floated around her like air. The straps were thin and delicate and the design cut very low on her back, showing more skin than she ideally wanted to display, but it had been the only black dress amongst her existing collection. She had set her mind on wearing black, hoping it would attract less attention than a bolder hue, not that it really mattered when Domenico always attracted so much attention, never mind with the addition of all sorts of swirling rumours...

He was waiting for her at the bottom of the staircase, his back to her, and her heart stopped at the sight of his broad back, sheathed in the pristine fabric of the expertly fitted tuxedo. It showed to perfection the raw strength of his body and Rae found herself gripping the banister for support as her knees suddenly felt too weak to keep holding her up.

Naked, he was mesmerising, a mouthwatering specimen to behold, but Rae had always thought that he was as much of a sensation clothed and the thrill of him in that moment did nothing to dispel that opinion. One of her favourite things about evenings when they'd attended some fancy soirée had been knowing that at the end of the night her hands would have the privilege of sliding the fine clothes from his body to find the hot skin beneath. Not that she had that privilege any more, or that she wanted it, she reminded herself sharply, hurrying the final few steps as though she could leave those feelings behind her.

Hearing the click of her heels against the floor, Domenico spun around, his eyes crashing into hers. Rae swallowed as his glittering gaze swept over her, his jaw tightening fractionally though he offered no comment.

'You should wear this too,' he said, turning to the table

behind him and lifting a velvet box that, when he popped it open, revealed a diamond choker.

'That was Elena's,' Rae breathed, stunned that he was presenting it to her.

'Yes. A much-admired piece of her collection. She wore it often, and you wearing it tonight should signal that everything in our marriage is perfect. I would hardly let someone I didn't love and was estranged from wear something so precious, would I?'

Rae swallowed again, unable to read beneath the hard glint of his richly dark eyes or the silkily lethal drawl of his words. But his willingness to allow her to wear such a priceless heirloom reminded her just how important this charade was to him and, as much as she wanted to refuse, she knew it wouldn't be a wise way to start the evening and so simply turned as he lifted the jewels from the box.

With deft fingers he fastened it around her neck, his hot fingers brushing her trembling flesh. The quivers racing over her skin sank even deeper into her and for the second time in as many minutes she thought her legs were about to give way. And it didn't help that he was standing so close that Rae could feel all the strength and heat of his body and she so badly wanted to press back against it, to feel the power of him enveloping her once more.

Domenico moved her by the shoulders so she was standing before an antique mirror.

'What do you think?' he asked, his dark eyes so steadily fixed on hers that he would see anything she felt.

Slowly, Rae met his gaze and, as she did, feeling throbbed in every inch of her. 'It's stunning.'

Their eyes held and her breath grew shallower. Could he feel it too? That pulse of passion and longing streaming between them. There seemed to be a million thoughts and feelings locked in the darkness of his gaze—emotions he had no intention of giving voice to. But Rae couldn't speak either, strangled by the heavy emotion coursing through her, thudding hotly in her sex in a beat that refused to be ignored.

She frantically searched his face with her eyes, wanting some sign that his blood was running as hot as hers, scared by the thought that it was and equally scared that it wasn't.

'We should go,' he said, stepping back easily and moving towards the front door.

Her skin instantly chilled, though her blood still ran hot and she cursed her stupidity. If she couldn't even *stand* close to him without turning into a puddle, what would it be like when he actually did touch her? The last thing she wanted was a repeat of what had almost happened in the upstairs corridor the night of Elena's funeral, when she'd gone up in sizzling flames at the barest of touches. The only way to keep that from happening, Rae realised, was to set some boundaries. *Now.*

'Before we go…' Rae began, seizing the moment to assert her will in a way she never would have thought to previously. 'I know everyone needs to believe that we are madly in love, but I was thinking we should establish some ground rules.'

Domenico arched a brow. 'Such as?'

'I know we need to be affectionate with one another and that's fine. But within reason. So I would prefer it if we didn't kiss on the mouth,' she specified assertively. 'It's not unreasonable, I think. Many other couples restrain from such displays in public.'

'I don't recall us being one of those couples,' he drawled, evidently finding the idea ridiculous, and he wasn't wrong. They'd never succeeded in keeping their hands off one another, but Rae had also never previously imposed her will on their relationship and look at her now. She was proof that things could change.

Holding herself steady beneath his unflinching regard, because she knew that he was expecting her to back down, she said in a controlled voice, 'I have faith that we can convince people we're happy without being overt in our displays of affection.'

'Hmm. Fine,' he agreed, his jaw locked tight. 'We'll keep kissing off the agenda for the evening. But let's make sure everything else is convincing, *sì*?' he added with a look of warning. 'Vincenzo D'Aragona is still in the city and it's likely he too will be attending tonight.'

Rae nodded, that tiny lump in her throat tripling in size. As if she hadn't felt enough pressure without knowing their judge and jury would there too!

The ballroom was full of people by the time they arrived and as they walked through the doors Domenico clasped her hand tightly in his. Rae wished it didn't feel so good, so right, to have his strong fingers wrapped around hers, to be claimed as his again. As expected, all eyes followed their arrival and beneath her beautiful dress Rae's heart thrashed against the cage of her ribs.

She tried to focus instead on the opulence of the venue. The high ceiling, the trio of glittering chandeliers, the string orchestra arranged in one corner and mammoth vases of fragrant flowers delineating the perimeter of the room.

She and Domenico exchanged polite greetings with

many of the couples in attendance before collecting drinks from the bar and standing at one of the high top tables. Rae was able to breathe for all of two seconds before she spied renowned socialite Luisa D'Amato strutting in their direction, her sights very much fixed on them. Behind her smile Rae's teeth gritted together, her body tightening even more. Luisa was the very last person she wanted to deal with. Their interactions had always been unpleasant, with every single remark she'd ever made designed to make Rae feel small and insecure and incompetent, and as hard as Rae had tried to withstand their power, they'd somehow always left their mark, chipping at her confidence and her sense of security as Domenico's wife. Not that Domenico had ever noticed, and Rae had never raised it with him, not wanting to appear petty or insecure, or as if she couldn't handle herself in his world. But it had just become one more pretence, one more truth she wasn't speaking, and one more brick in that ever-growing wall between them.

'Rae, so wonderful to have you back,' Luisa trilled as she reached them, air kissing each of her cheeks.

'It's lovely to be back,' Rae replied with a smile.

Luisa surveyed her through heavily made-up eyes. 'I must admit, we were starting to wonder if we would ever see you again, you were gone for so long. If only you'd heard some of the rumours going around,' she murmured, leaning in almost conspiratorially. 'That perhaps your marriage was over. Absolutely crazy, I said. But that's why it's dangerous to leave one's husband unattended for so long. Hopes, as I'm sure you can understand, were getting rather high. But I assure you, Rae, I did my best to keep some of the more predatory women away. No doubt you can imagine who I'm talking about,' she went on, gesturing not so subtly with her eyes to a passing female. 'But I suppose it's always nice to know you have options,' she added with a direct look of smiling suggestion at Domenico, 'should you ever want them.'

Rae's fingers clenched dangerously around the crystal flute of champagne in her hand, unable to believe what Luisa had just said, and yet not surprised at all. But after all the catty remarks and slights Rae had had to suffer from her, that was too blatantly disrespectful, too far over the line, and she wasn't going to just quietly accept it the way she always had before.

Throwing back her shoulders, she met Luisa's gaze. 'I'm very grateful for your help, Luisa, although I knew I had nothing to worry about. It's not as though anyone here is Domenico's type or he wouldn't have still been single when I came along, would he?' she mused, trailing a hand down his arm. 'But your care and attention towards him is much appreciated, especially when you could have been using that time to look for husband number three. Or it is number four? I've lost track.'

From the corner of her eye Rae was sure she caught Domenico's look of surprise, but she was more interested in Luisa's faltering expression.

'If you'll excuse me, I see Antonia and I need to speak with her. But it is wonderful to see you.'

'You too. Say hello from me.' Rae smiled as Luisa walked away. A small sense of satisfaction rippled through her, but she hated that she'd earned it by engaging in the same unkindness that Luisa practised.

'Are you okay?' Domenico asked in her ear, a low whisper that sent shivers rippling through her.

'I'm fine,' she replied, taking a sip of her champagne in the hope of shedding the nasty feeling snaking through her veins.

'Your hand is shaking, Rae.'

She looked at her hand to see Domenico was right, and then quickly up at him. 'I've never found Luisa to be the easiest person to deal with, that's all.'

He said nothing else, but placed a warm hand on the bare skin of her back, rubbing his palm up and down her spine, and within seconds she could feel the tension start to ease and her body begin to relax. Whether Domenico had intended it as an act of comfort and reassurance or as a necessary show of affection, Rae wasn't sure, and the answer did not prove forthcoming as her awareness narrowed to that mesmerising motion of his hand over her sensitive skin, streams of hot, sparkly feeling running in a dozen different directions.

She wanted that delicious feeling in the rest of her body too. She wanted those clever fingers to slide up her spine and graze her side. Wanted them to slip beneath the silk and curl over her breast, for him to touch and tease as he'd once loved to, and as she'd loved also. How many times had he brought her to screaming orgasm just by lavishing the hot attention of his lips and tongue on her breasts?

The bliss of imagining was dashed as she felt eyes scalding her skin. Across the ballroom, Luisa and her group of friends stared their way, murmuring intently amongst themselves.

'Ignore them.' Domenico's lips were against her ear again, his hand continuing to trace over her skin, skating a line up and down her spine.

'She's ghastly… To stand there and say those things

to my face.' Rae looked up at him. His expression was unconcerned and that rattled her even more, breath hissing from between her lips. 'Not that I expect you to care. You're probably delighted to know you have so many options.'

His eyes gleamed, dark and rich and completely devastating. 'A little late to be possessive, isn't it?' he remarked with a slight smile, sliding his hand to the curve of her waist and pulling her even tighter against his muscled body, and she hated that it did make her feel better. That each caress softened her mood that little bit more. That the nearer she was to his body, the more the rest of the room seemed to slide away. 'You never seemed to be bothered by the women and their comments before.'

Was he actually that obtuse? Rae thought with a frowning glance up at him. Or had her feelings really mattered so little to him that he'd never spared a thought for how those high society social occasions, in which she had no experience, could be difficult for her? It was hardly a new realisation, but it was jarring all the same.

'Of course I was bothered by them, Domenico,' she sighed, frustration loosening her tongue.

The look on his face was one she recognised: he was chewing over that information, trying to fit it in with all that he already knew. 'You never said anything.'

The words contained a mild accusation and Rae moved her shoulders in a small inexpressive shrug. She was regretting having said anything about it now and making it a bigger deal, highlighting her silly female feelings when she'd only ever wanted him to think of her as strong and capable, the perfect wife. The weight of his stare was unmoving, though, and Rae knew she had to say something to defuse the heaviness of the moment and diminish her confession.

'Most of the time there didn't seem to be much point in complaining about it,' she admitted reluctantly and uncomfortably. 'It's not like it's something you can control, Domenico. I just saw it as a reality of being with you. Of course other women were going to be catty or jealous or mean. You're a beautiful man. You're wealthy. You're powerful. One of those is catnip. All three together is a lethal combination. Naturally, any woman who looks at you is going to find you irresistible. Because you are.'

His hand had stopped moving. He stared down at her, a new light moving through his powerful gaze and, much to her annoyance, Rae realised she had done the opposite of what she'd wanted. Instead of brushing him off, she'd only made him want to dig deeper into her feelings. 'Irresistible?'

He repeated the word with a quirk of his lips and for the barest of seconds he looked like the Domenico she was used to—the Domenico she'd fallen head over heels for and married in a whirlwind. Charismatic and quick-minded, with that devastating slash of a smile. There was none of the cool distance, none of the well-bred politeness he'd treated her with on their few brief encounters since she'd been back.

'It's only the truth,' Rae replied huskily, feeling colour rush to her cheeks as she cursed herself for giving away something else that she shouldn't have. For giving him a first-hand look at the feelings she was alternating between ignoring and denying.

Domenico seemed to be on the verge of saying something else, his eyes dark with thoughts, before clearly changing his mind. 'We should dance,' he said instead, prising her flute from her hand and leading her to the centre of the room, where many couples were already taking advantage of the lilting music to move in smooth circles around the floor.

Domenico pulled her in close. His jaw brushed her cheek, the touch jolting through her like an electric shock. She caught the scent of him, strong and sharp, and it clouded her head completely and Rae had to fight the urge to brush her lips across his smooth, sweet-smelling skin, to sample his flesh with the tip of her tongue.

*Get a grip, Rae.*

This was only the first of many public outings that would demand their closeness. If she was going to simmer with unwanted desire each time, it was going to be a very long six months. She had to figure out a way to control herself. Had to remember that for all the reasons Domenico was right, he was also very, *very* wrong for her.

They imagined different futures. He wanted a wife permanently at his side and she wanted, *needed*, a life of her own.

Engaging in anything remotely physical, even entertaining thoughts of such caresses, would only muddy the waters and it would be far better for them both if they stayed unmuddied.

But as he moved her effortlessly across the floor, Rae's body continued to purr under their tempting closeness and the expert press of his hands against her flesh. His touch had always been her undoing and Rae could feel it starting to occur again, that unravelling of herself as her body slowly surrendered to his compelling touch of possession.

Had it not been for the eyes continuing to follow them, primarily Luisa and her friends, Rae would have drifted off entirely, but their predatory watchfulness kept her rooted in reality, their hard and hungry gazes making her stomach writhe and twist.

Because Luisa had been right. Domenico did have options, plenty of them. There was a queue of women waiting for a chance to be with him and once their charade was over, once it became public knowledge that their marriage was dead, a few of them would probably get that chance.

*If they hadn't already.*

That sudden burst of thought had tears pressing up against her eyes and an inexplicable emotion gushing through her and sticking at the back of her throat. She knew, however, that was how they wanted her to feel, insecure and vulnerable. It was the way she'd often felt at these events and around these ruthless, predatory women. But, as far as they were concerned, Domenico was still hers.

And her only job tonight was to show exactly how much he did belong to her, how his heart beat for her and his body hungered for her.

*Only her.*

Twisting her face inwards, the tip of her nose glided along his smooth, tanned jaw and Rae allowed herself to succumb to the scent of him, dark and strong. Playing along, Domenico tipped his head down, his lips within easy reach, just like that night in the hallway, but, unlike that night, Rae didn't hesitate, extending her neck so that their mouths met.

That first feather-light brush of their lips was shattering. He tasted better than she'd allowed herself to remember. Like desire and hope and passion. The gentle motion of their mouths changed as her hands slid up his powerfully muscled chest and curled around his neck. The answering press of his lips became harder, his mouth shaping to hers with more ferocity, seeking more of her passion, which she eagerly gave. Domenico held her more securely, the band of his arms around her back crushing her breasts to the solid expanse of his chest, and Rae very nearly melted, having forgotten just how amazing it felt to be held against the broad wall of beating flesh. As if nothing could hurt her ever again. As if there was no safer place for her in the whole world.

The heat crackling between them could have burned her dress right off her body and Rae didn't know if it was his heart or her own that she could feel racing. But she knew she wanted the kiss. Wanted it with every catch of her breath and every flutter of her pulse. Wanted it more than she remembered ever wanting any kiss, and she didn't want it to prove something, but wanted it for herself.

It was Domenico who drew back first, keeping tight hold and staring down at her, his eyes alight. 'What happened to your ground rules?' he demanded huskily.

*Good question*, Rae thought, feeling intoxicated, her mind fuzzy.

'It seemed necessary,' she lied, the words coming too slow. 'We were being watched. And I was under orders to be convincing, was I not?'

His eyes flashed as if he found her answer provocative somehow, and his face adopted the set expression that preceded an interrogation that always got him the answers he wanted. But then it was gone and he was drawing back and leading her from the dancefloor.

'I think that's enough for tonight,' he said as the music ended. 'We'll leave now.'

She blinked with surprise. 'But we've not been here that long.'

'Long enough,' he countered. 'And after that kiss, no one will find our departure strange. Everyone will assume we're in a hurry to get home and continue our reunion.'

Rae's cheeks flamed. But that was exactly what the kiss had felt like so it had most certainly looked just as passionate. Burning with mortification, she let Domenico take her hand and lead her from the ballroom, but, as soon as she could, she pulled her hand free. She said nothing on the journey back to the palazzo and, once they arrived, she ran up the stairs, tossing a hurried goodnight over her shoulder.

Domenico watched Rae fly up the stairs, his mouth still tingling with the incendiary passion of that brief kiss. The taste of her remained on his lips and the fever she had stirred in his blood with her unrestrained hunger continued to scorch his veins.

He had been doing his best to keep his attraction contained behind bolted doors, to avoid any repeat of the lapse that had happened the night of Elena's funeral, but with that unexpected kiss she had blasted the doors wide open, allowing the scorching desire to stream through him unchecked, and all he wanted to do was continue what she had started.

Wanted to tease her mouth with his, suck her lower lip

between his teeth. Wanted to slide the black silk from her body and see with his own eyes what she wore beneath. Wanted to hear her whimpers, then her pleas and then her screams as he drove her towards blissful oblivion.

He wanted everything he had tasted in that kiss and, before he knew what he was doing, Domenico was following her up the stairs, taking them two at a time, his feet keeping pace with the roaring and pounding of his blood.

Reaching her door, Domenico wrapped his fingers around the handle…only to suddenly stop.

Because suddenly he was outside a house and the door was being opened and the eyes staring back at him turned to the coldest stone when he stated who he was. And then, as if the words spoken hadn't been cruel enough, the door was being shut in his face.

A cold sweat dampening the back of his neck, Domenico released the handle and backed away from the door.

She could spurn his advance, deny the fire that had powered that kiss. Reject him. And he could not bear that. Not again, and not from her.

So he would ignore it. He would drag every last drop of feeling back under his control, close those doors and seal them with an extra bolt. He would bury that desire beneath pragmatism, smother the flames with the memory of her betrayal and keep himself safe from another stinging rejection.

# CHAPTER SIX

ANOTHER NIGHT, ANOTHER CHARADE.

They were attending the opening of a new restaurant overlooking the Grand Canal and being in such close proximity to Rae again, Domenico was once more struggling to keep control of himself.

In a fitted blue dress paired with open-toed stilettoes and a black leather jacket draped across her shoulders as there was a chill to the evening air and they were seated outside, Rae looked sensational. His heart had struck up a restless beat the moment he'd locked eyes on her back at the palazzo, a dizzying cocktail of heat and need moving through his blood and making his heart race and it hadn't stopped since. In the pearlescent glow from the low candles forming the centrepiece of the table, the alluring power of her vivid blue eyes was impossible to avoid and the fever stirring in his blood was only intensifying and there seemed to be nothing he could do about it. Nothing he could do to stop the sultry memories from cascading through his mind, one after the other, each more arousing than the last. Nothing to stop him thinking about how close he had been to charging into her suite and taking her in his arms the last time they'd been together and how he wasn't sure he had it in him to resist again.

In the days since their last public outing Domenico had barely seen her, not because of any special effort on his part but because his normal daily routine was so demanding. He rose early for a punishing workout before heading to his office, where it was customary to spend up to twelve hours, but, with the final pieces of a major deal still being worked out, those hours had been running closer and closer to midnight. By the time he returned to the palazzo most nights Rae had eaten dinner alone and was secluded in her suite, and though that lack of interaction had not been by design, Domenico was relieved by it.

Because he didn't trust himself around her at all. All it took was for him to catch her scent in the air and need unfurled within him like a fast-flowing river, and he hated the thought of being so tempted by her that he abandoned his good sense. That he forgot the lessons he'd paid so dearly to learn.

All he needed was her presence, her cooperation—for her to stick around for the next six months so he could retain ownership of what was already rightfully his. He required nothing else, not from her.

But even knowing that, even having told himself that every day since Rae had been back in Venice, he could not keep his eyes from devouring her or his thoughts from dwelling with heightened awareness on all the ways she was so very different from the woman he had married.

There was an aura of self-possession to her now that had been absent before. He could see it just by looking at her, in the way her shoulders were thrown back, her head held high. She refused to be intimidated by anyone or anything, and had proven that at the ball a few nights previously, when she'd handled Luisa's catty remarks with a cutting comeback of her own. Luisa had thoroughly deserved it and seeing her slammed back into her box had been satisfying, but it had startled him to hear Rae being so sharp with her words. But an even greater source of consternation was that Rae had felt she'd had to respond in such a way. Because her reaction had made it obvious that she'd suffered Luisa's unpleasantness in the past too, and that she had been wounded by it, and he had never known.

And he should have.

He should have noticed and taken action to protect her. Rae was his wife. He had brought her into his life and his world and it had been his responsibility to take care of and defend her. Only he clearly hadn't, and because of that failing Rae had been forced to act out of character, and that was not sitting well with him at all.

Not that he didn't appreciate her newfound strength and confidence. That flare of fire in her eyes when she'd refused to back down, and the steely determination to get her own way, even when up against his powerful will, were definitely intriguing new facets of her, but where those changes had sprung from and why she'd felt the need to change were questions running on a loop in his mind. Testing and troubling him. Driving him to question if he had paid enough attention, if he'd worked hard enough to discover exactly what had been swirling beneath the serene façade she had presented to him. After all, he hadn't known about her unease around Luisa, or how sensitive she'd been to the cruel society gossip. What else had he been unaware of? What else had he missed?

'How's your food?' Rae asked, seeing that he wasn't eating as his thoughts wandered.

He reached for his wine glass, taking a sip of the rich merlot to moisten his bone-dry mouth, and loosen the intensity of his single-track thoughts. 'It's good. You'll like it. Here, try a little.'

Domenico held out his fork to her, knowing it painted the picture of a devoted husband, but as her lips tightened around the fork and it slid between her mouth, he realised his mistake, realised that he had just poured oil on the fire simmering in his blood and, right on cue, he felt it, that sudden violent strain against his trousers. And as he imagined those perfectly ripe lips clamped around his throbbing length, sucking him deeper into the warm wetness of her mouth, his erection only grew more solid. More excruciating.

Heat raced along his veins, his skin suddenly too tight for his body as he worked to block out the erotic image in order to block the feelings it conjured, but it was too vivid, too potent. Hard as he tried, Domenico couldn't loosen the fixed image from his mind and, far from steadying himself, a wild, reckless abandon was mounting in him, urging him to take Rae's hand, slide it beneath the table and onto his crotch. Nothing in that moment seemed more urgent than letting her feel exactly what she did to him, and reminding her what powerful pleasure he could offer her in return.

Knowing he needed to change the direction of his thoughts and *fast*—before he did something he would majorly regret later—he searched desperately through his hazy mind for a safe topic of conversation.

'You were speaking with Imogen earlier?' Rae had

been speaking to her on the phone when he'd returned home to the palazzo. 'How is she?'

Rae stared back at him, her slim eyebrows halfway up her forehead.

'Why are you looking at me like that?'

'Because you hardly ever ask after my sisters,' Rae replied with her newly acquired bluntness.

'That's not true. I've asked about your sisters many times,' he insisted shortly, feeling defensive about the accusation because of course he'd asked about her sisters in the past. *Hadn't he?* 'And even if I didn't, I'm asking now.'

Rae softened her gaze and swallowed her small mouthful of food. 'She's good. She'd been at the library, studying for most of the day.'

'How is she getting on with her studies? Has she been enjoying her course?'

'Yes. She's doing really well.' Rae smiled, her pride in her youngest sister evident. 'Her classes finish at the end of the month. Then she has a few final assignments, but after that she'll focus on her dissertation. I want to try to coax her out here for a few weekends, get her away for a few days or she'll just work non-stop.'

Domenico watched her, seeing what she wasn't admitting in the pull of her lips and the concern momentarily clouding her beautiful eyes.

'You're worried about her?' Rae was always worried about Imogen and Maggie, but this was something else. 'Are you concerned she's pushing herself too much with her studies?'

'No. Well, yes, but it's not just that.' She offered no more, dropping her gaze and digging her fork back into her dish.

'We can't just sit here in silence, Rae. We need to talk about something. Imogen is a neutral topic at least,' he pointed out with cool pragmatism.

With a look that said she knew he had a point, she relented. 'Imogen got involved with someone last summer. I don't know who he was, I never met him and neither did Maggie. But she got in pretty deep with him pretty fast. And then he just walked away with barely more than a goodbye. Maggie and I didn't know about any of this until after it had happened, but it hit Ims hard. She became quiet, withdrawn. If she hadn't had her classes, I'm not sure she would have got out of bed.' Her forehead creased with a concerned frown. 'She's better now, a lot better, but I'm not sure she's completely over it.'

'A rejection like that, from someone she thought she could trust and who she thought she loved, she may never be completely over it. That kind of wound has a way of staying with you so that, even twenty years later, that sting of rejection feels just as sharp as the day it was inflicted,' Domenico imparted with all the certainty of someone who had experienced it himself and Rae's eyes lifted to his, the troubled blue of her gaze deepening to the colour of the darkest, deepest sea. It was that which alerted him to just how much he had inadvertently given away about himself. 'But she will move on. You just need to give her time. It doesn't happen overnight.'

Rae was still watching him, curiosity now burning in her gaze.

'What happened all those years ago that hurt you so badly, Domenico?' She leaned in closer, her eyes fixed on him with a compelling clarity and directness from which he felt there was no escape. 'You can tell me.'

'We were talking about Imogen,' he reminded her, growing more uncomfortable by the second under her intense gaze.

'Now I'm asking about you,' Rae responded. 'What happened? Who rejected you?'

Domenico looked off to the side. He had no intention of breaking his silence on the past. It was something he never talked about, but their conversation had unlocked an unpleasant memory that had started to snake through him and his usual tactic of pushing it aside was not working. In the strangest upending of emotion, he was struck by the desire to share it, to dispel it from his mind, and before he could examine that sudden urge, try to curb it, his lips were moving and he was answering her, information he had never spoken aloud before spilling out.

'My mother.' He faced Rae again. 'She lived here in Venice for a period when I was younger. By that time, I'd discovered who she was and when I found out that she was moving here I got so excited. I thought she had to be coming here because of me. *For me.* To see me, maybe have me come and live with her. It wasn't like I wanted to leave Elena—I loved her—but this was my mother. I'd been dreaming about meeting her for a long time.'

He paused, needing a moment, but the words were in a rush to escape. 'Every time the doorbell went during those days and weeks I leapt to my feet, so sure that it would be her. But it never was. She never came. Then one day Elena had taken me out for lunch and she was in the same restaurant. She walked straight past us and looked right at me. But, instead of smiling or stopping, she just looked right through me with those cold, hateful eyes and it was like I'd been burned. All I wanted to do was cry, but I didn't want to disappoint Elena, so I just held it in…'

Feeling emotion pressing at the backs of his eyes at the stinging recollection, Domenico shook his head, wanting to move on, erase that too intense moment. But looking across at Rae certainly didn't help. She was absorbed in all that new information. Having omitted all the finer details of his story, all she'd ever known about his childhood was that Elena had taken him in when his own mother had been unable to care for him. He'd never wanted her to know the whole ugly truth of how unwanted he'd been, fearful that with that knowledge she'd start to find him lacking too.

'But, like I said, Imogen will find a way to move on. She's strong. She'll be okay.'

Rae's eyes were stuck on him and he knew that, in spite of his attempt to draw attention back to her problem and her sister, Rae was thinking only of his story in that moment.

'How did *you* move on from that?'

Domenico was quiet for a second as he relived it, remembering the hurt and the confusion. Remembering how those emotions had spread through his body like a virus and how hard he'd fought against that anguish.

'I made the memory and feelings as small as I could and locked them in a little box where they could do no further harm,' he told her dispassionately.

Rae's hand had reached out and was curled around his fist, warm and soft, and the urge to twine his fingers through hers, to accept that comfort, was overwhelming.

'Did you ever see her again? Your mother.'

The lump in his throat was so large it was a second

before he could answer. 'Only from afar.' But those sightings of her were tattooed into his brain too, because she hadn't been alone. She'd had her children with her—the children she had kept, the ones whose existence she had welcomed and celebrated. Whilst he'd remained ignored. 'And no,' he added more sharply than he intended as he anticipated her obvious follow-up question, 'she doesn't still live here. It's been years since I set eyes on her.'

'I'm sorry, Domenico. I don't know what to say other than that.'

'You don't need to say anything.'

He didn't need sympathetic words, or platitudes. He didn't need to talk about it. It was a reality that he had borne for years and talking about it would change nothing, and yet didn't the burden of it suddenly feel a little lighter, its sting a little less potent?

His phone rang but, without breaking their eye contact, he swiped a finger across the screen to reject the call and, before Rae could cajole any more confessions out of him, he moved on. 'Are you ready for dessert? Your favourite is on the menu—tiramisu.'

Just as he reached for the menu, his phone buzzed once again.

'*Mi scusi.*' With a quiet growl of annoyance, he snatched it up, intent on giving the caller an earache for disturbing him, not once but twice. But then he sighed as he listened to the voice on the other end of the line, hanging up with a promise to be at the office soon. 'I'm sorry, Rae. There's a crisis with a new deal we're working on and I need to go and deal with it in person or it could fall apart.'

He was aggravated, and not just because his prize deal

had hit a snag, but because it meant cutting short his evening with Rae.

She smiled across at him. 'It's okay. Don't worry. I couldn't eat another bite anyway.'

Her words didn't dispel his niggle of guilt, or the feeling that he would prefer to stay with her, even though he didn't understand why he was feeling that sudden yearning for closeness with her.

'I'll sort the bill and walk you back to the palazzo.'

'You don't need to do that. You need to hurry. I can get myself home. It's not far.'

'You're not walking back alone. That's final,' he added when she opened her mouth to protest, the thought of her navigating the darkened streets alone sending trickles of fear seeping down his spine.

Throwing down a set of bills on the table, Domenico took her hand, leading her from the restaurant and making their goodbyes. Only a few of the photographers who'd been documenting the arrivals of Venice's social elite remained, but they eagerly snapped yet more shots of Rae and Domenico as they exited onto the street.

The night was dark and quiet. Venice's streets and bridges and waterways were almost empty. The dark water was still, reflecting the glitter of the lights from the surrounding buildings. Domenico kept hold of her hand as they walked in silence, the gentle brushing of his thumb feeling the crazy skittering of her pulse, making him wonder if she was also sensing that new intimacy between them, if she was as aware of him as he was of her, every brush of her arm, the nudge of her hip.

'Am I allowed to ask what the crisis is?' Rae asked after a few minutes of quiet. 'Or is it top secret?' she teased and Domenico saw it as a sign that she was feeling it too, that whatever had shifted had done so for them both.

'It's fairly top secret, yes,' he said, slanting her a quick smile to keep the light mood in place because he didn't want to disturb that connection blooming between them. It was the closest he'd felt to another person in a long time and whilst that normally wouldn't have mattered to him, in that moment it did. 'But for you I'll make an exception. The Ricci Group is negotiating a big deal that will see us expand into operating a cruise line.'

Her eyes popped. 'Like Raphael always wanted?'

Domenico was surprised that she'd remembered. Surprised, and pleased. 'Yes.'

'Domenico, that's incredible. Congratulations.' Her smile illuminated her whole face and Domenico's lungs squeezed. She was so beautiful, so much more than she knew, that it was actually painful. In the months that she'd been gone he'd encountered countless women, many of whom were eye-wateringly stunning, yet none had drawn from him a reaction that could compete with his response to Rae's smile.

'Thank you. It's been hard even getting to the negotiations. The company we want to partner with has a CEO who is notoriously guarded about who he deals with, but we've been making some good progress lately and I don't want anything to derail it.'

'Did Elena know about it?'

He gave a single nod of his dark head. 'She did. I told her a few weeks before she passed. When she took over Raphael's role as CEO she tried to realise that dream on a few occasions, but it never worked out.'

'I remember her telling me. I always got the sense that was a big regret of hers. She must have been incredibly touched that you were doing that.'

'*Sì*, she was.' The memory of that conversation, of all his conversations with Elena, rolled slowly through his mind, a million shards of memory causing a million throbs of pain.

He tried not to think about it too often—his default way of dealing with anything difficult—but he missed her. Missed her more than words could express. It was an ache that at times diminished but then always roared back into existence. At times he felt that, without her guiding presence, he had no sense of whether he was coming or going, no anchor tethering him to the earth.

It was an unpleasant snapshot of what his life would have been had Elena not stepped in and taken him in as a baby and it only sharpened his conviction that he had to succeed in this deal. He had to show Elena that she had been right to give him the chance in life that she had. Once more he needed to prove his worth.

'It must still be incredibly hard for you,' Rae said, watching his expression and reading everything in it, and abruptly he felt too exposed, too vulnerable, and he worked to shove those feelings back into the locker they'd sprung free from. Because he'd already told Rae too much, allowed her to glimpse too much of him. 'It's not been long since she passed. If you ever want to talk about it, about her, I'm here.'

As she made the offer, she watched him from those deep blue eyes and a potent emotional need stretched within him. A yearning to accept and tell her everything and deepen that tentative bond weaving itself around them like a magic spell. To reach out and grasp the comfort and connection she could provide and once more feel moored to something, someone. To feel that he had a place to call home, someone to call his family.

But they were dangerous yearnings that had to be cauterised. Ripped out, root and stem. Because chasing those feelings only led to heartache. That was a mistake he'd made already—he would not be foolish enough to do so again.

'I'm fine,' he said curtly, resuming a faster stride. If he said that enough times, believed it to be true, at some point it would start to be true, wouldn't it?

'Well, if at any time you change your mind, the invitation stands,' she said lightly, and was it his imagination or did Rae look a little deflated at his brusque dismissal? And why did that bother him?

They reached the palazzo. Lights burned in a few of the windows invitingly. Rae looked at the door and then back at him, a small smile on her lips.

'Thank you for walking me back. I hope you can fix whatever the problem with the deal is. Goodnight, Domenico.'

'Not so fast.' Domenico seized her hand as she tried to turn away. With a single step he moved closer to her, close enough to cause her breath to audibly hitch and her eyes to explode with colour. 'A man in love doesn't say goodbye to his wife for the night without a kiss.'

She swallowed and looked back at him nervously. 'There's nobody around, Domenico.'

There wasn't. But he didn't care. 'I'm not taking any chances,' he breathed, lowering his head towards hers.

It *had* been about making sure any lurking photographers or eavesdroppers had a show of them engaging physically. He was adamant about that, even though his lips had been tingling with anticipation of the moment their mouths would meet, but when the petal softness of her lips moulded to his and she responded with that gentle mewl of pleasing capitulation, his nerve-endings caught fire and the kiss became about something else entirely.

About coaxing more of that passion from her until she had no way of hiding from it. And revelling that in that heady, fevered pounding of his blood that she, and only she, could inspire.

Because this was something that Domenico understood and was happy to accept. Desire made complete sense to him, far more than those bewildering emotional yearnings that had surfaced with such strength only moments ago.

Banding his arms around her and drawing her tight against the wall of his body, he sought to squash those feelings into nothing, to incinerate them with the force of the heat blooming between their bodies, and with the passion of their kiss intensifying he could feel the confusion in his mind lessening, shrinking, until all made perfect sense again.

This was all that he wanted from Rae. Not her compassion, or comfort or understanding. He wanted the taste of her on his tongue, the feel of her arching and gasping beneath his hands. That was all permissible, the maximum he would allow himself to crave, to take.

And Rae was offering plenty of herself. Her hunger had overtaken her, her mouth moving against his with as much abandon and eagerness as his own, her chest grazing wantonly against his. She couldn't hide it. She sought everything that he did and as the flames of her desire licked against his own, they swirled into an even brighter, hotter, more treacherous fire.

Pressing her backwards into the wall of the palazzo, Domenico slowed the rhythm of their mouths, taking the kiss deeper as he slid his hands inside her jacket and around her body. Moving slowly, purposefully, they traced her waist, down over her hips and then around, exploring the toned peachiness of her bottom, the feel of her as exciting, as arousing, as dangerous as the taste.

He'd ignored and avoided this for too long, he realised with a burst of clarity. Too many nights he had lain awake, his sleep disturbed by his unfulfilled craving for the sweet connection with her body, and that had probably helped to cause the confusion in his mind, his body becoming overwrought with need and misinterpreting the signals being transmitted. But that was easily fixed.

'I think we may need to revisit the terms of our arrangement, *tesoro*,' he murmured against her lips, finding the power to momentarily break the kiss.

Rae's cheeks were flushed and she blinked a few times, a frantic look spreading across her face. 'What do you mean?'

'Us, Rae. *This*. We clearly both still want each other. We may as well take advantage of this time and enjoy ourselves.'

'No.' Rae shook her head, lightly at first but then with even more vehemence. 'No. Domenico. You're wrong. I don't…'

'Don't lie and tell me you don't feel it too, Rae,' he said huskily. 'I know your body, your kisses.' Even in that second, he could feel the hum of her blood, moving fast and hungry through her aroused body. 'I know you still desire me as I do you.'

An expression of panic shot through her eyes and she tried to put as much space as possible between their heated bodies. 'We're not having this conversation. We have an arrangement and the terms of it are fine. And now you should leave. You need to leave. There is a problem at your office and people waiting for you,' she reminded him sternly.

Domenico couldn't argue with that. The clock was ticking on his crisis. But if he didn't have to leave…

Using his finger, he angled her flushed and frantic face up to his. 'You may be able to run from this right now, but we will be talking about it again,' he promised, feeling the quiver skittering beneath her skin. 'What we have is too special to waste, Rae. So think about it…think about all the ways you know I can satisfy you. I know I will be.'

# CHAPTER SEVEN

TAKING A BREAK from the sketch she had been focused on for the last forty minutes, Rae savoured a sip of her cool water and, leaning back in her seat in her favourite corner of the palazzo's courtyard, tilted her face towards the sun, enjoying the heat that kissed her cheeks. However, she had no sooner closed her eyes than Domenico loomed at the forefront of her mind, just as he had numerous times since the previous night, forcing her to snap her eyes open again to keep her thoughts from wandering too far off the beaten track.

The previous evening had been...unexpected. After the kissing incident at the gala she'd been nervous about being so close to him again and had expected that the night would be edged with the tautest kind of tension, an expectation that had seemed on point when Domenico had been quiet, almost distracted, when they'd set out from the palazzo. But then he'd amazed her by asking about Imogen and from then the conversation had unfolded with incredible ease. Admittedly, he had stayed true to form and redirected the conversation when he hadn't wanted to say any more on the topic of his birth mother, but it had surprised her how candid he'd been about his shattering experience as a young boy.

Having waited so long for answers about his past, any answers, it had been hard for Rae to not be greedy, to refrain from pushing for more information, but she knew how difficult it was to draw him out to speak about his memories and she hadn't wanted to scare him into shutting down entirely and so had let him change the subject, content that he had opened up at all.

Rae couldn't remember a time when he had been as open with her. As they'd walked home, he had even offered up details about The Ricci Group, but it was what he had revealed about himself and the past, which he carried like an albatross around his neck, that had stuck with Rae the most.

Learning that his mother had actually lived in Venice had astonished her, because she'd never been given any indication that there had been any contact between him and any of his immediate family members. Hearing that she had completely ignored his presence had rendered Rae speechless, heartbroken for Domenico that he'd been forced to face such callousness and livid with his mother at the same time. It was a good thing that she no longer lived in Venice because, now that she was privy to that information, Rae was certain she would not be able to cross paths with the woman and hold her tongue. Of course there could be circumstances that Rae wasn't aware of, but, regardless, Domenico had deserved better than that. He'd deserved some acknowledgement of his existence at the very least.

She'd watched the pain flicker like a dying ember in his eyes as he'd recounted their encounter and the added admission that he'd crumpled the memory into something small and buried it away had torn at her heart whilst also explaining so much. If that was how he had handled any painful experiences over the years, he probably had a whole mental trunk stuffed with negative emotion that he never wanted to open again, hence why he'd resisted her every attempt to get him to open up. Perhaps he was afraid that once he let one thing loose, the rest would come tumbling out in an overwhelming tumult that would bury him.

It definitely cast his actions in a new light. In the past, Rae had taken his rebuffs personally, the rejection weighing heavy on her heart because she'd felt that he didn't want to share his secrets with *her*, that he didn't trust her enough to open himself up. But maybe his reluctance had always been more about his own fears. Maybe if she'd pressed harder, as she had last night, rather than backing off when he'd made it clear he wanted her to, they could have achieved that small breakthrough long ago.

Not that it mattered any more. The past was gone and their future extended only as far as the next six months, and, even if that deadline hadn't existed, Domenico still didn't possess the emotional openness that Rae wanted in the man she chose to share her life with. She wanted a partner whom she could talk to about anything, a partner who would be supportive and encouraging, who would meet her where she needed to be met, a partner who could share his feelings as easily as he shared his bed. That wasn't Domenico.

Their conversation last night had been good, and had reassured Rae that once she changed she could encourage change in those around her, but it certainly didn't mean that *he* had changed in any meaningful or permanent way.

Since a future together was not a viable option—and it absolutely wasn't—where was the sense in rekindling a sexual relationship that would only blur the lines of their arrangement? She knew with every rational breath she drew that it wasn't a good idea, yet…yet last night's kiss was playing over and over in her mind, like a song on repeat.

That hot, searing, purposeful claim his mouth had staked on hers had been like something from a dream. Tender but powerful. The full force of him had been contained in that encounter, making her feel as if the earth was shifting beneath her feet and she couldn't help but wonder if there was another man on the planet who could be capable of making her feel so much. Not that she was thinking about a relationship with anyone else. Her sole focus, for the moment, was on herself and creating the life she desired. When she'd left Venice, Rae had assumed that in time Domenico's mark on her would fade, but the more time she spent with him, the more confused she became because she realised how deeply her physical senses still belonged to him. Yearned for him.

It had taken far too long for her body to settle last night. *'Think about all the ways you know I can satisfy you,'* Domenico had said, and Rae had certainly done that. She hadn't been able to stop herself from thinking about it.

Those aching throbs low in her pelvis had continued to strike long after she'd showered and climbed into bed and, as sternly as she had ordered herself not to, Rae had yearned for Domenico to return and satisfy her in a way she hadn't ached for anything in a long time, even though she knew that was a path she must absolutely not go down.

But the tentative emotional connection that had threaded itself between them like a silken web had only made that physical yearning all the deeper. Because the time they'd spent together had highlighted how he could be a perfect partner. He'd listened so attentively to her concern over her sister and his response had been thoughtful and wise. After their conversation, the worry she'd been nursing had been somewhat allayed, his reassurance calming her.

She wasn't used to having someone to share her concerns with and it had dawned on Rae that perhaps that she hadn't always been the best at sharing her feelings or concerns either. Since losing her parents, she'd had to carry her worries alone. Her sisters had had more than enough to contend with in their grief and she'd never wanted to burden them more. Over time it had become her habit to keep things inside and to steady her fears herself.

So maybe if she had been better at sharing…matters would have unfolded differently. But there was no point in dwelling on that either. She couldn't alter the past and Rae knew that she had made the right choice in leaving. That was proven by the giant strides she'd made in building her own bridal collection in only a few short months. If she'd still been in Venice, still been a full-time Ricci wife, there was no way she would have had the time to outline her whole collection, source materials and design and produce nearly a dozen bridal and bridesmaids' gowns.

Her mother had made the choice to abandon her dreams of running her own catering company once she'd become a corporate wife. She had given over all of herself to the demands of Rae's father's busy professional life, and they'd enjoyed an enormously happy relationship, but where had it left her mother? She'd been devastated by her husband's untimely death and, without anything other than him to anchor her, had been swept away by a tide of grief and loneliness. Rae refused to follow her there. Refused to leave herself in a position for that to happen.

Whatever she was feeling for Domenico, she was unequivocal about that.

'I should have known I'd find you out here. It always was one of your favourite spots.'

Rae started, taken unawares by the low thrum of Domenico's voice, almost as if the strength of her thoughts had conjured him home, and as her eyes jumped to where the voice had come from, her heart leapt high in her chest.

'That's one thing that didn't change, I guess.' She smiled, her eyes rapidly sweeping over him, hungry to take all of him in all at once. In looking so close, Rae noticed how tired he looked. His dark eyes were ringed by even darker shadows, strain leeching out of his gaze. 'Were you working all night?' she asked with an undisguised note of concern.

She knew he hadn't returned by the time she'd fallen asleep in the early hours because her ears had been straining to detect any sign of his return. Upon waking that morning, she'd wondered if he had returned with the dawn to change his clothes before returning directly to the office, but, judging by this suit, which, although immaculate, was the same one he'd been wearing last night, Rae guessed that hadn't been the case.

'Pretty much.' Domenico rubbed at his jaw, dusted with uncharacteristic dark stubble, and Rae had the sudden urge to be close enough to feel it scrape against her skin.

'Did you manage to save the deal?'

'No. But I did get their CEO to agree to meet me in person to work out the problem.'

'Is he coming to Venice?'

'No. I'm going to him.' An alert sounded on his phone and he glanced at it, his fast fingers tapping out a reply in seconds. 'He has a luxury estate in Majorca and he's invited us to stay for the weekend.'

Having been ruminating on his absence over the weekend with a somewhat strange feeling spreading across her chest, it took Rae a second to process what he'd said.

'Us?' she repeated with an arch of her brow. Her pulse picked up as he began a slow stroll towards her.

'*Sì*. He invited me to bring my wife along and it would look odd if I showed up alone, don't you think?'

Her head started to spin as he drew closer, the scent of him hitting her first, and then the closeness of his body—forbidden, but welcome, oh, so welcome. Rae couldn't help but admire the outline of his chest through his shirt, the definition of hard muscle, coaxing her to touch. With superhuman effort, she dragged her eyes up to his, just in time to see the small smile playing around his lips.

'It also means we will have the opportunity to continue our conversation from last night.'

Rae knew that was her moment to tell him that conversation was closed. That it had started and ended last night. But, for some reason, her mouth wouldn't move and the words wouldn't form. And then his eyes were tracing over her face, pausing when they moved across her lips, and his fingertip was weaving a feather-light trail across her cheek and Rae was so close to forgetting her own name as she *ached* for him to lower his mouth to hers, to have the taste of him on her tongue.

'But later,' he drawled, leaving her lips still aching for that kiss as he dropped his hand. 'Right now, we both need to pack. We're wheels up in ninety minutes.'

Rae stilled, her heated thoughts draining away with the cold bite of reality.

*Ninety minutes.* She couldn't do that.

So far, there had been no conflict between Domenico and her growing business. She worked on her designs during the day when she was left to her own devices and Domenico had—unsurprisingly—never asked what she did with the hours she was alone. But she was going to have to tell him now.

He was already walking away and Rae took a deep, fortifying breath. 'I'm sorry. I can't leave in ninety minutes.'

He stopped, turning his head over his shoulder and a look of incredulity swept across his smooth features. 'You can't?'

'No.' Rae warred to keep her voice steady. 'I have an appointment.'

'Can't you cancel it? Rearrange it?' he asked too easily, too quickly, and it chafed at Rae in all the same ways and same places that it used to. Why did he always think her plans were of a lesser importance? That they could be *rearranged*? That she should jump whenever he clicked his fingers?

'No, I can't,' she said on a deep breath, making an effort to keep tight hold of her frustration, because an argument wasn't going to make this conversation any more palatable. 'I made a commitment and it would be rude and unprofessional of me to cancel at the last minute. Not to mention, the meeting is important to me.'

He stared down at her, his dark eyes rich with thought and his arms crossed over his broad chest as he considered her. 'What is this important meeting?' he demanded to know.

Rae mirrored his stance, folding her arms against her chest and meeting his assessing regard. 'It's a video call with a client.'

'A client?'

Rae nodded, acutely aware that this was a conversation she had shied away from having in the past—she shouldn't have, and wouldn't do so now. Her work was important to her. It was a priority, and Domenico would have to accept that, the same way she had always accepted his commitment to The Ricci Group.

'Yes. I've started designing a bridal collection.'

Picking up her sketchbook off the table, she handed it to him, holding her breath for him to accept it and start to flip through the pages. His eyes moved over each sketch, absorbing every detail with the same steady but indecipherable expression.

'Why didn't you mention this to me sooner?' he demanded, and there was something brusque about his tone that filled her with that old instinct to retreat.

But she wouldn't.

'You didn't ask, for one thing,' she pointed out sharply. 'But you're right, it was an error on my part to not tell you about it before now. Because this is very important to me and for the past number of months I've been working incredibly hard at it. My video call appointment this afternoon is with a bride who would like to talk to me about designing her wedding dress. She's seen others that I've been working on and is impressed.' Rae was aware that she was speaking to him in a way that she never had before, with unapologetic directness and clarity and as though she was his equal, and she sensed him regarding her in a new way in return. 'I understand the trip to

Majorca is important, but so is this. So I'm sure there's a way to compromise. How about if I fly out later this evening to join you?'

'No,' Domenico decreed after a moment's thought. 'I'll push the flight back so we can leave after you've finished your appointment. Arriving a few hours later won't make that much of a difference.'

'Really?' Rae struggled to hide her surprise that he was being so...*amenable*. 'That's... Thank you.'

'You're welcome.' He nodded, before turning on his heel and walking away and Rae could only stare after him, unspeakably proud of herself and unspeakably shocked by Domenico.

Rae was occupied for most of the flight to Majorca, her head bent low over her sketchbook, her hands moving fast and furiously. Domenico watched her, curiosity smouldering in his gut. She'd come off her video call with a bounce in her step and a sparkle in her eyes that he immediately knew had been absent during her final weeks in Venice with him. He hadn't noticed that change in her at the time but, having taken a hard look back, he could see now that she had lost something of herself back then, and that was making him question exactly how great a factor her desire for a career had been in her decision to leave him all those months ago.

He had planned to spend the flight working, preparing for his meeting over the weekend, but instead he spent it deep in thought, being plagued by questions to which he didn't know the answers.

And he loathed those types of questions. He had enough of them haunting him already.

As Rae sat back and surveyed her work with a critical eye, her lips curling up with a small smile of satisfaction, Domenico saw his chance to indulge that curiosity.

'May I see?' he asked, moving to a seat opposite her.

After a small hesitation she nodded, turning her sketchbook towards him. He cast his gaze over the beautiful sketches, taking in the care, the attention to every detail and her unique flair that he'd noticed immediately in the designs she'd shown him back at the palazzo. He'd undertaken a quick internet search earlier—something he'd started to do so many times since she'd walked out on him, only to always stop himself because doing so would indicate an attachment and interest that he'd refused to acknowledge in his all-consuming anger—and had quickly noticed the growing awareness around her name. After seeing her work, Domenico could see that she deserved every word of praise being sent her way.

'You're making your bride two dresses?'

'Yes. One for the ceremony, another for the reception.'

He forced himself to listen, even though all he wanted to do was grab her and not let go until she'd given him the answers he craved. That burning need he'd repressed for the past weeks and months had escaped its confines and was spreading like wildfire through him.

'This is the ceremony dress. All of it will be Alençon lace: very luxurious, very romantic. It's also very expensive, but it shapes beautifully and is durable enough to accept the beading she wants.'

'It's beautiful, Rae. All of these designs are.' He raised his eyes to hers, his stomach tightening as he saw it again, that gleam of unbridled joy and fulfilment. Given that he had once been responsible for that happy sparkle in her eyes, that he had been the man she'd wanted to share her life with, he couldn't fathom why she hadn't shared any of this with him. 'I have to admit, I'm curious how this all came about,' he said, sweeping an elegant hand over the book and the designs and keeping his voice more steady than he felt.

Rae hesitated again, her slim throat moving nervously and the tip of her tongue darting out to moisten her lips. The innocent act had desire firing to every corner of his body even as his mind was focused on getting answers.

'Do you remember Nell Parker—I was in Venice for her wedding when we first met? I'd helped redesign a dress for her...' He manged a stiff nod, coiled tight with anticipation, sensing answers were on the horizon. 'Well, she runs her own investment firm and she was so impressed by my design that at the time she said that if I ever had an interest in striking out my own, she'd be interested in investing in me. I called her a few months ago to see if the offer still stood, and it did but, coincidentally, she'd been trying to reach me too because her sister was in the middle of her own wedding crisis. Her reception gown and bridesmaids' dresses hadn't turned out how she wanted and she remembered loving Nell's party dress and so wanted my help. So I helped. And then, after her wedding, more people wanted my details. So I'm taking commissions whilst building a collection to show Nell before we make any partnership official. I figure that if I already have a client base and I can prove that there's a demand for my designs then I'll seem like an even better prospect for investment.'

'That's smart,' he commented, impressed at the savviness with which she was approaching the venture. 'Obviously, I knew you worked as a consultant at the bridal boutique back in London, but I wasn't aware that you wanted to design your own collection or have your own brand. You never told me,' he said, failing to keep the small quiver of accusation from his tone.

'I know.' Rae's eyes briefly met his and she swallowed nervously. 'The truth is I was afraid to. Afraid that a wife with career ambitions wasn't what you wanted.'

'You thought I wouldn't be supportive of you wanting a career?' he demanded, searching for clarification of what she hadn't said.

'Not really, no,' she admitted, and an uncomfortable heat swarmed into Rae's cheeks as she spoke that truth into the taut air between them.

Domenico's mouth dropped open. He was unable to understand what foundation she had to base that unflattering assumption on, because he had always been incredibly supportive of her. He'd…

But the silence in his head as he tried to root out examples to prove his point was deafening and as vehemently as he wanted to argue his case, he knew he could not.

'You liked our life the way that it was, Domenico, with me being available to you most of the time,' she expanded into the silence. 'I didn't think you would be eager to see that change, not when you had made it very clear early on in our relationship that you liked having me by your side and with you as much as possible.'

'And that's something I should apologise for?' he demanded, more agitated than he wanted to be, but the failings he'd just been awakened to were weighing heavily on his chest and her words had ripped through him like bullets. Because everything she said was right. He had wanted it to be exactly as she described. The pleasure and security of having her always by his side, always within reaching distance. Against all the odds, he had found someone he cared for enough to let into his life, some-one who'd cared for him in return, who had wanted him to be her present and her future, and he'd wanted to hold on to her as tight as he could. It had never occurred to him that'd he'd been holding on too tight. 'You were my wife, Rae. Of course I wanted us to be together all the time. That was the point of us getting married, wasn't it?'

'Yes.' Her blue eyes glittered, brimming with too many emotions for him to discern any of them. 'But I didn't realise that marrying you would mean surrendering all of myself to you. I thought it would be a partnership.'

'It was a partnership,' he insisted, even though he was starting to see that there had been some inequalities, for which he bore a heavy responsibility.

'Perhaps from where you stood. But for me... I was so busy living *your* life with you, I didn't have any time to live my own and I needed that,' she said, looking very close to tears. He had realised it already, but those shining pools of emotion in her eyes made it clear that this had been no trivial matter. He only wished he better under-stood *why*. 'I needed to have a life of my own, Domenico.'

Looking across at her, Domenico's throat felt too tight and too dry, his heart squeezing as if being tortured by invisible hands. He considered himself an astute reader of people, but he'd never seen, or even suspected, that Rae felt that way and he hated that he'd been so blind. So ignorant. That he'd failed her as a husband.

Failure had never been an option for him, not in any area of his life. Even as a young boy, long before he had learned the truth of his birth, he'd always known he was incredibly fortunate to have been taken in by Elena and he'd always felt the weight of that fortune, felt the need to prove himself, to make sure she had no reason to turn her back on him. So he'd made sure he was always as close to perfect as possible. He'd mastered every task, every skill, studying long into the night to overcome his learning difficulties and excel at academics, understanding all there was to know about the workings of The Ricci Group.

Upon marrying Rae, he had adopted the same mindset. Be the best man and husband possible. To him, that had meant formalising their relationship as soon as possible, claiming her as his wife in all the traditional ways and taking care of her financially, showering her with luxury.

Only that hadn't been enough, because it hadn't been right. That hadn't been what she wanted or needed from him and he hadn't known that because he hadn't taken the time to ask, to understand.

'I never knew you were unhappy with how things were,' he forced out, unable to keep the tremor from his voice as feelings twisted his insides.

Rae's blue eyes bored into his. 'You never asked.'

'And you never told me,' he shot back, suddenly as annoyed with her as he was with himself. Because he might have been ignorant, but she had been silent. She had known and hadn't given him a chance to fix the issue and make it better. 'If you ever needed or wanted anything, Rae, you only had to talk to me, to tell me.'

Didn't she know that he had only ever wanted to make her happy? To give her everything he possibly could. To make up for all the pain she'd had to endure in losing her parents at such a young age and selflessly and unwaveringly taking on the care of her two younger, grief-ridden sisters. Hadn't he shown how flexible he would be that afternoon, changing their flight arrangements so as not to disrupt her work engagement?

She gave a short laugh. 'Except every time I tried to talk to you about *anything*, you shut it down. You shut *me* down,' she exploded emotionally. 'In the end, there was no point in trying any more, because I knew what would happen. You'd walk away or you'd kiss me and we'd end up in bed and we'd never go back to the conversation. And if we couldn't talk about things, what kind of marriage did we really have?' She paused on a sad and heavy sigh, squeezing her eyes shut as though she had the power to blot out the painful memories. 'In the end, it was easier to leave.'

Domenico stared back at her, adrenaline pulsing through his veins and thoughts spinning through his mind, but unable to find any words in response. Unable to find his voice. Because Rae was holding up a mirror and forcing him to take a hard look at his own behaviour, and what he saw he didn't like at all. He'd made her feel shut out and disregarded and unsupported, and she had left because of that.

*Because of him.*

The realisation boomed in his mind like a roll of thunder, and on its heels frustration and guilt and self-recrimination tore through him, that conflagration of emotions so strong he felt as if they might burn him alive.

# CHAPTER EIGHT

DOMENICO BARELY SAID ten words to Rae for the rest of the journey.

He was silent as they disembarked the plane and settled into the waiting car, a silence that continued as they made the journey from the airport to the villa on the northern tip of the island. When the car rolled through the large gates marking the entrance to the private and luxurious estate and Rae turned to him to comment on that striking first impression, she received only a distracted murmur in response and their arrival at their villa—a sprawling two-storeyed, white-and-glass-walled modern construction with access to a private slice of beach—elicited little more from him.

Now she was moving through the mundane motions of unpacking her case in a desperate effort to banish the edginess jangling in her body and mind. But, no matter what she did, she still felt...*rattled.*

They'd finally had the conversation that Rae had run away to avoid having and it had been as uncomfortable and unsettling as she had feared it would be, forcing her to speak her truth and exposing all the fissures and fault lines than had run through their relationship. And now the matter of their marriage, which had felt like a closed book, felt very much alive and present again, with all those truths colouring the air and mood between them.

She hadn't thought it would be easy, but she also hadn't been truly ready for how hard it would be either. For that level of honesty and frankness between them, or the way they had put their marriage under a microscope for inspection and dissection. It was brand-new territory for them and to Rae it was terrifying, having to pry herself apart to get to the heart of the matter. She'd always considered herself quite an open person, but once again she was realising just how inept she had been, and possibly still was, at divulging her innermost thoughts and feelings. The discomfort churning in her stomach at that realisation about herself was substantial, because she'd harboured so much frustration and resentment towards Domenico for his unwillingness to let her in emotionally, but she was guilty of the same failing. She hadn't let him know her feelings, her scars and insecurities, had she? And, rather than divulge them to him, she had packed her bags and fled!

She hadn't even been as honest as she could have been—or should have been—in that conversation. Yes, she had bared more of herself than she had in the past, but she had not told him *everything.* She had not opened up about her mother and how affected she'd been by her husband's death, the deep depression she'd sunk into and never emerged from. And until Domenico knew that part of Rae's story, how could any of her actions make sense to him?

But baring that to him would require letting him in even further to her heart and soul, a prospect that was heart-stoppingly frightening. Because then he would know her in a way that no one else did. He would know all of her, even the broken places deep inside her.

Her anxiety levels spiking at the thought of generating such intimacy with him, Rae rose from the edge of the bed and wandered out onto the balcony, grateful for the gentle caress of the cool evening air against her too warm skin. Resting her arms atop the slim ledge, she closed her eyes, pleading with her body to settle down, but the peace was disturbed by the slap and splash of water.

Peering downwards towards the infinity pool, she saw Domenico slicing through the water, the span of his arms large and strong, his broad body a flash of bronzed gold in the clear water. Her body coiled, tensing with the rush of heated feeling, and Rae looked harder, wanting to see more of him, her heart kicking in her chest and, just like that, the memory of last night, of that solid body pressed up against hers, whipped through her mind, making her head whirl.

She imagined herself going down to him, quietly slipping off her clothes and joining him in the pool, letting the water carry her towards him until they were body to body, flesh against flesh. Until there was just the simplicity of desire, the complexity of all other emotions banished.

Alarmed by the force of the need pressing in on her, Rae hastily drew back into the shadows. That would be a very bad idea indeed. She wasn't there to relight anything and she didn't need to get in even deeper than she already was. What she needed was to remain detached enough to walk away intact at the end of the six months. So if Domenico was wounded and annoyed, maybe the wisest thing was to allow it, to let the issue wedge itself between them and prevent any further closeness.

*But*…her conscience prompted.

But…didn't he deserve a full explanation? Wasn't it only fair to both of them to clear the air completely, so that they could put the past to bed and move on? Based on the mess they were currently in, hiding her thoughts and feelings hadn't worked out well in the past, and as long as she concealed that piece of her past from him, wouldn't she remain uneasy, troubled by her cowardice?

She'd agreed to the arrangement to prove that she had changed and grown as a person, and perhaps learning to be more comfortable speaking her emotional truth was part of that journey too. And she could hardly continue to bemoan Domenico's emotional secrecy if she wasn't willing to be unreservedly honest herself. Even if the thought of letting him know her that deeply, that intimately, was absolutely terrifying…

But there was no time like the present, she decided and, without giving it another moment's thought, she turned and started down the steps towards the pool.

The swim had been a good idea.

Powering through length after length of the infinity pool had eased the spinning of Domenico's mind, and helped him to wrestle the demons and insecurities back into the box they'd sprung free from following all of Rae's startling revelations.

As he rested his arms against the edge and admired the glorious view as the sun disappeared into the horizon and painted the sky with streaks of sunset pink and red and wisps of fiery orange, he felt much calmer and in far better control of himself, which he needed to be. The outcome of the deal with Lorca was resting on the success of the weekend. There was too much at stake for him to be undone by his emotions.

And yet it was not the all-important deal that his mind chose to focus on as he relished those moments of the evening quiet. It was Rae. And their marriage. And all the ways he had screwed up.

He was a man capable of admitting to his mistakes. Elena had instilled in him the virtues of accountability and when he was wrong he could acknowledge it. And he'd been wrong in his marriage to Rae, neglecting her emotionally.

Every complaint she'd sent his way had been deserved. She'd had no reason to believe that he would support her aspirations because he'd never shown any interest in that part of her life. Never had he enquired about her dreams or ambitions for the future. He'd known she'd loved her job in London, but not once had he encouraged her to find a similar role in Venice.

Why hadn't he? Because he hadn't thought to. Hadn't cared to.

He mentally cursed himself again, the newfound awareness ravaging him in the same way it had on the plane. Over and over again he'd mulishly argued that there'd been nothing wrong in their marriage and that Rae had had no good reason to walk out on him, but the opposite was true. He had let her down in so many ways.

And he hadn't even realised that it was happening.

Hearing the patter of footsteps behind him, Domenico turned to look over his shoulder, his body tightening as his eyes landed on Rae walking around the edge of the pool. Her feet were bare, her hair was hanging down in loose waves and she wore the same white trousers and blue blouse that she'd travelled in. Heat raced through his veins as his eyes followed her. There was no point ordering himself to look away. He knew he wouldn't. Couldn't.

There was no way to escape his feelings for her. No matter what had happened in the past, he wanted her with a heat that could not be quelled or contained.

'Can we talk?' she asked, coming to a stop, and as he read the solemn set of her expression, his mood darkened momentarily.

'Haven't we dredged up enough of the past for one day, Rae?'

'It will only take a few seconds,' she responded, shooting him a look that signalled she would not be deterred and he knew that, fired by her new grit and determination, she would not be.

*'Bene.'* He placed his hands on the side of the pool and levered himself out, completely naked. He reached for his towel, wrapping it around his waist before turning back to Rae. But as he did so he caught her widening stare, full of wonder and hunger.

She wiped her expression clear and started to speak. 'I want to apologise to you. Since our conversation, I've not been able to stop thinking about everything that happened between us and I realised it was wrong of me to run away. It was cowardly and unfair. I should have talked to you, told you what I was feeling and thinking. However hard it seemed to be, I should have tried, at the very least. And I'm truly sorry that I didn't, and that it's taken me this long to apologise.'

'Thank you for saying that,' he said, his voice quiet

as he absorbed the depth of emotion in her expression. But she was not the only one who had been engaged in some serious self-reflection and although he could sense there was more she had to say, he couldn't allow her to go a second longer feeling that she bore sole responsibility for the demise of their relationship, so he pressed on. 'But what you said about me on the plane...you weren't wrong. I did like having you by my side all the time and I wouldn't have wanted that to change.' He lifted his shoulders, trying to loosen his thoughts. 'I wasn't trying to restrict your life, Rae, or you. I didn't even think of it in those terms. I was only thinking that I didn't want to lose that sense of complete belonging that I had with you. Because I'd never had that feeling before. I'd never felt like I belonged anywhere or to anyone.' His mouth was dry with the effort of speaking those words, those feelings dragged from the closed-off heart of him.

But Rae had every right to know why he had behaved as he had, where his ignorance and incompetence had stemmed from. He *wanted* her to understand. He wanted to understand it too and by the way she was hanging on his every word, whatever she had been on the verge of saying forgotten, he knew she was just as eager for that explanation.

'Did you feel that way because of the situation with your biological parents? Because you weren't raised by them?' she asked tentatively, as if she were tiptoeing across a minefield, expecting an explosion at any second.

Was that really what he'd done to her? Made her think she couldn't ask him anything? Fresh recrimination speared him, sharp and deep.

His nod was quick, an admission he didn't want to

make and yet knew he had to. He had to start making amends, undoing these patterns that he hadn't known existed but that had proved so destructive. Moving to one of the nearby loungers, he sat down, gesturing for Rae to do the same.

'I was only a few days old when my mother abandoned me. She left me on the doorstep of Palazzo Ricci for someone inside to find.' He heard Rae's shocked intake of breath, but carried on. If he looked at her, if he paused, he wasn't sure he'd be able to continue. The only way for him to get through this was to keep going. 'She hadn't given me a name. She hadn't registered my birth. On my birth certificate it just says *genitori ignoti*—parents unknown. I've never been able to find out who my father is and my mother, whose identity I obviously did know, didn't want any connection with me.' His heart burned uncomfortably with that admission. 'I had no sense of belonging to anything, or anyone, not the way most children do. I had Elena and all the love she gave, and for that I was lucky, but she wasn't my mother and I always knew that. I was always aware that I didn't belong to her in that traditional sense and other children were very good at making me even more aware of that.'

And the steps that could have been taken to instil him with that security and sense of belonging had never been actioned. He didn't hold that against Elena. She had given him so much, but that additional piece of paper would have offered him a lot too. Instead, he'd grown up always feeling unsure—denied and rejected by one family and always fearful that it could happen again because there was nothing official, nothing legal, binding him to Elena.

The first time he'd felt completely secure in a relationship, he realised with a jolt, was when he'd met Rae.

She'd been so open and giving of herself, so whole-hearted in her acceptance of him. He'd liked how everything she felt was written across her face, how her arms opened to him whenever he walked in the room, the eagerness of her kisses. He'd felt so certain of her love for him.

Maybe that had been the driving force behind his whirlwind proposal, why he'd felt that loosening of feeling around her, why he'd been so impatient to marry her. Because all along he'd been clinging to that rarefied feeling, having finally found what he'd spent his whole life hungering for. Love and acceptance and belonging. And he'd wanted it legal and binding before it could be taken away.

Rae was quiet, absorbing the overwhelming weight of all that he had shared as the darkness swelled around them, cocooning them in its mystical embrace. When she did open her mouth to speak, he was expecting sympathy and platitudes but she just smiled sadly across at him.

'If only we could have found our way to talking like this four months ago,' she said wistfully.

'Would it have made a difference?' Domenico asked, unsure why he was asking the question or if he really wanted to hear the answer.

Her lips twisted as she thought about it. 'I'm not sure. Maybe. Knowing that we had the ability to talk things through would have helped me to feel a lot surer about our relationship. That we could have the big conversations. And I like talking to you, hearing the sound of your voice.'

'You didn't like the way we spent the time not talking?'

Her burst of laughter was quick and genuine. 'I had no problem with that. The physical side of our marriage was never in question. That was always incredible.' Her eyes glowed with the memory and her accompanying smile was almost shy. 'It's probably why I let myself be distracted by it so many times, because it was so good. Because it was in those moments, lying in your arms, that I felt closest to you. But it shouldn't have been a substitute. It wasn't. It's not.'

He heaved out a sigh, feeling the reproach. 'I'm not a man who wears his heart on his sleeve, Rae. I never pretended to be.'

'I know you didn't. But I thought that after we were married you would lower those walls a little, show me some more of yourself. That you would talk to me about…anything. Everything. The way my parents did.' She hugged her arms around herself, smiling nostalgically as she thought of them the way she always did, with that mix of happiness and hurt. 'I used to listen to them after we'd gone to bed. In the summer I'd leave my windows open and they'd be outside and I'd drift off to sleep to the sound of their voices. My mum talking about whatever naughty thing Maggie had done that day, my dad telling her about work. I stupidly assumed all marriages would be like that, and that ours would be too,' she confessed and Domenico felt a twist in his chest that he'd ruined such a simple dream. 'I didn't understand the amount of work that went into getting to that place. And when you wouldn't talk to me, I saw it as a rejection of me. That you didn't want to talk about things with me, you didn't trust me. Sometimes I even wondered why you'd married me, if you'd started to regret it. That's why it hurt so much.'

'Rae, no,' he assured her hurriedly before the words had even finished leaving her lips. 'That couldn't be further from the truth. I trusted you more than I ever trusted anyone. Before you, I had never considered letting anyone so deeply into my life. I just...'

The sledgehammer of guilt cut off his words as he was confronted by another of his inadequacies. The way he had shut her out.

He'd never liked talking about the past because experience had taught him that no good ever came from raking up dirt and searching for skeletons. And delving into emotional waters held no appeal, because his were cold and dark and he was scared of drowning in them. He'd blocked those conversations to protect himself, but he'd failed to consider how that would be perceived by Rae. How it would make her feel. How it would affect the rest of their relationship. But he could see it now. See the walls he'd erected, the doors he'd sealed shut, locking her out completely. Domenico knew how that felt, and that he had forced her to feel that same dismissal was agonising.

'I never meant to shut you out, Rae. To shut down our conversations. But I'm not sure that I knew how to let you in either,' he admitted with a wince of discomfort at such profound self-analysis. 'When things have been hard, I think the way I've always dealt with them is by compressing my emotions into something small and manageable and locking them away. They're not easy doors to unlock.'

'I think I've started to understand that about you already. And the things you've told me… I understand why you would want to bury them, keep them out of sight and out of mind.' She reached out to him, just a small touch of her fingertips against his bare knee, but he felt it everywhere. 'You didn't deserve to be left like that, to be burdened with those feelings. And you didn't deserve to be left the way I left you either. If I caused you more pain, I'm sorry. But I appreciate everything you've chosen to tell me. I know it's not easy for you.'

It wasn't. It was like drawing poison from a wound, but if opening up earned him that soft and loving glow in her eyes, he'd gladly tell her more. Anything, to keep her staring at him in that way.

'I'm sorry I let you down so badly.'

'We let each other down,' she said on a sigh and, as she looked across at him, Domenico could see a tempest of emotion swirling in her eyes, threatening at any second to spill over. She chewed at the inside of her lip, deliberating about something uneasily, hovering on the edge of speaking, of telling him something he sensed was important to her, but then she just shook her head, shaking the storm from her gaze. 'We both made mistakes.'

He wanted to tell her that his mistakes were tearing him up inside, that he'd never wanted to lose her, that if he could go back and do it all over again, he would in a heartbeat. But he didn't know how to get those words out, didn't know if it would be wise to speak them aloud, so he just reached out, curling a hand around her cheek and drawing her face close to his. He touched his mouth to hers softly, a kiss that said everything he wanted to say but couldn't. And then he let her go.

'Did you think there was someone watching us?'

'No,' he said with a smile. 'That kiss was just because I wanted to kiss you.'

Her breathing changed, quickened. Heat exploded in her eyes, as if he'd set something loose inside of her, and then she asked, 'And if I wanted to kiss you back?'

'I wouldn't stop you.'

He wouldn't be able to stop himself. He couldn't tear his eyes from her, his hands were burning to feel her skin beneath his.

Rae moved at the same time he did, reaching out with as much urgency, so when their bodies collided and their lips fused together it was like a giant starburst, with pops of colour exploding behind his eyes and rivers of feeling pouring down his body as if a dam had broken.

# CHAPTER NINE

THE PASSIONATE CLAIM Domenico was staking on her lips was making Rae's body tremble and her blood sing with delight. She'd missed this, she thought in the tiny part of her brain that was still capable of thought. Missed the masterly glide of his firm lips against hers, missed the bite of his hands into her tender flesh, and the feel of every line and contour of him pressed up against her. The moment was almost too overwhelming, every sensation fighting for dominance, and she couldn't decide which to revel in first…the imprint of his firm, masculine form or the deepening probe of his tongue, turning the desire already racing through her into a swirling inferno that was so potent it had the power to burn her from the inside out.

The last place that she had expected to end the evening was in Domenico's arms. And yet it felt right. More than right. *Necessary.* As he'd opened up, Rae had felt herself falling deeper and deeper into him, her body yearning to reach out to his and envelop him in her comfort. He had been so open and honest and she had wanted to be too, but when the moment for her transparency had arrived, Rae hadn't been able to do it. She had kept her secret locked inside, and chosen not to feel bad about doing so because, whatever it was between her and Domenico, it wasn't substantial enough to require the baring of her heart and soul. Their relationship was neither real nor lasting.

But then he abandoned the glorious assault on her mouth and feasted instead on the super-sensitive skin of her neck. As he scraped his teeth against the very spot he had just finished sucking on, Rae curled her fingers into his hair and snatched in a desperate lungful of cool air, needing that burst of oxygen because she was already drowning.

*In him.*

The feeling that speared through her seemed to be a direct and defiant repudiation to her stance that their relationship wasn't real. With every swipe of his mouth and every sweep of his hands Domenico was taking her over, inch by inch, kiss by kiss, and as he did, the parts of Rae's world that had felt out of sync for reasons she hadn't been able to identify began to shift back into perfect alignment.

She had spent so much time and energy trying to convince herself that she was okay without Domenico, that there was nothing missing from her life, but in that moment, with the imprint of his hands all over her and the sharp masculine scent of him surrounding her, she had no choice but to abandon that lie. Because she was coming alive again under the possessive pressure of his fingers against her skin and the hungry scrape of his mouth, and something very *real* was unfurling within her, something with a potent, glittering, unfamiliar power.

His hands moved to her blouse, reaching for the buttons, and as he did, he drew back enough so that he could stare at her. The look in his eyes was so hungry and yet so tender that Rae suddenly found it harder and harder to breathe. Because whilst they had done this many, *many* times before, for some reason it felt like the first time again. There was the remembered thrill and anticipation, but every other feeling spinning up inside her was so new, so profound and piercing, that she felt, just for a second, so wildly overwhelmed.

She could feel the thuds of her heart in her throat and they only grew heavier as he pushed the fabric of her blouse open and gazed down at her, hunger darkening the glow of his already dark eyes, turning them molten.

'You're so beautiful, Rae,' he breathed, and the sentiment seemed infused with so much loving and open feeling that tears hit the backs of her eyes.

'So are you.' Lifting her hand, she stroked it across his face, caressing the strong jawline and noble chin, brushing a finger across his full lips. It was a face she knew well, a face she would be able to find even in the dark, but now, as she looked into his eyes, for the first time she felt as if she could see into him, into his heart and soul, and she trembled. Because she had always wanted all of him, and now he was giving her exactly that. Only there was danger in that as much as delight, because the connection crackling between them was now all the more poignant and powerful. And it would be so much harder to extract herself from.

However, there was no question in her mind about turning back now. She wanted this connection with him. She was craving it. She needed it.

'Take me inside, Domenico,' she commanded in a whisper, knowing they needed privacy for all that she wanted to unfold.

He inhaled a sharp breath as though he hadn't dared imagine he'd hear those words, and then raised himself to his feet and carried her with him, her legs curled around his waist, her body cradled in his strong arms.

They didn't look away from each other, but neither of them spoke. To do so would have interrupted the feeling flowing unspoken between them and, finding his way inside, Domenico set her down on the nearest flat surface.

The light in the room was dim, casting a dusky glow, and his mouth wasted no time in reuniting with hers, his lips asking questions that she answered with her own. Their kisses deepened, the effect sinking deep within her, making the honeyed river of lust flow with more speed, more ease. When he drew back to take a breath his chest moved up and down in an uneven rhythm and Rae's heart and pulse were just as restless, running riot beneath her skin.

Reaching out, she traced her hands over his chest, revelling in the smoothness of his skin, the unbelievable strength of his body. His was the first, and only, male body she had ever touched and tasted and explored, and although she had no comparison, she knew there could be none. Domenico had no equal, and definitely no superior. It was not a theory she'd been in any rush to test, but she knew without question that no one would be capable of making her feel all that he did. Lightning, after all, did not strike twice.

She kissed a pathway across his chest, her lips settling over his heart—the heart that had been twisted and torn by the cruel actions of others. He thought he'd never belonged, but he belonged with her. In that room, in that moment, there was nowhere else on earth he should be and Rae was determined to use all the power of her body to show him that.

Hands gliding downwards across the corded muscle of his stomach, she loosened the tie on the towel and let it fall away, a breath quivering from her mouth as his arousal jutted into the space between them. Her chest hitched, her mouth running dry as her blood ran even hotter. She'd forgotten what a magnificent sight he was and the jagged, restless feeling cut through her again, and she could almost *feel* how good it would be to have him inside her once more, filling her, completing her. Owning her.

Watching her breathless reaction, impatience fired in Domenico's eyes and he reached for her clothes, sliding the blouse from her body, pulling the trousers down her legs and tossing them over his shoulder, and then he moved into the space between her thighs, running his sultry gaze down her body.

Lowering his head, he pressed a line of kisses down her throat and along the cup of the bra. Her reaction was instant, her flesh swelling against his mouth, her nipples tightening.

'Rae…' he groaned against her skin. 'I want to run my mouth all over you, but I don't think I can wait to be inside of you.'

'So don't wait,' she urged, pressing herself into him, as desperate as he was to complete their joining.

With a single move, he positioned himself at her entrance and then, eyes locked with hers, he pressed powerfully into her, her body accepting every inch of the sweet penetration. He filled her completely and Rae gasped, not just with the joy of his possession but because of how different it felt. Rawer, deeper, more…just *more*. Her breaths crashed from her mouth, the moment feeling too big, too powerful, too moving. But then all she could feel was the exquisite familiarity of Domenico stroking inside her, tenderly but firmly propelling her towards her orgasm with the powerful thrusts of his body.

She clung to him, tilting her mouth up to receive his kiss, and he obliged, touching his lips to her mouth, her earlobe, her jaw, her neck, his breath like fire. His hands clasped her butt, urgency in his fingertips and his rhythm changed, the drive of his body becoming more powerful and possessive, and he surged deeper inside her, deeper than ever before, pressing her back to accommodate that exploration. With every move of his body, he obliterated her defences, taking more of her for himself, and the connection was electrifying. The beginning and the end. Everything that Rae had ever needed and felt like she would ever need.

He held on to her tighter, hitching her leg higher up his waist, and that was when she started to feel it, the onset of that wild, unstoppable ecstasy spiralling up through her body, consuming all of her with flagrant ease, and Rae clung even more pleadingly to Domenico's shoulders, her mouth biting into his skin.

His own release was beckoning. Rae could feel him resisting, wanting them to hit their explosion point together, and seconds later they did exactly that. She broke apart with a cry of unadulterated delight a moment before he gave his own shout of release and, although they had made love a thousand times, the eruption was like nothing Rae had ever felt before and for an infinitesimal, heartshaking moment she pulsed with the sense that nothing would ever be the same again.

# CHAPTER TEN

RAE WAS HAVING the most exquisite dream.

Domenico's skilful mouth was marauding across her neck, swiping and sucking and nibbling. Where his lips and tongue touched, her skin tingled and sparks of glittering, explosive pleasure ignited by the blissful contact streaked along her veins, arrowing to the very centre of her body, where the most intense feeling was building. She arched her neck, offering him even better access, and speared her fingers into the thickness of his hair, purring at the back of her throat as his teeth and tongue played on the same spot, making her nerve-endings shiver and dance.

Then he began to tease more of her body. His hand slid languidly up her ribcage and curled around her breast. His fingers were warm and tender and her senses stirred even quicker at the intimate contact, straining beneath the touch, seeking more of it. His fingers brushed across her nipple, the large pad of his thumb circling the ultra-sensitised and begging point before flicking across it once, twice…a torturous three times. Her body arched and a gasp of wanton pleasure escaped from her parted lips, every inch of her now feeling alight and alive.

Enraptured by the caresses, Rae desperately wanted

more of them, more of that heady, obliterating feeling he conjured within her. But, feeling the tug of consciousness, she squeezed her eyelids tighter together, wanting to stay in the dream as long as possible, not wanting to wake yet again to a darkened room and a cold, lonely bed. But the golden light of day was already infiltrating her gaze and as the pleasure of Domenico's touch built towards a crescendo her eyes flew open…and she realised it wasn't a dream at all.

Domenico's hands were skating across her body, his lips making her shiver as they trailed down her neck and towards her collarbone. Feeling was fizzing in every inch of her, her blood was humming and her body purring at his touch. Fragments of the previous night returned to her in bright flashes and Rae realised that it had happened. She hadn't only imagined it.

*'Buongiorno bellissima,'* Domenico murmured against her lips. They were the words he'd greeted her with every morning of their life together and Rae smiled, having never expected to hear them uttered again.

'I thought I was dreaming,' she whispered as he held her close. 'And I didn't want to wake up.'

He kissed her again, slow and long and deep, only pulling back to stare at her. 'Did you spend many nights dreaming of me?'

'Yes,' she admitted, tracing the sensual contours of his mouth with her finger.

During the day she'd never permitted him entry into her thoughts. During the dark secrecy of the night, however, when her consciousness had relaxed, she'd had no control over what—*who*—came into her thoughts. And Domenico always had. In the moment when it was said a person's deepest desires were revealed, he had always been hers. Rae had reassured herself that those mental slips were acceptable, normal even, and that with time her subconscious would relinquish its yearning for him.

But here she was, months later, in bed with him, and the feelings were as strong and imposing as ever. The shift of his hair-roughened leg against hers stirred detonations of delicious tingly feeling along her skin. The bulk of his body, so close, made her want him pressed up even closer. It made her question if her feelings for him would ever fade, but that was a worry she had no desire to dwell on in that moment. Worrying could wait until later. Much later.

'And what exactly was I doing in these dreams of yours?' His smile grew wider and wicked as a blush burned in her cheeks. 'Something like this, perhaps?'

Drawing her against him, Domenico buried his long fingers in the tumble of her hair and nuzzled his face in her neck and made her every wish come true as his naked body pressed up against hers. Rae moaned as his hard length moved against her, instantly suffusing her with the need to feel him inside her, filling her, claiming her. She pulled his head down, opening her mouth to his, excitement brewing within her as his tongue thrust between her lips in a dance that she knew only too well. A dance they had moved to several times during the night and, just like all those times before, the intimate slide of his body against hers transported her to heaven.

Later, she was resting, sated and sleepy, with her head on his chest and his fingers stroking up and down her back in a lazy rhythm when Domenico's phone rang and he reached for it with his free hand. Rae already knew it would be Nico, Domenico's assistant, with his morning round-up.

'Morning, Nico,' Domenico greeted him, and Rae smiled as she felt the rumble of his rich voice vibrate deep within his chest. She'd missed that burr of his voice, missed the early part of the morning resting in his arms. It was in those moments that she had always felt most content, when her heart had felt beautifully full and her worries about their marriage had been diminished by the warmth and closeness of Domenico's presence.

However, her peacefulness was disturbed when Domenico vaulted into a sitting position, his body suddenly rigid.

Rae sat up too, clutching the sheet to her chest, concerned by the quick-fire chatter she could hear at the other end of the phone.

'Did you...? No... No, it's fine.' Domenico dashed a hand through his too long hair, shoving it back off his forehead and, based on that agitated motion and the stiffening line of his spine, Rae guessed that whatever it was that was going on wasn't fine at all, a theory confirmed by the heavy sigh he emitted upon disconnecting the call, followed by the torrent of blistering Italian.

Vaulting off the bed, he snatched at the first piece of clothing he found, anger infusing his every jerky movement as he pulled on the drawstring pants and started to pace backwards and forwards, hands planted on his lean hips. His Italian blood had always run red-hot with passion, and in recent days she'd seen him overwhelmed with feeling about his past, but Rae had never seen his temper heightened to such a degree and she was immediately wondering what had set it off.

'Domenico, what is it? What's happened?'

But he was already pacing away from her, brushing the flowing white curtain aside with an impatient hand and striding out onto the terrace, and Rae could only stare after him, bewildered.

Because in the space of thirty seconds the whole mood of the morning had changed and Rae was utterly unsure of what to do next. Not so long ago, she would have thought twice about rushing after him and querying his upset because she was so wary of being rebuffed. But things had changed a lot since then. She had changed, and the landscape between her and Domenico was shifting as well. The ground they had broken last night had been significant, and it was those moves that they had made to know each other better, *to trust each other*, which gave her the confidence to follow the instinct firing from her gut and follow him outside, where she hoped he would tell her what was bothering him.

The morning view was stunning, but all Domenico could focus on was the pressure pounding at his temples. The call from his assistant had delivered the worst news possible and with so much importance and emotion attached to the deal, and so much of his own self-worth tied to its success, his frustration was lodged so deeply he could barely think straight.

Hearing the gentle sound of footsteps on the tiles behind him, he emitted a sigh. 'Go away, Rae. Please.' The last thing he wanted was her witnessing the state he was in. He understood that he needed to be more open, and he was proud of the barriers he had been able to bring down last night, no matter how painful doing so had been, but this cut to the deepest and darkest of his fears and he was in no way ready to cast them into the light.

'Sorry. I can't do that,' she replied, her voice soft as she came to stand beside him. For a woman who bordered on being petite, only five-foot-four in height, he felt her presence immediately. 'Do you want to tell me what's going on?'

*Absolutely not.*

Turning his dark head towards her, Domenico was ready to repeat his earlier command, but as his gaze caught on her and he was hit between the eyes with the bright shine of her blue eyes and her long hair gleaming with the kiss of sunlight, he felt the knots around him loosen and, to his shock, heard himself start to speak.

'Lorca cancelled our sit-down today. His assistant phoned Nico ten minutes ago. She said that Lorca no longer has the time to meet me and that he sends his sincerest apologies, but still hopes to see us at his party this evening.'

Rae's brow furrowed slightly. 'You don't believe that?'

'He invited me out here to have that meeting, so why cancel it at the last minute?' he grated out, his voice frayed with aggravation. 'Unless he's stalling the deal on purpose.'

'Why would he do that?'

Domenico pushed his long fingers through his dark hair. 'I don't know. But every instinct I have is telling me that's what is going on.'

Rae's eyes rested on him, gentle and kind, and yet they seemed to burn him with their scrutiny. 'This deal with Lorca obviously means a lot to you. A lot more than any other deal I've ever seen you make,' she observed, and he could see her thoughts ticking over, trying so desperately to understand. She really was incredible. He'd neglected her emotionally, failed as a husband, but she was still standing at his side, trying to help him. Heal him. If it hadn't been clear to him before that moment, it suddenly was—he hadn't appreciated her enough in the past. Her strength, her kindness, her loyalty. He'd been so focused on his feelings, on the void in him that she had obliterated, he'd overlooked entirely the sensational woman he had been lucky enough to find. 'Is it because this was Raphael and Elena's dream? You're trying so hard to make it happen·for them?'

'Yes, that's exactly it.'

'No, it's not,' Rae challenged gently, after a long moment studying him. 'You should know by now that I know when you're shutting me out, Domenico, when you're holding something back. What is it?'

In front of him, his hands curled into tight fists as he felt the truth bludgeoning its way to the surface from the depths where he had tried to bury it. 'I do want to do this for Elena and Raphael. I just also want it for myself too. To prove that I am deserving of the life that Elena gave me, that she was right to keep me, right to give me the position of her son and heir.'

He stared straight ahead, his eyes fixed on the neutrality of the sky, but all he could feel was the poison of that feeling slinking through his blood, making his heart race with the fear that it was the truth.

'Why would you need to prove that?' Rae asked on an aghast breath. 'Elena left you in charge of the company because she trusted you so much, and she gave you everything that she did because she wanted to, because she loved you.'

A muscle worked tightly in his jaw as the insecurity continued to needle at him 'She never made it official though, did she? She never formally adopted me, so there must have been some doubt in the back of her mind if I was worthy of all that she had to give.'

'Domenico, there could be a dozen reasons why Elena didn't adopt you, and none of them have anything to do with you not being good enough,' Rae argued. 'You are deserving. You are worthy. Your mother choosing to abandon you as a baby is a lot more damning of her character than of yours. You were just a baby, you did nothing wrong...'

'But maybe...'

'No maybe. You did nothing wrong. Look at me.'

Abandoning his forward stare, he turned his head.

Rae moved a step closer and pressed her hands to his chest, her eyes blazing with vehemence. 'You did nothing wrong,' she repeated, slower than the first time. 'There was nothing wrong with you. And even though your mother couldn't or didn't love you, Elena did and you have nothing to prove to her. But if you feel that you need to make this deal happen to believe that, then let's make this deal happen. Forget about the cancelled meeting. You'll speak with Lorca tonight at the party instead,' she said simply. 'All you need is a few minutes to talk through whatever is bothering him and sort it out. I've seen you close deals in less than fifteen minutes, Domenico, so you can do this, no problem. Don't let him cancelling today be a big thing. Take the opportunity to have a day to yourself, to take it easy. Enjoy the island.'

'I'm not someone who spends a lot of time taking it easy,' he muttered. 'You should know that.'

'I do know that. Which is all the more reason to do so now. You've been under a lot of pressure. You need some time to rest and destress so you're relaxed for tonight.'

She might be right, Domenico conceded with his eyes on the water below. He had been pushing himself harder than usual, partly because of this deal but also to avoid dwelling on his grief for Elena and his feelings about Rae's return. Maybe a day of leisurely pursuits would restore him to his usual pragmatic self and release some of the strain from his coiled body.

'What do you have in mind for this day of relaxation, then?' he asked her.

'Look at this beautiful island we're on. I'm sure we can come up with a few ideas.'

She smiled up at him, her eyes as blue as the waves rolling into the cove below them, and the tempo of his body shifted once more. Heat crackled in his veins and the simmering frustration melted away, only to be replaced with an entirely more pleasurable burn. They had shared a night of mind-blowing sex but, as satisfying as that reunion had been, Domenico was hungering to do it all over again.

He moved closer, succumbing to temptation and taking possession of her body with his hands. 'I actually already have a few ideas,' he shared as his fingers loosened the tie at her waist and delved beneath the silky fabric of her bright robe to meet the warm, soft skin beneath. 'And none of them involve you wearing clothes.'

'Wow.' Domenico went hard all over as Rae emerged from the bedroom. He'd thought she couldn't look any better than she had that afternoon when they'd spent a few hours on their private beach and she'd played in the waves in an emerald-green strapless bikini. However, in a pale gold sequinned wrap dress, with straps that curled up towards her neck and a neckline that dipped low enough to hint at the full swell of her breasts, she was a sight capable of setting him on fire. 'You look incredible.'

His eyes devoured every inch of her as his gaze swept from her head to her toes and then back again, a single look not enough. The dress showed off her figure to perfection—her toned legs, the sexy curve of her hips and slim waist, the globes of her breasts. The reaction of his body was immediate, his thoughts leaping ahead to when he could skim his hands across her body and peel away the material, sampling each piece of tender flesh as it was revealed.

'Is this one of your own designs?'

Colour bloomed in her cheeks. 'It is. An idea I was experimenting with that didn't quite work out, but I loved it anyway. How could you tell?'

'I can see your touches in it.' Lightly, he touched the fabric between his fingers and then her, tilting her chin up to accept the graze of his lips. The taste of her as addictive as ever, he had to force himself to take a step back before he started to act on his fantasies and they never made it to the party.

'The car is outside. We should go. It would be poor form for us to be late.'

The journey to Lorca's home was brief, a short drive along the winding coastal roads with amazing views all around, the rocky outcrops on one side and the drop to the glittering blue waters on the other. It pleased Domenico that he was able to enjoy the view, his relaxed mood a drastic change from the tension that had been simmering in his blood for days, and perhaps weeks.

As much as he wished he could credit himself with the turnaround of his mood, it was Rae who had calmed him, reminding him of who he was and what he was capable of. It was her advice to take the day for himself, which had been the right thing to do, and it was her company that had made the day as fun and relaxing as it had been. It didn't surprise him but it did trouble him because, as his guard dropped, he was revealing more and more of himself to her. His deepest and darkest depths.

Rae had proved to be the balm he'd so desperately needed so he couldn't say he regretted sharing as much as he had, but he detested that she had witnessed him at his most vulnerable, when he was lost in the darkest reaches of his mind. It was not a place that he liked to go to, so to have shown it to her was…unsettling at the very least. He had never wanted anyone to know how damaged he was inside…but now she did. And if that valve on his emotions loosened any further then she would know almost everything, all the ugliness that he wanted to hide.

If their relationship had been secure, perhaps he could live with that, but right now she was his wife in name only. At least that was all she was supposed to be, but he knew a part of him had *wanted* to open up to her that morning. To let her in that way, to feel more of what he had felt the previous night. The peace that had come from sharing.

*'You need her, Domenico,'* Elena had insisted after Rae's departure, as she had tried to encourage him to go after her. *'You need her.'*

He'd denied it being true then, because how weak would a man have to be to admit to needing the woman who had turned her back on him? So, as happy as he was to have her by his side as they exited the car and walked up to Lorca's house, he was determined to resist it again now.

Because she *was* his wife in name only and in a matter of a few months she would leave Venice and him. So there would be no more sharing of his emotional secrets. The only intimacy they would share from now on would be physical.

# CHAPTER ELEVEN

RAE GAZED OUT at the mesmerising view, staring at the spot where the indigo sky merged into the glimmering expanse of the sea. The stars were out in their thousands, the night air was balmy and so far it had been a wonderful night, following on from an idyllic day with Domenico.

Their seafood lunch at a waterside restaurant and afternoon enjoying their private beach had reminded her of the better days of their relationship, where everything had been so easy and carefree.

There had been a void in Rae's life before she'd met Domenico. In spite of her sisters and friends, her job at the bridal boutique and her dreams for the future, Rae had always felt as if something was missing. Something vital. She'd assumed it was the void left by losing her parents and the suddenness with which they'd dwindled from a family of five to one of three. But then she'd met Domenico and that void had evaporated. Suddenly everything had been dazzlingly, beautifully bright. She'd felt happy again, excited and hopeful in a way she hadn't in the longest time.

The same kind of happiness that was streaming through her as she stood there, enjoying the evening. Had she been that happy after leaving him and returning to London? she caught herself wondering. Rae hadn't allowed herself to consider it at the time, but she knew it would be a lie to say she had been completely content. She'd made herself busy and forced herself to focus on the future, but without Domenico that chasm in her heart had opened again and she was only aware of it now because, after their day together, she felt it a little less keenly.

But she wasn't sure what she was supposed to do with that. As happy as Domenico made her, it could only be temporary. Because their time together had an expiration date, and once they hit it Rae would be returning to London.

*Even though you have already thoroughly blurred the lines of your arrangement with him? And with each hour that passes you're only growing closer.*

Rae's heart raced with her thoughts. They had grown closer, closer than they had ever been in the past. Even their intimacy had been different, charged by their emotional vulnerability with each other. There was only one matter that Rae had not yet shared with him—the truth about her mother's death—and that was proving to be a weighty burden. The guilt she felt about her continuing silence was immense because Domenico wasn't holding anything back. He had been raw and unguarded, answering any question she asked, and Rae felt that she was truly starting to know him, the real, beautiful, complicated man that he was.

At the outset she'd thought that getting answers to her questions about his past would help her reach a place of closure, where she could walk away and leave him behind, but with all that she was learning her heart was opening up to him more than ever. And that was alarming to realise because one day their situation was going to end, and the more engaged her feelings became, the more likely it was that her heart would break into a hundred pieces when it did. Maybe that was another reason why she was clinging to her secret, because once Domenico knew everything she would belong to him in a way that was undeniable. And she wasn't ready for whatever it was between them to be anything more than what she had agreed to—a fake and temporary marriage.

'You're looking very thoughtful, Signora Ricci.' Drawn from her pensive moment, Rae looked up to see their host, Santiago Lorca, approaching at a leisurely pace. She had met him briefly when they had arrived and her first impressions had been of a warm and welcoming man.

'I'm just admiring these stunning views of yours,' she lied. 'The plot of land you have here is incredible.'

'It has been in my family for generations,' he shared, leaning back against the curved stone wall, 'apart from a brief period. When my father was a young man they went through some hard times and lost almost everything. It was a mission of mine to get it all back for him.'

'Was he here to see you achieve it?' Rae asked, hoping for a positive answer.

'He was, but he sadly didn't live long enough to enjoy it.'

'I'm sorry. That must have been very hard.'

'It was, but the upside is that I always feel connected to him here.' He paused, watching her with friendly eyes. 'Have you enjoyed the evening?'

'Very much.' In the ensuing silence, Rae's heart thudded. It wasn't her place to do so, and she had never before dreamt of meddling in Domenico's business dealings, but as she spied the opening to raise the topic of the deal, Rae knew she couldn't let it pass by. Although Domenico had recovered well from his troubled state that morning, and had so far charmed everyone they'd met that evening with his confident smile and magnetic charisma, she knew he was still singularly focused on getting the deal done. If there was any chance she could help, her heart was compelling her to try because the last thing she wanted was to see him mired in more despair. And now that she knew why it mattered so much to him…

'Although I noticed that you and Domenico haven't had the chance to talk yet.'

'Unfortunately not. Hosting duties are keeping me rather busy.'

'Is that the only reason?' Rae pressed, trembling within at her boldness. 'Domenico is worried that you're getting cold feet about the deal.'

'I do have some concerns,' Lorca admitted, much to her surprise. 'Given that history I just briefly touched upon, my company matters a great deal to me, and to the rest of my family. I am very conservative about if and who I enter into partnerships with. And your husband is in the middle of an emotional transition.'

'Because of the death of his aunt?' Rae queried.

'Precisely. And also, if you'll forgive me for being so blunt, the rumours about your marriage.' With those words a hole slowly started to gnaw open in Rae's stomach. 'I'm not asking for an explanation; your personal life is private. But whilst Domenico always had a reputation for being pragmatic and unemotional, I worry that in having to contend with such issues he could become emotional. And emotional people are known to exercise poor judgement and take risks—the type of risks I don't want my company involved in.'

For a moment Rae couldn't speak. Her fingers had grown clammy around her champagne glass as all she could feel was the weight of the future of the deal on her shoulders. If she said the wrong thing in response, it could blow it to pieces. But if she could explain to him who Domenico really was, could she perhaps save it? And save Domenico from drowning in that fear of not being enough?

'Domenico would never be reckless with The Ricci Group,' she responded, the need to defend him rising in her like a tide. 'No matter what's going on in his personal life. The company belonged to the aunt who raised him, and before that her husband, and it means everything to him. Now that they are both gone, Domenico treasures it even more. He wants to make this deal for them, to fulfil a dream that they had. That's how you can be sure you can trust him, because he's just a son trying to make his parents' dream come true. And after what you just told me, surely you can understand that.'

'I can.' He nodded slowly before smiling across at her, the action sincere. 'I'm glad to have met you, Rae. You have given me an insight into your husband I didn't previously have.' He fixed his gaze on something over her shoulder. 'Your wife is delightful, Ricci.'

Turning her head over her shoulder, Rae's heart flipped to see Domenico sauntering closer. In his pale-coloured suit and open-necked shirt and with his hair gleaming in the starlit darkness, he looked almost too good to be true.

'She is. I'm a lucky man,' he agreed, sliding an arm that felt almost proprietorial around her waist.

'I don't want to interrupt your evening, but do you

have a moment to talk now?' Lorca asked him. 'I have a fifteen-year-old Scotch I've been meaning to try. We can slip away for ten minutes.'

Domenico glanced down at her. 'Rae?'

'Go. I can amuse myself for a while.'

He pressed a feather-soft kiss to her lips before walking off in step with Lorca and Rae watched him go, happy that she had been able to help, yet uneasy about that happiness. Because there was only one reason that she would be so delighted for him, Rae recognised with a lump swelling in her throat. Because she still cared for him. More than she really should.

More than was safe, or smart.

More than she had actually realised when she'd agreed to their crazy charade.

But Domenico had always been quicksand. She only had to recall how quickly she had fallen for him in the first place. It had taken only hours and days for him to steal her heart. It really shouldn't surprise her he would be a stubborn presence to erase from it.

Feeling her pulse start to skip out of control with her escalating worry, Rae attempted to comfort herself with the thought that it was different this time around, that *she* was incredibly different…but it was then that it hit her—because of those changes in her, *everything* between her and Domenico had become different too.

What they had now was not the same relationship that she had run away from. It was an entirely different beast, and that meant she was in entirely unchartered waters.

Later that evening, once they had returned to the villa, Rae was watching herself remove the delicate drop earrings from her ears in the mirror when she spied Domenico approaching in the reflection. Coming up behind her, one hand gently brushed her hair to one side before he touched his lips to the sensitive skin of her neck and feeling erupted along her skin.

'Thank you,' he breathed, his breath moving across her skin like a tender flame. 'For whatever it was that you said to Lorca.'

'All I told him was the type of man that you are,' Rae said, her eyes drawn into meeting his in the reflection by a magnetic pull that she couldn't fight.

'Whatever you said, it had some effect. We're meeting tomorrow morning to finalise the details of the contract.'

Happiness streamed through her again, making the nervous pit in her stomach grow wider, but she smiled back at him. 'Good. I'm happy for you.'

This time when he pressed a kiss to her neck it was open-mouthed. His tongue flickered against her hammering pulse point and it was like a flame being held to a tinderbox. Feeling exploded inside her. She wanted to hold back, to find some much-needed space to claw back the intensity of her growing feelings, but her body craved the opposite and as his lips trailed a line of fire up her neck and to her ear, and his hands started their slide of possession around her waist, Rae's eyes fluttered closed, her battle already lost. Her heart thundered with desire a hundred times stronger than anything she had ever felt before and all she wanted was to drown in the glorious feeling he conjured within her. To float in that space for ever.

She turned in his arms and he slowly lowered his head, but impatience ruled her actions and she rose to her tiptoes, speedily closing the distance between them and relishing that sinuous slide of his mouth against hers, need mounting frantically in her already, a hot and needy throb pounding in her molten core.

But whispers of warning continued to swirl around her mind. Where exactly would this leave her? She'd returned, amongst other reasons, to find some closure, but now all she was doing was drawing back closer and closer to Domenico, stripping back layer upon layer in a quest to know and understand him so much better. And the bond between them was intensifying, deepening... Would the boundaries of their original arrangement still be able to keep her safe? Or was she deluding herself, hiding behind an agreement that was no more stable than a sandcastle?

'Domenico, is this madness? Us doing this?' she breathed against his mouth, too needy for him to pull away but unable to quieten those thoughts.

'Possibly,' he murmured with a laugh. 'But it might be madness not to do it too.' His body seemed to move closer to hers. 'As long as both of us are clear on the terms and time limits, I see no danger in it.'

Rae was almost certain she could see bright flashing red danger signs up ahead but they were dim, and with the sinuous slide of his hands taking her to a place where there were no negative feelings they seemed too far away to be of any immediate importance.

'Do you want me to stop?' he asked in between swipes of his lips over her neck.

The answer was on her lips before he'd even finished asking his question, rising from the very heart of her. 'No.'

Even if it was madness, it was a madness Rae wanted. Badly. With every breath she took and with every beat of her heart. Surely if she focused only on this physical need for him and not on the possibility of anything more significant, there could be no harm done.

Reaching for his mouth again, Rae responded to the gentle probe of his tongue by parting her lips and granting him entry to her mouth. She slid her tongue against his, hungry and needy and wanting. His fingers searched for the fastening on her dress and, with a deft move, undid it, gently sliding the straps from her shoulders and down her arms until the dress slid down her body to the floor in a whisper of sound. Domenico tore his mouth from hers to survey her body and his eyes burned with a shimmering flare as he took in the ivory lace lingerie set.

'I'm so glad I didn't know you were wearing this. I would never have been able to keep my hands off you,' he purred, his fingers lightly, teasingly skimming up and down her sides, touching and then melting away.

'You not being able to keep your hands off me was the whole point of wearing it,' she replied, laughing, the sound turning to a gasp as he turned her, his strong arms banding across her middle as they faced their reflection in the mirror.

Her need for him was painted all over her face. She had never been able to control it. There had been times when she could hide it, but now…now her longing was too big, too overpowering for her to exert any power over it. From the moment Domenico had started to dismantle his walls, she'd been lost to her desire completely. Lost to him. And she was sure he could see it too.

Eyes alight with a wicked kind of fever, he lowered his head to her neck and dusted her skin with light kisses, simultaneously moving his hand lower and lower, sliding it under the thin line of her panties in search of that bundle of exquisitely sensitive nerves. Pushing back her slick folds, he stroked a fingertip against her pulsing flesh, drawing a shattered sigh from her lips.

Domenico had always known how and where to touch her to make her scream, always seemed to sense how she wanted to be taken by him, but lately his touch had assumed a new power. It was reaching all the way into her, erasing her fears and caressing her soul. It was a way of being known that made her feel completely safe and yet utterly terrified.

Because surely that was everything one could hope to find in a lover. There was no greater connection, but if that was true... Rae was in even more dangerous territory than she'd thought. If only the danger wasn't so addictive.

Her mind sent into a spin by his touch, her head arched against his strong shoulder as his probing and caressing fingers sent the most magical, fluttering feelings unfurling within her like a flower responding to sunlight. The rhythm of sensations built, soaring higher and faster, and her knees were slackening with each beautifully torturous second that passed.

'Domenico,' she gasped out brokenly, unable to withstand it any longer.

'Open your eyes,' he commanded throatily. 'I want to watch you when you come.'

Rae hesitated. No doubt he had watched her orgasm before, but that was *then*. To do so now, to be looking into his eyes as she came apart under his caress would be extremely intimate and exposing, the forging of another deep connection, another unbreakable link between them, and that was the last thing she needed.

'Open your eyes for me, Rae. Let me see you.'

The silky murmur of his words worked their magic and, her resistance overridden, she slowly opened her eyes. The first thing she saw was his face, his eyes dark and commanding and fixed on her, ready to devour. She wanted to look away, look anywhere but at him, but she couldn't. With the devastating flash of his smile, Domenico sent his finger in a long, powerful stroke and that was all it took for Rae to implode, stars exploding behind her eyes and her whimpers filling the air around them.

His strong arms cradled her as she floated back down to earth but hunger was still yawning inside her and so she turned, fastening her hands behind his head, pulling his mouth down and kissing him greedily, hoping to distract them both from her ecstasy, which had filled her expression.

*Sex. It was just sex.*

But the reminder felt hollow and so Rae poured everything into the kiss in a bid to prove it. Evidently as eager as her, Domenico's fingers moved to his shirt, ready to tear open the buttons, but Rae stilled his hand with her own.

'No. Let me,' she said, thrilled at the thought of undressing him, of revealing him inch by inch, the way she most loved.

Moving his hands away, Domenico stood still, breathing deeply as Rae smoothed her hands up to his broad shoulders and pushed his jacket off them, letting it fall to the floor. His eyes followed her every move and revelling in the freedom to touch him and determined to do to him what he had done to her, to make him feel as unsteady and exposed as she did, Rae traced the outline of his chest, her fingertips playing over the solid muscles and the hard ridges of his ribs. Each time she felt him quiver she danced her fingers a little further, her vulnerability diminishing with the thrill of feminine power rolling over her.

Had she ever before realised what she could do to him? Unsurprisingly, Domenico had always been the dominant sexual partner, but Rae was suddenly understanding that she had underestimated her power over him, that he was in thrall to her as well, and that was intoxicating...

She undid the buttons of his shirt slowly, one at a time, feeling his impatience mount, his breathing change as her fingers grazed purposefully against his bare skin. Once all the buttons were open, she pushed the sides of the shirt apart and pressed her lips to his warm chest. Domenico tensed and hissed beneath her, his fingers flexing at his sides as she teased a path of tender kisses down his hard stomach, following that line of faint dark hair that disappeared into the waistline of his trousers.

'Rae...' he groaned warningly as she neared the band of material, a plea she ignored to kiss her way back up his chest and manoeuvre him free from his shirt.

She tasted his lips again, her fingers continuing to roam across the planes of his upper body until his breathing was ragged and his chest was heaving and only then did she move her hands lower, unbuckling his belt, sliding down his fly and guiding his trousers and boxers down his strong legs.

And then he was completely naked, proud and erect before her eyes, and Rae had no desire to draw her gaze away. Only looking wasn't enough, not by a long shot.

She needed to touch, to feel him, and so she pressed her hand against him, her body jolting in response.

When she felt him grow harder under her touch, that feeling only arrowed even deeper and her need to conquer even more of him, *all of him*, intensified to a treacherous degree...

Domenico couldn't comprehend what was happening. Sex with Rae had always been incredible, the best of his life, but he'd never been overpowered by those feelings. But as her hand slid slowly down his length, her touch consumed him in a way it never had before, blasting open everything inside him.

Lust. Desire. They were not powerful enough to describe the feelings unfolding within him and all he knew, all he could think, was that if he didn't have Rae back in his arms, back against his body in the next five seconds, he would implode.

Before she could act out her next intention, which Domenico read easily in her small, catlike smile, he clasped his hands to her hips and dragged her against him, seizing her mouth with a bruising, fevered kiss. Kicking his feet free from his trousers, he walked back towards the bed, bringing Rae tumbling down on top of him and keeping possession of her mouth, desperate to ease the hunger clamouring inside him, a hunger that seemed to emanate from the very centre of his being.

With her hair, her scent, her body, Rae surrounded him and that was driving him even crazier. No matter where he touched, how much sweetness he drank from her lips, it was not enough. Nothing satisfied the rushing of his blood, nothing helped him find that control that had always been present in his previous sexual encounters. That piece of himself that had always remained separate and safe. Untouched.

Reaching behind her, he tried to unclip her bra, but the force of his need was making his fingers unsteady and Rae had to help. Together they tossed the scrap of pretty lace aside and Domenico didn't waste a moment, taking the weight of her breasts in his hands and lifting his mouth to lick one and then the other, a worship that he had engaged in many times before, but that now felt different, more profound, for it was not just her body that he was adoring, but all of her. Her heart, her bravery, her passion. Everything that she had been generous enough to share with him and that he'd failed to appreciate for far too long, and her actions that night had clarified it even further.

His ministrations continuing with unrelenting expertise and feeding off the satisfied moans breaking from her lips, Domenico kissed the soft skin and sucked at her rosy nipples until she was writhing. That sight of her astride him, above him, her head thrown back as she fought the torrent of pleasure pulled a smile from his lips, but still, it wasn't enough.

An even darker, more urgent surge of passion rose up in him and with a single smooth movement Domenico flipped her over, trapping her under him. As he parted her legs, elation spread throughout his body and it startled him, as if he had finally found the place he recognised as home.

Rae was wet, as aroused as him, and for the first time in memory he couldn't hold back. He didn't even try, his actions being driven by a greater force than he could understand. He drove into her with ease, welcomed by her velvet heat, and the moment they joined together he felt something within him unlock. As if she was the solution to a problem, the answer to a code. It felt like the moment he had been waiting for, only he hadn't known it.

Trying to dislodge that unsettling poignancy, to focus only on the physical, Domenico started to move, following the urges of his body. Slowly he withdrew from her and then powered back inside, and Rae moved with those motions, her body sinuous and sensual against him. As they moved, she watched him from her bright eyes and, as their gazes held, he found he was incapable of looking away. Some new power within her gaze compelled him to maintain that connection and with each thrust of his body, with every answering lift of her hips, their eyes held, emotion starting to swirl amongst that physical tempest. Such fierce, unexpected emotion that Domenico could feel the last of his walls crumbling beneath its power, exposing everything that he was and leaving all of him open to her, to see and to take.

Beneath him, Rae began to shudder and as the tremors rocking her body spread into his own, the ripples of pleasure grew more powerful. They rushed through him so fast that they rammed into one another, becoming a single shattering orgasm that, for the first time in Domenico's life, left no single piece of him untouched.

# CHAPTER TWELVE

'You are going to tell me where we're going at some point, aren't you?' Rae asked, smiling at the mysteriousness with which Domenico was acting.

'In about ninety seconds, you'll see for yourself,' he answered, at the exact moment the car drew to a stop.

They had arrived at a marina and as she saw what sat at the end of the dock Rae's eyes widened. The yacht had to be at least fifty feet long, with four levels, dazzlingly bright white against the darkening sky. The captain welcomed them as they stepped aboard, explaining that they would circle the island before introducing them to the crew, who were waiting to greet them with warm smiles and a glass of champagne.

As they pulled away from the dock, Domenico led Rae up to the third deck, where a tapas feast and a candlelit table for two was awaiting them.

'I cannot believe you did this,' Rae exclaimed when they were sitting at the table.

'We had to do something special to celebrate. With your help I finalised a very significant deal for The Ricci Group today.' Domenico had met with Lorca for two hours that morning and had returned to the villa with a completed contract and a triumphant mood. 'I only wish that Elena and Raphael could have been here to see it.'

'I have no doubt that wherever they are, Elena and Raphael are incredibly proud of you tonight.'

'I hope so,' he said quietly, a shadow scudding across his expression.

Rae's heart rippled with pain for him. 'You're still doubting yourself. Even after everything you've achieved today. You still think you have something to prove?'

'I've always felt it,' he admitted with a press of resignation to his lips. 'And I always think maybe if I do this, or if I achieve that...but nothing is ever enough to erase the feeling. I'm starting to think nothing will ever be the cure.'

'The cure is you, Domenico,' Rae beseeched him. 'You have to believe that you're deserving, that you're good enough. You have to ignore that voice that tells you you're lacking or worthless and trust that Elena would never have left you in charge of The Ricci Group if she didn't believe in you and trust you enormously. You have to believe that she loved you with all of her heart. I believe that. I saw it every time she looked at you. And you have to know that it doesn't matter one bit whether there is a piece of paper stuffed in some drawer that names you as her child or not.'

His eyebrows lifted, the slant of his gaze disbelieving, and Rae wished so badly that she could make him see that his belonging and his worth were defined by so much more than a completed form.

'In every way that mattered, you were Elena's son. It was you who had dinner with her every Sunday night. It was you who went with her to her hospital appointments. It was you she turned to when she had a problem. That is what belonging to someone is about. All those small, everyday acts. Not a name on your birth certificate.'

Domenico nodded, but he could hide little from her now and the flatness of his mouth, the way he cast his eyes down was telling.

'But it's not just that, is it?' Rae deduced. 'It's not just your mother leaving you and Elena not adopting you… What else happened?'

Pain flashed like lightning across his handsome face and for a split second Raw saw, to her shock, all the anguish that he had so adeptly hidden from her. It was right there on the surface.

'She had other children. My mother,' he stated in a voice breaking with repressed emotion. 'The reason she moved to Venice was because she got married and they had children—children whose births she announced and celebrated, welcoming them into her life in the way she never did with me. She even had stepchildren whom she happily accepted. And I was…ignored. I watched it all… watched her embrace those babies, giving them the security of family and parents…and each time I saw them I found myself asking what was so wrong with me that she hadn't kept me. Why I was so *unlovable*.' He shook his head, emitting a low curse in his native tongue. 'I shouldn't have cared. I had Elena and she gave me her name and a home, protection I would never have had. It shouldn't have hurt me.'

'Of course it should,' Rae reassured him, reaching out to curl her hand around his tense arm. 'You're not wrong to be hurt by what happened. Anyone would be.'

Rae's throat was clogged as she considered what those circumstances must have been like for him. Watching from afar, having that same bruise pressed upon day after day.

'You'd think I would have been smart enough to learn

my lesson that day she looked right through me. But I wasn't. I went to her home once, to try and meet her.'

'What happened?' Rae asked, almost holding her breath, because she knew by the hollow look in his eyes that it had left a wound.

'I'm sure you can imagine.'

She nodded. 'I can. But I think you should tell me anyway. Then maybe you can let it go.'

'I knocked on the door and an older couple answered. Her parents, my grandparents. It was the first time I'd ever seen them, but I think they knew who I was straight away. I introduced myself and a look of such contempt came across both of their faces. I told them I wanted to see my mother, they refused. They said that she wasn't my mother, she'd never wanted anything to do with me, that I was a no one even if Elena had given me her name, that I was nothing more than a mutt and none of them wanted anything to do with me. Then they hissed at me to leave and never come back and slammed the door in my face.'

Rae gave a small shake of her head. To have experienced such cruelty from people who should have loved and cared for him. Accepted him.

'But that wasn't even the worst part. As I backed away, I looked up at the house and I saw her—my mother— watching from a window. She'd known I was there, she'd heard everything they said and did nothing. She just looked right through me again before turning away. Like I really was nothing.' He smiled grimly. 'I've never told anyone about that before.'

Was that when it had started, Rae wondered, his habit of burying everything so deep so he could pretend it had never happened? How it all must have festered in him, turning every thought dark and black and hopeless, making him worry that every relationship would end with a closed door.

'There's no way to defend their actions, but I will say this about your mother. She was only very young when she had you and if her parents weren't supportive that can't have been easy. So maybe when she left you on Elena's doorstep she knew she was leaving you with someone who would take care of you, the way she wanted you to be taken care of. Maybe that was an act of loving you.' She saw by his expression that he was listening. And hearing. 'And maybe…maybe when she saw you again, well…'

'Maybe she had consigned that to a box that she didn't want to open either,' Domenico offered, finishing her thought with a sigh of willing acceptance.

'It's possible. But what I know for sure is that you're definitely not nothing, Domenico. Your grandparents could not have been more wrong. You are remarkable. You're intelligent and generous and kind. You stepped up when Elena needed you to. You've spent every day of your adult life honouring her and Raphael's legacy. Those are the actions of a wonderful man.'

'It's a little strange to hear the wife who walked out on me declaring how wonderful I am,' he remarked with dry humour, but beneath that veneer Rae heard his vulnerability. Saw the hurt etching itself into his profile in spite of his efforts to hold it back.

And for the first time she could see the far-reaching consequences of her hasty, panicked decision to quit their marriage. Could see how that had cut to the deepest part of him, inflicting a fresh wound over an old one. And she knew she could no longer withhold what truly lay at the core of that decision—the truth of her mother's passing. She had let it remain a secret for too long and now that Domenico had taken the monumental step of laying his soul completely bare, Rae had to find the courage to do the same. She had to be as brave and vulnerable as he had been. Only then would he be able to understand everything about her, and she knew what a beautiful gift that was.

'I didn't leave because I thought you weren't good enough, Domenico,' she admitted, steeling herself with a quick breath because she knew there was no going back from this moment. 'I left because of me. Because I was scared.'

'Scared?' Domenico repeated, unmoving as he absorbed her confession and tried frantically to make sense of it. 'Of what?'

Colour drained from her face and she scraped her teeth over her lower lip before answering. 'Of being like my mother.'

Domenico frowned in confusion, her words making no sense to him. 'Explain,' he commanded softly.

Rae took a small breath, glancing off to the side, but she wasn't quick enough to hide the sheen of tears coating her gaze. 'When my dad died, my mum gave up completely. Her whole life had revolved around him and with him gone, she didn't know who she was. Each day that passed, she slid deeper and deeper into a depression that none of us could pull her from.'

'I thought she died of pneumonia,' he queried gently, trying to assemble all these new facts into the right order.

Rae gave a small, stiff nod, meeting his eyes for only the tiniest moment. 'She did. She got caught outside in a storm without a coat and she caught a chill that went straight to her chest and eventually ended up in hospital. But she shouldn't have been outside…' She hesitated, her face filling with a ravaged kind of hurt. 'She wasn't strong enough. Since he'd passed, she'd barely eaten, barely slept, her weight had fallen off her. She was like a ghost.'

He moved closer to her, wanting to offer comfort with his presence, the promise that she was safe from that past. Seeing the tremble of her body, he slid his jacket from his shoulders and draped it over hers.

'It was awful, Domenico. Watching her waste away like that. Day after day. And I couldn't do anything. Then, when I realised how empty my life was in Venice, all I could think was that the same thing was going to happen to me, and I couldn't let that happen. I couldn't follow her down that path. I couldn't put Maggie and Imogen through that agony all over again, put myself through it.'

He pulled her into his arms, holding her securely against his chest as her body shook with emotion. Not only did he ache for the losses she had suffered, but for the agony she'd had to go through in watching it happen and being powerless to stop it. He hated that he hadn't known any of it before that moment, that in attempting to keep his pain buried, he had forced Rae to be silent about her own. He knew nothing good came from keeping pain boxed inside, but at no point in time had he considered it was his role as her husband to try and tease her secrets from their hiding place, but it was not a new realisation that as a husband he had focused on all the wrong things.

On formalising her position as his wife, on gifting her jewellery and various other material luxuries, but not what she'd really needed and wanted. A husband attentive enough to know that she was battling a deep-rooted fear, a husband who would listen and share in return, a husband who'd make the effort to find out her needs and prioritise them.

But he was no longer in the dark. He understood why she had left him, why she'd felt it had been her only choice. Why she had seen no future in their marriage.

That she trusted him enough now to tell him her truth, after everything, was incredible. Obviously, he had somehow managed to start to restore the connection that had once bound them together, but it burned him to know that he could have known these truths sooner and spared them both a mountain of pain. If only he hadn't been so intent on keeping their relationship as a primarily physical connection, so scared of going any deeper than the surface and dislodging everything that lay below. If only he had done as Elena had urged and gone after Rae the second she'd left. He should have chased her to London and banged on her door and refused to leave until she'd talked to him. *Dios*, it was what a large part of him had strained to do…but he had been too proud. And too scared.

It had been too easy to believe that she'd deserted him because she didn't love him any more. Too easy to recall his past and heed those dark thoughts that rose in his mind like smoke. He'd let himself be convinced that all that awaited him in London was a closed door and another rejection and had idiotically fallen prey to that fear of not being enough.

Although Rae had been the one to leave him, Domenico knew now that he was the reason she had stayed lost to him.

Rae was right. He needed to silence those ugly thoughts in his head. He needed to look to what he knew to be true in his heart and trust that or he would be doomed to stumble again and again over that same fear.

Holding on to her tighter, he pressed his lips to the top of her head and inhaled that light scent she always carried with her. She drew back slightly, pressing her hands to his chest and looking up at him.

'Surely you see now it was as much to do with me as it was you. And if I'd had any idea what that my leaving would make you think...' She stopped, raising a hand to his face, her warm palm curling around his cheek, a touch of such tenderness he found himself leaning into it. 'You're not unlovable, Domenico,' she whispered, gazing up at him with all the magic of the stars above reflected in her eyes. 'You're the furthest thing from it.'

Her words held such feeling and such quiet power that the only thing he could do in that moment was claim her lips and it was a kiss that contained everything. Joy and passion. Forgiveness. But also regret and sorrow. Because, as badly as they wished it, neither of them could change what had happened, their many mistakes and the many hurts.

And yet, amongst all that wreckage, there was a single revelation sticking in Domenico's mind. That Rae had never stopped loving him, and that made his heart feel fuller than it had in a very long time.

# CHAPTER THIRTEEN

Rae woke from her sleep with a jolt.

Her skin was sticky and her heart was pounding, a hot and sickly panic gushing through her veins.

She lay still, waiting for the threat of the dream to fade, for her breathing to settle into a more even rhythm, for the drumbeat of fear to grow smaller and shallower and her limbs to unfreeze and, as soon as she was able, she swept the covers aside, casting a quick look at Domenico to make sure he was still sound asleep before carefully extracting herself from his tight embrace and slipping out of the bed and the room.

Her feet carried her down the stairs and outside and she welcomed the waft of the cool, clean morning air against her face and the feel of the sand beneath her feet as she walked across their private horseshoe-shaped beach towards the gentle froth of the waves.

Taking a seat on the sand, Rae hugged her knees up to her chest and rested her chin on her knees, her mind going back to her dream. No, not a dream—her nightmare. It was one she'd had before, but not for many months. In it she was lost, casting around for any kind of anchor or raft to grab on to, but there was nothing apart from an encroaching blackness, looming thick and dark and growing even greater the nearer it came. It was blinding and choking, strangling her screams and sucking her in, no matter how hard she fought it, until it was all around her, taking her over, pulling her down. That was when she'd woken up. That was always when she woke up.

Pulling her knees in tighter, Rae sucked in a shuddery breath of air, feeling the surge of a fresh wave of panic. Because she knew exactly what that dream was about, and she knew exactly why she'd had it again.

Because of last night. Those emotional, transforming few hours in which everything had changed.

*Everything.*

She and Domenico had become closer than they had ever been before. Closer than she had ever felt to another person, than she'd ever believed it was possible to be.

There was nothing standing between them now. Nothing pushing them apart or holding them back. There was just the two of them, their defences lowered and their hearts open. Together, they had ripped down the last few walls that had stood between them and dragged all of their secrets and fears into the light, but what had endowed those moments with even more power, even more meaning, was that they had *chosen* to do that. Individually, they had each decided to be more honest than they'd ever previously been, decided that they wanted the other person to know all of their heart as if they had been holding it in their hands. That they had both found themselves in that same place at the same time, both of them filled with courage and willing, seemed to Rae to be incredibly beautiful and incredibly poignant.

All she had ever wanted was for them to be reading

from the same page, and for the first time in a very long time they were.

And with every new piece of himself that Domenico had revealed to her, Rae had fallen more and more in love with him. Because, with his whole story out in the open, she was able to see how strong and determined and noble he truly was.

She'd always been in awe of his strength, that ability he possessed to carry everything and even more on his very broad shoulders, but knowing that he'd been rejected and abandoned and broken and was still upstanding in spite of that was mesmeric. That he had found the perseverance to go on, to retain the trust he had in Elena, and to believe in Rae enough to want to marry her, spoke volumes about his capacity to feel and the fact that didn't understand how remarkable he was only made Rae's love for him so much greater.

But that meant her fear was that much bigger too.

Because the love she was feeling—the fierce, intense, passionate devotion to him—was anchored too deep and consumed too much of her. It had the power to be utterly devastating and that was terrifying.

It was a risk that Rae wasn't sure she could live with.

She knew too well what followed devastation. The darkness. The swallowing, surrounding, smothering darkness, which had been hunting her in her dream. The one that she feared coming for her in reality, just as it had preyed on her beautiful, strong mother. And as long as she loved Domenico as much as she did, that was a worry that she would carry with her each and every day. What if she lost him? How would she cope? Would she even be able to?

As those questions mounted, a cavern opened in her stomach, filling with the bitterest kind of dread, so strong that she could suddenly taste it in her mouth. And all she wanted to do was run. Run fast and far and away from all of those feelings.

As much as Rae had loved her mother, she didn't want to follow in her footsteps. She didn't want to force her sisters to watch another person they loved suffer and there was no way for her to reel in her feelings. They were too powerful, with a force of their own. Intense. Enthralling. That was the way it had always been between her and Domenico. She didn't believe it could be any other way. Their love had been forged in the sizzling flames of their instant, scorching passion, and the many ways they had opened up to each other in recent days had only fanned those flames.

It was everything that Rae had once wanted with him. A soul-deep, unshakeable, unbreakable bond…but back then she hadn't known how deep that fear was anchored in her, hadn't fully comprehended the consequences of such a connection. The power and sway it held over her. Now she did, and she knew those consequences could be catastrophic, and that scared her more than she could say.

She didn't want to live with fear shadowing her every move. She didn't want to feel fragile every minute of every day, worrying about what lurked around the corner. It had been hard enough last time and even with all the work she had done to make herself strong, to make her life fuller and become more robust so that nothing could ever break her the way her mum had been broken, it wasn't enough. Nothing was powerful enough to counter Domenico's presence and power over her. She still felt vulnerable and afraid.

*Too* vulnerable. *Too* afraid.

She felt it when she spotted Domenico striding across the beach to join her, felt it as she watched him work on the plane going home to Venice, his head bent low as he typed out email after email, occasionally looking up to send her one of his slow, devastating smiles, and she felt it when he kissed her goodbye at the airport before he went off in one direction to the Ricci offices and she returned to the palazzo.

Every time she looked at him, she felt that overpowering wave of love for the man he had become in spite of everything he had had to endure. And then a deep, threatening stab of fear.

It was a relief to have some space from him and some time to herself, a few hours without that frantic back and forth of feeling. But once back at the palazzo Rae became restless, unable to settle peacefully to even the smallest of tasks, and so when, mid-afternoon, her phone rang with an incoming video call from Nell, she leapt to answer it, eager for the distraction that a friendly conversation would provide.

'I have some very exciting news for you,' Nell announced after they'd exchanged pleasantries, launching into a description of the conversation she'd had with the owner of New York's biggest and world-famous bridal boutique.

'Are you serious?' Rae gasped in disbelief when Nell had finished. 'They want to stock my dresses? Even though there aren't even samples of all my designs yet, only sketches?'

'They like what they see,' Nell said, beaming at her through the screen. 'It also doesn't hurt that your name is quickly becoming one of the hottest new names in bridal design. And they don't just want to stock your dresses, Rae. They want to have your designs exclusively and offer their brides a custom service with you. It will be like having your own boutique within their store.'

Rae gave a gob-smacked laugh and lifted her hands to her mouth. 'That's incredible. I can't believe it. I... I'm speechless.'

'It's a huge opportunity, Rae. An unbelievable one. And with all the hard work you've done recently, you really do deserve it. So how do you feel about coming and living in New York for a while?'

Rae opened her mouth to reply, but no words came out. Because the reality of the offer was only just sinking in, the understanding that accepting it meant relocating. To New York.

*New York.* It had always seemed like such a frenetic and overwhelming place to her, never a city that she'd longed to visit, but that wasn't the foremost thought in her mind. No, at the centre of her mind was Domenico. The heart-slowing realisation that if she was in New York, she wouldn't, *couldn't*, be with him because his life was in Venice.

And although excitement was absolutely what she should be feeling, how could she feel any excitement in her heart about being somewhere he wasn't, when her heart so completely belonged to him?

'I don't know,' she stammered on a nervous laugh, realising her silence had dragged on a little too long. 'I guess I'm a little taken aback. It's a lot to take in.'

'I know.' Nell nodded sympathetically. 'It would be a

big change for you. But they wouldn't be looking for you to be in New York until some time after the New Year, so nothing would happen immediately. You and Domenico would have plenty of time to figure things out,' she offered as an attempt at reassurance. 'But, if you are interested, the owners would like to meet with you as soon as this week, just to talk through all the particulars and start the process moving. So think about it. It really is an incredible opportunity for you, Rae.'

'I know,' Rae managed, her throat growing tighter by the second. 'I'll talk to you later, okay.'

Ending the call, she dropped the phone onto the desk and sat back in her chair, her teeth nibbling on the inside of her lip as thoughts sifted through her mind at a mile a minute.

It was, as Nell had said, an incredible offer. Perhaps a once-in-a-lifetime opportunity. And it would give Rae everything she wanted. Success. Security. Something that could sustain her should the worst ever happen. There would be no need for her to worry any longer about falling into that black abyss. She should be thrilled, overjoyed. A month ago, she knew she would have leapt to accept it without a second thought, but now…now there was Domenico to think about too.

There was her and Domenico.

They had finally reached the place in their relationship that she had always wanted, she thought, her heart racing with renewed feeling. They were poised on the edge of their own opportunity to start over and, as frightening as that was, as much as she had spent all day fretting about it, there was a part of Rae that wanted exactly that. To spend her life with him. To build a family with him. To be there when he was struggling, to share in his success and share hers with him. Everything meant so much more with him. Just last night she had fallen asleep with images of the life they could build together swimming before her eyes.

She believed wholeheartedly that they could make their marriage successful this time. They had both grown so much, changed in so many ways, big and small, that she had no doubt that they could make their lives together work, managing their marriage and their careers.

But if she went to New York, none of that would be possible. Everything between them would be severed. The possibility, the hope, the connection they had both fought to forge.

*But you wouldn't have to live in fear of losing him, you wouldn't have to feel scared and vulnerable. You'd feel strong and safe and successful.*

Her heart skipped several beats, tempted by that possibility, except…

She wouldn't have Domenico and if she didn't have Domenico, she wouldn't have her heart. She would only be half alive.

A glimmer of movement caught the corner of her eye and Rae looked up, her heart ramming straight into her ribs as she saw Domenico's reflection in the mirror, standing in the doorway.

For the longest moment she was frozen, a thudding fear pulsing behind her breastbone as she stared at him, trying desperately to read his face, to gauge how much he had heard and what thoughts were running through his mind. Had he already jumped to the conclusion that he was being abandoned again? Was that why his face was set that way, so flat and unreadable, his eyes as dark as night? Were his wounds tearing themselves open again?

She turned quickly. 'How long have you been standing there?'

He didn't move, and that stillness strummed at her nerves, making them jangle with ominous feeling. 'Long enough.'

She swallowed. 'Did you hear all of my conversation with Nell?'

'Most of it, yes.'

It was difficult to speak over the panic hammering in her throat and chest, but she managed to do so. She took a slow step towards him, scared of moving too quickly, as if he were an animal that could startle.

'Then you know I didn't commit to anything. I wouldn't do that without talking to you.'

'Nell said the job wouldn't begin until the New Year,' he said without any inflection and that flatness made her unease mount even higher. 'Our arrangement ends well before Christmas, Rae. You don't need my agreement on whatever you do after that.'

She blinked, stunned by his words. Why he was saying that? As if her future was no concern of his, of no interest to him? It made no sense to her, especially not after everything they'd shared last night, after the beautiful way they had given all of themselves to one another and in doing so blasted open a door to their future.

'I don't need it, no,' she agreed, frowning and picking her following words with care. 'But I would like it. I would like to talk about it with you. To know where you stand, how you feel.'

*To know that you love me as much as I love you. To*

*know that you are in this as deeply as I am and that you want me to stay and be your wife. To know that you believe we can make our relationship work this time, that you too believe we are stronger and better than the people we were before.*

He looked at her directly, but the eyes staring back at her did not belong to the man she had come to know over the past seventy-two hours. Not the eyes that had looked deep into hers as he had moved slowly inside her last night, sealing their emotional bond with the sharpest and sweetest physical joining of her life. Not the eyes of the man who had stroked her hair back from her face as they'd lain face to face afterwards.

'I think you should accept the offer and go to New York,' he responded without a single beat of hesitation, and Rae could only stare back at him harder, nonplussed and sure, *certain*, that she had misheard him.

Domenico thought that saying the words would break him. That forcing them out of his mouth would cause him to shatter into pieces, or at least be struck by a bolt of lightning because they were such a big lie. But they flowed from his lips without a single tremor and, once they had, he felt a brief sense of relief, because he knew the hardest part was over. He had started down the path. Now he just had to keep going.

Because he owed Rae this. The freedom to follow her rainbow to the end and find the success and happiness that awaited her there. It was what she wanted, after all. What she wanted—and needed—more than anything. And he had denied her too much and failed her in too many ways already to allow her to turn down the opportunity.

For a large part of the day that was all he had been able to think about—the poor husband he'd been. Grappling with a profound sense of guilt, Domenico had questioned if his mistakes would be too great to be overcome, if his and Rae's past would prevent them from reaching the brighter future he knew with absolute unflinching certainty that he wanted with her. He'd known it as soon as he'd woken that morning, drained from his emotional outpouring of the night before, but with that weight of the past lifted from him, all the murkiness and insecurity bled out of him, he'd felt a freedom and clarity unlike anything he'd known before. And his every thought, every skip of his heart, had been for Rae.

He loved her. He always had. He'd just been so lost in the darkness of his thoughts that he hadn't been able to realise it. Elena had been right. Rae was the only one for him. She did make him the best version of himself. She had healed him. Because of her, standing beside him the whole time, telling him it was okay, reminding him that he was safe, assuring him that he was not what he feared, he had finally found the strength to face his painful past and at long last been able to view it, not through the eyes of a shaken and hurt little boy, but a man who understood that people were complex and flawed.

Because of Rae, he finally understood that love was not contained in a single act of claiming or acceptance. It was something that was given and felt day in, day out in a thousand small ways. And, adopted by her or not, that was the way Elena had loved him. And the way Rae had loved him too.

Beautiful, wonderful, incredible Rae.

It was because of how wonderful she was that he knew

he had to say those words again and tell her to go to New York. Because it was what she deserved, but she was so generous of heart and so used to putting others before herself that she was already hesitating to seize it.

Because of them. *Him*.

He'd listened to her reaction to the news, heard her uncertainty about relocating to New York, and with a sharp twist of his heart and gut had realised that she was veering on the edge of turning the offer down. And he couldn't allow her to do that.

Rae had already sacrificed so much for him. She had given up everything she'd ever known and worked for to start a life with him in Venice, a sacrifice that he hadn't appreciated at the time, but he did now. And then she had denied her own wants and needs so as not to upset him.

Standing in her way again was not an option. He couldn't do it. He *wouldn't*.

No matter how much he wanted to hold on tight to her, to keep her with him for ever, never again would he be the one to hold her back, not when the emotional cost to her would be so very high.

'I'm sorry, I don't think I heard you correctly,' Rae breathed out quickly.

Domenico knew that she had heard him, but he repeated himself anyway, forcing himself to ignore that pain in her blue eyes and the weight hurting his chest.

'I said that I think you should accept the job in New York.'

She looked bewildered, her forehead creasing, her eyes crinkling as they narrowed disbelievingly. 'Why are saying that?'

'Because you asked for my opinion. And that's what

I think you should do. It sounds like it's an amazing opportunity for you.'

'But if I take it, it would mean I would be living in New York, Domenico. Permanently. I wouldn't be here. We...we wouldn't be able to be together.'

Domenico kept a tight check on his emotions. He had to, or the words he really wanted to say would spill right out of him. Only he couldn't let that happen. He couldn't dwell on the empty landscape that awaited him without her. He had to let her go. Whatever that meant for him afterwards was something he would just have to deal with.

He nodded blankly. 'I understand. But we won't be together in the New Year anyway. We'll be divorced by then, remember?' he said, his voice cool and calm and sounding like it belonged to someone else. 'Our arrangement only lasts for six months, Rae.'

'Our arrangement?' she exclaimed. 'Domenico, nothing that has happened in the last few days has been about the stupid charade I agreed to! The things we've shared with each other, everything we talked about last night— that was all real. You can't tell me it didn't mean anything, that it hasn't altered anything between us.'

'No, I won't deny that,' he agreed. 'Last night changed many things. I think we understand one another far better than we ever did. But one night doesn't fix a broken-down marriage, *tesoro*. And if last night revealed anything, it's that we both want and need different things from a relationship. Things we can't get from each other.'

She was shaking her head indignantly, colour rising in her cheeks, and she was all the more beautiful for it. He longed to reach out, place his fingers against her skin, feel that delicious combination of silk and heat.

'No. You don't mean that,' she whispered. And then in a stronger voice, 'I don't believe you.'

'Have you ever known me to say anything that I don't mean, Rae?' he parried calmly.

'So that's just it?' she demanded of him. 'None of this has meant anything to you? You're just happy to walk away from this? From us?'

He shoved his hands into his pockets, to keep himself from reaching out for her, and faced her with a sigh. 'There is no us, Rae. Our marriage stopped being real a long time ago. This has just been a way to…close the door for good.'

It was in that moment that she faltered, his purposely cruel words cracking her spirit and her willingness to fight. He watched the colour in her eyes and cheeks fade, watched her start to splinter inside, and he wanted so badly to go to her, but he held himself firm. Held himself back. Weakening was not an option, not when her happiness was at stake.

'You're right. I don't know what I was thinking.' She looked away, placing a hand against her chest. 'If you'll excuse me, I would like to be alone. I need to call Nell back and make arrangements for my trip to New York.'

Nodding and turning away, Domenico sucked in a silent breath that caused his heart and lungs to burn. He'd achieved what he wanted, but there was no sense of triumph in it, only misery.

# CHAPTER FOURTEEN

RAE KNEW HER flight to New York would be boarding soon, so she cleared away the wrapper from her sandwich and, after a last glance at her phone, tucked it safely away in her bag. In ten hours she would be in Manhattan, building her plans for her future. A future that didn't involve Domenico.

Her heart squeezed, the pain so acute that she felt it everywhere, but she breathed through it, knowing that leaving was for the best. This way, she would be safe and secure, taking a big step towards making herself invulnerable.

And Domenico didn't want her anyway.

*'There is no us, Rae. This has just been a way to... close the door for good.'*

The memory of those words carved through her, almost as cold and sharp as the first time. With them, he had made it clear where he stood, the sentiment rolling off his tongue without a single beat of hesitation.

*Do you really believe that, Rae? That he doesn't care for you? You know what you felt in his arms and saw glowing in his eyes—do you truly think that was all a lie? Or did you just accept the escape that he was offering because it was all becoming a bit too real, too scary?*

Rae tried to swat away the thought, but it stuck, forcing her to examine its veracity and grudgingly acknowledge what motivations had driven her actions. She had been scared in that moment, standing at that crossroads that would set the tone for the following years of her life, a crossroads she hadn't expected to come to, especially not so swiftly. But she would have chosen Domenico. She had wanted to choose him.

*Then why didn't you? Why didn't you fight back against his words and tell him how much you love him and that you wanted to stay with him?*

Because…a baseball-sized lump formed in her throat.

Because of fear. Because, faced with her rupturing heart and the pain exploding in every corner of her body, it had been easier to not fight. To accept his words, his rejection, and let it all go.

*You promised to not be a coward any more.*

Rae hissed out a breath, frustration with herself burning deep within, making her feel all twisted up inside. She had let fear win, allowed it to dictate her actions, and if she kept going, if she got on her flight, she would still be running, and not towards something she wanted, but away from something she was scared to want.

In that second, she knew what she needed to do.

She had to go back. She had to tell Domenico exactly how she felt, one final act of vulnerability, and probably the hardest one. But she had to do it. Her fear would never go away completely. With love there would always be fear. But if she faced it, it would shrink and its power over her would lessen. And maybe, in leading by example and putting her heart in Domenico's hands, he would feel safe enough to put his in hers and conquer whatever it was that had made him hold back.

And if he didn't love her, if everything he had said the other night was the truth, then Rae would just have to live with it. She wouldn't be scared of that and she wouldn't allow herself to fall apart, because she was strong and she was brave. She might not always remember that when she needed to, but that was who she was. Strong and brave, and it was time she started acting like it.

Overhead, the speakers flared into life, announcing that her flight was ready to board, but she was already on her feet and hurrying in the opposite direction, towards the exit. And, hopefully, towards love.


Domenico was relieved when the meeting was over.

His head hadn't been in it. More than once he'd had to be prompted to answer a question that had been asked of him and that he hadn't heard as he was too busy thinking about Rae, wondering where she was and what she was doing at that very moment, if she was missing him as profoundly as he was missing her. Not that that was likely, not after the words he'd spoken in their last conversation. But he'd had to make her leave and he hadn't known any other way to do that.

Rising from his chair at the head of the long table, he knew he needed to get his thoughts in order before his conference call later that afternoon. To focus on the matters at hand. But it was a struggle.

He'd made a bad habit of stuffing his feelings down and never dealing with them and he didn't want to do that any more, not after realising how all those unresolved emotions had festered in him like a contagion.

He wanted to be better, to manage his emotions with more maturity so they didn't constrain and control him as those childhood ones had, but allowing himself to feel his pain was agonising.

More than once he'd noted the time on his watch, calculated that he had time to race to the airport and stop Rae, tell her he hadn't meant any of what he had said and plead with her to stay, but then his better sense overrode that emotion and for the hundredth time he sternly reminded himself that he had let Rae go for a reason, and a good reason at that—because of what was best for her, and that was a life with her career at the centre of it.

*Are you sure you weren't pushing her away more than letting her go?*

Domenico wanted to reject the thought out of hand, but the twist of his gut forced him to concede that, yes, maybe he had been pushing Rae away to a certain extent. Because embarking on a future with her would require him to trust that he could be enough for her. A good enough man and a good enough husband, who wouldn't screw up as epically as he had last time. And trusting in that, *in himself,* was not easy…not after everything he'd been through, all those years of pervasive doubt and insecurity. It lingered like a decaying stench and when faced with that very big question mark about their future, about his ability to give her a good future, that fear had blown up in his mind and he had reacted to it. Because he couldn't bear to cause Rae pain again. To be the reason she was unhappy. He could think of no worse fate.

As he strode back to his office, Domenico passed his assistant at his desk. 'I don't want to be bothered for the next hour, Nico. No exceptions,' he commanded wearily, sensing that Nico had words on his lips, but closing his office door before he could get them out.

He leaned back against the door, closing his eyes and giving himself a moment to buckle under the magnitude of his pain.

'Having a bad day?'

His eyes snapped open. Sitting in his chair, behind his desk and looking right at him with her bright blue eyes was Rae. He blinked quickly, making sure he wasn't imagining her.

'You're meant to be on a plane on your way to New York right now,' he managed, his voice hoarse.

'I know, but the thing is, Domenico, I don't want to go to New York.'

His heart stuttered. *She didn't want to go?*

'But the job with the bridal store—it's a huge…'

'It's a huge opportunity, I know,' she sighed, as though she was tired of hearing those words. 'But I'm not sure it's the right one, not if it means leaving you.' Words failed him, especially as she pressed herself out of his chair and moved around the desk towards him, her footsteps sure, her eyes fixed steadily on him. 'I love you, Domenico. I love you with every breath that I take and I want to be your wife now even more than I did when you first asked me to marry you. Knowing exactly who you are has only made everything I feel for you stronger and I want spend the rest of my life with you.'

The sparkle of her eyes intensified, the truth of her words easy to see, and his heart quivered, threatening to burst open with the delight streaming into it. 'The only reason I even set that meeting for New York was because I was scared of everything that I was feeling, scared of the fear that comes with loving you so much, and when you told me *repeatedly* to go, I thought, okay, maybe it's better this way. This way, I won't have to live with that fear of making the same mistakes as my mum. But I realised that I was only making a different one. Because, by trying so hard to not be like her, I was going to the other extreme—a life without love, a life controlled by fear. And that's not what I want either. Because a life without you just isn't a life.'

She moved closer, hope brimming in her face. 'What I do want is to stay here and be your wife. Not just for a few months, but for ever. And I know it won't be easy, making our marriage work with both of our careers, it will take a lot of work, but I believe in us enough to know that we can.'

He moved like a bullet, darting towards her and taking her face in his hands, kissing her long and slow and stopping only because there were some words he needed to say. 'I want you to stay too, Rae,' he murmured breathlessly, the words in a rush to get out. 'I only told you to go because I didn't want to stand in your way again. I didn't want to be the reason you would one day wake up unhappy. But telling you to leave nearly killed me. I've been in a fog ever since.'

'That is the most selfless, sexy and stupid thing you've ever done for me. And I forbid you to ever do something like that again,' she said strictly, but with a dazzling smile up at him. 'We need to be honest with each other if we're going to make this work, Domenico. We have to always tell each other what we're thinking and feeling, however hard it is, however scared we are that the other won't like what they have to hear.'

'I'm scared that I can't be enough for you,' he admitted roughly, not wanting to hold anything back from her. 'That, however hard I try, I won't ever be the man you deserve.'

She reached up her hand to his face and cupped his jaw with her warm palm, empathy shining out of her eyes because she knew exactly why he thought that without him having to say anything more. 'You're already everything I want, Domenico. I'll tell you that every day if you need me to. And as for you standing in my way—you're not. I'm making a considered decision about what I do and don't want. That's different to how it was last time. And New York is just one opportunity. Hopefully, there will be others and when they come we'll talk about them. If we can make it work and how we do that.'

'I actually already have a thought about that,' Domenico said, detaching from her reluctantly and moving to his desk, withdrawing a file from his top drawer. 'For you,' he said, placing it in her hands and watching as she opened it and withdrew the sheets of paper inside, a puzzled look racing over her expression.

'You bought me a building?'

'A three-storey building on the corner of Salizada San Moisè, so lots of windows, lots of beautiful natural light. I thought, to start with, it would be a good studio. You could bring brides there for consultations and fittings and then, eventually, the ground floor could be a store. Your first store.'

She looked overcome, her eyes moving from him to the paper and back to him. 'I... I can't believe you did this.'

'I had Nico start looking after our conversation on the plane to Majorca. I wanted to do something for you, to make everything up to you. And to show you how much I believe in you and support you.' He slid his arms around her waist, drawing her against him. 'I didn't always in the past, but I do now and I will every day going forward. Because I love you. More than anything.'

He rested his forehead against hers, contentment sinking down the length of his body. 'You're my home, Rae. You are where I belong. And we will make this work. I will not allow anything to come between us ever again.'

She smiled up at him, the words bringing palpable relief to her body. 'And I won't run any more, I promise. Whatever problem or fear I have, I will come to you.'

'And I will always make time to listen and be there for you and whatever it is that you need, I'll make sure you have it.'

'Right now—' she smiled, sliding her hands up his chest and around his neck '—I think I already have everything I need.'

'As do I, Signora Ricci,' he said, smiling that long, slow, devastating smile. 'As long as I have you, I am complete.'

# EPILOGUE

*Three years later*

THE RICCI BALL WAS in full swing. It had become one of the biggest nights in Venice's social calendar and the gilded ballroom was packed with guests. The chandelier high above glittered in splendour, rare jewels sparkled at every table, but as far as Domenico was concerned, nothing and no one shone as brightly as his wife. As his eyes found her among the throng, he cut an eager path towards her.

'Are you having a good time?' he whispered, slipping his hands around her stomach and resting them on her protruding bump, which even her cleverly designed dress couldn't completely hide.

'Yes. But it's even better now that you're back at my side,' she murmured, stroking a hand across his jaw.

'Would you like to dance?'

'As if you need to ask. I told you I want to make the most of tonight before I'm too big to do anything...'

'You'll still be ravishing,' Domenico cut in.

'And before these babies get here and drastically upend our lives.'

The pregnancy had been planned entirely, but the news

that it was a double pregnancy had stunned both of them. It had taken Rae a little time to adjust to the idea.

He smiled down at her, pulling her in close. 'I think we're going to handle it fine. We'll do it the way we do everything—together.'

It was how they had navigated the whirlwind that the past few years had been, juggling both of their busy careers and their marriage. The Ricci Group had continued to flourish, with the maiden voyage of their cruise line setting sail a month earlier to a hail of praise, and Rae's career had gone from strength to strength. She had opened her first store in Venice two years ago, in the building Domenico had gifted her, drawing in brides from all across Europe, but as her renown had grown, so had the global demand for her bridal gowns. Partnering with a high-end department store in a deal facilitated by Domenico, six months ago she had opened her first boutique in their London store, with a second one set to open in New York in four months' time. It hadn't always been easy, but with communication and love they had managed it, their marriage growing stronger than ever.

'I love you, Domenico Ricci. My life wouldn't be complete without you.'

'You're everything to me, *mi amore*. And I can't wait to meet our two babies and tell them how perfect and how loved they are.'

Seven weeks later, Domenico was able to do exactly that. Their newborn daughters arrived several weeks early, but thankfully healthy. They named them Elena and Raphaella, names he and Rae had agreed upon very easily, and cradling them in his arms for the first time, Domenico murmured to them just how loved and precious they were.

As he gazed down at them, unable to tear his eyes away, he could feel his heart overflowing with so much love, and he found himself marvelling at how far he had come from the man he had once been, the man who'd married his wife without knowing how madly in love with her he was.

He had changed so much, and it was all because of Rae, he thought with a tender glance at her resting form. Because of her, he had learned to accept himself, to make his peace with the past and seize the future. Because of her, he felt safe, waking each morning without a single doubt in his heart or mind that he was loved, that he had *always* been loved, even if he hadn't been able to see it, and would continue to be for the rest of his days, and he never allowed a day to pass without making sure that Rae knew exactly the same thing.

* * * * *

# MILLS & BOON MODERN IS
# HAVING A MAKEOVER!

The same great stories you love,
a stylish new look!

## Look out for our brand new look
# COMING JUNE 2024

MILLS & BOON

# COMING SOON!

We really hope you enjoyed reading this book.
If you're looking for more romance
be sure to head to the shops when
new books are available on

## Thursday 6th
## June

MILLS & BOON

# MILLS & BOON®

## Coming next month

### MY ONE-NIGHT HEIR
### Natalie Anderson

'You stunned me into silence.' His expression softens. 'I was trying to stay in control. I couldn't do this there.'

'This?'

The brush of his lips is balmy, teasing. His tenderness takes me by surprise as does the moment he takes to lean back and search my eyes. I realize he's seeking my consent.

I can hardly think. 'This is…'

'What I've wanted to do all night.' His gleaming gaze bores into me—intense and unwavering. 'You're why my pulse is racing.'

I just topple right into his arms. He scoops me close and then his mouth is there again—on mine. And I melt.

It turns out that kissing is the best ever way to neutralise panic. The best way to stay in the moment, to not give a damn about anything else in life—not even imminent death. Kissing is the best ever thing full stop.

*Continue reading*
### MY ONE-NIGHT HEIR
### Natalie Anderson

*Available next month*
millsandboon.co.uk

# LET'S TALK

# *Romance*

For exclusive extracts, competitions and special offers, find us online:

- MillsandBoon
- @MillsandBoon
- @MillsandBoonUK
- @MillsandBoonUK

Get in touch on 01413 063 232

# MILLS & BOON

## THE HEART OF ROMANCE

---

## A ROMANCE FOR EVERY READER

---

**MODERN**
Prepare to be swept off your feet by sophisticated, sexy and seductive heroes, in some of the world's most glamourous and romantic locations, where power and passion collide.

**HISTORICAL**
Escape with historical heroes from time gone by. Whether your passion is for wicked Regency Rakes, muscled Vikings or rugged Highlanders, awaken the romance of the past.

**MEDICAL**
Set your pulse racing with dedicated, delectable doctors in the high-pressure world of medicine, where emotions run high and passion, comfort and love are the best medicine.

*True Love*
Celebrate true love with tender stories of heartfelt romance, from the rush of falling in love to the joy a new baby can bring, and a focus on the emotional heart of a relationship.

**HEROES**
The excitement of a gripping thriller, with intense romance at its heart. Resourceful, true-to-life women and strong, fearless men face danger and desire - a killer combination!

From showing up to glowing up, these characters are on the path to leading their best lives and finding romance along the way – with plenty of sizzling spice!

To see which titles are coming soon, please visit

**millsandboon.co.uk/nextmonth**

# GET YOUR ROMANCE FIX!

Get the latest romance news, exclusive author interviews, story extracts and much more!

**blog.millsandboon.co.uk**